MURRAY HALL

A Novel

MILO ALLAN

Black&White

Black&White

First published in the UK in 2025 by Black & White Publishing
An imprint of Bonnier Books UK
5th Floor, HYLO, 103–105 Bunhill Row,
London, EC1Y 8LZ

Owned by Bonnier Books
Sveavägen 56, Stockholm, Sweden

A CIP catalogue record for this book is available from the British Library.

ISBN (HBK): 978 1 78530 462 0
ISBN (TPBK): 978 1 78530 620 4

1 3 5 7 9 10 8 6 4 2

Typeset by Data Connection
Printed and bound in Great Britain by Clays Ltd, Elcograf S.p.A.

MIX
Paper | Supporting
responsible forestry
FSC
www.fsc.org   FSC® C018072

www.blackandwhitepublishing.com

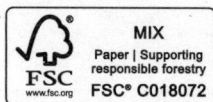

To those who live, regardless.

PROLOGUE

THE TALL MAN IN THE black frock coat and polished shoes was lingering. He hovered outside the storefront, now with one foot on its stone doorstep, now back out on the frosted sidewalk, his breath forming clouds around him. He was dressed in a navy-blue three-piece suit, with a starched high collar and deep burgundy necktie; on his head was a top hat, which he touched unheedingly as people made their way about him, hardly glancing in his direction.

The frost made Manhattan sparkle that Thursday, although few were so idle as to stop to look at the bright, cloudless sky as it wrapped around the city's skyline, or to appreciate the low sun as it illuminated the gold lettering embossed on the store's large window, which read: *C. S. Pratt, Bookseller*.

He knew he was drawing more attention to himself idling on the pavement than he would if he simply stepped inside, but he could not yet quite commit himself to entering such a place. To those in the know, particularly in his line of work, C. S. Pratt's was the place to come to if you had a request for an unusual title. The bookseller stocked all the run-of-the-mill biographies and popular romance novels, but further into the depths of the place, past the well-lit shelves by the window and into its darker, dustier corners, one could find texts that were banned or rejected elsewhere, books imported from Europe or discreetly ordered by special arrangement.

It was for this reason that the man was so hesitant to step inside. It was one thing if it was for an investigation – for that he would happily stride into the most insalubrious of establishments – but if a colleague from *The Times* were to see him here, he would have no real reason for his presence other than personal curiosity. It was as these thoughts ran through his head, and as he was making his short, nervous journey back from doorstep to window, that through the polished glass he caught sight of a familiar figure.

Behind the displays of the latest releases and rare editions, obscured slightly by the gold of the window lettering, he could make out the silhouette of a small man in a bowler hat and slightly shabby oversized coat, his back turned. Instantly, he forgot his hesitations and slipped inside, hoping not to be noticed by this small man as the jangling bell announced his entrance. Inside, the shop was warm, musty and subdued, its expanse of wooden floors populated by only a few patrons on this cold day. He made his way as quietly as he could towards the geography section, picking up a title at random on the mountains of the Himalaya, all the while straining his ears to overhear the conversation that was now taking place between the small man and what appeared to be C. S. Pratt, Bookseller, himself.

The shabbily overcoated man tapped on the floor with his blackthorn cane. The book on top of the pile was one he had perused just moments before. The image he had seen inside its pages, a monochrome plate showing cancer cells, had rattled him, stirring something in his chest as if someone were pinching at his flesh.

The bookseller's words added to that feeling of being prodded and irritated.

"... can't let you have all these. I know we have an arrangement, Mr Hall, but if you'll recall you have yet to settle your tab for Watkin's *Compendium*. And that was a first edition! This is a business, and a bookselling business at that, not a public library."

The bookseller was broad-shouldered, a light blond beard shadowing his muscular jaw; he looked more like a bartender than a scholar. His substantial arms were folded in front of him as he addressed Mr Hall, but his tone was playful.

"Damn you, Pratt," Mr Hall said. His fingers dug into the skin just above and to the left of his sternum, betraying the fear plucking at his rib cage. "You know I'm good for it. And

3

besides, I haven't decided if I'll keep it yet. My eyesight isn't what it was, and there's all that small print ..."

As Pratt hesitated, Hall snipped: "I can't imagine you get much custom for this kind of specialised text. Why not let me have it, and you know where I am if someone else comes asking after it?"

His slim fingers reached out for the smooth leather binding as if it were some kind of religious text, a talisman, a lifeline from which he must not let go.

As soon as the reporter heard the shrill voice attached to that compact body, he knew his suspicions were correct. Murray Hall. Of course, one would expect a man like him to be found in a place like this. He had been right to debate his entrance. Hall was not the kind of figure one would want to be readily associated with, though now he had an excuse to blame his presence here on his profession.

An excuse he was grateful for; as the century reached its turn he had become increasingly aware that the popular opinion of journalists was not one of trust. This wasn't unfounded – the birth of the yellow press meant stories were becoming ever more sensationalised, so their writers could turn a quick buck as they spun tales from scandal and prurience. But Samuel Clellan, which was the byline he went under, considered himself above that sort of thing. If people were to trust his writing, then they must trust his character, he thought – particularly when his articles often exposed the more unsavoury goings-on of the city. This angle of his work hadn't made him many friends, Hall being one of those who took an antagonistic stance towards him.

At the risk of exposing his presence, Clellan decided to draw closer to the two men. He moved as silently as he could towards the polished oak counter where their exchange was taking place. It was almost comedic, this physically imposing man with a smile playing on his lips and an air of easy, rough-hewn bonhomie leaning over Hall's tight, angry body. The disparity between the figures reminded Clellan of one of *The Times'* satirical cartoons. Hall was hunched over and seemed even smaller than the last time they had encountered one another, his body nearly collapsing around his black cane. The great shapeless coat he always wore hung about him so it was impossible to tell his true build, only his height, and a guess at his age from the grey curls peeking out from beneath his hat. His cheeks and nose were red with the cold, and from years of drinking, but his flinty eyes were as acute and piercing as ever. Clellan was glad that he seemed too engrossed in his debate with the bookseller to notice him; the two hadn't last parted on the best of terms.

In front of the men, atop the wooden counter, lay a pile of five large books. Clellan couldn't imagine the diminutive Hall carrying them all away with him, but he had heard that he was stronger, wirier, more physically resilient than he looked. From all the stories of Hall's nights of poker and whisky at the Iroquois, Clellan had no doubt he could pack the punch of a man half his age and twice his height. On top of the pile lay the most impressive of the tomes, its cover dark green and gilded with small gold lettering. Clellan shuffled as close as he dared and peered over, trying to make it out. It read,

The Science and Art of Surgery: Being A Treatise on Surgical Injuries, Diseases and Operations.

Clellan was surprised; he had expected to see something far more salacious, and from what he knew of Hall, the man didn't strike him as the academic type. But then, he himself had also come in here with an unusual request.

By now, Hall and Pratt seemed to have come to an agreement, and the bookseller was wrapping up the weighty pile in butcher's paper and twine. Clellan turned back to the shelves so as to avoid detection, and realised that he was now facing Conan Doyle's *A Study in Scarlet*. He turned swiftly away. As a journalist, a wordsmith, he believed that in order to be a good writer, one must first be a dedicated and insatiable reader, but he drew the line at novels such as those – when one's writing deals with facts, it does no good to get caught up in debaucherous fiction.

Hall was now making his way across the shop floor, the package of books hanging curiously from his outstretched arms like a labourer might carry a heavy stone. It was not particularly gentlemanly, and only Clellan's desire to remain undetected stopped him from attempting to assist him. Luckily, one of the other few patrons was quicker to the door and held it open for the man, who shuffled out into the cold without a word or gesture of thanks. Not so much as an inclination of his head. What an odd, ungracious fellow, Clellan thought.

Now that his chief distraction had left, Clellan was faced with the task he had come here for. He looked around, glad not to recognise any of the other faces he saw. The motive for this much-considered outing was his recent investigation into the Slide, a joint that had earned itself the moniker of New York's "fairy resort". He hadn't written those words himself, but he had contributed to the bank of articles that had led to the establishment being shut down. It was, in his opinion, one of the most depraved, immoral places the city had ever produced. Even as a journalist, he had never actually dared to visit the Slide, but had heard the stories; of men dressed as women, women as men, of liquor and drugs as freely available as the clientele. It represented for him all his fears about this new century that approached, one where money and sex, avarice and lasciviousness, ruled with wanton abandon above the laws of civility and of God.

The Slide's closure, and Clellan's contribution to its demise, had spurred him on to a spate of research into sexual deviancy. This was not his only area of interest – his work seeking to expose the corruption of the Tammany boys, Murray Hall chief among them, was evidence of that – but, slippery as a Hudson oyster, those men had proven frustratingly difficult to take down, whereas the Slide offered a more satisfying conclusion. He was hoping that, in his research of the subject, he could learn more about these individuals' proclivities and therefore predict – and block – their next move. In his experience, when a den as debauched as the Slide finds itself with padlocks on the door and its licence revoked, somewhere new, somewhere equally dissolute, springs up almost overnight. Already he had been hearing whispers about a new club, the Excise. Clellan's interest in this topic had begun to overtake his duties at *The Times*. It had become something of an obsession, and that is what had led him to the door of C. S. Pratt, Bookseller.

It was not Clellan's usual source of literature, but Pratt's warranted its reputation as a store where one could get hold of books that were not sold elsewhere. If there was gossip or outrage around a publication, Pratt was sure to stock it. Clellan wasn't after anything particularly obscene, but Havelock Ellis's *Psychology of Sex* had proven elusive, presumably owing to its rather novel and contentious theories around the origins of sexual inversion. If anywhere in New York were to stock it, here would be the place.

After Hall's departure, Clellan began to scan the back shelves of the store, where Pratt kept his more discreet titles, but he was yet to come across Ellis's name. He sighed. This scenario was one he had hoped to avoid. He looked around the store once again and was relieved to see that he was now the only customer remaining. He made his way to the counter and coughed gently, causing Pratt to look up from his receipt book and smile.

"Yes?" the bookseller questioned.

"Good afternoon, sir. I am looking for a title ... It's by an English doctor, name of Ellis."

"Ellis? I'm not sure ... Could you tell me what it is about, and perhaps that will jog my memory?"

The bookseller's face was animated by that perpetual half-smile of his, and Clellan knew he was being toyed with. Presumably the man could sense his discomfort. He resolved not to rise to his sardonic teasing and answered his question matter-of-factly.

"Certainly. It is on the psychology of sex – quite a recent publication, I believe."

"Ah, Ellis! I remember now. Havelock Ellis. No, we don't have that in, I'm afraid, though I'd be happy to order it for you."

"If you would. The name is Clellan."

"Clellan. Not a problem, sir. Ellis's text will be here within the month. Is there anything else?"

"No, I don't believe so. Although—" he hesitated, a little of his confidence ebbing away. "Was that Murray Hall whom you served before?"

The bookseller's smile grew to a grin that revealed two rows of small, yellowish teeth.

"Hall! Indeed, it was. A funny old boy, that one."

"Do you have any idea why he was buying a book on surgery? I happened to notice it on top of the pile, you see, and I was curious. I was under the impression he worked in the political field."

"Did you, now? Well, Hall has been interested in texts of a medical nature for a while. Interested in all sorts of books, as it happens, though I believe his wife was once studying medicine. Perhaps he buys them with her in mind."

"Ah, perhaps. Well, sir, you have been most helpful."

"No problem at all, Mr Clellan. Now, let me take down some details for this order ..."

As Clellan turned to leave the bookshop, he had the rather unpleasant feeling that Pratt had learned more from him than he had intended in their exchange.

He stepped back into the chill Manhattan air, the first few flakes of snow beginning to fall, and turned to make his way towards the offices of *The Times*. Though the beauty of a winter day usually raised his spirits, Clellan couldn't free his mind of the strange image of Murray Hall, his stooped frame hobbling out of Pratt's store with his unusual armful of books.

PART I

MURRAY HALL WASN'T A STORY I broke. In truth, that particular week I was so busy poking my nose into the filth behind the latest police corruption case, I didn't even register his death till the day after, when I was gazing distractedly at a slump of morning editions of the *World*. My eyes landed on a sketched face, peering out from the wall of words. Thick hair, side-parted; a crooked, closed-mouth smile that turned down at the corner, and above, the headline:

VOTED TAMMANY FOR THIRTY YEARS. DIED A WOMAN.

"Died a woman?" I said under my breath.

I hollered over to Irving, the deputy, inside his own gated editorial pen. This is how we speak, like neighbours either side of our picket fences, pausing now and again in our raking to gossip.

"Say, who wrote this Murray Hall piece?" I asked. "Astonishing disclosure of the death of Murray H. Hall. Supposed to be a man. But, in fact, a woman."

13

Irving looked up from his strikings and underlinings, as if distracted from the pruning of some small herbaceous shrub. His face was a wry smile. "Magee. Why?"

"Is he following it up?"

"No, I've put him back onto Bosschieter."

I looked again at the sketch of Murray Hall that accompanied the article and, still staring at it, wandered over to the swing gate by Irving's desk where I stood for a moment, paused.

This was the face; the very same. But supposedly a woman's. It felt to me as if I was staring at one of those optical illusions that could be seen as first one thing, then another. A woman at her dressing table who morphs into a skull before your very eyes. Yes, this was Hall's face, but now I searched its lines and creases, looking for the tell-tale signs that would transform it from that of a man to the softness of a woman.

"What is it, Sam?" Irving asked.

"Nothing . . ." I said, shaking my head as if to rid it of the surge of thoughts flooding in.

My memory flew back to that first time I saw Hall up close, sliding into the seat opposite me in the back corner at Fatone's, an exaggerated smile stretched across over-sized porcelain teeth and, its contradiction, menacing steel-grey eyes. He had seemed to me, in that moment, like an image from the parlour game Heads, Bodies, Legs, an unsettling arrangement of parts that did not belong to one another.

"Mr Clellan," he had said, and in an instant the forced grin dropped.

The events leading up to that moment at Fatone's tumbled through my mind again, starting with the walk south from the sun-baked square at Jefferson Market Courthouse, where I'd had that haunting feeling I was being followed. It was one that had been dogging me for days. A shadowy form that seemed to repeat in the pattern of ever-shifting New Yorkers. A distinctive narrow-legged suit with chest-hugging jacket that appeared in my periphery again and again. Thinking that I had noticed him on my tail, I had sped up and taken a quick left off Sixth Avenue, dodging through the crowd, trying to melt into the mass of humans. The steamy heat rose from the pavements, filling the air with a halitosis of urine and sweat. I took a left after Washington Square, then another right, zigzagging east and into the cacophony of Little Italy, darting between carts piled high with blushing New Jersey peaches, until I finally ended up on Mulberry Street and decided to duck into Fatone's to cool myself with what was, for me, a rare tall glass of lager.

The place wasn't yet busy, and I ordered at the long sweep of a bar littered with trays of leftover "free lunch" crostini, before heading to the back of the room to take a seat under the gaslight. There, I looked over my notes from the day at the courthouse. It was while I was scanning my shorthand that I heard the sound of a chair being dragged from under my table, and felt the prickle of an unexpected threat.

He wore a charcoal sack coat which seemed to dwarf his small figure, loose and literally sack-like, in contrast to the form-fitting fashion of the moment. Clean-shaven, barber fresh, sweat dripping down his cheek, he wiped his chin with the back of his hand. His unwavering glare lasted several beats before he turned to his companion, smiled again, then swivelled back to me.

"Mr Clellan," he repeated, as if my name itself were some kind of menace, but delivered in the warble of a pubescent boy, an oscillation between low growl and needling falsetto.

I tried to place the accent. Was it Irish?

"Mr Hall," I said. "Mr Murray Hall."

There was a sharp tap on the sawdust floor beneath the table and I noticed its source: the dark reed of a blackthorn stick, whose pale handle he rubbed in his palm. With his left hand, he reached across the table and pulled my notepad towards him. "We hear that you have been conducting a few interviews down at the courthouse. Asking questions. That's what we hear, is it no, Joe?"

The two could not have looked more different. This other man, tall, muscular, dark hair streaked with iron-grey, wore a suit cut tight to emphasise his broad chest. Perfectly pressed; the antithesis of Hall's neglected attire. My immaculate shadow. A well-oiled moustache gave him the air of a man still clinging on to his sporting days, but his face was warmer than Hall's, in spite of the livid scar that splintered his cheek.

Another tap of that stick on the sawdust; a call for attention.

"Let me see what we have here ..." Hall said. "Ruby Stile, arrested whilst merely visiting an alehouse with a friend, paid all her savings in bail." He read slowly, in that piping voice. "You would listen to the words of brothel workers now, would you? These women who will wrap you up in any old story for a dime? That's no way to get the proper idea of the keeping of law and order in this town. That's what I do with my bonds, you see, as well as the helping of certain unfortunates who would otherwise end up in that hellhole, the Tombs."

No, I thought, Scots.

The man was a Scot.

He read on. "James O'Hare. Crippled former railroad worker. Some of this I cannot read, of course, since it is in the secret code of shorthand. Well now, he seems to have spun you quite a tale about me. I hope you are not thinking of publishing any of this balderdash."

He closed the book and slowly pushed it across the table to his friend. "Joe," he said, and his companion picked it up and put it in his jacket pocket.

I was distracted again by Hall's right hand, which was stroking the handle of the blackthorn stick with clockwork regularity, rubbing it repeatedly as he spoke.

"You will know, Mr Clellan," Hall said, "that we Tammany brothers have many friends. There are brothers everywhere in this city." He leaned his stick up against the side of the table and smiled his porcelain smile again. "The benevolent hands of this party reach everywhere. I'm sure you are aware of that."

He dug inside his pocket to pull out a yellowed handkerchief, wiping it across his forehead. The sweat had pooled on his brow, yet he removed neither his hat nor his coat, which remained buttoned, framing a loosely knotted tie. I felt my own sweat gathering in the pits of my shirt.

"Are ye not?" he asked.

I did not reply.

17

"I'm sure we can trust Mr Clellan not to publish such lies. Can't we, Joe?"

The man next to him nodded, wordlessly. His head cocked to the side, and he looked at me as if he were studying some strange insect or animal specimen; his eyes drifting over my damp brow and down across my frayed shirt collar, the uniform of a journalist not quite hitting the big stories. His hands pushed against each other, knuckles pressing in and releasing – not fists exactly, but the suggestion of them.

"Yes." Joe finally spoke in a low, soft growl, turning back to look at Hall. His eyes caught mine again. "Ah would say so."

Murray Hall picked up his stick and rose from his chair. His companion mirrored the movement, rising now so it was clear he was almost a foot taller than the little man.

"Ah would definitely say so," Joe said lazily, nodding his head.

Standing by Irving's swing gate in the smoke-clouded office of the *World*, I heard that reedy voice ring through my mind again, singing out the words: "Mr Clellan."

An old fear prickled across my shoulder blades.

Hall, I thought, as I studied the inky sketch, was everything that was wrong about this city: in thrall to Mammon, an absence of moral principle, vice almost endemic. A perverse and violent malaise of masculinity dominating the streets, the police precincts and the factory floors. But this particular revelation – about Hall's true sex – seemed like a crack in the façade, something that didn't fit, or even seem quite possible.

"What is it, Sam? You look stuck . . ." Irving interrupted my reverie. "Something on your mind?"

I waved the paper at him. "I'd be interested to follow this up. I met Hall a couple of times. Never liked the man . . ." I trailed off, realising what I had said. "But I never suspected this."

"If you think there's more to it, go ahead," he said, almost absentmindedly. His hand was already reaching towards the candlestick of the telephone in front of him, his awareness caught in some other, more urgent mission. "Make it yours. It's certainly a yarn. The readers are bound to want to know more."

He picked up the mouthpiece and spoke into it. "Morning, Eleonora. Can you put me through to the DA?"

As I put on my Kersey, glad of the warmth of the coat's plaid lining, I became aware of a tightness in my chest and let out a release of air. Before leaving my desk, I put a call into the 15th Precinct, hoping to access one of the few men I knew for sure might want to share some tales of Hall with me.

"Can I speak to Officer O'Connor?" I asked the bored-sounding secretary on the other end of the line.

"He's out on beat. Won't be back till lunchtime. You could try then."

"Can you tell him Mr Clellan called?" I said. "And that oysters are in season at around one p.m. today."

I walked onto the World's viewing platform. That balcony is where I like to go to think. The platform draws tourists and visitors, and today several women were out there, cooing at the outstanding spread of the city's grid below them, the green of City Hall Park now dusted with snow, wispy trees skeletal against the sky. The women wore the same long cinched dresses with lace collars as was the current fashion, in varying deep shades of green, red and tan. Tiny flakes of snow were floating through the air. One of them glanced at me with a warm, broad smile of pleasure, then shyly looked down and away.

Most often when I'd take a chance to gaze at that view, I'd think of all the thousands of people going about their day, wondering at the intricacies of their ordinary lives, or of the darkness hidden behind the city's glittering lights. Now I only could think of one. Murray Hall.

My thoughts drifted back to Fatone's, and those two figures, the oddest of couples, sat in front of me ... That was when the feeling began, the tiny, pulsing knot of dread I carried in my gut, the one that would grow, tightening and tangling itself over the following months. I shouldn't worry, I had told myself at first. Those were straw threats from a man who made his living from bluffs. I shouldn't let them, or the loss of my note-book, intimidate me or hold me back. I should write what I had always intended to write. The truth.

How naive I had been! How arrogant to imagine I would be free from harms aimed towards me, or that the institution of the press – as a buttress of integrity – was there to protect me.

I felt that knot in my gut again, an old stab of hurt. The same feeling was tightening inside my head, contracting around an image, a memory, of the *New York Times* editor, frowning so fiercely his thick eyebrows became one. "About this bail article, Clellan. A source, this railroad worker, says he never spoke to you." He sighed, as if this was a needle of real disappointment to him. "But also, the truth is you spend too long on these investigations which are, I understand, a personal mission for you. The *Times* is not some arm of your City Vigilance campaign. Our readers don't want moral sermonising on this city's pleasures, which are their pleasures too."

And that was it. With a thump of the editor's meaty fist on his polished, ink-stained desk, Murray Hall had, almost effortlessly on his part, a major – and detrimental – impact on my life.

If nothing else, Murray Hall had taught me a lesson in New York life.

Though at least I was now finally back in on the job at another paper, and a sensationalist Pulitzer rag at that. I was no longer quite the wet-behind-the-ears reporter I had once been.

As I gazed out over the pulsing arteries of Manhattan, my father's voice came, as it often did, like a sermon running through my head, an insistent murmur on the breeze.

Look at this city. It ought to be a city of light! Instead, it is rum-soaked, Tammany-debauched, lecherous and corrupt. It is nigh impossible for a young man to be in the midst of this and retain his natural temperate and clean character. God alone knows why we left Wayne County to come to this heart-sickening place.

The women waltzed back into the building and I followed, jumping into the crush of the elevator, a silent bystander as they chattered among themselves in refined English accents. Once out into the chill of the January day, I walked briskly down Newspaper Row and headed for the Park Place elevated railway, galloping up the steps two at a time and emerging into the ashen light of the platform.

The familiar smell of coal smoke and sulphur caught the back of my throat, and I pulled a scented handkerchief from my pocket, pressing it up to my nose.

The station was quiet, with only a small crowd braving the chill, and it felt as if the world had already begun its retreat indoors from the grey of the day. I scanned the winter-paled faces of the commuters, mentally noting them. A habit gifted me by Murray Hall. Even now, I still look over my shoulder to see who may be behind.

Breathing a welcome drag of violet, I edged up the platform to position myself near the front of the train, to better view the passing windows and upper storeys of the looming city. Once inside, the train pulled swiftly away, rushing onwards. The cloud-scraping palazzo of the Broadway Chambers building loomed and was gone, a flash of Washington Square, then a snake to the left and the ornate spike of the Jefferson clocktower. As the track swerved along, the buildings shrank and grew then shrank again. Smaller, middle-class brownstones, stores, offices, the buzz of upward mobility, of trade and reinvention. Fire escapes cascaded down; signs shouted from roofs and windows. The tips of tele-graph poles reached skywards, like skeletons of winter saplings.

The train drew to a halt, its brakes whining. Under the dank, geometric shadows of the track, its iron supports cast this way and that. I walked a block down to a line of three-storey houses, pinned like a patchwork quilt with shop letterings and slogans. Among them was a feature I recognised. Emblazoned along the base of a roof were the bold words "Mrs Hall's Intelligence Agency".

I had seen this text before. I had called in at this office during my weeks of bail investigations, purely a fact-finding expedition, nothing more. We call these places intelligence agencies, but that is far from what they are. "Employment office" might be a better term, "labour shop" probably closer still.

The sign appeared differently to me now. Recent facts brought a new slant to it. I had always assumed that it referred to Mrs Celia Lowe Hall, the brisk and efficient woman who ran the agency. But now I wondered whether it was not she, but her husband, Murray, whose name it proclaimed. All the while, a truth had been hidden in plain sight, as if Hall were making a joke, laughing in the face of all those he had deceived.

For a moment I stood there, looking up at one of the upper windows – slits of eyes only partially open. A narrow, vertical rectangle of light was framed by curtains. A silhouette of a head appeared in that space, peering out for a moment. Whoever it was had let her hair down and was brushing it in rough, jerking strokes. She turned in profile and I saw the smooth slope of a nose and the square thrust of a jaw. Then she looked out again, as if studying something below, and pulled the curtains closed.

It was her, I thought. I remembered the determined set of that jaw. *The Hall daughter.*

My eyes drifted back down to the darkness of the crepe-draped agency window in front of me, which offered no more than a reflection of myself and a blackboard sign listing, "Live in Domestics. Hire servants. Cooks. Seamstresses. We want you. References essential."

Leaning against the wall of the agency, I watched the flow of winter pedestrians pulling their collars tight up to their necks, heads ducked down against the frigid breeze. A man dressed entirely in the black of mourning and a towering top hat passed into a door to the left of the office. I watched as he left the door slightly and deliberately ajar, jamming a block of wood into the space. Open, I thought as I stared at the dark crack, as if to let death out. Open, perhaps, in the carelessness and chaos of grief.

I stepped towards the darkness of that door and paused in the slit, looking upwards beyond the shadowy staircase. The corridor was as chill as the street.

I could hear footsteps on the stairs above.

Gently, I called out: "Hello!"

"Hello!" I said again, slipping inside.

Already I could hear muted conversation. The low tones of people exchanging information.

"... tomorrow ... Around ten. You need make no decision right now." In those words was the solemn tone of mourning, or at least its pretence.

"The body shall be quite safe at the morgue, I assure you. And it shall be returned to you post-haste," said the other voice.

"One would hope that now the coroner's physician has seen, *ehm*, the body, all will be in order for the inquest. As soon as his office has given permission, we can arrange the funeral." He paused. "You may want to think over the choice of clothing. I suggest the dress of, *ehm*, a lady would be most appropriate."

This voice had a strange coughing tic, one that was quite annoying.

A woman spoke now, her voice hoarse but fierce, with a strong Irish lilt. "Mr Hall in his life never wore no dress."

"No doubt you could find one that would fit. If not, perhaps we can help you with that. We will, of course, *ehm*, prepare the body, as discussed, so only the face is visible."

"So as not to upset Miss Hall. Yes, thank you."

"I assure you, my assistant, Mr Rinning, can be trusted with all matters."

"She is desperate, as you'll have heard, to see him – though I worry the shock would be too great."

"You have done right to keep her from this. No one else should enter the room till we finish tomorrow. It would be too, *ehm*, upsetting."

"She will not believe it's true."

"None of your, *ehm*, privacies shall be shared," the man's voice said.

There was the creak of a door, then footsteps on the stairs once more. I stepped soundlessly back down a few steps to give the impression I had only just entered the building. Two men appeared on the landing, one of them carrying a small case. Both were dressed in black, and the second I recognised as Mr Partridge, the undertaker and sexton of Grace Church. This was a man who had buried some of the leading lights of Manhattan, whom I had encountered when covering the death of the society man Lawrence Kip; Partridge was one who carried the hush of death in his every delicate step. He tipped his head at me, gave another of those odd coughs, frowned, then walked on.

When I reached the interior door marked "Hall", I found it closed, and knocked loudly. It took some time for it to be answered. An elderly woman appeared, jutting her head out from a dimly lit hallway, eyebrows arched, as if expecting someone else entirely.

"I apologise for this intrusion upon your mourning," I said.

The woman stared, eyes focusing, gunmetal hair pulled tightly back from her broad-boned face.

Her dress was more grey than black, so faded was its colour.

"My very deepest condolences," I went on. "You see, I heard of your loss and, also, of some peculiar circumstances around it, and I wondered if you might verify a few details."

"Verify?" Her eyes narrowed, her voice chewing over the syllables.

"Check with you," I said, uncertain if she was thrown by the word. "Yes, you see, there are a few things . . ."

She was one of those older Irish women who seemed to have the measure of all people. "A few things about what exactly?" she asked.

"Mr Hall," I said.

"Mr Hall is not in."

"As I said, I am sorry for your loss."

"Esther, who is it?" a voice broke from down the corridor. I could now detect the long low sound of a moan, like the baying of some animal.

"Another gentleman!" she called back along the corridor. "I am about to send him on his way!"

"Tell him this is not the day!" the distant voice, tired and flat, called out.

"He says he has heard of the peculiar circumstances surrounding our loss."

Another voice rose up, livelier, calling out in Yiddish, "Neyn, neyn."

"No one else today!"

The woman they had called Esther nodded, as if to say, yes, you heard it there, be on your way. "You will have heard what the lady said. This house is in mourning. We are not taking visitors."

"I'm a reporter," I said quickly, recognising that in seconds the door could be closed. "I heard the shocking news. The story has already, of course, been covered by many newspapers today – but I wondered if Imelda Hall may like to tell her own version, for readers to hear her own words."

"Well, now," the woman said with a sigh. Her hand was on the door and she gripped it, ready to push it closed. She looked back into the corridor as if to call out again, then seemed to change her mind. "I can tell you now that the mistress of the house doesn't want to see you," Esther said. "She has already decided as much."

"I only wish to ask a few small questions. Perhaps I could return another day?"

She lowered her voice. Her eyes glinted out of the shadow. "Sir, I must say again that this is a house in mourning. I don't think it's right that you come here asking such questions. Write what you like in the papers, and I'm sure you will, but Miss Hall will not speak with you." She was slowly closing the door, but I leaned into the crack and heard her words, now muffled through the wood: "She will speak to no one."

"May I simply leave my card? Mrs . . . Esther . . . In case she changes her mind?" I sensed this was my last chance, slipping my hand into my pocket and thrusting an arm through the door. Such forcefulness was unusual for me, and I surprised myself. Was it the desire for information on Hall? Or was it a desire to see that woman whom he had presented to the world as his daughter?

She shrugged wearily. "Leave it if you like. I don't see it doing much good. This house has no need for newspapermen. We are, as you see, in a state of loss."

The snow was thickening on the ground. Chastened by the exchange with the old woman, I wrapped my scarf over my chin and walked through the gleaming white carpet to the shelter of the railway. New York cleaned by snow; all its dirt and grime hidden momentarily from sight.

It always felt like a new beginning. The smoothing out of a fresh page.

There were others now gathered on the sidewalk opposite, where a public bench had been installed under the shadow of the railroad track. It was a knot of six or seven people, mostly poor working folk, judging by their clothes, perhaps on their way to, or from, one of the ale houses. They had stopped to look upwards at those same windows.

"Remember how he used to sit there on this bench with his dog ... There'd be him and sometimes a couple of the younger lasses from the agency. He liked to bring them along. Sometimes the older ones too." A woman spoke, the snow melting into the cloud of her hair. She didn't seem to mind the cold, despite the thinness of her coat and skirts.

"*She*," said another woman wrapped in several layers of shawl, so that only the window of face between her mouth and her eyes was visible. "*She* used to sit there."

"He ... she ... I don't care. I just know Murray Hall was good to me."

"Good to you?" A dishevelled figure in a battered and frayed peacoat was standing over her. "Well, you'd be a rare one. I'll tell you a story about Murray Hall. I'll give you a proper story."

"Oh, Artie, shush. Not that again."

"I bet you haven't heard the body in the basement story?" the unkempt man went on.

"The body in the basement?"

"It's nonsense." The woman with wispy hair was shaking her head.

"Nonsense? I saw it with my own eyes."

"Pure nonsense ..." she said again.

"You say that, girl, but you wasn't there. I was the only one who was there, and I saw what I saw and I won't forget it. You want to hear this story or not?" The man was clearly gearing up for a monologue, and I saw some folk who had seemingly heard the story before drifting away. I was intrigued, and shunted myself closer to the edges of the crowd.

"This was twenty years ago, at least, and Mr Hall was clearing out his home and offices and moving from one place to another. I was hired to help. We were clearin' out the basement, and the one thing he said was we shouldn't go anywhere near the large box that was down there." He was really getting into his story now, his eyes far away in memory.

"But I looked at that box and I saw the size of it. Somethin' about it made me want to look in. You know that feeling? Someone tells you not to look somewhere, so it's the only place you want to look ... I guess it was the fact it was man-sized. So, anyway, curiosity got the best of me and when I was alone, I went over and pried it open – and what did I find?"

"A body!" the threadbare woman shrieked, rolling her eyes.

"Damn it, Mary McBride! Let me tell my own story. Yes, a skeleton." He shuffled himself taller in his peacoat, conferring authority to his tale. "To my eyes, it was the skeleton of a woman."

A blond man who had been silent until this point smiled. "My wife always swore Mr Hall was a woman. Always. When I think of how I laughed at her."

"Your missus said that? She will be laughing now."

"From the moment she first met Murray Hall, that was what she said. And it was all because of that damned dog. That noisy goddamned dog. It made some racket. The whole neighbourhood would tell you about it. And then the savage creature bit our Clara."

The interrupter, Mary McBride, laughed. "I knew it too! And none knew Murray like I did. I'm telling you. I know more than most."

"And me!" said a younger man with a dark pencil of a moustache, dressed slightly more respectably than the rest. The crowd was working itself up, and I began to wonder how many of these claims were being made up on the spot.

"First time I ever met him, I was working over at the Armory Hall. This was before it got closed due to the City Vigilance and for 'encouraging prostitution', as they said. That was in the days when we had all kinds of people coming in, and there was no bother about women – though mostly they were of the fast and fallen type.

"Anyway," he said, facing away from me and leaning conspiratorially into the crowd so that I had to bend closer to hear, "on this particular night there was this party o' three came in, and I looked at them and all I saw was three women, one of them dressed in a man's suit. We were used to all kinds at the Armory so I didn't think much of it. They came in, the three of them, this little person in a suit and two tall women on either side, and sat at a table through the back. So, I just got on with taking the order from the party and the two ladies

31

ordered the grog. Then I says to the one in the suit, 'And what will you have, little old woman?'"

He laughed loudly at the memory of it, slapping the older man, Artie, on the shoulder.

"I've never been one for mincing m' words. Well, ah can tell you all hell broke loose then. This little woman flew into a rage. This person was cussing and cussing and calling me all kind of names, which I would not repeat in front of the ladies, but they were such as you might only normally hear from rogues and coves. Then this person – who I later learned was Murray Hall – picks up this bottle from the table and starts waving it at me, like he's going to wallop me in the face. It was lucky the ladies calmed him down. Course, now that I know the secret, I can understand what roused Hall. It was that I'd seen the truth. He or she was short, skinny as a rake – and effeminate. With no one telling you she was a man, it was clear as day she was … well, a *she*. There was not a hair on her face, which was wizened like an autumn apple in a hayloft, and she was continually smiling, like an old woman might be expected to smile."

He looked from face to face, a huge grin stretched across his own features. "There's a big difference between a man's smile and a woman's – and it's not just about how much we do it."

I knew what he meant. It wasn't a man's thing to smile. I'd learned that young. A man has to know when and where to smile.

"How's it we all knew the truth and never shared it?"

The voice of Artie, the man in the peacoat, rose again over the rest of them. "Don't you want to hear the rest of my tale?

This is tavern gossip. But what I have to say might mean somethin'. I was there. I was there. I thought that body in the box was Hall's wife. But you know what I think now?"

There was a hushed silence.

Mary McBride rolled her eyes.

"I think it was Murray Hall himself. Which means his wife could have killed him and taken his place!"

A concerted grumble issued from the others. Mary McBride sighed and turned to the crowd. "This old cadger has changed that story to fit the facts. Which of you people are gonna come with me to Skelly's? A drink in memory of Murray."

"I mighta changed the story – but there's no changing the fact there was a skeleton in there, and I saw it! And he did have another wife – that's true and nobody knows what happened to her. She just disappeared."

"Went out West," said the blond man.

"I heard she came back now and again to try and get some money out of the scoundrel. Come on, let's shoot. I'm thirsty for a drink."

"I heard he met her out there when he was in California searching for gold," said the woman wrapped up in scarves.

Mary McBride tugged at Artie's arm, pulling him away from his oration. Some of the crowd peeled away, but most of the group started towards the bar in unison. As they moved away, I heard Artie's voice start up again.

"I'm telling you, Murray Hall must have put that body there. I looked into that box and there were human bones – a human body!"

MA'S BASEMENT OYSTER BAR, MACDOUGAL STREET

17TH JANUARY 1901, 1 P.M.

Y POCKET WATCH REGISTERED JUST before one o'clock as I turned the corner onto MacDougal Street and saw that O'Connor was already there, kicking snow off his boots. He grinned. "Oysters in season, I hear," he said.

"So I've heard." I returned his smile and reached out to shake his gloved hand.

"Good to see you, Mr Clellan," he said. "I imagine you'll be wanting to talk about our man-no-more Murray Hall. Am I right?"

"You certainly are, Officer O'Connor. And perhaps a catch-up, too, on matters regarding our Captain Herlihy?"

"Now Herlihy – that's a more difficult matter."

We descended a narrow set of stairs and passed through a pair of swinging doors into Ma's; hers was the kind of dive where you could fill your eyes and your belly for less than twenty cents.

The restaurant, formerly a den that swarmed with fallen women, had been cleaned up five years ago by Ma, a formidable woman, whose parents – so I'd heard – had been slaves in Alabama, with a presence fierce and generous enough to keep the place reputable, and a talent for serving the best oysters in the district. During the years of my bail investigation, hers had become the go-to joint where O'Connor and I would meet, a location and an exchange that was acceptable to us both. Oysters for tip-offs. Back then, Ma's oysters were often, as we said, in season.

The policeman was more than a yard in width, with a chest so broad it strained the brass buttons of his uniform. He filled the entire doorframe as we entered. Heads turned, as they always did, when the bulk of this man entered the room. He never seemed to know what to do with his size, though, and was constantly knocking over glasses as he spoke. It was as if he had never quite caught up with the growth and heft of his own body.

Within a minute of us taking our seats, Ma was standing over a table, singing out. "Raw. Stewed. Fried. Pickled. Smoked. Ketchup. Horseradish?" Her eyes caught ours and she made a swift movement of her hand to direct us to just get on and make our order. She hadn't been a fan of O'Connor and his uniform on our first visit, but now that we were regulars we were tolerated.

The great thing about Ma's was that we could almost guarantee to be the only white-skinned people in the place, and could certainly find a corner far from any potentially prying Tammany ears. It was a joint so raucous that our conversation was sure to go unnoticed. Ma's voice would boom across the room and a symphony of noise would barrel out of the hectic kitchen, where pans crashed and her son

36

Henry, only eighteen years old, would swear and sing like a one-man orchestra as he shucked.

We were settled at a pew in the corner. The policeman disregarded cutlery and scooped an oyster out with his thick fingers as soon as they arrived, licking the salt from their tips afterwards in a thorough, deft movement like that of a preening cat.

"You saw him," he said. "You saw what he was like. Or I suppose I should say she. You shoulda written about it back then."

I shook my head with regret. "I'm a coward, Michael. I don't have your courage." Or your morals, I thought. O'Connor was one of the few policemen I knew who shunned the graft protection system and hadn't tried to buy himself up the ladder – which was why, in spite of his talents, he was still a lowly beat officer. "How are things at the fifteenth?"

"Same as ever. Feels like the system never changes, as corrupt as ever. Though everyone is looking at what is happening with Herlihy. Officers are nervous. They sense secrets about to come out."

"Those with hope in the Lord will renew their strength," I said, but even as my father's words fell from my mouth, they felt hardened and trite. "I'm sorry," I sighed.

"I still pray every night for the end of the graft," O'Connor said. He scooped another oyster out with his thumb, wiped his hand, and placed the napkin down on the table. "But I believe it less."

"Such a simple word, graft." I said, drawing its single syllable out. "As a youngster I thought it just meant work.

But this, here, in Manhattan, is the opposite. This *graft* is designed so the rich and powerful can skim money off other people's real work."

O'Connor nodded. His solemn eyes locked mine from under his thick reddish brows. "I've often thought about that day with Murray Hall," he said. "An' not just because o' what we've learned about who she was, but also because of the blinker Hall left me with. This mark ... here ... Below the eye." He pointed towards a line, like a deep wrinkle that ran under his lower lashes. "You see it? It's still there if you look close ... The spot where the little man, who I now read in your paper was a little woman, anointed me. A scar from a woman? The shame. I can't get my head round it. Murray Hall, a woman."

"Who of us can?"

"You should go down to the Iroquois club and ask if any of them knew. If any of those Tammany had even a hunch there was a woman in their midst."

"I'm not sure any of them would admit to it even if they did know."

"Barney Martin would, I'm sure, have something to say."

"He does give a choice line."

O'Connor shook his head. "I've been thinking back. I don't know why Cross chose me for the job of going down to the club that night an' arresting him. I know what I'm good at. I can bust up a brawl, chase down a man over a mile. No sweat. There's many a touch been stopped by me. But this was another thing. A different thing. Hall was just this little man."

"Platter of ten," Ma declared, as a new plate of oysters landed on the table in front of me – raw and seasoned with pepper, salt and vinegar.

"No ketchup?" Ma asked. "No horseradish?"

"You should get the ketchup," O'Connor said.

"Ya like the new ketchup?"

"Best ketchup in town, Ma. Best in town," O'Connor said, a sparkle in his tawny eyes. "I believe this fine place of yours gets better every time I come here."

"You sayin' we were no good before?" Her tone was rough, but I could almost see a smile playing at the corner of her mouth. Almost.

"No, Ma." He turned the expanse of his chest to her. "Yours was always the best."

I sprinkled more pepper over the plate. "I remember that story about how you picked up Hall at the Iroquois. You said he was looking smart, full evening suit. Croker was in at the club that night, and he'd been concerned for there not to be too much fuss. You took him straight down to the station."

He chuckled. "Not exactly. I remember I said, 'I've a warrant for your arrest, Mr Hall. On grounds of presentation of fictitious sureties as bail.' He blinked for a moment, takin' it in. 'I'm accused of straw bail?' he said, eyes wide. 'Straw bail? Hell's bells. I've been working in this town as a bondsman for three decades. And I'm now accused of straw bail. Who is the source of these goddamn lies?' I tried to coax him, go easy, y'know. He wanted to stop for cigars on the way. So, I let him. To me,

39

Murray felt like a boy. Like a gnat. But I knew this gnat was said to have some temper. I didn't want to spark it."

O'Connor stopped for a moment to spoon more ketchup onto his plate. I relaxed and picked up one of my oysters, tipping it gently so the viscous form slid into my mouth, a briny gulp of sea. You don't swallow oysters – they do it for you.

"We got the cigars," he went on. I got the feeling he wanted to run through the whole tale. "Meyer's cigar shop. Then after that it was on to Skelly's. Murray sayin' how he'll furnish me bail and we can have a quick drink. 'I'll buy you a beer, Officer O'Connor, I'll make sure you're looked after. A quick drink before we get to the station.' Maybe it wasn't my smartest move, but I went with it. I was in no rush to get back to the station, or upset Hall. You know Patrick Skelly's?"

"Sure, I do," I replied. "Round the corner from Hall's place. A fine free lunch – the pickled fish is worth the cost of a nickel beer. All the champs on the wall. I can see why Hall liked the place. That was how Skelly got involved?"

I knew at least part of this story – that Patrick Skelly had ended up down at the police station where they'd found Captain Cross, a man as corrupt as any officer now caught up in the Herlihy case. The captain was particularly glad to see Skelly, a man renowned for possessing a readiness to pay out. An envelope of graft from the master brewer was often more than generous. It wasn't long before Cross was declaring the arrest a mistake as he tucked the hefty brown envelope away. All of them enriched by the transaction.

"I'll always remember what they said when they left the precinct office," O'Connor went on with a grin. He licked his thumb once more. "'Now, go straight home, old boy,' Mr Skelly said, 'and don't stop to drink any more, or you won't be able to get around to court in the morning. Straight home.' 'Home?' Mr Hall replied. 'And pass the Old Grapevine without a glass of Blooming Grove?'"

O'Connor took a long, gulping drink himself as he recalled the evening's events. "It was later during my rounds that I heard about trouble going on at Teddy Ackermann's – a Tammany crowd up to nonsense. I could hear the commotion even as I turned on to the street. I could hear commotion out front at Ackermann's. I was soon close enough to see, in the glow of the door, some kind of brawl was picking up."

O'Connor paused, took another slug of his beer, and wiped the heel of his hand across his lips, readying himself to continue. "Murray Hall was outside, o' course. He was swayin' as he pushed to get back through the door again, but he was bein' stopped at the entrance by a man of some width, who was blockin' his way an' pushin' him back. There was that crowing again, that quail-pipe voice. I'd no idea what words he spoke – he was that drunk – but I could tell Mr Hall was objectin' and he was in some overheatin' fury. I was glad to see there was already another officer approachin'. I could tell it was Perchet – a man who, though he may be stringier than myself, can hold himself ... Then in the doorway appeared the white apron of the saloonkeeper, shakin' an angry fist. More shoutin'. All the foul-mouthed words. Hall was waving that black cane of his, flailing and trying to knock the others back. It did not deter Perchet, who lunged past to try an' grab 'im. The cane clattered to the ground, and there was this whirlin', bodies turnin' over, and Hall was on his feet again, and started hammerin' into Perchet, who curled like a stepped-on beetle. Never seen anythin' like it!

"'Send for the patrol wagon!' I hollered good and hard and thundered towards Hall, who was now standing in empty space, like Shanklin waitin' to take a punch. Before I could get there, Perchet rose to his feet, but Mr Hall was on him again. The little man flew at him, like some ragin' bat wrapping its wings. I lunged down in between, trying to grab him, to grasp hold of his arm, but somehow missed. 'Mr Hall!' I cried, as I at last seized his wrist. 'It's time you went home.'

"Hall hurled a torrent of words at me, pure drunken Scots. Damns and blasteds and suchlike. He wriggled out of my grasp and curled his hands into buckets. I let him pummel me, and leaned in, my arms grasping over to grip the black frock coat, but the wily little man slipped under. I tried to grab him as he did, twisted to catch him, but felt my face slam into something. A sharp jab hit me under the eye. The space around me went black with the force of the pain right there, and I staggered. The man had hit me, I realised. He had hit me square in the face. I reached a hand to my eye. But I could see nothin' other than a darkness and the colour of blood. I could sense the man still dancin' around and I could hear him laughin'.

"I felt the skin below my eye. Wet and sticky. I wasn't sure if it was blood or tears. The little man got me, I thought. Damn him. And damn the shame o' it. It was this that dizzied me much as anything else. I cupped my hand over my eye and closed it and found that at least I could now see through the other eye. I could see Mr Hall, runnin' again full tilt towards Perchet. It was as if he did not care who or what he was fightin', as if all he saw was shadows needin' defeating.

"Perchet was stepping back from the blows. I could hear onlookers laughin' and hollerin', like they was at some vaudeville show. The mocking sound maddened me, and I pushed myself forward. I got a grip on his shoulder and pushed him to the wall. I pressed down on him there so his face was turned up against the rough brick. He breathed hard. Grunted. And I pulled round his arms, then tugged the cuffs from my pocket. I clipped them on. 'It's all a damned plot,' Hall cried in his wretched, reedy voice. 'Call Barney Martin. Call him. Call Croker.'"

O'Connor shook his head, pausing for a moment to catch his breath. He picked up his beer and glugged it back. "And damn it, Mr Clellan, we find out now that that damned rascal was a woman!"

The noise around us had dropped and I wondered if the tables nearby were listening. The policeman leaned into me, pointing again at the crease below his eye, and growled quietly. "Even then, when I thought it was a man who did this to me, just that pipsqueak man, I felt nothing but shame. 'Well, that's a fine storm cloud draping in the making,' is what the night officer said. 'Did the little fellow do that to you?' It became the precinct joke – the night Murray Hall knocked out the big man, O'Connor – and I was its punchline."

"Literally," I said with a smile.

O'Connor frowned, and I wasn't sure he had got my point. He threw his hands in the air, almost knocking his platter upwards. "Of course, the story has changed now. It's no longer the night the little man gave me a storm cloud; it's the night a little woman did. That little woman, Murray Hall. God himself, I sometimes think, is mockin' me."

I shook my head. "God is mocking all of us. I keep thinking today that Murray Hall is laughing at me, showing me some kind of lesson."

O'Connor chuckled. He picked up the fresh beer Ma had put before him and drained the glass. He placed it back down and there was one of those pauses, so typical of him, in which I knew he was thinking, chewing something over, and it was best not to interrupt. "But on that night, Murray Hall was not laughin'. Far from it. Most men when they are drunk seem not to care what kind o' floor you throw them down on. They see it like a welcome bed for the night, a place where no more trouble awaits. But Hall, when we locked her up, looked real terrified to be there."

He shook his head, thoughtfully. "See ... when I checked the cell before leavin' that night, she was cowering in the corner as if she didn't want no one else near her – as if she was scared an' wanted to make herself so small no one would even see her. Was she like that when you came the next morning?" he asked, his expression curious. "I always wondered that."

"She was sleeping," I said, a memory flashing clear in my mind of how, when I'd visited the cell, she was passed out – how peering through the door all I saw was what looked like a crumpled pile of clothes in the corner. "I couldn't work out if that was her at first. Then I saw that the black cape was covering her. Just those shiny, worn-down shoes sticking out . . . Like a child blanketed by a father's coat."

"I always wondered what it was that made her do that," O'Connor said, staring down at his plate, empty but for its debris of shell and streaked ketchup. "Now I think I know. It's 'cause of what she was, and what she was hidin' . . . Think how damned terrifying that must have been. The fear and the terrible shame. The endless anticipation of exposure. P'rhaps that's what drove it all – that big man attitude, the wheeling and dealing, the hustle, the gambling, the political thuggery. Perhaps it was all just a way she could hide."

Yes, I thought. A child curled up under a blanket. Hiding.

THE IROQUOIS, WEST 13TH STREET
19TH JANUARY 1901, 1 P.M.

I
T'S SOME BUILDING, THE IROQUOIS. A four-storey brownstone, with a portico of iron that appears to writhe, vine-like, out of the masonry. Then as you enter, you get the scent of it. The sweat of man. The rude, animal energy – along with the ever-present undertone of strong liquor. Yes, it's a political club, but it operates more in the manner of a saloon bar – billiards in the basement, poker and pinochle in the back. Alcohol of all types on tap at all hours of day and night.

It's not, in other words, the kind of establishment that any ordinary woman would choose to access, nor would it welcome her; unless she were the invisible kind, scrubbing its floors, washing its glasses, or cooking its highly rated clam chowders.

All this was on my mind as I passed under its arch and into the heart of the place. This and the thought that here was a fortress under threat – spooked by the idea that Herlihy might spill all, or that the district attorney might swoop in and catch them at it. The tables had been turning on the party and the backhanded way it operated for some years – and now it was attempting to rebrand itself as some kind of moral institute. Nothing to do with the debauched "combine" of police, gambling and nightlife power! I wasn't sure anyone was buying this unconvincing pivot.

You know you are heading towards a victory when your enemy starts to use your language, when they talk of a "clean-up", when they believe their own lies to such an extent that they invent their own committee to execute them. The demise of this place can't come soon enough, was my view.

It says it all that the man I was hoping to see, the club's sachem, Senator Barney Martin, was also the one-time owner of the notorious Burnt Rag saloon, friend of the burglar Red Leary, and a defender of the open city of New York, a metropolis in which the faucet of vice is never turned off.

"Member?" asked the door boy.

My father's voice whispered towards me through the hallway:

Harpies, under the guise of governing this city, are day and night feeding on its vitals. They are a liquor-addled, lecherous lot. Do not let them lure you in.

"No. Just a visitor. I was hoping to see Senator Martin."

"Who shall I say is asking for him?"

"Mr Clellan, of the *New York World*." I knew there was a strong chance that Martin would know of my City Vigilance past, of my anti-vice stance and my involvement in the closing down of certain establishments on Bleecker Street, but I hoped he might still be generous enough to grant me a brief audience. It seemed there was no point in pretending to be anyone other than myself.

The door boy, a charmless, sallow youth in an ill-fitting suit, led me through. Barney was smoking a thick Upmann at a mahogany table. The senator looked up and waved as if we were close friends. Like so many of the most adept politicians in this city, he had a good memory for a face, if not always a name.

"Ah, Mr Clellan! I hear you want to talk to me about my close associate, Mr Hall!"

There was an emphasis, a threat on the word *Mr*. As he moved his chair to the side, I sensed the irritation at my presence that moved beneath the façade of his hospitality.

"It's a surprise to find a reporter of your persuasion showing an interest in our dear friend. I thought you had more interest in the business of the courts and police department."

I hadn't seen Barney up close for a few years, but my immediate impression was that he had widened in girth since our last interview. Veins had crept across his prominent nose. He had thickened further about the neck. The flesh around his jaw had melted downwards, and the digits holding it were almost as wide as the cigar itself. The saying that Barney Martin is fat of body, fat of fingers, fat of neck, fat of face, fat of head ... well, it was truer than ever.

A bottle of wine was open on the table, and one glass already poured – a second sat empty. "You'll take a drink, won't you?" he said. "I'd say a drink is the only way to deal with events like these. We've got some fine French Burgundy, just arrived on the ship yesterday. You will take a glass, won't you, Mr Clellan? I have already been toasting the sad loss of a friend."

He began pouring generously into a wide, fashionably pressed glass, then raised his own. "She's dead, poor fellow!"

49

I raised mine and took a restrained sip. "Indeed. Poor fellow," I said, rather awkwardly. There was a tear quite visible in the corner of his right eye.

"So," he said, "what are you trying to uncover? I am happy to talk if what you want is some glowing tale about our friend Murray Hall! But I'm not sure how much I can help you. Much of the story has already been told by the *New York Times*."

"I'm simply curious. I met Hall a couple of times and I'll confess I never guessed. But all of you ... How is it that the men here had no idea?" I pulled a notebook out of my pocket.

The senator frowned and gestured. "As you like – but if I say something is off the record, it's off," he instructed. He leaned towards me and his voice dropped. "And, by the way, I'm not interested in payment; just a story I'd like you to tell that might put Tammany in a more favourable light. I hope that is what you are here for. Or are you, Mr Clellan, on another of your puritanical, anti-corruption missions to expose Tammany Hall?"

He smiled that winning smile again, looking for all the world like a kind, fatherly gentleman.

"These vicious resorts," he said, beaming, "I am sure you are aware, are not run by Tammany Hall. They are run by a combine who cloak their workings by pretending to be Tammany. I am confident that our leader, Mr Croker, has not received one single cut of this blood money."

I raised my hand to halt the speech that he was no doubt going to develop. I had heard, and put in print, far too many such protestations before. "Please. I'm just interested in Murray Hall," I said. "I met him a couple of times and I'm intrigued

50

by this tale. Aren't we all? Isn't all of New York? Let me ask perhaps an obvious question. I take it the revelation came as a surprise to you?"

He laughed, and the rust-coloured wine formed concentric ripples in our glasses. "There are those who would make out that this is a scandal. But truly it is most wonderful, don't you think? Murray Hall, a woman? And none of us guessed at his secret. I knew him well. A member of the Tammany district organisation, a hard worker for his party, and always had a fierce argument to put up for any candidate he fancied. He'd come in here to pay his dues, and occasionally he would crack a joke with some of the boys. Like, Joe here ... You probably knew him better than most of us, didn't you, Joe?" he said, raising his voice for the benefit of another man who was settled at a nearby table with an open newspaper, but who was clearly listening in.

I turned towards the man to whom he gestured, who lowered his shield of print. A tall, tailored figure, muscular, and with the thickest of handlebar moustaches, grey at the edges and black towards its centre, shining with oil. The contrast against his white skin was quite striking, But what struck me most was the fine, thin scar that stretched the length of his cheek.

I felt myself stutter out a noise which sounded more like a cough than a word. This man was so familiar that I wondered for a moment if he might greet me in recognition. But there was not even a smile. He tilted his head and shrugged. "He was one of us boys. A sport. Liked a game of cards. Ah think the last time I saw him was over a game of Widow here."

Barney nodded sagely. "Say, when was the last time he was here? Do you recall, Joe? I hadn't seen him for many months. He'd been ill. I don't think he even voted in the last election. Joe, you would know."

"Ah don't think so. Ah could check the records." You could barely see the man's mouth move as he spoke behind his moustache. If he did indeed recognise me, then that was some poker face. His eyes met mine before drifting blankly across my face, as if he were merely observing the pattern of a piece of wallpaper. The look was unreadable, and then he broke away. "Ah'll get the book."

I watched as he left the room, a bold swing in his stride, every movement controlled, right down to his neat closure of the door behind him.

Barney talked on, oblivious to my upset, or at least pretending to be. "Something happened to Murray that sent him downhill. Some folks said it was a bicycle collision, but others said he had suffered a beating – and by a convict, William Reno. A thorough beating, they said."

I was now barely listening. All I could think of was this strange, elegant brute of a man, and the circumstances that led to our last meeting. My mind reached back to that afternoon at Fatone's ... to the man in the chair opposite, to that face, that livid scar.

"Suspect he was a woman?" Barney went on. "Never. He dressed like a man and talked like a very sensible one."

The senator was a born politician, I thought. He paused for a moment as if trying to call something to mind. "The only thing I ever thought eccentric about him was his clothing. That old coat he wore no matter the season was always far too large."

The words seemed to sink and muffle as if caught in the dense velvet curtains of the club room. Still, all I could think about was when Joe was going to come back, and whether I should be gone by the time he did. Barney paused to observe me. "I take it I have given you enough?"

I saw something tighten in his jaw. I was under no illusion that I could trust Bernard F. Martin, or that his words were anything other than smoke and mirrors, the smoulder of political arithmetic. You had to be suspicious of a man who counted among his friends the likes of Billy Vosburg. There was a warning in his tone that made me want to leave.

The door creaked, and I realised I was too late for a swift exit. Joe was there again with a book under his arm. He laid the thick leather-bound slab on the table between us and pulled up a chair, opening it at a page he had already bookmarked. He smelled of cigar smoke and wet leather. "Ah was trying to remember when he was last in. He hadn't been for a good while."

I looked down at the page, a series of columns of names, payments and voting numbers. I was surprised that the senator would be so willing to let me, a journalist, glance over such key party information, and I wondered if this was some kind of trap.

"Ah liked him," Joe said. "Ah liked the way he played his cards."

I noticed as I watched his finger drift up and down the page, the bright cuff of his white shirt, the chunk of gold rings on his fingers. Another scar, too, across the back of his hand, grooving his right knuckle.

He lifted another book onto the table and opened it. "Ah thought he had voted last year, but in fact he did not get round to registering in time to vote for Bryan, perhaps because of his illness. His last vote, you'll see here, was in November 1899. You can see for yourself that he is enrolled that year, enrolment number one-seven-six ... A woman? Murray Hall? Why, he would line up to the bar and take his whisky like any veteran, and didn't pull faces over it, either."

He titled his head and looked me directly in the eye for the first time. I noticed the deep furrow of another light scar across his chin. This was the kind of man who most likely did his own share of street fighting back in his youth, perhaps until fairly recently. The type you would cross the street to avoid.

"Are you fond of the Widow, Mr Clellan?" he asked. "Ah like a game myself. Murray did. Perhaps you will stay for a few rounds and ah'll tell you some tales of my own about our Murray Hall."

"A champion idea!" The senator's booming voice caused the wine to dance once more. "I must leave you gentlemen, I'm afraid, as I have business to attend to. But Joe here will keep you entertained, won't you, Joe?"

Joe Young's eyes gleamed green in the electric light of the card room. I had remembered them grey, like Hall's, from our first meeting, but I now saw the depths of them like a briny sea.

"Ah take it you know how to play the Widow. Thirty-one? It's a simple game but it was one of Murray's favourites. Better to play with three or four, but we can play it fine enough with two."

A pack of cards danced between his hands, fluttering like sparrows taking to the air, then caught between his deft fingers.

"I've played it a number of times," I replied.

My father's voice murmured through the back of my mind as the cards spread like a lady's fan at the opera, then closed again. *We must, as we battle for reform, not allow ourselves to be deformed . . . Gambling, cards, disorderly houses, the pool room, all these can divert us from holiness.*

"The aim being to be the player who has collected cards closest to a total of thirty-one," he said as if he sensed my uncertainty. "A dollar note on the table, and each life you lose, you fold the corner. No more than a dollar lost in the whole game." He chuckled. "Ah sense you're not a gambler, Mr Clellan. Ah know, of course, your aversion to such base pleasures. But if you'll permit me a game, ah'll tell you about my friend Murray Hall."

The two candles of the bouillotte lamp bathed the mahogany surface in light, sharpening Joe's features as he leaned inwards to offer the deck towards me. "Cut," he instructed, and I did as he said.

"The Widow," he repeated as his muscular, nimble hands dealt three cards to each of us, then slid a further three down onto the centre of the table. "Strange how many card games are named after the female cards, don't you think, Mr Clellan?"

The man leaned back into his chair and inhaled deeply. He appeared to be studying me, just as he had those few years ago in Fatone's. He hadn't changed much, save the hint of grey in his moustache. I wondered for a brief moment if I had. He drew a box of cigars from his pocket and offered me one. I raised a hand and shook my head, then watched as, with a smirk, he lit his own.

"They say Murray Hall fooled many shrewd men. Well, you can count me as one," he said, taking a long draw. "Your start."

I turned my cards towards me. On the table, flipped upwards, the flop contained a further three: a five of diamonds, a seven of clubs and six of spades.

"Murray loved this game," he went on. "First time ah ever saw him was in the back room of the saloon on the corner of fourteenth and sixth in the run-up to the 1883 senatorial election. Ah hadn't gone in there looking for a poker game, just a drink and to eavesdrop on the gossip of the County Democracy crowd. Ah drifted into that room because the whisper in the bar was that they were back there, playing, and there was a big pot already building. This, ah figured, might be a game of some interest. Quite how much, I could not have imagined. Needless to say, ah played him at cards that night and lost.

56

"Always remember the first glimpse ah had of the little fellow with the hat, silhouetted at first by the lamp behind him. Watchin' him play, ah soon realised that this was the fella people had been talking about. Murray Hall. Ah remember how he played, cigar between his teeth – though I don't believe he lit it. At one point he held out a trey, a three, for a 'kicker', and, blame me, if he didn't pull another three and a nine spot."

"I heard the woman was a remarkable shark – a killer instinct," I said, fighting to resist a smile as I stared at my cards. There, already, was an ace of spades and a Jack of spades, an early score of twenty-one. On the table, a further six. I waited for a moment, as if assessing my hand with uncertainty. If I could have knocked right then in the first round, I would have.

"That night he beat out three aces and swept up over a hundred dollars," said Joe, cigar smoke obscuring his face for a moment. "And this was a woman, a fella who stood two raises, on only two nines? Ah don't believe it ..."

I reached forward and pulled the six of spades towards me, replacing it with my nine of hearts. The man opposite smiled and plucked his hand off the table. He glanced at the cards for barely a second before he took my nine of hearts.

"It seems, over time, you got to know her better than most," I tried as I rearranged my hand. His manner was so casual that I wondered if he could possibly have forgotten our first meeting, if the incident was so frequent, or myself so unmemorable.

"Did ah know him well?" he said, resisting the feminine pronoun. "You reporters and your questions! What does that mean? Ah knew his style as a poker player, what cigars he smoked, who he would lay a bet on in a fight, and what he was like to come up against in an election match, but if you're asking me for details about where he came from and how he ended up in the city, you need to look elsewhere. Ah reckon most of us Tammany boys would say the same."

I studied the face, the scar like a pencil line leading up to those jade-coloured eyes. Could he truly have forgotten me? No, I thought, it was more likely the man was playing me, waiting to see who would cave first. But I was far from caving. I knocked gently on the table. My heart pounded and I spread the three, the ace, the jack, the six. "Twenty-seven," I said, now allowing myself a flicker of a smile.

"Nice," he said, as he laid out his own spread of nine and ten of hearts. "A lucky first hand." Joe's fingers reached forwards to pick up his dollar bill, flattening it on the table before turning one corner inwards. "One life gone," he said as he creased it with all the precision of Japanese folded paper. "Ah'd say Murray was one who lost a few lives along the way. So be it. Lives are made to be lost." Those eyes held my gaze for a moment and he pushed the deck of cards towards me, his hands hovering a moment longer than I expected before he pulled away. "Your shuffle, sir," he said. The eye contact did not waver.

"Ah'll say this about Murray – he was a genuine sport. He liked his cards and his pool and going to the big fights. He wasn't so much into the horses. Always said that wasn't for him. Ah remember in the late eighties, he and a few of us went up to Boston to watch the Dixon–Lyman fight. Little Chocolate,

Dixon was called then, and ah don't think anyone expected he would win it. Did you ever see Dixon fight?"

"Never, no," I said, concentrating now on the cards, but also attempting to suppress my displeasure at the sport of boxing. I never had much of a poker face. The skill of shuffling is not one I have ever developed either. I picked up the pack and mixed them overhand, passing them several times, then clumsily dropping them back onto the table. The man opposite me did not react. He simply kept talking.

"Ah noticed then," he said, "how Murray would lean in towards the ring, his head pushing forwards, his arms jerking as if in response to the movement of the fighters on the canvas. His limbs were echoing them. When Dixon's head was suddenly against Lyman's flesh just above the eye, cutting a nasty gash, ah saw how Murray jerked back as if he'd been hit himself. Ah've known a few blows myself. You'll see for yourself ah've been in fights that involved more than fists. And I feel it every time. That's what I felt about Murray. He, like me, held the fight in his body, as if he was right there in the ring. He was in the fight, moving within it, with its rhythm ... Will you take a whisky, Mr Clellan?"

I looked at Joe's hands, one fist rolling on the table, the other tapping restlessly on his leg. I wondered if what I saw before me was some nervous tic, a sign of a surfeit of energy – or a conscious threat.

"I'd rather just a water."

"You won't take a nip in memory of my Scots friend?" he said. "No, ah imagine not." He walked over to a small cupboard at the side of the room, turned a key and pulled out a bottle as I continued the deal. Was that a hint that he had a handle on my anti-vice principles? Or just that, somehow, he sensed a teetotal man?

"I had been watching Murray throughout the Dixon–Lyman fight, and as we left the building, and I'd been fascinated. It wasn't how sore he was that he lost the bet, or how he growled his way to the tavern about match fixing and injustice. It was how he responded, how he watched. It was how he leaned right into that ring as if he was studying every move. He was in there, as if he were a fighter himself. 'Were you once a pugilist yourself, old boy?' I asked, as we stepped out into the darkening street. 'Me? No,' he said. 'I've gotten into a few scraps over the years, but I never fought in the ring. Still, I like to watch. Not just for the sport. You learn things by watching.'"

There was a glug as Joe tipped the bottle, pouring himself a generous shot.

As I listened, I wondered why he was giving me so much attention – what the point of this audience was, or if I was nothing more than a fresh ear for his stories about a lost friend. We all want to tell our tales, sometimes feeling closer in the telling than ever we do when the deceased were alive.

"I have my regrets – that I didn't see Murray in his last months," he said, wandering back over to the table where he placed his glass. "You see, ah knew he was struggling. Ah feel some regret now that ah didn't do more to help. Maybe he mighta reached out, confided, asked for assistance despite his pride. He was surely struggling. You could see it."

Joe swirled the whisky in its glass, lost in thought.

"Ah don't know what sent Murray on a downward spiral. The death of his wife, the death of the dog? I have to say I couldn't understand how much he wept over that dog. That damned dog. I couldn't stand the creature. Too many dogs in this city, and their shit is waiting for you to put your foot in it everywhere a man walks. No one cleans it up. Maybe your paper should pay attention to that problem, huh? You who say you wanna clean up the city." He raised the whisky towards me and winked. There was a pause as we regarded each other cagily, two men from the same city but different worlds. "Ah know of your efforts on behalf of the League. And ah detect your judgement, Mr Clellan. You are a very judgemental man."

He settled back into his seat, his air of nonchalance dissipated. My heart was pounding. Was he saying that he remembered who I was from the Fatone's encounter? Or was that something else besides? I did not dare look up to catch his eye now as I dealt the flop, which was low at only a two, a three and a five.

All I could think about was this question of whether he really knew, if indeed he really remembered.

"That's not such a terrible thing," he went on. "P'rhaps it is even a sign of discipline. But anyway ... our friend Murray. It was back in the summer of 1898 that ah first started to notice that he was off form. Ah wasn't sure what the source of it was, and certainly he had told none of us. Gossip had it that he had been sandbagged by an ex-convict, though ah was never sure if it was true or groundless. Others said he had been knocked flying by a bicycle. Then his goddamn dog died.

And, of course, the loss of his wife. That hit him hard. Ah always thought that was the source of all his pain. Ah've seen it before. Some men can't take it when their other half goes. They wither. You start to wonder if the woman, the wife, had been their source of energy, a spark of electricity that kept them going – lit their bulb, as it were. Ah've never had much time for women myself."

Joe paused and slid the highest card, the six of clubs, towards him. Raising his eyebrows momentarily, he then placed down a six of diamonds. I let out a breath. I already had two diamond cards and one was high.

He continued talking as he stared across the table at me. "But, looking back, ah realise now there were also some physical symptoms. Murray, always small, seemed shorter even than usual, his back bent in a stoop that curled in on itself like one of those ammonite fossils. His gait was cautious and wincing, and he was using that cane of his for support more than style. Ah couldn't tell you how old he was when he died. He was an old man already when ah met him."

I listened. Instead of picking up immediately I stared thoughtfully at the three cards of the Widow for some time, absorbing his story.

"Ah don't tell you about his illness for publication – but just so you can have some kind of understanding. Gradually he came less frequently to the club, and to Skelly's too, or the Old Grapevine, where he was once as much a fixture as the musty ale and the sticky tables. Ah liked his company. And ah called at his house one or two times but was always turned away, with the explanation that he was out on business or indisposed. Then he stopped paying his dues to the club and didn't even vote that last year."

There was a lull in his narrative and I picked up the diamond, then nodded at him to play, which he swiftly did, taking my four of spades.

"Some people want to share their woes with all, every tiny ache and pain, but Murray was not one of those. I took that as being what his nature was. Private."

I knocked once more, a short hollow rap. I saw his eyebrows raise.

"Again?" he said.

"Perhaps," I said, spreading out a neat fan of six, ten and nine of diamonds.

He looked at his cards. "You certainly have the luck ..." He pulled his dollar bill towards him and began carefully folding over the second corner so it was now shaped like a distorted hexagon. As he did so, he continued talking. "Ah look back with some fondness, though, on one of the last times I saw him. It was that summer, a memorable trip we boys took to Coney Island. A group of us went, end of the season, to see the Sharkey–Ruhlin fight. It was one of those riotous trips that sticks in one's mind as being what life is for: the good times.

"There were seven or eight of us travelling together, though many familiar faces were heading that way, and Murray was among the group who took that early train out. Ah remember how he kept banging on about his dog. 'I miss Nick ...' he said. 'I even miss the way he would howl each morning to be let out.' 'Your block certainly won't be missing him,' ah said. For Nick, the hound, was known in the neighbourhood and there were many who didn't like the racket he made."

The hands, ringed on both pinkies with silver and blackest onyx, slid across the table, gathering in the pack. Again, the cards fluttered between his fingers, something alive beneath his control.

"As the day wore on, the whisky flowed faster," he said, switching to the other hand and performing the same deft riffle. "Murray seemed to perk up. Sharkey–Ruhlin, as you'll know, was a much-anticipated fight, but it ended so short you almost wanted your money back. Dramatic, though. Wild. The sailor knocked Ruhlin out in one round with a hard right cross to the head. Just two minutes and seventeen seconds of fighting it was. First time we'd welcomed Tom Sharkey to New York, and we knew we were seeing a terrific hitter.

"The energy of the fight seemed to have got Murray going. He was back on form as we arrived at the Streets of Cairo, and cheered noisily at the hootchy kootchy. He threw a load of money at a shell game in one of the gyp joints, insistent that he knew where the pea was, though even he knew it was all a con, but, hey, he seemed to be loving it. Onto Perry's, and he was soon ordering generous rounds of drinks, more generous than was his character, an' flirtin' shamelessly with the waitresses, who we could all see were taking him for his money."

The cards slipped smoothly across the table, each arriving as if fired from a gun, right in front of me. Another widow dealt, this time with an irresistible ace of hearts, which I immediately picked up.

"Finally, we ended up at the beach," Joe continued. "It was almost midnight, and one of those indigo skies, with the moon casting a gleaming path down into the water, as if invitin' us in. The surf was rolling, like lather, glowing and churning. There were twenty of us by then, and we all knew what we were there for. It had been Hackett's idea. He suddenly stripped off naked and rushed into the water. Ah'm not sure if it was the warmth of the day, or if it was the alcohol that charged us onwards.

"Ah saw Hackett's scrawny, pale ass bounding towards that sea, disappearing into the darkness and into those white horses, and ah started to unbutton my shirt. Ah knew Murray had tried to quash the idea as we all moved like sand flies towards the water, and ah sensed him loitering towards the back of the group.

"'Are you coming, old sport?' ah asked. He was standing still on the sand, frozen to the spot, backlit by the lights of the buildings behind. His face, in shadow, was hard to read. 'No, no,' he insisted, shaking his head.

"'Come on,' ah urged, reaching out to him.

"'No, Joe. See, I canna swim.'

"'Ah,' I said, 'you don't have to swim. It's just a splash in the waves. You never played in them?'

"'No, I never have,' he said. 'It scares me too much. And I'm an old man now. Too old to swim, too old to splash.'"

There was a distant look in Joe's eyes as he spoke, staring down at the table, as if transported back to that moonlit

65

beach. He was an excellent storyteller, and I found myself transfixed, my fear of the man dissipating in my desire to hear more.

He went on: "'You can just stand at the edge,' ah told him, 'feel the waves. It's quite something feeling the waves, the power in them. It's like it passes into you. Fires you up.'

"'No, I couldna,' he said.

"Ah sensed there was no persuading him. So, ah left him there on the shore." Joe picked up a card and stared at it for a moment, as if barely registering, before inserting it into his hand and nodding towards me to play on. "The surf that day was astounding, the kind of surging water that makes you grunt and whoop, bashin' you and almost knockin' you over, and ah realised it was probably best he didn't join us. White bodies lunging this way and that through the waves. You didn't have to get deep to get churned and knocked about by the force of the water.

"There were others there who couldn't really swim but who went in. Ah remember Moran, drenched, and laughing and hollering in near ecstasy when he was thrown over, and then dragging himself up onto the shore. Ah remember looking back over my shoulder as ah ran towards the waves. There was Murray up on the sand, leaning down over his stick, his huge coat turning him into a black boulder, surrounded by all the piles of our clothing scattered across the beach.

"He looked so alone. Ah remember wondering why he was quite so scared. There was something he feared. Ah thought then that he must have some terrible dread of the water, as some do. But ah see it now. Ah see what that was. It wasn't the water at all."

I waited a moment before I knocked gently on the table.

He smiled and simply passed the dollar bill over. "The game, I feel, is yours, Mr Clellan. Thank you for listening. As it happens, ah don't quite have the appetite for another hand."

I waved the bill away. "I think we could say we are quits, Mr Young. I won your dollar, but you told me a tale, which is of more value. Keep your dollar."

He nodded. "Take it, Mr Clellan. You won it fair. Mah words have never cost nothin'. Ah gave you that tale of dear Murray gladly and for free. Ah give it because that's what's on mah mind now. It's what ah keep thinking of. Mah friend so alone on that beach."

WASHINGTON SQUARE SOUTH
19TH JANUARY 1901, 3 P.M.

AS I STEPPED BACK INTO the sharp street air, I felt
I had been in another world. I suppose that's how
those windowless card rooms are designed – it could
be any time of day or night inside. They are meant to disori-
entate, to disconnect you from your life and responsibilities and
tempt you to stay for just one more hand. It was stifling. I was
glad to be out of there.

I mulled over the conversations that had taken place,
wondering why the senator and Joe Young should be so willing
to tell me so much of what they knew of the late Murray Hall.
In my days with the City Vigilance, I'd found that these
Tammany types aren't wont to give anything away unless they
think they can get something in return, and yet what could I
possibly offer them for their stories? They had seemed genuinely
glad to reminisce about their old friend, and I had seen another
side of Young. Among all the tales of drinking and hard sports
there was a tenderness in his memories of Hall, and he had
seemed moved when he spoke of that night on the beach.
Perhaps the telling was all they wanted. In talking to me, these
men could hope to get a good word out, to clean up their

friend's name a little in the papers and humanise him away from the scandal. The cynic in me also knew that, in doing so, they would protect the name of Tammany.

I had been pondering this as my feet took me roughly southwards. As useful as the elevated rail can be, I walk as often as I can. It gives me a sense of the city, helps me to keep a grip on the place as rapidly as it changes, and in doing so I bring clarity to my mind. It's why an hour or two on foot doesn't bother me, even in the winter months.

I could never be described as a particularly sociable man, but when a story takes its grip, I find a conversation can help me to shuffle my thoughts into order. The person whose opinion I hold highest in that regard is my sister. She married well, and the streets around me began to give way to the well-kept and comfortable brownstones of Manhattan's wealthier district – though I am told the city's real elite are now making their way even further north. Leafless trees encircle stretches of bare grass, and there were few other people around when I turned in to my sister's square.

Grace was in, as I knew she would be. She feigned annoyance at my calling without advance warning, but as always she was secretly pleased to see me. A bookish type, sharp and engaged with the politics of the day, she has never really settled into the social circles of parlour gossip and high society that marriage has introduced into her life.

"I suppose you better come in and have some coffee. You should never play poker, you know, Sam. You wear it right on your face as soon as something is troubling you."

"I'll have you know that I have come here from a successful game of Widow."

"Widow! Then it's a story that's troubling you. No brother of mine would be tempted to a game of cards unless there were a story at the end of it. Who were you playing?"

I could see the movement of my sister's servants through the doorway as we took our seats. They always made me slightly uncomfortable, these silent figures in the background, and I wished we were truly alone.

"A gentleman by the name of Joe Young, down at the Iroquois. I'm looking into this Murray Hall business – have you heard of it?"

"I can't believe you were welcome enough there to be invited for cards! Maybe things really are changing at Tammany." She gave me a quizzical look. "Hall was the bail bondsman who was found out to be a woman, wasn't he? Yes, I read about it in the *World*. It didn't strike me as your writing, though – what made you take it on?"

We were seated in my sister's tastefully decorated parlour, surrounded by dark, polished wood and elegant lighting. The quiet of the street was even more noticeable inside, highlighted by the distant ticking of a grandfather clock in the hall. My eyes rested on the piano by the window, its lid raised. It had been a long time since I had heard Grace play.

"I came across Murray Hall before. Or we came across each other. I met him a few times, in my work around corruption in Tammany." I had never told my sister the real reason behind my leaving the *Times*. It was around the time leading up to her wedding day, and I hadn't wanted her to worry, not that it had stopped her.

"You're right; that article wasn't mine, though I believe there's more to learn about Hall, about where she came from. If someone like Hall can reach such a position of influence in society, I think it's worth investigating how she got there, what she was like. Otherwise, who's to say such a deception couldn't happen again? There seems to be an air of comedy about this story, but imagine she wasn't just a bondsman. Imagine, say, she had run for election herself. She was good enough at pulling in the voters. She could have done it."

"Samuel." I could hear the exasperation in Grace's voice. "You always were so doom and gloom. There are plenty of corrupt men at the Iroquois; I don't see what difference it makes if one of them happened to be a woman. It rather makes me like the whole lot of them more, I have to say."

"You would say that. Doesn't it bother you how things have changed, even in our lifetime? I know New York is a special case, but even back home . . . We're in a new century, and I'm not sure I recognise the world around me any longer. Morals, religion, manners – they're either inverted or they seem not to matter at all. There's drunkenness, gambling, prostitution on every corner. Women passing as men in the world of politics, and it comes up only as an amusing little oddity in the news-papers upon their death. Aren't you frightened?" I demanded, strident now. "By the sinfulness of it all?"

"Oh, Sam! You sound just like Father. Who are you to say any more than I what is sinful? Sure, it sounds like this Murray

Hall was no saint, but I would guess he did what he thought was right by Tammany. And didn't he have a daughter, and a wife?

"I'm sure there's as much sin in the world as there's always been, only more of it gets printed in your paper nowadays so that it seems an epidemic. There's as much good as there's always been, too, and by good I don't mean your City Vigilance boys – I mean honest, ordinary people living the best lives they can, doing their best with the cards life's dealt them." She looked at me, more gently now. "It does you no good tying yourself into knots over other people's ills. Why don't you focus on your own life?"

"This town is rotten with rottenness," I said, refusing to relinquish my high ground or to succumb to her softer tone. "Remember how Father used to say that."

Grace sighed. "Perhaps not everything in this city is rottenness. I've found rather a nice life here myself, even if it is quieter than I'm used to. I don't miss what we once had."

This was a rare reference on her part to our childhood, and I glanced up at her, trying to read her expression. She was staring out the parlour window, her face bathed in the sombre afternoon light. Her maid came in with the coffee on a silver tray, blushing at the intrusion. She was a red-haired girl, a slight thing, but Grace seemed fond of her. She smiled her thanks.

I looked out the glass myself at those bare trees swaying in the breeze. It wasn't often that I allowed myself to think of the past either, although I felt it with me always.

"I keep thinking that even the fact I'm now at the *World* would be a disappointment to him," I murmured half to myself. "My failure to instigate reform would be a disappointment. He wanted us to do good in this world, Grace, not stand by as sin takes root."

That voice again, whispering in my ear:

We live in a wicked world. Ask yourself, my son, what can I do?

"It's time you stopped dwelling on whether you are a disappointment to Father," she told me sharply. "He doesn't deserve your devotion."

It was never any use, I knew, arguing with Grace. As much as she claims to be above the religious moralising she believes I have inherited from our father, she is just as passionate about right and wrong as I am. But, alas, we have different definitions. I knew that if I carried on down this road my visit would more likely than not turn into a searing fight, so I did my best to bite my tongue.

"What you don't realise, Grace, is that I *am* focusing on my own humble life. I am doing what I can to make my time on this soil count for something. But perhaps you are right. Perhaps it is unfair to use Hall as a cipher for all the ills of this world. That's why I would like to learn more about her. I'd like to know what made her the way she was, what kind of life she had. That's why I went to the Iroquois, to speak to some of those men who worked with her."

Grace pursed her lips, accepting the olive branch I had offered. "Accomplices and drinking-mates are fine, but you ought to find out about the wife and child. They will tell you more about the true character of this Murray Hall."

I was glad of my sister's input, and I sought, too, to avoid the dangers of the past. She had a clear journalistic eye, and I thought if she hadn't married that she might have found success as a typist. She would've been right at home amid the buzz and intrigue of those smoke-filled offices.

Although the conversation had moved on, my sister's comment about our father had gotten under my skin, which I knew was as thin as a sheet of newsprint on such matters. His voice was ever present in my memories, and I suspect in hers too, as little as we spoke of the past. Our father's sermons were not limited to within the walls of his church, and everything we were taught as children was through the words of the Bible. My sister is no longer led by religion. Though I no longer attend church, the principles of the Lord's Word still guide me; they are how I make sense of the world. But for us, once there were no more ties to that hard, rural upbringing, the more it felt like a dream. A nightmare, Grace would say.

I am grateful for it now. I understand why our father could be so harsh with his words and his hands – he had to be. There are so many dangers out there, so many temptations waiting for the inattentive. One must be vigilant, alert. The devil does not knock – he slips in at night through an open window. He hides in laziness, in lust and gluttony. He preys on the weak minds of those who are suffering.

Mark said, "What comes out of a person is what defiles them. For it is from within, out of a person's heart, that evil thoughts come."

75

Do not be tempted to believe that sin lives in the world. It is already within you – you must fight it every day.

I could still hear his words so clearly, even now. The quiet of that house made them harder to ignore. Grace must have noticed that I had slipped away, because her voice softened and she placed a hand on my arm.

"Have you thought any more of my offer? I know you and I don't always see eye to eye, but you do bring some of the city's energy to the place. Henry is so often out on business, and I know he adores you really. There's space enough for you to have your own office too, if you wished. Here, with us."

The plainness of Grace's words took me aback. When she had mentioned my moving into this house before, I had assumed it was out of pity – it was during the time I was out of work, after my unfortunate first encounter with Murray Hall. But perhaps her life was lonely enough for her to actually miss my companionship. It was a strange feeling. My sister had never been the lonely type, always content with her own company and the lost souls she seemed to pick up along the way.

"Oh ... I don't know. It is kind of you to offer, and I can't say I haven't thought about it. But my apartment serves me fine, it's modest, cheap to run and is near the World. Anyway, you don't need me turning up in the early hours after some fire or gang fight that I've had to rush out to cover. I don't want to put you out like that."

The silence hung a little awkwardly between us, so I continued with a change of tack.

"What makes you think knowing more about the wife will be of much use to this story anyhow? As far as I know, she's been dead for several years now."

"Ever the bachelor. Marriage changes a person, for better or worse. And that's what'll interest the readers – surely she must have known his secret. Did she know before they were married? Were they happy together? These are the things you must find out."

"I suppose you're right, as ever. I do believe a sister survives the wife, though I don't think she can have been close to Hall. As far as I'm aware, she hasn't visited the house since his death. I wonder if she would talk if she knew I wanted to write about the wife's story a little."

"Mm." Though I had re-engaged her for a while, Grace was once again facing out of that tall window and the grey light it let into the large, comfortable room. She drew her feet up onto the velvet couch, folding her skirts around her.

"Do you remember the preacher, back in Wayne County, who used to stand at the corner of the street opposite the general store?" she asked suddenly. I wondered where her mind had been wandering to conjure this particular image.

"Joseph Lobdell," I said. In an instant, the face had conjured in my mind, and I was on the streets of home, the broody skies and flat, brown landscapes.

Thick, close-cropped dark hair over a smooth round face and intelligent eyes. Though they were the words of the Bible, I never did recognise the wild phrases Lobdell would shout in an endless refrain. He was always plainly dressed, but held himself with such a confidence that he was hardly ever moved along from his corner, even when he would bring out his fiddle and hop like an imp to the music, holy verses still streaming from his lips. Father was afraid of him, I think. He used to call him the false prophet.

"The Reverend Lobdell." Grace nodded. "Who turned out to be a woman. They called her the Female Hunter of Delaware County."

"You used to like to watch her."

"Father hated it, but I was fascinated by what I thought was this magnetic man. I followed Joseph Lobdell's story over the years afterwards. He ... she ... ended up in an asylum. Did you know that? So, of course, Reverend Lobdell is who I thought of when I heard your Murray Hall story. There are others, is what I'm saying, and that's what interests me most. I even bought a paper written by Dr Wise of the Willard Asylum in which Lobdell was a case study. I could find it to show you. But, you see, my books and papers are such a mess ..."

At last, I understood why the subject of Hall had caused such a wave of reminiscence. It wasn't unpleasant; we continued to discuss the wild preacher without touching too much on the painful aspects of our past. It was an unspoken agreement between us, and one of which I was glad.

We parted on good terms, and Grace made me promise to call again soon. There was a sadness in her eyes even as she waved me off, and the silence of her home struck me again. I pictured my brilliant, lively sister in stasis in that big house, like a light that was only lit when Henry or I were around. It made me feel guilty, and a little hollow.

When I returned to the comfort of my small rooms downtown, I relished the rattle of the elevated rail outside my window and the chatter of the greengrocer's downstairs. The walls seemed to hum with life, with the hustle of the city.

I sat down to consider my initial telegram to Murray Hall's sister-in-law. A good telegram, I knew, to a prospective source must be concise but warm – you only get one chance at a first introduction.

As I was sitting at my writing desk to mull this over, my eye caught sight of a pile of books by the fireplace. I have spent many contented evenings in front of that fire with a pot of coffee, listening to the world pass by. If I could read for a living, I would; writing is the next best thing. At the bottom of the pile lay a book I hadn't picked up in weeks. It was Ellis's *Psychology of Sex*, and in an instant that day at C. S. Pratt's returned to me, and the encounter between the bookseller and Murray Hall to which I'd been privy. I recalled his stooped, painful form, the weight of his bulky coat about him. The cancer must have been through him already, I realised. And yet he made no complaint as he carried that haul of tomes through the door. I gazed at the book's dark leather spine and wondered. Such a memory was surely not a coincidence. I did not believe in fate – how could I? – but this was too much of a sign to ignore. I began to compose a second telegram, this time addressed to Havelock Ellis.

THE EAST RIVER
20TH JANUARY 1901, 11 A.M.

RUMOUR HAD IT THAT THE funeral date was set, but that Hall's body was still lying on the cold slab of the morgue, untouched since the coroner's examination. Meanwhile, I had been growing increasingly frustrated in my search for those who knew Murray Hall. Sure, there were plenty who claimed to have known her and would rush to tell you their piece of gossip – and who would invariably claim that, of course, *they* knew her secret all along – but it was proving more difficult to find credible sources, and even more so to find ones that I believed exposed some of Hall's true past and character. That was what I was really interested in. The paper disapproved of the time and expense I was spending on this story, but I was convinced there was more to learn, new angles to explore. I had persuaded my editor to give me a little more time, but I had a feeling that the patience of the higher-ups was wearing thin. Still, it was a risk I was prepared to run.

That is what led me, on a damp and misty morning, to the city's morgues. I have never been fond of the morbid, and whenever my work takes me there, I bring a little of Dr Pinkard's mint balm to smear under my nose. The smell is truly something awful, and the pertness of the balm scarcely staunches it.

I had held off on this particular journey, not only because of its unpleasant location, but out of respect for the deceased's family. Hall may have been an invert and a rogue, but it is not my usual method to rubberneck at corpses. Still, I couldn't shake the notion out of my head that if I could only see her, this story might make a little more sense. How it could be that, for so many years, so many people were fooled by – or if not fooled then reticent to challenge – her façade. Even in death I believe the character of an individual is shown on their face. I remember the sight of my father in his coffin, his face as stern and unreadable as ever. He did not look peaceful then, as I always thought he would. His soul was with God, but his body remained trapped in unyielding condemnation of a world that had always disappointed him.

I wasn't sure I could stomach it, but nevertheless I found myself heading towards that hall of death. The keeper was known to be willing to show a body for a coin or two. I had found throughout my time in New York that there was very little that a show of dollars could not buy. No matter how moral people claim to be, everyone has their price.

After a hushed and hasty conversation, and feeling considerably lighter of pocket, I was led into the dingy old building that balances precariously on a pier running out into the East

River at the foot of 26th Street. Though I have been here before, it never fails to make me shudder. All the streets of New York are cold this time of year, but there's something when you enter this place that makes you feel the chill in your bones. It's a damp that you take home with you and can't shake off no matter how many logs are thrown onto the fire.

The keeper is an unsettling, stooped man, a jangle of bones like a skeleton himself. He led me briskly to the main display room, a lofty space with the atmosphere of a hospital, where light glanced through high-up windows down to bodies arranged on slabs. The chamber echoed with the sound of trickling water, washing bodies from taps placed above in an attempt to cool and prevent the process of decay.

"Take care." The keeper's voice bounced back at me from the marble as he gestured to the floor, their tiles shining with pinked water.

Wearing a sharp-toothed grin, which seemed to indicate his amusement in my discomfort, he took pains to show me some of the more gruesome arrivals as we passed. Those victims of fire and violence, horribly disfigured and pitiful.

"Thank you, but I only want to see Hall," I informed him, perhaps a little curtly. His smile wavered.

"Come along, then. You're just in time – they're to collect the body this afternoon."

I followed him past rows and rows of marble slabs, each with a body laid on its back, sometimes covered, but most open to the elements save for a white cloth draped over their genitals. I have never understood those who say the dead look as if they are sleeping. To me they look absolutely dead. There are those with injury and illness, clotted wounds and jaundiced skin, and then there are the lucky ones, fat old men with a face full of white whiskers and the robust look of a life fully lived. The children are the hardest to walk past, and I avert my gaze when I notice a small body laid out on the slab.

Too often the deaths of those children have been grisly – and now they lie there waiting to be claimed, to be identified by parents who never come.

"The coroner was here first thing," the keeper informed me. "Came here with the doctor to look 'im over, not that anything had changed since the last time. Maybe a bit stiffer."

His pointed grin had returned. "Here we are. One Murray Hall, past 'is best, by all accounts."

The keeper had stopped abruptly by one white slab, indistinguishable from the others. I wondered how he kept track of so many bodies, so many human beings now turned to mere flesh as they passed through these doors and into his lifeless kingdom.

In front of me lay what I knew to be Murray Hall, and yet I could not align the person I saw with the Hall who existed in my mind. The figure on the slab was slight, pale and with waxy skin that seemed to stick to their bones. Only the genitals were covered. The face was smooth, true, but there was nothing about it that was particularly feminine. Perhaps it was the muted January light, and the shadows of that drab building, but I could have sworn the face shifted even as I looked at it. I couldn't stitch together the meaning of what I was seeing.

For a moment, I felt a surge of anger and frustration. What had I come here for? Murray Hall was dead. Any truth she had to speak died with her.

I cursed myself for my sentimentality. This was a waste of time, time that could have been spent in the land of the living, in search of answers there. I looked down at the frail body below me and for a second saw the face of my father in that glassy emptiness, saw in Hall's place his pallid, bony joints, his lank hair, his unreadable expression. I blinked, looking up into the light filtering down from the window, and the swirling dust making patterns in its beam. I shouldn't have come here.

I glanced around at the keeper, but found he had now walked on several bodies along and was occupied with adjusting the water system that washed the bodies from above.

In this moment of privacy, I allowed myself another, truthful look at Murray Hall. At the blistering wound in the centre of the chest. It was impossible to ignore. I could barely tell that she had been a woman, the breasts were so overcome by the disease. Around the mound of cancerous flesh the body had collapsed, creating a vacuum within which only disease could survive. While the rest of her skin was milky, almost translucent, the cancer was a hungry patchwork of dark purples, reds and yellows, eating its way almost through the flesh. I felt the bile rise in my throat and was glad I was yet to have breakfast that day.

I wanted to recoil, to avert my eyes, yet I stared into that wound. Some dreadful part of my curiosity was piqued. I looked down the body, across the greying skin towards the loin cloth.

Its folds rose and fell in a way that made no particular sense, revealed nothing obvious.

My hand, almost without me bidding it, reached to pull at the edge of the fabric and tug it upwards.

But even as I pinched the cloth, I heard the keeper's footsteps.

"That will be all you're wanting to see then, sir?" he asked.

I heard, and heeded, the warning note in that voice.

"Thank you. That's all I need to see."

I don't know what I had expected to feel on looking at Hall, at the devastation of her human form, but what I noticed most strongly then was the absence of feeling. I felt nothing. I was an observer, watching.

As the keeper led me back down that cursed aisle, I passed an old man weeping like a child by the side of what I assumed must be the body of his wife. "Annie, Annie, Annie," he murmured through his sobs into her neck. She made no reply.

I felt the intrusion of my presence. I had learned nothing, only the lengths I was willing to go to settle my own mind, to complete the story I had started to construct for myself. But there was nothing more here.

As I turned away from that intimacy, I felt unclean, not from the place I was leaving, which was pristine, but from my own actions.

I, who always preached such purity. Could I really claim to be without sin when I was so drawn to it, spent so much of my time rubbed up against it, both in body and mind? Did this compulsion to uncover the sins of others disclose some unplumbed sinfulness in myself?

Outside, I looked into the misty sky, and wondered again about the God who lived there, what He thought of the man-woman, destroyed by a secret cancer, lying on that slab. The tender-limbed children abandoned in death. The heartbroken grief of an old man.

Behold, God is exalted, and we do not know Him;
The number of His years is unsearchable.

146 SIXTH AVENUE
20TH JANUARY 1901, 1.30 P.M.

MY FATHER'S VOICE WAS WARNING me. Words were showering down from a pulpit, hovering somewhere in the clouds above, words remembered from a Sunday service, yet now directed solely at me.

Curiosity is not a virtue. It is so often a path away from holiness. There are places in this wicked world that it is better not to look.

Every man's face I passed, every woman, buttoned up to their chins, velvet-collared, bonneted or bowler-hatted, seemed to morph into Murray Hall. Some stared me down with accusing eyes.

We live in a wicked world. Ask yourself, my son, what can I do?

I continued walking for some time, as if through my steps, through merging with the hundreds of other faces passing by, I could rid my mind of the lingering image of Hall. But even as I walked, I sensed I was being drawn back towards her. Compelled, unthinking, I followed the roads across the East Side until I ended up back again at Sixth Avenue, and below the Hall apartment.

The block between 10th and 11th Street jostled with people, but the rooms above the agency were as still and dark as ever, betraying no sign of light or activity. I watched the curtains, half hoping for another glimpse of the building's residents; for one, indeed, in particular. My eyes drifted, scanning the building alongside, taking in the lights of some upper-storey windows, and were caught by a small sign in red. Hung from the window, second floor to the right of the Hall residence on Sixth Avenue, the sign read:

Mrs Porter. Clairvoyant.
Offering answers to all YOUR questions.

The words were, surely, issuing an invitation. Here, the sign claimed, would be answers.

Curiosity lured me in.

Curiosity is not a virtue. It too easily leads us astray.

It took several pulls of the bell before it was answered by a woman, just over five foot tall, but with heaps of curled red hair, piled high atop her head. She was dressed in emerald velvet and wearing an extraordinary gold pendant from which an eye of aquamarine stared out. She had the air of a performer preparing for a show, poised as if about to step on stage.

And then she led me through the hallway to her half-lit rooms, which appeared, though it was still daytime outside, like a darkened cave. "I apologise. My head is often filled with noise, a chattering. I don't always hear the bell," she said. Her voice was low and trance-like. "You'll have come about Mr Hall. Am I right?"

I was not surprised, nor impressed: such is the way of clairvoyants. They are always delivering something that could be easily guessed so as to make it sound like a profound psychic perception. Their nonsense is not something I would ordinarily entertain – in fact, theirs is a belief system my father had no tolerance for, believing it to be a satanic practice.

I knew what Father would say of this woman.

Beware of those who claim they can speak to the dead. Most are frauds, false prophets, and their faith is deformed. Only listen for God, not the spirits who have left us.

I shook my head briskly, once, dispelling his diktats. In the pursuit of a story, I am obliged to set such qualms aside. The woman – this Mrs Porter – nodded as if she discerned the meaning of my actions, then drew a deep breath and passed through the curtained doorway ahead of me. I noted, as she did, some small patches of mousy hair at her roots, presumably missed by the dye. "I knew him quite well, our Mr Hall. As a matter of fact, he came to me for a few readings, which were, shall we say, revealing."

She pulled a velvet-cushioned chair from under a table, which was covered in a mustard cloth with extravagant tassels. "Sit down. Sit down. Now, what is it you would like to know? You must understand that what is said inside these walls does not, in general, get spoken outside of them. I am a professional. I uphold a certain confidentiality."

"Even when there is payment on offer?" I said, placing a note carefully on the ugly tablecloth. The corners of the bill curled upwards, and I recognised it as my winnings from the previous day.

"Well," she said, pausing to press the folded edge down with a finger, "that looks like a lucky bill."

She watched as I slid another note out of my wallet.

"Even luckier. Now ... of course," she said, "there is the fact that the person in question is deceased, which makes things a little different."

"They are no longer around to feel the slight."

"Though," she said, leaning towards me with a sly grin, "they may still be hanging around and listening ..." She laughed, entertained by the idea. "Even so. I believe Murray will not mind."

I smiled and sank a little more comfortably into my seat. I paused. "There is, of course, the obvious question. Did you know she was a woman?"

"No, no ... It's been quite a shock, as you can imagine! We mediums don't perceive everything; we see beneath life's surface, but there are those whose aura can stand in the way of our visions," she said, her heavily jewelled fingers moving to the pendant around her neck. "A woman, living as a man, just next door? It's been very much an unexpected piece of news, though when I reflect back, perhaps there were ... signs."

She breathed in deeply, as if trying to summon something – not from memory, but from the spirit world. She had a curious way of pausing between her words, and one got the impression she was only half present, and taking part in another conversation simultaneously.

"There was one memorable occasion when he came round for a reading. I remember he was late, and I had already got caught up with some other presence making themselves known. It took me some time to notice the bell. In any case, when I heard the door, I peered into the night to find Mr Hall grinning, one might almost say leering, lopsidedly from under his hat.

"'My apologies, Mrs Porter, for my lateness,' he said, a slur to his voice. He was drunk. Apparently, there had been some business down at the courthouse and then he carried on to the club, and before he knew it, had found himself at the Pug's Hat. There was a jubilant energy to his words, and although I cannot do my true work with those who are intoxicated, I felt compelled to converse with him. 'You were at the Iroquois?' I asked. 'I hear they are all in fear of this new investigation. The City Vigilance League will not let it drop. Your chieftain, Mr Croker, must be worried.'"

I sensed that this Mrs Porter was embarking on quite an extended story, and keen to tell it in detail. I pulled my pen out of my pocket, flicked open my pad and readied myself to begin taking notes.

She smiled and nodded. "Then we sat at this very table and talked for some time about politics, and the matter of loyalty. Murray was very fixed on that idea. Loyalty to friends and family. Loyalty to the people who support you. Loyalty above all."

"Loyalty is indeed the mantra of Tammany," I observed. I could hear the bitterness in my own voice. To me, this code of loyalty was the enemy of moral rectitude. A man who is under its command will commit any number of sins in its name and protect, too, the sins of others from their proper accountability.

"One of the things," Mrs Porter went on, "I enjoyed about Hall was how he talked politics to me – as if I, too, were a man. He treated all of us women that way, though he was never keen to broach the subject of suffrage, not in the manner in which I could sometimes engage Mrs Hall."

"The wife?"

"Yes, Celia. Such a fine, admirable woman . . . and a suffragist in her own way. Anyway, Murray was clearly very drunk that day. It was obvious from how he drifted across the room. At first, I thought he had been disoriented by the dimness. I keep it this way so it might be more possible in the shadows to see the spirits; but, no, I realised, he really was that inebriated."

"You would call Murray he?" I asked.

"He . . . she . . . I don't mind. Lamentably, the masculine pronoun is used to cover both sexes, as if there only were one. Why, even the Constitution of this land seems to have it that we are all 'he'; as if one half of this population did not exist, or were of so little importance that our differences matter nought. Or are too mysterious, too alien, to address the inconvenience of our existence. Sometimes I sense we women are ranked so low in life's ladder that those in power have decided it prudent to push us off it entirely."

The clairvoyant, I now realised, was one of those commanding suffragists who love nothing more than to expound on the rights of women. I recognised the type. We had grown up surrounded by many of them in the revivalist county where my father, as a staunch Wesleyan Methodist minister, opposed their arguments and protests with his hand on the Bible and his sermons full of godly edicts on the rightful, most becoming place of the weaker sex.

"But that, Mr Clellan, is set to change," Mrs Porter strode on, a little intoxicated now by her own words. "One day, for example, a woman will be president. There is already much debate among us suffragists around this issue."

I had stopped taking notes. "Very illuminating and worthy," I said, my tone dry. "But perhaps we could return to Hall?"

"Forgive me." She gave me a teasing smile, not asking in the least for forgiveness. "I am always talking about suffrage one way or another, especially when I have a captive audience, but you are here for a different tale. Where was I? Yes . . . He was drunk. 'Mr Hall,' I said, 'careful there. Take a seat.' I reached a hand to guide him away from that cabinet over there, and he swayed slightly before tumbling onto that red cushioned chair. Had he been any other client I might have ejected him straight back out into the street. But this was Mr Hall."

She leaned towards me. "I felt sympathy for my neighbour. I sensed his loneliness, his despondency, his isolation from the world. It was, however, about all I detected about him. All these times he had been to see me since his wife's death, and he had revealed very little about himself. The man was so perplexingly defended. With the ball, or the tarot, I usually find it only takes only minutes for a person to reveal something about their past and the questions they are bringing to me. But with this little man, the walls around him were impenetrable. There was nothing. Only what I knew already.

"I decided to begin with small talk. 'I saw your Minnie in the street the other day. How is she doing?' Hall slowly shook his head. 'That girl,' he said. 'She's such trouble.' 'Oh, but Mr Hall,' I said, 'your daughter dotes on you. Allow her a little freedom. Your wife would want it. Minnie is in her twenties now – oughtn't she be finding herself a husband, before she ends up an old maid?' There was a flash of anger in his eyes then. 'There's time enough,' he said. 'Besides, I need her . . .'"

Mrs Porter paused, leaning in towards me and eyeing me from above her small round glasses. "I had seen that anger before, and it made me uncomfortable. You see, there were stories that I could not entirely discount about how he once flew at a man for just looking at Celia, or how sometimes it was his wife he flew at – and beat. Though these things, of course, are so common, and they could have been nothing more than rumours. My years in this business have taught me to treat them as such, to pay more attention to the less spiteful tales. People are often kinder than others make out. And there were such stories I had heard of Murray Hall's kindness, his generosity – of how he took in that dear girl, Minnie. So, you see, one must reserve judgement.

"But that day . . . Yes now, that day. I asked Mr Hall what he would like me to do for him. A tarot reading? Some palmistry work? Or maybe he would like me to seek contact with his dear wife?

"'Do you think she's in the room?' he said, looking around. His tongue was loosened by the alcohol. 'Listening to us now. Do you think she hears us? Do you think she is whining about the burial I gave her? Let's do those cards of yours. Give me a reading of your cards.'

"I rose, crossed to my cabinet and slid out a pile of three card-decks, my precious Petit Lenormand all the way from Paris, the Madam Morrow, and Dr Jayne's Egyptian set. I selected Madam Morrow. They are my favoured pack, and I can identify the cards even when I cannot see them well. I placed the pack on the table and slid them towards him.

"'I am sure your wife is not whining,' I said. 'I don't recall her being a whiner. I will listen for her. Shuffle,' I instructed. 'I will see if she has anything to say. Shuffle, and think of what you would like to ask.' I watched the man as he lifted the cards, without a glance down at the table. 'You may tell me the question if you like.'

"Mostly I choose to read the cards blind, so as to impress the client with my powers of divination, but on this occasion, I wanted more from Hall. I realised I wanted him to reveal himself. Murray hunched forwards as he shuffled rapidly, like a man for whom cards were merely an extension of his hands. Even as drunk as he was, they whirled through his slender, confident fingers. He laid them on the table as if he had forgotten where he was, and was at a card table playing a round of the Widow. 'A question, a question,' he murmured, speaking

97

more softly than he had since his arrival. 'Well, all right. Here is one. Will there be another woman in this life of mine? Will I find myself another wife? Or will I die a lonely old man?'

"I admit, I was shocked at the frankness of this question. 'You are looking for another wife already?' He closed his eyes and breathed deeply. 'Aye, I am lonesome without a wife. I have had several in my life. Is my Celia to have been my last?' I felt my breath catch in my throat. I had heard from one of the old servants of the house that he had been married 'at least' twice, and was both fiercely jealous of and devoted to Celia. 'You're still grieving, Mr Hall. I wouldn't be so fast. I have been listening in recent weeks to Celia and she tells you not to worry. She is fine where she is. She is waiting for you.'

"'Indeed. Indeed. No one will replace her.' Was that a tear welling up in my neighbour's eye? 'But the woman left me. She left me here on my own.' Hall seemed lost in a reverie as he slipped the cards through his hands, soothed by the repetitive movement. I felt he was forgetting from one moment to the next the subject of his inquiry."

She paused. "Would you like a refreshment, Mr Clellan? Perhaps a cup of tea?"

"No, no," I said, "please go on."

"I took advantage of his loquaciousness. 'You never talk much about your past, Mr Hall, and I'm sure you have some stories. Where, for instance, are you from? If I had that information, I might be able to map out the astrological chart we have discussed on previous occasions, at a mere dollar for consultation. My special rate for you, Mr Hall.'

"'From Scotland.' He laughed. 'Can you no tell?' 'Of course. But where exactly?' 'Here and there,' he said. 'It would mean nothing to you. My family had land near Dundee. Stolen from us. My years there are merely a dream now. They have the air about them of another life. As distant as one of those past lives I've heard you talk about. That was another person. The Murray Hamilton Hall you see here was born when I came across the Atlantic to America, when I stepped off that putrid, rat-riddled ship and into the New World.'"

I was gripped. For here, finally, was a story that reached into Murray's past, into where she came from before she arrived, fully formed, as a bondsman on Sixth Avenue. "She told you about her youth in Scotland?"

"Only some small hints," Mrs Porter said. "I didn't follow up on that element of his past. For the conversation instead ran on with tales of how as a young man he went out west, as one of the Forty-Niners. Declared he had 'seen the elephant', as they say."

"A Forty-Niner?" I said, astonished, my mind adding up the years. "But surely that would make her at least seventy ..."

"I know, I thought the same. Surely not. But this was what he said, and I saw no reason to question. He had been part, he said, of a company working the Tuolumne river, though he didn't stay long. He said: 'It became clear to me that the graft of the work outweighed the value of any treasure we found.'"

"No, that can't be true." I said. Hall, with her mop of thick curls and smooth skin, looked far too young for such adventures.

"Well," said Mrs Porter, "I must say, his story was highly convincing."

As she spoke, I imagined Murray out west, sleeping in a tent alongside rough, opportunistic thugs, brawling with them, gambling, drinking. Gold country may well have been where she learned her card skills and swift, coarse tongue.

"He told me how one day, at near twilight, when most of the rest of the men had headed back to the camp, and he was getting ready to do the same, he was bathing his tired hands and face in the cool water when he saw the corner of something glint in the fire of the dying sunlight. At first, he thought it was his eyes fooling him. But it turned out this was real. He reached his hand deep into the river and pulled out a nugget, the size of his thumb, just sitting there in the silt."

Her own thumb, gnarled and swollen at the joint, twisted in the air between us. "I recall exactly the words he used," my hostess said now, quite convincingly adopting the pose and voice of Hall. "'It went straight into my underwear,' he said. 'I'd been among those gold rushers long enough to know a find like that might be once in a career, once in a lifetime. And that any other man would relieve me of it quicker than death.'"

My pen raced, in rapid shorthand, to keep up with her words. The tale seemed extraordinary.

Mrs Porter went on, eyes closed as if moved by the spirits of her trade: "'I was young and foolish enough to give that thumb of gold away to a young girl I thought I would marry,' he said. 'Oh, I thought a lot of things back then. But though she took the gold, she married another man. Perhaps I'm not much wiser than I used to be. I'm sure if I had my life over, I'd do it all the same. Young love never leaves you, they say.'

"He was dismissive," Mrs Porter said, her voice returning to its previous tone, "of the whole endeavour. 'The venture,' he said, 'was a failure. Sure, some got rich, but many were muddle-headed dupes, and I was one of them. The work there was so hard, so hot and heavy and endless. I suffered, my body felt broken by it – and my back has never been the same.'

"He returned within a year, which was when, as he told me, he found work in a drug store. That was where he met Mrs Hall. He didn't like it. 'Too much like women's work,' he said. He didn't speak much more about his past. At some point in this conversation, he asked if I had any whisky in the house. 'All this talk about my youth is giving me the thirst for a dram.'"

The woman sat back, satisfied with the climax of her story, some wisps of steam still rising from the delicate rose-painted teacup she held clasped between two hands. I put down my notebook.

"I have been trying these past few days, of course, to contact him. Often you find the spirits stay close around their homes for at least a few weeks after their death." She cupped her hand around her mouth and pitched her voice high. "Mr Hall! I'm here if you fancy one of our chats!" she projected, then lowered her tone again. "No? Perhaps not today."

"Perhaps not," I echoed.

Mrs Porter put on an impish grin that took years from her face. "There's things troubling you, my dear. There's a cloud all about you."

I shifted in my chair. I never like it when my investigations require me to step outside of my role of observer.

"I'm not sure about that. I'm a little tired. That's all."

"Give me your palm. Free of charge, of course."

Hold firm. Resist those that would tempt, my father whispered and I pulled my hand closer to my side.

"Oh, come now. Give me your hand. I won't bite."

I sensed there was no point in resisting and, in any case, I told myself that if I did not believe, it meant nothing. The clairvoyant had been generous with her time. I stretched out my hands and reminded myself that I do not believe in the supernatural.

As soon as we touched, her eyes closed, and her expression changed. She stiffened a little. "I feel you have suffered a loss, Mr Clellan."

I smiled at the cliché. "Who has not?"

"True. But, Mr Clellan, this loss is significant for you."

I sighed. "My father died. Some two years ago."

Her forehead wrinkled into a frown and she leaned forward to peer more deeply into my palm. "That may be it. But I am not sure . . ." Her eyes caught mine. "What interests me is how I can help you with your grief."

I said nothing, uncertain of what help she could offer – or I could take.

"When there is an unresolved grievance, there is grief," she said, her voice soothing. "You might not want to call it that,

102

but that is what it is. That is what I sense I am reading: your grief at the loss of someone, or something. A path not taken; words unspoken. Am I right?"

I shook my head. "I have no grievance."

This world, my father whispered, *is rotten with rottenness.*

"No? Are you sure? If it is your father we are talking about, then I can tell you that in my experience most people have grievances against their parents. And where there is grief and grievance, where better to direct one's anger than against oneself? Think it over. The anger you hold so tight does not serve you. It is time you let it go."

THE WORLD BUILDING
20TH JANUARY 1901, 4.30 P.M.

FROM MRS PORTER'S I TOOK a hansom cab along Sixth Avenue, the streetlamps and windows igniting one by one all the way as we hit Canal Street. Cloaked figures were caught in the beam of a passing streetcar, a young couple, laughing as they skipped prettily out of its path. Snowflakes floated like pale fireflies. At the corner of Mott Street, we slowed for a crowd so dense we came to a stop. Manhattan looked like a glittering organism coming to new life.

The city lived for the night and yet also lived in fear of it, its incandescent bulbs burning at all hours, obsessively, to keep away the darkness. They were the flames to which the luna moths of vice were drawn.

At Park Row I tipped the cabbie, keeping back a few coins as usual for the old Russian, who was there by the side entrance, sitting on his stool with his crutches propped against the wall. He was cocooned in fabric, his fur hat pulled down over his ears, blankets over legs and shoulders and his beard so long it almost functioned as an insulating scarf.

He nodded and mumbled, "Spasíbo. Thank you, sir." The only words I had ever heard him speak.

I slid into the side entrance of the World Building, then ascended the elevator into the familiar whirr of the newsroom; its clatter of typewriters also beating back the terrible silence of night. I began to type, drumming out words to meet a 7 p.m. deadline. Murray Hall, the story of a gold-rush veteran; a kindly father; but a drunkard and a card shark too. I wondered, even as my fingers flew over the keys, if I believed that he was in truth any of these things. But, as the editors would often say, that was not my concern. My concern was the story. *Story trumps facts.*

I pulled my last sheet of paper from the typewriter and leaned over the editorial fence into Irving's area to place the copy on the newsdesk tray. He nodded without looking up from behind the precipitous hedge of books and papers lining his desk. "Cutting it fine, Sam!" he hollered.

From there, I wandered over to the pigeon-holes filled with correspondence to check my mail. I picked up a wad of envelopes addressed with my name – one of which was wrapped in heavy cream paper. I turned its weight over in my hands and checked the postmark. Waterville. The thickness of the envelope, its bold script, all spoke of someone desperate to be heard. Impatient to open it, I slipped a thumb under its closed flap and pulled it outwards. I turned swiftly, without looking, and collided with the copy boy. "Careful, sir!" he said, then scurried onwards towards the newsdesk. I glanced around; the sketch artist was humming as he drew, a sports writer was chattering with the speed of a racing commentator, mid anecdote. As I slipped along the desk-lined alley back to my corner, I turned over the sheets of paper, looking for the name of the correspondent.

It was a Mrs Ellen Elba Hobbs.

Dear Mr Clellan,

Thank you for your message. I read today some of what must have been your work in the World *– and I do think you have captured some of my brother-in-law's personality. Or should I say, "sister-in-law"? Though the word "law" would hardly be appropriate if this is the case. I have written to you in haste, however, as there are key facts I feel require correcting. I am glad for the opportunity to present them to you.*

There was no love, as you must already know, for Murray Hall on the part of our family. He certainly had none for us. These past few years I have tried hard not to think about my sister's husband, but it seems that fate and recent revelations have conspired to make that impossible.

We Lowes are respectable people, enmeshed in farming and community life here in Waterville, but we now find men of your profession knocking at our door; men who want to caricature my sister as if she were some oddity or witless fool, men who treat her life as nothing but the key to unlocking the mystery of her woman-husband. I would like you to understand she was much more than that.

We were much surprised to read that Hall was dead, and more so to learn that "he" was anything other than the man he had always passed as being. This is not something we ever suspected, though, of course, after such a revelation one is inclined to review past conversations, letters and exchanges, to appraise one's memories in a different light.

Nevertheless, I am as yet unused to referring to Murray as "she," so forgive me if I stick to the pronoun "he" while I explain our experience of this particular character and his influence on my sister. I am yet to be convinced someone of his nature could possibly have been a woman.

Hall first came to visit the farm here in the summer of 1872, following what we came to call my sister's nervous depletion. Celia, as you'll know, was once a medical student, and a talented one at that, prevented from graduating only by ill health. Such an education is a remarkable feat for a woman now, but it was even more so then. She was quite a star at the local school, and only improved her reputation when she began to study with the late Dr Nathaniel Boutelle of Waterville.

I have often had cause to think on how one with so much talent and drive could have ended up with such an odd, stunted person as Hall. I loved my sister and believed that she would make her mark on the world, and whilst I do not wish to belittle Mrs Hall's Intelligence Agency, I can say it hardly stands in comparison with her ambitions as a girl. When she was a child, Celia would say she wished she had been born a boy, so that she might enjoy a man's freedoms. She believed from an early age that she was destined for a fate beyond the scope of "ordinary" womanhood.

Her path through life would have been smooth, I believe, had she not left Waterville for Boston and New York. I'm not sure what happened in her time there, when she was studying in New York at such colleges as then admitted women, as well as the leading hospitals. I recall how during that period her letters home grew more and more infrequent. I assumed it was simply because she was doing what she wanted most, studying hard, reaching for the heights she knew were in her grasp. Of course, now I wonder at the signs I missed, at what else I might have done to help her.

The woman who returned to us from Boston in 1871 was not the sister who had left the year before. Study had so undermined her health that she was like a ghost. What shocked us most was her sudden arrival at the door only a few months before she was due to graduate from her schooling. She was pale and diminished, her skin washed out, her bones protruding, and her hair lank and unkempt. In a state of constant distraction, she would murmur to herself and alternate between marching back and forth, and collapsing in bed for hours. She spoke of dizziness and of itching of the scalp.

We had the doctor to visit and he immediately diagnosed neurasthenia. I had wanted Dr Boutelle, who knew her so well, but he was on a sabbatical carrying out research in France. I remember the shake of that doctor's head, and the way he talked over Celia as if she were not really there. "Your daughter, I'm afraid," he told our mother, "has over-extended herself. Unfortunately, she has taken on too much, reached too far. Women have sensitive nervous systems, and stress and over-education can leave permanent damage. As I myself know, medical studies and the arduous work that follows are really *not for the weaker sex. If she rests enough, however, I think it possible she will pull through."*

This doctor prescribed a "rest cure" for my sister, which involved weeks confined to her bedroom. He advised simple, bland foods. He also, and this is what shocked me most, recommended that she limit her "intellectual life" to just two hours a day. She should refrain from reading books and should not lift a pen for three months. "The exercise of her brain has overwhelmed her," the doctor said.

He questioned my mother on how many hours Celia had spent studying in her youth – then shook his head solemnly when she described its intensity. He advised we purchase a book titled Wear and Tear: Or Hints For The Overworked. *He quoted from it: "At seventeen, healthy girls are as well able to study, with proper precautions, as men; but before this time overuse, or even a very steady use, of the brain is in many cases dangerous to health and to every probability of future womanly usefulness."*

I have since read this book and its comments on women. "If a woman," the author writes, "matches herself against a man, it will be, with some exceptions, at bitter cost. Her reserves of nerve force have become depleted – and women have less of these than men."

How Celia would have raged, I thought as I read this, against such an inhibiting notion. But, I considered, perhaps the author was right. I had witnessed my strong sister felled in an extraordinary way. And previous letters she had sent me spoke often of the difficulty of being a woman amongst so many men.

110

The doctor's concern was that it might already be too late, and that Celia had "ruined" herself. His rest prescription was absolutely vital, he added; without strict adherence there was a danger she might become an invalid, of no use for anything, and particularly as a wife.

My mother and I took this to heart. I wanted to believe that Celia would return to her medical work, but more than anything else I wanted my forceful, entertaining, fiercely intelligent and wilful sister back. I found myself wondering whether something else had happened in Boston or New York that had driven her thus, or if some mysterious infectious disease had her in its terrible thrall.

In the weeks that followed, my sister's condition did seem to improve, though she continued to speak of aching muscles and fatigue, and seemed to have lost all ambition – lost all drive for anything. She cared for nothing. Even our sunlit garden with its blue and purple violets that once delighted her now passed under her glassy eyes without comment.

Was Murray Hall the key to my sister's unravelling? I do wonder if Mr Hall identified and saw as an opportunity the vulnerability of her time in Boston. Had he seen her as someone on the edge of sanity when they first met, and taken advantage of her susceptibility?

It was in Boston, not New York, that she first became acquainted with Mr Hall, though later when she moved to the city she met him again, and they began to spend time together. He was then working at a drug store.

111

I recall how, during the months of her recovery, Hall's letters began arriving, and how much they lifted my sister's spirits. I think we all imagined a handsome, well-mannered aristocrat from the way she spoke of him. A Scottish nobleman, she said.

But the man we encountered was infinitely different from the charming vision I'd allowed myself to believe in. He was quite an eccentric fellow, with thick dark hair, and always wearing that baggy woollen coat and straw hat. Always clean shaven, and with a small-featured but expressive face and wide smile. I admit it may be hindsight tarnishing my memory, but I can remember never quite trusting the authenticity of that smile.

He had left his job in the drug store when he came to visit us and was dismissive of it, saying it was women's work, a menial position he had only taken to keep himself afloat while he was awaiting funds. He told us he was a nobleman and had been deprived of his estates and title in the old country. There were many grand stories of familial wealth, how he had learned the profession of detective and was working to have the moneys restored, and how he would soon be in possession, so he declared, of a fabulous sum.

It was a tall story, a fanciful yarn – and I was sceptical even then.

I was glad, however, at the way his presence brought my sister out of her stupor. I was pleased to see her going out for long walks in the woods and by the river – though also concerned when she would return flushed and ragged, exhausted by such little activity as she had refrained from for so many months.

The man, I worried, was a womaniser. There was something knowing and, forgive me, uncomfortably priapic in his manner. He was also an enthusiastic drinker. This my father observed from their evenings, two men together, discussing the news and politics of the day. He commented on the way Mr Hall would knock back one drink and then urge the pouring of another, manners be damned.

I learned later that when he returned to the inn where he was staying he would drink until he collapsed, which now explains why he never arrived for his visits until late the following day.

He was frequently tardy and so Celia would be standing by the window waiting for him when he arrived, fretting that he was not coming. It was so unlike her. This fear of rejection, of abandonment, this desire for the glow of his attentions. You must understand that my sister had never previously shown much interest in romantic matters. The kind of chiselled, broad-shouldered men who made me swoon had no real impact on her, and she could be quite charmless with male visitors, almost appearing bored by them and their gallantries. But here she was pining for this strange little fellow. We all thought it must be an aspect of her illness.

But before Hall left, he approached my father for permission to ask Celia's hand in marriage. My father's immediate reaction was to tell him that this was all rather sudden, and not quite appropriate given Celia's health. I think he had already *been guided by my mother not to encourage the relationship further.*

But Celia, too, insisted this was the man she wanted to marry.

My parents were opposed to the very idea of such a marriage, as was I. We were also keen to keep her calm, given that she was still barely out of her nervous depletion. Mother was concerned that she followed doctor's orders. Fresh air, long walks, a little soothing music and simple foods ... nothing more complicated or heightening of the emotions than that.

That autumn, Celia left in a whirl for New York, purportedly for a short visit. When several weeks later she had not returned, we began to fear scandal. The next we heard, our fears were confirmed – she had indeed married the man, in a ceremony on Christmas Eve. Snow had fallen all around, Celia wrote to me, and the occasion was so beautiful it made her cry.

"I've never known anyone like Murray," she wrote.

At first, I wondered if this was a shotgun wedding. But no pregnancy materialised, and of course, now, we understand that would have been physically impossible. Such conception was an impossibility throughout their marriage. I grieve for this too.

And so, the baby we thought might come never arrived, and I understand now why Celia was always so keen to avoid the subject of children. I thought perhaps she was barren and did not wish to discuss the matter, or that, as she had done in her youth, she rejected the idea of motherhood as a limitation rather than a fulfilment of her sex. In her adolescence she had been known to say she would be happy to live a spinster's life and find purpose in healing the sick, forgoing the domestic "traps" of motherhood and marriage. I know she did become a mother in the end, but I don't know how much she ever felt like Minnie was really hers. That girl belonged so much to Hall that I think my sister felt she was not needed, or even that the child was her competitor. She felt a sense of duty towards her, yes, but they never had a close bond. I only met Minnie on a few occasions and was never introduced as her aunt. I regret that now. It was remiss, spiteful of me. She didn't choose to be that man's daughter – and now she's all alone.

When once I asked Celia if it was the lack of a child that made her so unhappy, she shook her head. "No," she said. "It's not that. My unhappiness is greater than that."

I feel I must now stress my true feelings. I have come to understand that Hall's principal characteristic was his supreme meanness, his miserly, tight-fisted ways. Quite how miserly he was, we would only learn as the years rolled on and his falsely promised fortune did not appear.

The Intelligence Agency at least was a success. You will note that it was called Mrs Hall's, not Mr Hall's. It was Celia who ran the service and did so with her own impetus and drive. She still read occasionally around medical subjects, and sometimes spoke about returning to the profession on which she had once been so doggedly set, but as the years slipped by, she had little time for such interests save as a hobby. It was only when my daughter, already an enthusiastic medical student herself, would visit that her passion would reignite. They would swap *and share medical textbooks and argue over pioneering new treatments. Celia would blossom in her role as Ethel's wise mentor. I saw flashes of her shrewd brilliance revive.*

It is the sad truth that my dear sister led a most unhappy, cowed life, and that Hall's treatment of her, without doubt, contributed to her early death. I came to realise that she had a terrible, unshakeable fear of him, and often said when we urged her to leave that she would if only she dared. I cannot forgive him for this; this limitation of his own sprit which he inflicted, as violence, upon my sister's body – breaking her soul and her heart.

You will have heard of Hall's drinking and that he was an incorrigible flirt. But it was not just that; it was the gambling. He was a sport, as they say. A jovial word for a cruel disposition, one tied to womanising and the jealousies of that type. Celia mentioned in her letters the matter of other women and the amount of time he spent with them, the attention he bestowed upon them. At one point she did leave him for a matter of a month, on account of his shameless courting. She pointed out one such woman who had incited a particular malaise – a domestic servant, almost half her age, but far from prepossessing.

Meanwhile, in addition to the cruelties he inflicted upon her emotions, he controlled aspects of her life in a way that was most surprising to me. I was astonished that a woman with the independence of spirit possessed by my sister, a woman with her intelligence and spark, would allow such ignominy. But I suppose she was helpless, trapped, as many wives are. The power – and status – is all with the man. And her own wits are no defence against such power wrongfully wielded. For instance, the key to the room containing her jewellery, wedding gifts and personal property, even down to everyday clothing, was always in Hall's possession. He kept her watch and silverware, as well as everything else he could get his hands on, locked up in a room in the house and would not allow them to be used by her at any time. This behaviour cannot, I am sure of it, have been motivated by anything other than a brutish desire to entrap and diminish my sister. To control her by the basest of means.

One occasion stands out, one that took place during a visit the family made to their home around fifteen years into the marriage. There had been an altercation at the dinner table. I'm not sure what the subject at issue was, but it felt like some unpleasant niggle had been bubbling away all evening, as if Hall had been looking for an excuse to fight, prodding away with one small provocation after another and waiting for someone to crack.

The conversation had drifted first through political issues; the Sunday licensing, the necessity of hard labour among the working class, justifications of the corruption of Tammany, and through each of these a clash was successfully averted, and the course rerouted onto matters more genteel. This was proving harder and harder to orchestrate, and conversation had somehow switched back around to a lightning-rod issue.

It was ever thus with Murray Hall: a bellicose verbal pugilist, his tendency to aggravate and jostle and set himself loose from rationality escalated by each glass of wine.

I think the final blow-up might have come over a remark Celia made about his visits to a certain saloon bar. As frightened as she may have been of him, the spark of her central character was never fully extinguished, and she could not help challenging – and thus provoking – him when she felt herself wronged. He slammed his crystal down on the table, so forcefully that red wine droplets splattered out over his plate and the cloth. Then he turned and pushed his small face within a breath of hers, and spoke in a menacing flurry of blasphemies which I find myself unable to repeat. I was shocked that he would do so in front of us all, shocked that he would speak like this, with such foul contempt, to his wife. I wondered with horror how he might act when the family was not there to witness it.

The following day we were due to leave, and I implored that she return with us to Shawmut. "I've seen now what I have long suspected. I have seen the truth of Hall's cruel and irascible personality," I said. "You cannot go on living with this."

Celia's head dropped and she let out a low sigh. She sat on the edge of her bed for several minutes, then began to shake her head, saying it was impossible. "I fear what might happen," she said softly. I sensed what she meant, that she feared the violence I had seen flash across Hall's face could harden into a more concentrated brutality. There was something in that thrust of the head, the tension in his knuckles as he raised his hand away from the glass, that suggested his aggression could be physical as well as verbal. He was a man who wouldn't hesitate to attack a woman if he felt his dominance threatened.

"Does he hit you?" I asked. "Tell me, there is no shame in it."

She was quiet. I watched as she wiped silent tears from her cheeks with the heels of her hands. She stood, then, in that room and looked out over the thronged street. I felt she was about to say something, but the moment passed.

"If you come now, we will protect you from him," I said.

She nodded. "But I have nothing ready."

"Just pack a few things in your bag. We have plenty at Shawmut."

Celia went to her wardrobe and pulled a small case from the bottom of it, throwing two of her dresses inside. They filled the case almost immediately. Then she gathered the few trinkets he had allowed her to keep. There was not much, and I saw how little of any beauty or pleasure she had to hand.

"Your pendant?"

She shook her head. "It's in the room. It's locked away in that room."

Then, as we were almost ready to exit her bedroom, Mr Hall blocked our way. He was standing there, suddenly, his baggy coat taking up all that space in the wood-panelled landing, his eyebrows gathered as dark shadows. "What in hell is going on here?" he demanded.

"I'm going to Shawmut," Celia said, folding a shawl and pressing her skirts down into the case. "I'm going home to see my family. It's long overdue."

Hall stepped into the room. His movements were slow and calm despite the anger in his voice.

"What about the business?" he said in that high-pitched tone that suggested it might break any second. "Your intelligence agency. You would leave that?"

"Esther can look after the agency, or it can close for a while," Celia said. She was yet to look up. She was tall, but in that moment she seemed to shrink down into herself. I recoiled to see such instinctive belittling of her own presence in the world.

"You would go without me?" he snarled.

She nodded slowly.

"No!" he said, and it wasn't clear whether this was an expression of despair or an order for her not to leave. He was shaking his head vigorously. "No, Celia. No." His hands were clenched once more, knuckles white as he circled the room, suddenly coming to some internal conclusion and abruptly departing.

Celia had never ceased in her task. She went to her drawers in search of some final item. She pushed down on the piled-up fabric and pulled the lid over the top. Finally, she began to clip the buckles into place, her hands trembling, but never slowing as she did so.

Before she could finish, Hall was back in the room, stilling the air again with his rage and moving towards her at speed. In his right hand was a glint of metal.

I stared at it and gasped, astonished to see a revolver.

Celia's eyes opened wide and round, meeting his gaze. I heard a strangled, almost animal sound emerge from my sister as she backed away towards the window.

Hall skirted the side of the bed. I tried to reach out and stop him, but he was too deft on his feet and knocked me aside. He was pointing the gun directly in her face. As she backed away, he grabbed her by the arm with his free hand.

"You're not leaving me," he said as he dragged her through the door. "I'll not let that happen. I won't let you leave me. Not ever, you hear?"

In the commotion I found myself pushed against the dresser.

I stood there for a moment panting, unsure of what I had seen, or what to do next.

I could hear grunting as the steps receded into the room next door. Then sobbing, or some sort of guttural cough. I could hear my sister crying out with the last of her strength. "I mean it." I was now shaking and quite terrified, but determined to get Celia out of there, so I gathered my wits and marched through. When I swung the door open, his head was thrusting up to her, and despite her physical stature she looked utterly weak and defeated.

"How can I trust you when you would threaten that?" he said. "Tell me! Tell me, now! How can I trust you?"

Celia dropped to the floor on her knees in front of him. Her chest convulsed with an awful, heartrending sob. It shocked me more than I can express to see her like this. "I won't," she cried. "I won't leave you."

"Celia," I urged, but in that moment my voice didn't sound my own.

"I won't leave you." She looked up at her husband. She reached up and touched the fabric of his jacket. "I won't."

"Celia, you must come now," I tried again.

"Promise!" he said. His voice had dropped to a cold whisper, sure now of his victory.

Hers was more of a wail. "I promise I won't leave you. I promise." She repeated this again and again, dissolving into a cascade of tears.

"Come!" I was shouting, horrified. "Celia, please. You must." But I felt she hadn't heard me. After some moments she turned, and her glazed eyes met mine. What I saw there will stay with me for ever. I was looking into the shadow of a person, into a soulless void, worse even than during her illness all those years before. I pleaded, my hopes ebbing from me. "Let's go, Celia. We must leave now!"

"Don't you dare!" Murray roared, his fury splitting the air between us.

"I can't. I can't," Celia moaned, her voice a scratching whisper. She was shaking her head, rocking back and forth, broken.

I looked across at Hall's face, his features twisted into a smug, animalistic smile. He shrugged, as if to say that the matter was a mere trifle, which was now sorted to his satisfaction.

Then he simply walked out of the room.

My sister's eyes did not meet mine as she straightened up to standing. She smoothed the creases of her dress down. "I can't come. You see how I cannot come. You go now. It's better, safer, that I stay. Safer for everyone."

I tried so many times to make her leave. So many times, I failed. But this was the worst. This one hurt the most. This one tore me to pieces.

In all this time, I had no idea. Never, until we read in the newspapers of Hall's death and the discovery of his sex, did we know anything at all about it. I think it was from fear of Hall that my sister never told us. He – she! – had a remarkable, poisonous power over her, and that must be why she never spoke of it. Either that or pride – and its shadowy companion, shame.

There is more I could write here, so much more, but the pain of it is exhausting. Some things I find too hard to tell. They are still, even after these years, too raw. Perhaps I will write them someday, but for now I send you a few of Celia's own words, her letters to me, so you might glean for yourself who she was and what kind of marriage she became entrapped within.

Yours in hope,
Ellen Elba Hobbs

By the time I had finished reading the letter, the typewriters had stopped their strident clacking and only the deputy and production editors were still murmuring in the kind of soft tones most people reserve for a library. I felt sunken, depleted, but with a dark instinct thumping inside me.

"Any news on the Hall burial?" asked Irving, breaking into the murky swirl of my thoughts.

"Rumour is it's tomorrow, but there is no official release of details. It appears the family don't want guests," I said, managing to match my tone to his brusqueness.

He nodded. "Head along and see what you can get out of it; general impressions will do. You don't have to invade privacy, keep your distance. Then you can switch back onto the Committee of Five. That story could do with an injection of your moral high ground!" He chuckled, smokily. "You all right, fellow?"

"Fine, yes, fine."

"If you say so," Irving said with a sharp glance. "You look like you could do with a bit of shut-eye and a visit to the barber's. This Murray Hall story getting the better of you?"

I nodded, which was no answer at all, still reeling from the letter's harrowing details. The Murray Hall it described was like so many men willing to stray from the path of decency to protect their own self-interest. I looked beyond the window out at the darkness of the city that night.

SIXTH AVENUE
21ST JANUARY 1901, 10 A.M.

THE SUN WAS STRIKING A band of slate behind the spear of Jefferson Market Courthouse, edging the clouds with its coral glow. I stepped once again onto the dirt-and-oyster-shell carpet of Sixth Avenue, making good time for the departure of the rumoured burial of Murray Hamilton Hall at Mount Olivet.

At the corner of 10th Street I paused for a moment, my attention drawn by a stand of old telegraph poles, spindle branches leaning this way and that, amidst a cat's cradle of wires. They seemed, now most of the city's cables had gone underground, like the last avenues of a near-extinct species of tree. For all the chaos of New York's disappearing canopy of wires, I almost missed them.

I could see as I reached my destination a flock of black-clothed figures on the sidewalk, milling under the geometric shadows of the elevated railway, faces and limbs caught, here and there, in the rectangles of light that penetrated the rails from above.

Though the family had expressed their wish that there be no guests at the funeral, some had turned out to see her off. As I got closer, I realised I recognised a few. One, Artie, the labourer, smartened up in a bowler hat and black suit; another the blond man who had sworn his wife had always known Murray's truth. But no sign of that cackling woman, Mary McBride.

I sidled up to a small group and leaned awkwardly against the iron pillar of the railway strut. The woman next to me laughed, randomly, as if to disrupt the chill. All eyes were focused on the opposite side of the street. As I listened to my companions gossiping, I realised that while some were voyeurs like me, others were there to pay genuine respect. "Whatever Murray Hall was, he was generous to me," one woman whispered.

The sign above the door advertising "domestic servants" creaked in the breeze. A distant thunder rose in volume, as the El train approached like a gathering storm, then screeched to a halt. A momentary twitch jerked the curtain at the window above.

"There's someone in there, for sure ..." said the blond man.

"The old aunts ..." said Artie. "Ain't they jus' like that – a family of strange old aunts."

"Apart from the girl."

My timing had been good. Barely had I waited more than a few minutes when one and then another black carriage slowed to a stop outside Murray Hall's home. The carriages stood, for some moments, stationary. There was no movement save for one of the ebony horses tugging restlessly at its harness, pawing the road with a hoof from time to time.

Briefly, the wan ghost of a face appeared against the window. It seemed to be watching us, studying from above, pausing pressed against the glass, then retreating. Several minutes later, two women emerged, one dressed in the voluminous black of deep mourning, the other in a stiffly functional black outfit, buxom and brisk.

"Oh my! Is that Johanna Meyer there?" said the woman next to me. "And with Minnie Hall?"

"My wife was telling me Murray and Mrs Meyer were close friends," said the blond man. "Murray wrote to her asking her to come over just the night before he died. And not, surely, looking for his last Rose O'Cuba. But the woman had the grip and did not go. Imagine. What if he were about to tell her all?"

"Imagine that conversation," said Artie. "My dear, my Johanna, I oughta tell you we have more in common than you mighta thought."

The crowd burst out laughing.

"He wouldn't have told her and not the girl."

"I've always told you."

There was movement to my right. A flat-capped fellow, who had been standing some yards down the street from me, strode up and said a few words to Minnie Hall, pressing her hand tightly with apparent affection. She turned away, shaking her head. As she walked to the carriage her body appeared to weaken beneath her, and she reached out to clutch the steadying hand of her older companion.

I yearned to rush forward to question her, but it would be unseemly on such a day as this. Three more women, with the stiff posture of the elderly, emerged from the same door and mounted the second carriage. One of them I recognised as the old woman who had refused to receive me at the door those few days ago. "These other ladies?" I asked the fellow next to me. "Who are they?"

"Servants who worked for the family and lived with them," the gentleman said, as if he'd been awaiting my question. "Louise Perkins and Esther O'Donoghue, and one there I don't know. Hall practically pensioned them."

"A strange household they were," observed another.

It was then that the hearse arrived, driven by the top-hatted Mr Partridge from Grace Church, and the two coachmen nodded to each other. Partridge's presence suggested some care and seriousness about the matter, yet the hearse that arrived was clearly his cheapest and simplest. No doves or angels. No plumes atop the horses' statuesque heads. Only the modern plain frame, supporting a glass box through which it was impossible to see, for the curtains had been dropped.

Murray Hall was hidden from sight. No gawkers permitted.

"Well, would you believe it? In there is a woman's body!" said one stout onlooker, craning her neck towards the hearse as if hoping to see through the heavy fabric.

"I heard," said another, "they dressed her in women's clothes. It was Mr Partridge himself who did it."

"Murray Hall? In women's clothes?" said Artie.

"Well, blame me, I thought they were going to be dressing him as a man!" said the blond fellow. "I was imagining him lying there in his big sack coat. I can't think of him otherwise, whatever it was he kept under that coat."

The street turned silent. The hearse rumbled onwards, its draped cabin turning down 10th Street. I could see the young woman's veil silhouetted against the window as it passed.

The stout woman ahead of me started talking again. "Don't you think that if Murray Hall had died a man, all the ward would have been at that funeral, all his Tammany brothers crowding to pay their respects. Now see who is going. None but the old servants. The old aunts as you call 'em."

"That's it, then," the blond man said decisively. "I'm going to Riley's. It's got a back room for you ladies if you'd care to join, and Murray always seemed to like it."

"Sure, I'll come with ye, Bill. For ol' times."

The small crowd was beginning to make its slow way towards the alehouse, but something was preventing me from following in their footsteps. It was the look on Minnie Hall's face.

She had been so tantalisingly close; the one living person who knew Hall the most. An impulse overtook me as I watched the other onlookers amble down the street and, as they turned the corner, I hailed myself a hansom cab.

The chill air bit at my cheeks and I wrapped my scarf around my face, tipping my hat down over my eyes, as we headed across town towards the Mount Olivet cemetery. Down Sixth Avenue the traffic was slow, but as we approached the cables of the Brooklyn Bridge the driver cracked the reins and we picked up speed, climbing the granite hill in a surge of other vehicles, before descending into Brooklyn and its cobbled streets. Out in open country, the cab bounced and rattled over potholes and a road that was barely a dirt track.

The wind had kicked up as we reached the lower slopes of the graveyard. Snow was swirling between the gravestones and above the bare earth, and the site looked desolate – not the place for a fond farewell to a loved one. Dark studs of headstones pierced the thin carpet of white that was descending on the landscape.

"Will you stay, driver?" I asked, as I stared out across the bleak hilltop, wondering why I had come so far, and for likely so little.

"How long would that be? It's been quite some job already."

"An hour."

"It will cost you more than a few cents."

"That's fine, it'll be on the *World*."

I peered out of the window of the cab. I could not yet see sign of the funeral party. My eyes swept the vast, undulating cemetery and fell only upon the scattered shapes of monuments to the dead and wintry vegetation.

I wanted to be sure, however, that they were not already there, so I descended from the cab and began the walk up a gentle incline. I had only walked about thirty yards when another flurry of snow swirled up around me. I sheltered from the wind in the shade of a mausoleum the size of a small home, regretting my decision to follow the trail to this place beyond the city's familiar comforts.

I considered heading back to the hansom cab. There would be trouble in the office over the wasted expenses, and I might be better paying it myself, but this seemed now a fruitless mission. Through the cold breeze I heard my father's voice. *The law of the Book is above the law of the land. Go forth and know yourself sinful.*

Then the muffled sound of hooves caught my attention. I looked down the rise to see the hearse wending its way up the track. Behind it was the second carriage, moving sedately, the horses gathered to a gentle trot.

The hearse, I now noticed, was moving towards an empty area where I could make out a solitary figure already waving. The gravedigger most likely, I thought. I began to walk in that direction, bent forward against the wind, my arms wrapped about myself. My intention was to come close enough to watch, but not to intrude upon the party. When I got to within fifty yards, I stopped to watch the carriages empty, the women helped out one by one by the funerary assistant.

To my relief the snow had taken a breath of pause, as if out of respect. The world stood still for a moment, even the wind slowing until all was silent. The Reverend Partridge, a stark, distinct figure with his towering hat, stood at the foot of the grave. No family, I observed, was there to carry the coffin, nor close male associates to act as pallbearers. Only these women and their paid service, joined together in a cheap graveside committal.

I soon realised the difficulty in maintaining my anonymity given the intimacy of the service, and I shifted uncomfortably in the cold, hoping the group were too engrossed in the proceedings and their own grief to look up and spot my uninvited, loitering presence.

Five figures now stood at the graveside, gathered at the foot of the dark space in the earth. If they were talking, I could not hear them, nor could I identify their faces from this distance. I shifted slightly closer until I came to a tall headstone, against which I crouched.

The gruff, authoritative voice of Reverend Partridge drifted out as he spoke over the grave. I recognised that solemn tone fighting to be heard over the wind as it whipped up once again. His voice rose and fell with the same cadence I had heard in my father. Now that I was closer, I could pick out Minnie Hall too, dressed in a black coat covering her mourning dress and a small hat, her veil lifted. Her face appeared pale even from such a distance.

The young woman leaned in on the taller, stooped figure next to her, as if weakened by the task of bearing in its entirety the mourning of her father's death.

It seemed to me now that these people were so caught up in their personal drama they would not notice me there, so I took the opportunity to stand up in order to see better.

"God grant her an entrance into the land of light and joy," came the voice, faint in the wind.

I moved closer again.

There was a low, choking sob.

To my horror I noticed then that the tall, elderly woman was looking directly at me. I sensed the heat of her glare, and I recognised the face, too, from its pinched frown and the forward crook of her neck. This was the servant who had guarded the door on that first evening. The one they had called

132

Esther. The dark pins of her eyes held my gaze for a heartbeat. Then she turned away, leaned in towards Minnie to touch her arm, and gestured towards me.

There are a couple of things a newspaper man can do when caught in such a situation. I considered approaching them. It was, perhaps, my only chance to engage the young Miss Hall. But that seemed an invasion too far, a tipping of the scales that wouldn't do me any favours were I to attempt to visit them again.

Besides, I thought, it was just possible this servant may not have recognised me. So, I turned up the hill and walked as if I had merely been there looking for something else, perhaps in search of another grave. I thought of the warm inn where I might have found more fruitful gossip than this chill, windswept scene. When I thought I had walked far enough, I looked back down.

Some of the party had returned to the carriages.

Only the young woman was left now at the grave, which lay unmarked, with no headstone. Only a heavy mound of earth against the snow. She stooped to lay something at its foot. Her show of grief moved me. I tried to read her movements, to work out what it was that the language of her body revealed. I don't know what I hoped to reveal. All I knew was I was sure that if anyone held the key to the truth of Murray Hall, it was Minnie.

The young woman's gloved hand flew up to cover her mouth, and her neck twisted downwards. Her back seemed to curl in a wave, as if hit in that moment by an invisible punch to the abdomen. She tottered back a couple of steps and then recovered, like a boxer righting himself to rejoin the fight.

I saw her lips move, her hand reaching out in a stab of grief. I heard only the moaning of the wind; her words were lost to me.

THE PAROLE CLUB, DEY STREET
22ND JANUARY 1901, 3 P.M.

T HE FEELING OF GUILT AT my intrusion haunted me for the rest of the evening. I had gone too far; I had stepped outside my usual code of conduct, and I couldn't quite work out why. Again and again, I saw the young woman's hand fly to her face. Was I, in truth, so obsessed with the story of this man-woman? Or was it something about Minnie Hall that had captivated me?

When I wrote up the funeral report, I felt more of that guilt, a twinge of buried pain spreading through me as I spelled out her name. The next day as I read my words in the paper, I felt it again. What was that pang, that regret? What did it mean? I found myself wondering, again and again, what that young woman really knew of that old man with the painful stoop, of the secrets he took to his grave. I yearned to go back to the apartment and knock on the door once more.

But there was other work to do. The battle against the protection combine did not stop for a peculiar human-interest story like that of Murray Hall. I found myself dressed in a borrowed suit and flat cap, on a dimly lit staircase, knocking at the Parole Club. The hour, 3 p.m., was one that had been passed to me as a tip through my City Vigilance contacts. I was to say I was meeting a man called Des.

"Would you like to join a game?" asked the sharp-featured floorman. "There is poker about to start in the side room, and I would say, knowing the players, the pot will be big."

"No, thank you," I replied, as he led me into a large room, arranged with battered wooden tables, around several of which a card game was already happening. "I've got some friends joining me. We'll have our own game."

"The bar serves only beer, brandy and Scotch," he told me with a nod. "Can I get you anything?"

"Just a small beer."

"You can take a seat at the side tables till your friend arrives. Or perhaps you might like a quick spin at the roulette table?"

"I'll read my paper till my friends arrive." I pulled out the copy of the *Sporting Life* I had tucked under my arm, and wafted it through the air, suddenly feeling awkward at the fakery of my prop. But it was up there now, swiping the space between us.

I took a pew at one of the side tables, from which it was possible to watch the room with its long, emerald-clothed main table and two smaller poker tables. There was also a view, from my placement, into the room to the right, where a man, in white shirt and crimson braces, was stretched over the pool table, his left leg balletically extending through the air. For a short while I sat casually browsing the results pages of *Sporting Life*.

From time to time, I looked up to observe the small, noisy group of young sporting men gathered around a poker table on the other side of the room.

A clean-shaven young man with a defined jawline and straw-blond curls was pushing chips across the table, an unlit cigar in his mouth. Though not exactly the twin of Hall, he made me think of Joe Young's description of him. I imagined the bondsman there, resolutely retaining his shabby coat and hat, cigar unlit all game. The young man's flickering eyes caught mine for a moment and his small smile provoked a desire to be there, over that side of the room, stacking my chips. I wanted no longer to be always the watcher, but rather part of that fun, that lively scene they were creating; the bubbles of laughter that spilled out across the room making their group seem like the club that anyone might long to be part of.

The floorman, dressed in black waistcoat, with a red garter slashed across the white of his shirt arm, crossed the room. He carried a tray of liquor shots, held high and gliding through the air, before swooping down to be shared round the table, eliciting a series of masculine whoops of bonhomie.

I was aware that I shouldn't appear to be studying them too closely, but my paper's tales of new baseball signings weren't holding my interest, nor were its stories about trap shoots, so I pulled from my pocket an envelope I had picked up as I was leaving my apartment. I needed something else to draw my attention, and it's always wise, when on a job in which you know there will be waiting, to bring some correspondence, or other reading, you are keen to catch up on.

This was a thick envelope postmarked Waterville. The group of sporting youths soon disappeared from my view as I unfolded the heavy sheets and began to scan the words.

Dear Mr Clellan,

There was a story I omitted from my previous letter, which I should relate to you. I mentioned that there was more I wished to convey, matters I found too painful to write. I now find myself ready to do so, perhaps propelled by the desire to right a wrong. Day and night I am troubled by memories of my sister, comments she made, her smile as it aged and faded. I hope that in writing this out for you I can purge them. I might almost say my sister haunts me. Certainly, she was a ghost by the end of her life.

My belief, as you know, is that Mr Hall's jealous nature and miserly ways, as well as his general ugliness of character, made my sister's life a hard one. I have a long list of grievances and I will not elaborate on them all here; but I must speak of what I found most unforgivable: his conduct towards the end of her life and after her death.

It pains me even to write of it. I am wracked, indeed, with guilt. For whilst I blame Hall, I also blame myself for not trying harder to extricate my dear Celia from the circumstances, the utter calamity of her marriage, a hardship of spirit and of body that I am only now beginning to understand.

I felt helpless, I admit, to come to her aid. She had told me she was unhappy, but I did far too little; it might be I was driven by my own fear of Hall and some deep assumption that any marriage, even a flawed one, must be in some way fated by God. I assumed at first that some of this unhappiness might be her own tendency towards melancholia, some of that lingering illness that had afflicted her as a student. But I was fooling myself; I knew it was more than that. She had told me she could not leave him, and I assumed that was because she feared he would kill her. It's the thought of this that has kept me awake at night since, the depth of the fear that my sister lived with.

I knew that my sister was ill from early 1896. Though her letters had become increasingly infrequent, she had written a number of times describing first a mysterious back pain, then some swelling. When I heard during April that year that matters had worsened, and of the exhaustion and bleeding from which she was suffering, my daughter and I (she is herself a doctor, to my sister's eternal pride) took the train over to New York in order to visit her. Ethel almost immediately recognised from the symptoms described that she was highly likely to be suffering a cancer of the womb, a catastrophically painful, creeping and almost always incurable disease.

Upon arrival, however, we were turned away by the housekeeper, who informed us that Mrs Hall was much better, and that all she needed was rest. That servant, by the way, held an extraordinary position in the household, almost as if she was a second wife.

Visitors, she said, would only exhaust my sister and hamper her recovery. My daughter protested, insisting she could help, but we were told that "Mrs Hall is already receiving the attention she needs from Dr Gallagher". You'll recognise that name as the man who is now quite famous for bringing Hall's secret to light.

There was little we could do save storm the place, and so we left the city after a brief visit to some friends the next day. I never like to spend too long in that dirty, crowded environment at the best of times, and I was too enraged to make some entertainment or enjoy the delights of Bloomingdales, as I might have more usually done.

Three months later, in that exceptionally hot July, I received another letter, written in a hand so weak it was almost unrecognisable. It said little more than the words, "Gravely ill. Please come." I remember reading them again and again, hoping that I might read something different, or more, in that shaky hand. I must be mistaken. But, no, my husband verified – that was what it said.

Those words cut like a knife, the blade of the sharpest sword. I was determined to go immediately, though my husband tried to persuade me not to take the trip. "If she's gravely ill," he said, "you won't be able to bring her back. And, in any case, Hall won't let you take her away. She won't be able to be moved. Remember how he is. Remember when you last tried to persuade her to leave ..."

Contrary to my husband's desires, it was precisely that memory which compelled me east once more.

As I said, I am not fond of spending time in Manhattan. The heat was stifling that day. We thought about catching the elevated railway from the central depot, but in the end hailed a hansom cab. One of the reasons I always have hated your city, Mr Clellan, is because New York stole Celia. It devoured my sister long before Hall did. It felt, sometimes, as if it would swallow me too. Everything about it baffles me – and it doesn't help that by the time I arrive I am always exhausted, irritable and enervated from days of travel.

The city seemed that day to have become even faster and busier than the last time we had visited, more and more of those motorised vehicles swerving along the roads at reckless speeds. When we reached 145 Sixth Avenue, my nerves were so rattled I almost tripped out of the cab. All I remember is looking upwards at the sturdiness of the big black door, the door through which I was determined to pass.

It was Ethel, standing behind me, who noticed the closed curtains. She pointed upwards, but by then I had already rung the bell and one of the servants answered, of which there often appeared to be many – so many that there was never room for any of us to stay, and we would feel as if we were the invaders in some strange domestic den.

The woman's face paled in shock as she squinted out into the bright sunshine. Her jaw dropped. "Mrs Hobbs," she said.

"I received a letter saying that my sister was gravely ill," I said with purpose.

Then, as I looked into that woman's face, I knew the worst had happened.

Her hand lifted lightly up to her bosom. "You know the news already, don't you?" Her voice was almost a whisper. "You have heard?"

I felt it as a thumping blow in the chest, and everything after washed over me as if I were in a dream. My sister, we were told, had only three days previously passed on, quietly in her sleep, though not without some agony in the days leading up to her passing. Mr Hall, the housekeeper said, had in fact written to us, not only telling us of this news but also that Celia's body was on its way, that he had shipped her already to Shawmut, by express.

The words were abstract and unreal, as if that phrase didn't quite fit together. Celia and dead. Celia and body. Celia and shipped.

Celia and – express.

"Mr Hall arranged for her body to be sent in a casket to you," the woman said.

"He did not accompany her?" I asked. In my imagination, I saw her once tall and handsome body being carried across the country. My sister inside a shoddy box, as if she were some unloved piece of cargo.

My poor, lonely sister!

"My understanding is that Mrs Hall requested this. Her instructions were for her body to be returned to Shawmut, to her home and family. This was what she wanted. Mr Hall would not have done this, were it not for that."

I nodded. If this were true, this in itself was a message. It spoke to me of her suffering, of how not even in death did she want to stay with her husband. She had wanted to come back to us.

But I also found myself doubting it. I asked if, since we were in town, I could see Mr Hall. "Grief is a thing best shared," I said. But the woman stayed planted right there in the middle of the doorway, telling me that he and Minnie, the daughter, were in mourning and had seen no one for the past few days. They had given her strict instructions that they would receive no visitors till the end of the week.

"Please," I begged. "You can't send us away like this."

"These are Mr Hall's orders. They are to be obeyed," she said, her voice as unreadable as her eyes. "He has just lost his wife, ma'am."

As you can imagine, this only enraged me further, and I insisted once more. There was some animal part of me that wanted to enter the house, to see her empty bed, to witness her absence, to draw the lost scent of her into my lungs. To allay a fear, perhaps, that I was being lied to again. I harboured a small, secret hope that all I had heard was simply not true, was some inexplicable act of subterfuge, of revenge.

"What was it like?" I asked.

She seemed to understand what I meant and on this at least offered a shred of comfort. "Your sister had been in great pain for some months," she said. "I think in the end she was glad to go. She is better off where she is now."

I remember how long that journey home felt. The Stonington line seemed to move with agonising slowness, each minute dragging into eternity. Every passing mile of countryside was *a new torture. I was desperate to get back to Shawmut as soon as I could, to be with my sister, yet acutely aware that such a reunion came far too late.*

My little sister, I thought.

I couldn't shift the grim idea, as I stared out the window of the train, which had kept me standing on that doorstep. What if Celia had not in fact been dead at all, if she had still been in that room on the third floor, still lying in that loveless, godforsaken room where I had last seen her? Surely my sister could not disappear just like that.

"Does he hit you?" I had asked.

I knew what her silence meant.

But, of course, she had gone from me long ago. I had lost her in the past when our lives as sisters gave way to our lives as wives. I had lost to her to this person called Murray Hall.

"We should have demanded he give us her things," I said to Ethel as the train rumbled along. "All those possessions he kept of hers, the wedding presents, the clothes, the jewellery. All those things of hers, those feminine things, he would keep locked away in another room to which only he had the key."

But I knew this would have been pointless. Of course, the clothes, and the jewellery, hadn't been seen in decades. The dresses, for one thing, would not have fitted her for many years. The way he locked them away had been such a source of pain. I had seen it as his way of rejecting us, of loosening Celia's ties to us. And, of course, of tightening the chain of his control — over himself and her.

144

"It's better that I stay," she told me. "Safer that I stay. Safer for everyone."

By the time I reached Shawmut, the coffin had already been placed in the parlour and flowers arranged on the table beside it. The delicacy and fragrance of the flowers could not disguise the shocking flimsiness of the box. It was indeed shoddy. I remember as I leaned over it, when my knees buckled and I reached for support, how it yielded. It bent under my hands. It felt that if I were to put all my weight onto it, it might splinter and crack.

That box felt like an insult. The thin, unadorned wood, barely fit for a pauper. The smell, too, for since that July was so hot there was already the scent of decay like an unpleasant mist through the room.

"It's really quite eccentric," my husband said.

"Eccentric?" I said. I was flabbergasted. "Richard, it is ugly!" Eccentric seemed an entertaining and inappropriate word. Everything Hall did was ugly. Everything he had done since the first moment we met him was ugly. This was simply the latest and final ugly episode. An ugly spectacle, yes, but a truthful display of the ugliness of his treatment of my beloved, beautiful sister.

Flies hovered, as if sensing that here was some rich home in which to lay their eggs. I know, of course, that decay comes to us all, but this lonesome, anonymous journey my sister had made, in nothing more than a glorified shoebox, felt specifically humiliating.

Despite my anger towards Hall, what I felt now was relief. I felt relief at knowing she was here, at having her back finally.

I think I even uttered the words out loud: "Finally, you are home." I had the feeling of having some stolen item returned, only now it was broken irreparably.

I recall that my husband was still talking in the background, but his voice was thin and distant. I only picked it up again when he started to talk once more about the coffin. "The driver advised not to open the casket. They said Mr Partridge had advised that it should, as soon as possible, be lowered into the family plot, such would be the state of decay. Particularly in these summer months. She has not been embalmed. But I knew from the telegram you would want to see the coffin before she was put in the ground."

Hall, I realised, had acted solely to minimise his costs. I have learned since that he went to the sexton of Grace Church and said, "My wife is dead and I want to ship her remains to her old home in Waterville, but I don't want the cost to be over fifty dollars all told." The undertaker's bill was around sixty dollars. So little for a man of his wealth, and for a woman who gave the best of her life to him. I feel that old, uncomprehending anger rise as I write of this to you now.

Hall, as I have said, was a miser who always looked for a way to save a dime. He made sure to spend the minimum possible on his own wife. What shocked me, however, was that any reputable undertaker might be willing to do such disrespectful work. That, surely, is New York for you.

I wanted to look inside and see my sister's face for one last time. I insisted. Hence it was that Richard did open the box,

146

in part so I could be sure it was her, that this wasn't some cruel joke played by Mr Hall.

After some prising, the lid came open and I looked at the body. The face was hers, and yet not hers. It was like one of those waxworks that had become all the rage in the city. It was shiny, expressionless, pale.

For some time that face occupied my memory. It would be the first image that would float up when I thought of her. It replaced the sister I knew. It obliterated her. But lately I have gone back to remembering her as she once was, as I always think of her. The vibrant, clever Celia of our youth, before she met him.

As I mentioned, I have made up my mind not to come to the inquest, though I am well aware of its relevance to me. Celia left me $1,500, but she left far more to Murray and to their daughter, Minnie. That portion, some consider, should come to me, since, as is well known in scripture and in law, woman cannot marry woman.

But it's not the money that troubles me: it's what he did to her. And it is my belief he did that as a man. I will never forgive Murray Hall for the life he gave my sister. I felt this even before I learned the news of that person's sex – if indeed that be true. There was so much secrecy in his life that his sex makes only a small difference to how I feel.

Hall always disturbed me. I felt there was some element of him that was out of place. Now I feel I know why; what it might have been I was reacting to. For years I have seen him as the man who ruined my sister's life; the man who stole her

away from us. Now I learn he is something other than that –
and I do not know what to do with that knowledge.

I find myself grieving all over again. So, yes, I am bitter.
My hate deforms me. I cannot get over it. I cannot forgive. I
doubt I ever will.

Words linger in my mind. They haunt me.

"I would leave," she once said. "But I fear him too much."

I sprang at the sound of a sudden whinny from the table opposite. "Damn it!" the muscular man with the over-oiled moustache was saying. "I was sure I had that!" I was aware of how absorbed I had been in the letter that now dropped into my lap. I looked again at those last lines with recognition. Hate, I thought, had deformed me too.

My mind jangled with those words.

Across the other side of the room, the blond man stood up and performed a theatrical bow, before returning once more to his seat. The gentleman beside him rolled his eyes, unseen by his friend, and knocked back another glug from his glass. I glanced at my pocket watch and saw it was nearly quarter to four. Time had passed. Perhaps they were no longer coming; the swoop had been called off.

At another nearby table, several Wall Street types had taken up seats and a dealer slapped cards rhythmically down in a circular motion. But now I could hear voices at the door, the floorman calling, "Keep them out!" A rattle and a rush of movement as bodies, dressed in black, flooded the room. The Committee of Fifteen and its officers were finally here, two of them dressed in flowing opera capes and top hats, as if calling in on their way to the theatre – and, as it turned out, they were.

There were a few yelps and a rumble. One of the young men cried, "Run for it!" and several dived through the side door into the pool room. The rattle of counters being swept from a table; the rustle of bills; the tumble of liquor glasses.

"Stay where you are," said the gaunt, bearded figure of the district attorney, Philbin, in his long black mackintosh, shiny with rain. "You will no doubt have heard about the raids currently being carried out by the Committee of Fifteen. This is one. We will be taking the names of all present here. Please do not remove anything from the tables."

Behind him were several police officers, topped by their bowl-like helmets, one of them a broad-set giant, glinting with brass buttons. Philbin tipped his head, white-tipped at the hairline, and gestured towards the officer. "Check the side rooms! No one else move."

The young man knocked back his drink, and in one swift movement chucked his glass over his shoulder. He grinned as it smashed on the floor behind, never turning his head. Another sank into his chair and under the table, disappearing like some mischievous child.

"Nothing going on here, sir!" the young man said. "Just a little parlour game. Hand of Happy Families? What harm is there in that?"

I nodded towards Philbin and followed two of the officers through to the pool room, where there was one man attempting to climb out of the window, and another peering through, was shouting, "Bejabbers! It's a long way down!"

"Jump! Jump! It's only one storey."

"I would advise you not to jump!" said the tall police officer as he hauled the dangling man in and pushed the other to the side. "We don't want any broken bones."

This is a corrupt world, my father whispered, *and we must be the antiseptic that is to be rubbed in to resist the process of decay.*

Philbin dipped his head into the room. "Make sure the space is secure and keep them all in here, then we'll go through them one by one. Has anyone found Ridge Levien?"

"He's here, sir," said the second policeman, pointing to one of the men who had been egging on the others to jump. "Mr Percy Levien too."

The two men, so physically similar they might have been twins, were standing at the window and looked intent on making the jump themselves. Ridge Levien, owner of the Parole Club, and his sibling Percy, a high-up in Tammany, so key to the party's machine that he was frequently called "Commissioner".

"Keep them all in here," commanded Philbin again, and he swept back through to the central room, turning briefly to me to say, "We are going to take names and statements here. No one leaves before they give one. You are welcome to take a seat a little back from the table and make notes."

Judge Jerome was already poised with his elbows propped on the poker table, hands folded, thumbs twitching impatiently. He wore, with his trademark playful informality, a mustard-yellow spotted bowtie. His dark eyes, scowling through rounded spectacles, flashed with anticipation.

The first suspect to come through was one whose face I immediately recognised as the director of the board of public improvements.

"Name?" said the judge.

The gentleman, bowler-hatted and generously grey-whiskered, smiled. "I see no need to give my name."

There was a brief chuckle. "I see," said Jerome. His head thrusted forward, projecting a clean, athletic jawline. "We are not letting anyone leave this room without giving their name and a statement. But you need not fear, Mr Holaban, we are doing no more than collecting witness statements. Name?"

"John Doe."

Justice Jerome frowned. "Come now, Mr Holaban. Let's not play this game. I want it understood – and if this could be conveyed to those present in the adjoining room, that would be helpful – that all persons who refuse to give their true names will be committed to the House of Detention for witnesses. If true names are given, it will be in confidence; they will not be made public." He glanced my way. "Understood, Mr Clellan?"

I nodded.

"Now, Mr Holaban. Name?"

The man sighed. "Maurice F. Holaban."

"Now, you get the idea, Mr Holaban. You will see here I have brought a Bible along, so that we may take witness statements without leaving the establishment. We are not interested in prosecuting you, merely those who run this place, or in some way profit from it. May I ask you to swear in?" He pointed to his copy of the Bible on the table. "You can regard this room as a court of law."

"This room?" asked Holaban, a brow raised. "A court of law?"

"Yes indeed, this room, Mr Holaban. I do have the authority," affirmed Jerome, leaning further across the table to push the battered book towards him. For a judge, the man was unconventionally confrontational and pugilistic.

Holaban groaned and pulled the small, worn Bible towards him. He placed his hand on its front cover and said rapidly: "I swear to tell the truth, the whole truth, so help me God!"

"So, Mr Holaban, am I right in thinking you are currently director of public improvements for Manhattan?"

The man nodded. "I am."

"And what were you, director of public improvements, doing in this establishment? What were you hoping to improve?"

"I was here for a business meeting."

"Ah, yes, a business meeting in a gambling house. I have a note here that you were found in the poker room, playing cards."

"Just a relaxed game, no money exchanged. We were in the poker room, but it was not poker we were playing."

"A relaxed game? What game would that be?"

"Bridge," he said, in a wavering voice.

"I wonder if the other players will say the same about your game."

Mr Holaban smiled. It was possible to see the nervous sweat, even in this cold room, on his brow. He pulled out a white silk handkerchief and mopped his forehead. "Actually, I remember now. It wasn't Bridge. It was poker. But no money exchanged."

"A game of poker, no money exchanged. I see. And were you aware of others in the building placing bets on their games?"

"I have no idea what other patrons of this establishment were doing. That is their own business. I am not in the habit of taking note."

"Thank you, Mr Holaban. I can see this is going to be a long afternoon. You may leave now. I hope work on the new Public Library continues apace. My wife is most excited about it."

There was a silence around the table as the man walked quickly towards the door. "Percy Levien next?" asked Philbin.

"No, let's get the Wall Street crowd out the way," said Jerome. "They have less to lose. Then the others will start to fear that too many of their associates have already told all and there is no point in lying. The longer they are in that room, the more nervous they will become."

"Those Wall Street fellows have been swearing they did nothing wrong and beggin' to go without giving their names," said the police officer. "The young one was close to tears, going on about his father."

"We'll see," said Jerome. "Bring them through. I think I know the young man's father. Let's go hard for another hour here, then we should adjourn to Church Street police station. My fear is this could drag on all night. But we are making progress. The element of surprise is, I believe, most efficacious."

153

That night I went to bed early after filing my copy just in time to meet the deadline for the morning's edition. As I left the editorial floor, I called out to Irving, "I'm likely late in tomorrow. Contacts to meet!"

This was, at least, partially true. But the contact I referred to had nothing to do with the vice investigations. I had an appointment at the cesspit of the New York Tombs.

"Most likely he'll be making his lace, sir," McAveety, the jailer muttered as he guided me through a gloomy passage that smelled of the deepest sewers, then out into the morning light of the courtyard beneath the Tombs' Egyptian-style façade.

Through various inquiries I had ascertained the whereabouts of one William Reno, the man who had reputedly "sandbagged" Murray Hall. Such were his numerous crimes, he was now confined to the city's worst hellhole of a penitentiary. I felt sorry for the man, as I did for anyone incarcerated in those notorious walls.

"Lace ...?" I said, wondering if I had misheard.

"He's our lace man. You never heard? Bill Reno sits there day after day after day making lace. Used to be one of our noisiest inmates, howlin' and mutterin', till we gave him his table and a thread. Now that's all the fool does – makes lace, and it's quite something, I might say. He gave me some few pieces for my wife and now all she's wanting is more of the stuff. Earned him a few dispensations, as it were, that lace."

The smell of the Tombs was what assailed the visitor first: the stink of human misery, a noxious combination of urine and stagnant water, with a faint undertow of blood. Its sounds were the next assault. Grunts and wails, like the braying of asses and the groans of cattle. Murky and disease-ridden, it was, like all places relating to our penal system, run in the most corrupt fashion.

We passed a small group of men loitering outside the lower cells. Their clothes were ragged and hardly thick enough to face such weather as we were having. Most of them, I knew, would barely be worse than petty thieves. Many were merely awaiting trial. They were those presumably who could not afford bail, or for whatever reason had not been given it, those not favoured by Tammany bondsmen such as Murray Hall. It was, I always thought, a most desperate place to end up for those who had not yet been found guilty. It was no wonder that many who entered here innocent soon found themselves drawn down an inexorable path of crime.

We walked across the central yard, and I stared up at the three storeys of crumbling façade as men wandered desolately, passing their hour of exercise, as if they were the dead risen from their graves.

I followed the jailer, a heavy-browed jackdaw of a fellow, up a set of stone steps to the first tier. There were four tiers of cells, with a narrow gallery running outside the cells on each level. "Reno will be in his cell," he said. "He won't be out here. Never does come out anymore. Used to sit in the corner there, in the light, till one of the convicts ripped his lace away from him and stamped it into the dirt. After that he never went out again."

I peered through the window in the door to the cell. A man was sitting in a thin shaft of light that was penetrating the room from a small window above. He held a piece of white fabric in his hand. He was so absorbed he did not turn as McAveety called out, "Visitor for ye."

"One moment." The man spoke quietly without looking up.

I observed, as my eyes adjusted to the low light, that the fabric was in fact a piece of very dainty lace and that he was working on it with a fine needle.

"Beautiful, isn't it?" he said, as he held it up in the narrow sunbeam.

I nodded my appreciation and stretched out a hand to shake his, but he pulled away. "I try to avoid touching anything other than the thread and lace," he said.

"I wrote to you about Murray Hall," I told him. "You may have heard his story. It's been in all the newspapers."

"The newspapers?" he said. "I do not read newspapers here."

"Murray Hall, though," I prompted. "I wonder if you might remember him. Murray Hall? The Tammany bondsman?"

There was something in this man's frailty that made me hesitate from detailing what I understood of his story, which was that he was quite possibly the individual whose extreme violence, so Murray Hall had claimed, was to blame for his cancer.

"Murray Hall," he said slowly. He was still staring, as if transfixed, into the intricate patterns of his own lace. "Yes,

Murray Hall . . ." I saw now that tears rolled silently down his cheeks. A guttural croak rose in his throat, and then he swallowed. "I'm sorry, sir," he said, weakly. "This . . . This . . ."

He put his lace down on the rickety table, picked up a pair of heavily worn dark leather gloves and carefully put them on, finger by finger. He gestured for me to come over. "Please, take a seat. I will sit on the bed . . . You want to know about Murray Hall?"

I observed now the bed and other furnishings in the room. It was remarkable, too, that he had this table, since no cell I had ever visited had more than a bed, though occasionally there may be a stool or chair. I assumed this addition must be one of McAveety's dispensations.

Reno's sleeve wiped across his face, pushing away the wet trickle of tears. "I should warn you that this is not a short story. You have some time?"

"Of course," I said. The chair creaked as I dropped my weight into it. I was glad to find a man who wanted to talk.

Reno began to speak. I sensed from the start that he could bear no interruption, so I remained in silence, only nodding periodically throughout.

"I like to keep my hands occupied. I have found in recent years some distraction from my restless energies in the making of lace."

He stared at me for a long moment, eyes drifting over my face, as if contemplating some new piece of lace. Another tear welled.

"It must be lonely here," I said.

"No … It's too noisy," he said, cupping his hands over his ears. "Too many people. I would rather be on my own."

I attuned my ears to the sounds from outside – distant, despondent wails and cries, the angry, futile shouting of an inmate.

"I learned to make lace in Dannemora prison from a fellow convict. A Chinese man, who called his style and method Oriental. When I first looked at what he had made, the twist and turns and detail of it, the patterns, it had me under its spell. Those long-beaked birds with chequered wings, flying amidst simple-petalled flowers. A whole, enrapturing world conjured up out of thread. My wonder prompted me to start to learn from him the craft. I began to practise daily. My skills now include both bobbin lace and fine Chinese needlework. I can do almost anything a client might request."

As he spoke of such exquisite craft, my eyes glanced once around the room. I noted how it was a mere couple of feet wide, with only room for the bed, the chair and the desk, all of which were of such greying, dirtied wood that I could not imagine how he managed to keep anything clean, never mind his lace. There was no mattress, only a thin, folded mat on top of the wooden-slatted bed.

"There has," he went on, "been some virtue to spending so long inside these walls. It has meant I have had the hours to practise, to work again and again on these skills, till they now seem almost second nature. I have the same feel for the thread as some men have for wood. The rhythm and movement have worked their way into my limbs, and they soothe me. I can say it calms whatever memory or unhappy thought arises. When

I'm mad-angry with the world and what it keeps doing to me, I pick up my work with the bobbins and all that ebbs away."

I listened, imagining the power of such craft to distance a person from their body, their mind, their wretched surroundings, even perhaps its smells, such as the urgent one that now assailed my senses and distracted me from his words. I saw now its source in the darkness of the corner: a water closet, open and stinking of recent faeces.

"Sir?" he said, as if he had discerned my inattention. "Perhaps you need to see more to understand."

The man reached under one of the mats atop the wooden slats and pulled out a green canvas pouch. It was fastened with a button and even in the low light I could see that it was embroidered with his initials, W.R. He took off his gloves, one by one, then began pulling out pieces of fragile white lace, holding them up, then putting them back in again.

He sighed and ran his hands over his own skeletal head. "Why him? Why him?" His left hand now held out a fragment of lace, three or four inches long, so intricate in its detail, I had to lean in to see the pattern.

"Why Murray Hall?" he said, distracted now by some fresh thought. "Yes, Murray Hall ..."

I saw that the tears had returned and I felt the urge to reach out and put a reassuring hand on his knee, but he pulled away.

"I'm sorry, sir," he said at last, blinking and swiping at his eyes with the heavy gloves. "Perhaps you can come back another time. Today is not a good day. Some days are better."

In the distance, doors banged and keys rattled, followed by dull footsteps, reluctant and plodding. It seemed as if Reno was about to say something more, when a figure tumbled in through the entrance to the cell, his profile silhouetted in the light. I soon saw it was a slight, young man.

"A visitor!" this youth said on observing me, and I realised as he took up a spot further down the slatted bed, that this was with whom Reno shared his cell.

"Is he tellin' you one of his tales?" the youth went on. "You'll be a while then."

"No, no," Reno said. "Not today. I am not in the right mind today."

My instinct was to be annoyed by Reno's change of heart, but more than that I was shaken. Not just by the mystery of this man's tears, and the marvel of his lace, which made me feel that no human who could create such beauty should be languishing in jail, but also by the sights and sounds of the Tombs themselves. They echoed with anger, shame and pain. They spoke of a lost tranche of society. And yet here was a man in the centre of it all, spending his days in this fine, exquisite, timeless art.

"Another time," he said. "I will tell you, sir, another time."

"Any time," I said. "I would be very glad to hear it."

A tear dripped onto the white circle of his lace, darkening it. I watched as it spread. I left him to his weeping, nodding to the guard as I headed to the door.

T HE NEXT MORNING, I WOKE up still thinking of the bald wraith of a lacemaker crouched in his cell, squinting at his creation as it dangled in the light. I recalled that teardrop darkening the fabric; those hands over his ears to block the noise. I wondered if such a man could really have been responsible for the beating of Murray Hall.

So haunted was I that I dropped into Mendel Goldberg's store, said, by my sister who knows such things, to be the finest source of fabric and thread in Manhattan. There, I bought the most expensive reel of lace thread I could find on their shelves. The young assistant smiled patronisingly at my inquiry and explained, as if to a child, that silk is the best for lace, since it is less inclined to break than cotton.

Well, one learns something new every day.

When, later, I called by the Tombs with my bounty, McAveety grinned. "He will cry like a baby when he sees this. Never seen a man so in love with a piece of thread."

"And also, please do give him this," I said, handing over an envelope containing a printed card with my address and several sheets of paper. I had been struck by the gentleness of the man in as unloving a place as this. "I assume he will have access to a pen. Tell him he may write to me if he wishes."

"I doubt the man will pick up a quill when he has needle and thread."

I dug inside my pocket for a dime. "And here is payment for the post. I trust you will see that it is delivered."

All of this took longer than I had intended, and as a result of these errands, I arrived late again at the World offices, mentally formulating an excuse that I had been working on the Committee of Fifteen. Instead of a reprimand, however, I came across Irving waving an envelope in my direction as soon as I came into the room; he had that twitch about him that indicated he thought he had a big story. Even his hair seemed electrified.

"It's the lead you've been looking for," he proclaimed as I approached the desk. "This lady says she has information pertaining to the previous identity of Mr Hall. You might want to look her up. See if it's for real."

I unfolded the page and read the short note. It was signed by a Mrs Canning and directed "the *World* reporter" to a residence in Brooklyn, stressing that there was no telephone, but that, since she was elderly, she was at home most of the time and would welcome a visit.

"I have information," I said, reading the note out loud now, "that might be of interest to you regarding Murray Hall's early years in Scotland. I believe I knew him, that I worked with him."

162

I felt Irving's pale eyes studying me. "What do you think?" he said.

"Early years in Scotland ..." I said doubtfully. "I'm not sure."

"Not sure?" he countered. "He was a Scot. Most people agree at least on that, don't they?"

"Perhaps. But I've begun to think the whole Scottish thing is a fabrication, a fraud. This identity, that of the wealthy Scottish nobleman, it's one he made up to woo his wife – a bravado for her family's benefit."

"So, you don't think this woman is credible?" he asked.

"She's old," I mused. "She may have read the articles and jumped to some conclusions. Could be a wasted journey, all the way over to Brooklyn."

"I'd say it's worth looking into. If you get across the river at top speed, and the story stacks up, it could make the morning's edition." Irving cast a glance up at me. A frown creased his brow.

I nodded, still staring at the paper, and the old woman's trembling script.

"Lord, Clellan, move will you, man? You've been stuck to this story like flypaper, and now you don't want to follow a decent lead. You can't rely on goodwill from the boss for ever. And when you get a chance, treat yourself to a damned shave. I'd like copy in before the end of the day. I need a page three. Then I want you back on Herlihy and Devery. Go!"

There is nothing like an escape over the East River to clear the mind. Glimpsing the great flow of water acts as a jolt back into life, a reminder that we are part of some bigger spate, something more than the noise and ever metamorphosing bricks, mortar and steel of Manhattan.

The Brooklyn transit car juddered and pulled away, gliding rightwards and then rising up the long hill of track and onto the bridge, that eighth wonder, a mountain of granite and twisted steel. To my left, bowler hats advanced resolutely, dipped and gripped against the biting wind; to my right, horse-drawn carts and bicycles processed. Then ahead loomed the Gothic towers, like gateways to heaven.

All around I saw that vast and dazzling spider's web of cables, the words of Walt Whitman running through my mind, "Bring your freight, bring your shows, ample and sufficient rivers." A man next to me reached out and clasped the bar as we jolted forward, dropping a pamphlet he had been reading to the floor. It landed face up on the dusty slats, so I could read the words, "Meat vs Rice".

I stared at the piece of paper for a moment, before reaching to pick it up for the gentleman. Underneath the title was a clearer anti-immigrant message: "American Manhood against Asiatic Coolieism". What exactly, I wondered, did meat have to do with American Manhood? I thrust it into the man's hand, and held my tongue, as we gripped tight to the bar until we descended again, away from heaven now, past the bright-painted signs for Quaker's Oats and a Broadway billboard, through the cavern of Brooklyn station and out again into the light of its hall.

Twenty minutes and a cab ride later, I approached Jefferson Street. I was struck by the aroma of hops which hung in the air like a rich cloud, smelling of warmth and comfort. In spite of my loathing of the vice of alcohol, I find the smell of the brewery is like a soft embrace, particularly on a day when the cold bites. A young boy with a toy popgun ran across my path. "Sorry, sir!" he cried, his voice light and free of worries.

The door was opened by a young woman, who introduced herself as Mrs Canning's granddaughter. She seemed unsurprised by my appearance, and I wondered if I wasn't the only journalist whom the old soul had contacted. The granddaughter showed me through to the parlour where the elderly dame was sitting. The apartment was frigid in spite of the small fire, and she was tucked under a knitted blanket neatly folded over her lap.

The room was spartan and functional, with few of the ornate trinkets found in the homes of the middle-classes. "You newspaper lads work fast," she said approvingly. "I believe my grandson only dropped that note round this morning."

"We are very interested in what you have to tell us," I said.

"Aye. And so you should be. I am dumbfoonert by it myself." She shook her head, somewhat theatrically. She had a pointed face, with eyes that seemed to contract and expand from tiny creases to full moons. "But what I'm wondering, first of all, is if there might be any reward in my telling you it."

The woman was a shrewd player.

"There would be some small recompense, yes."

"I thought as much. Maggie, can you make this laddie a cup of tea? You look like you could do with one. There's a chill in the air today."

"That would be wonderful, thank you," I said, desiring the warmth of the tea as much as its flavour. A slug of it might also drown out the smell of boiled potatoes and coal smoke that lurked about the place.

Mrs Canning picked up a set of round spectacles from her side table, along with a newspaper she had folded there. I tried to imagine her as a younger woman. Taut, capable, precise: exactly the kind of woman you would want to run a household, though perhaps a little unsympathetic and lacking in human comfort.

"I always get the *World*. And there I was, reading your paper the other day about this Murray Hall, and I was struck by the similarities between this man and one I knew back home. Was it you that wrote this?"

I nodded as she held up the spread from my Sunday article, and turned it so I could see the sketch of Hall in silhouette. "I couldnae believe the similarities. I just kept thinking, it sounds like Johnnie as we knew him back at the hospital. We called him such, Johnnie, though we knew his story, because he was really more like a lad than a lass."

I sank down in the worn armchair and pulled out my note-book. "Do you mind?" I asked, raising my pen.

"Aye. Go ahead."

I observed her as I waited that brief moment for her story to begin. She wore a black shirt with a high neckline and a small brooch pinned at its centre. The hair was pinned back, no tufts astray. Everything about this woman and her environment spoke of capability.

"In around 1870 I was working as nurse in the Edinburgh Hospital near Duddingston, and this fellow Johnnie, as we called him, was helping out there. Not nursing exactly, but more just doing whatever jobs he could."

She frowned a little as she recalled. "This was around the time of the smallpox in the city. Johnnie was a decent lad and always helpful, always caring – somewhat kinder to the patients, I would say, than I was myself. Soft on them. As I remember, when he first arrived in the hospital the story was that he was a woman, suffering from smallpox, though recovering well. I ignored the stories. I am not fond of gossip. Anyway, this woman as she was then, Mary, kept on insisting on being called Johnnie and asked not to be called 'she', so I called her thus. 'Johnnie.' None of us made much of it. It was just what he was like. And, in truth, he seemed more like a boy. He was Johnnie, and we called him a lad. And we noticed as he recovered from the smallpox what an obliging soul he was. After a wee while he was offered some work."

The granddaughter entered the room with a teapot and two cups, as well as a pretty china bowl of sugar. It seemed out of place in its unfussy surroundings. Her hands shook a little as she began pouring the liquid out into plain cups.

Mrs Canning glanced over at her sharply. "Shortbread," she said. "Two pieces."

"Johnnie one day told me his secrets, the story of his past. It turned out wee Mary and her brother were orphaned when she was just twelve years old. I believe the surname was Anderson, which was the name she kept. Or was it Campbell? In any case, the story Johnnie told me was a tragic one involving the death of a brother. You can read it in the newspapers, if you can get hold of them. The *North British Daily Mail*, the *Evening Post*, the *Dundee Courier*, they all published it."

"It was covered by the newspapers?" I said, astonished, and now quite thrilled by the story I was uncovering.

"It was indeed, by many. Johnnie was a big story. A big and shocking story."

She took a sip of tea and a quick bite of shortbread before resuming. "Back then, I almost felt as if there were two Johnnies. The kind lad, so good around the patients, and then the other who would smoke and drink and swear like a sailor. This was one of the things that stood out for me with your Murray Hall. All that smoking and drinking, playing cards and playing women too. Johnnie did them all. But then that's what men do in this city, isn't it?"

"That does indeed sound very like Hall."

"Aye, so much the same. Particularly the women. I believe it was on account of his affairs with so many different ladies that Johnnie's wife reported him, and the papers covered the story, and all that had happened came out in such a public way. After that, the head nurse said she could no longer keep employing him, that he was bringing disgrace to our profession. I remember how upset he was. He said the only option he had

168

now was to leave the country. And I suppose that's what he must have done."

I nodded, sipping at my own powerfully brewed tea. I wondered how many stories like this were out there, how many people were wondering now if they perhaps knew, or had once known, the famous Murray Hall.

"But the other thing is, Mr Clellan, the thing that most made me think it was him was the name. Murray is very like Mary, aye? And here's the rub. There were two sections in that hospital in which we worked. One was known as Hamilton Hall, and the other as Murray Hall. Johnnie was assigned to work in Murray Hall."

I paused in my writing, my pen hovering over the paper. The coincidence did truly seem astounding. "May I ask, Mrs Canning, what was the physical build and look of this Johnnie?"

"He was less than an inch shorter than me, a wiry wee creature. He brought life to any room he entered, despite his stature. I liked Johnnie. He always knew how to make a woman laugh, to lighten the mood – and you need that when you're nursing, even if you don't always let the patients see."

She looked at the sketch of Murray Hall from the *New York World* and smiled, shaking her head as she did so. "All this way ... Strange to think we could've been in the same place all these years and never known. I'll admit to having found something quite fine about our Johnnie myself. He had this way of looking at you. Like he saw the truth of you, like he had a playfulness, a mischief about him. You could say he knew how to charm a girl with his jokes and his attentiveness."

She nodded at the newsprint. "Have you taken your notes from the story?" she said, her sharp eyes misting as she drifted into the past. "Aye, I can see his face right now. That way he would look at you."

Mrs Canning craned her head towards me and looked me right in the eyes, her mouth an almost coy smile, and her expression one of mild and curious enchantment.

PART II

10TH STREET

8TH JULY 1896, 9 P.M.

I T WAS THE TIME FOR transition from the business and order of the day to the revelries of night. The market vendors were still packing away their wares, but in the saloons and alehouses raucous laughter could be heard, occasionally broken by the odd word shouted in anger or joy.

It made Clellan nervous, all this noise. This was only his second month in New York, and he was not yet used to the unending movement and commotion that seemed to flow about him no matter the hour. He felt the familiar heaviness in his coat pocket, the book comforting in its solidity. He ran his fingers up and down its spine, tracing the pattern of the leather and gold lettering with his thumb.

The Vigilance League had stationed him here for the next hour; he was to wait and see if he could spot the pickpocket who had supposedly made this corner his familiar haunt. Clellan wasn't sure what he would do if he saw him – probably just take note of his appearance. It was not as if he had the strength, or the authority, of a policeman. He was simply doing his civic duty. A man stumbled out of the saloon to his left and promptly painted the sidewalk with his vomit,

173

leaning one hand on the building's wall for support. Clellan raised his own hand to his face to block the smell and looked to the sky. What choices had brought him to this godforsaken place? His thumb ran over the spine of the book over and over again. Inside, in a sloping script, read the words, *To my son; fear not, for I am with you.*

He sighed and dropped his arm. Perhaps this was a waste of time. He was more likely to be picked out for a fight here than to do any good. He suspected that the committee had in truth stationed him here to test his obedience, his moral fibre, before offering him anything of real value to do. The drunk began to stagger away, wiping his encrusted face on a filthy sleeve before bellowing out what sounded to be an old Irish folk song. Clellan was afraid of these places, not only for their obvious moral depravity, but for the intensity and heat of human life they held. The people within, fuelled by whisky and false confidence, could do anything, be anyone. There were many times that he yearned for the quiet stillness of a summer evening at home, reading by the fire while his mother and sister completed their needlework, and his father was out visiting parishioners. He knew those memories told him a false story of home, but he replayed them, nonetheless, letting his mind wander away from the careless squalor of this place.

Another stumbling man passed through the doors of the alehouse, briefly allowing the steady commotion of its patrons to rise to a roar, and Clellan followed him in. He made his way to the bar, which was populated by a heaving mass of bodies, mostly of Irish men, and almost all in a heavy state of intoxication despite the relatively early hour.

For a moment he hovered, awkward and out of place, not even sure how to summon the attention of the barman in such a crowd, let alone what to order. Ahead of him at the bar a man slammed down his glass, making a cracking sound on the wood.

"We'll have another!" he growled. He was perched on a stool, flanked on both sides by a young woman. He seemed to be drinking two whiskies for every one he ordered for them, though as he was paying, they didn't seem to mind. The trio struck an odd sight, his legs dangling down from the bar stool and his feet only just brushing the floor. Though he was swaying slightly, his derby hat remained firmly planted over his hair.

A man could seem possessed by liquor, Clellan thought, and this one was. There was nothing in such a face one could connect with – almost little sense of a person peering out at all.

"Tell us one about your boxing days, Murray." One of the women turned to him, brushing a curl from his cheek.

"Oh aye." He grinned at them each in turn. "I've always been a mean dinger. You'll know I took out Paddy Ryan with one punch?" His words came out slurred, but his eyes remained alert.

"Oh, come off it!" The other woman gave him a gentle push. "I've never met a bigger fibber than Murray 'one punch' Hall."

If she had not been a woman, and a pretty one at that, this would have been a dangerous thing to say, but the man only smiled and held her bright gaze.

"It's true, I tell ye, every word. He was twice as wide as me and three times as tall, but I dodged him real quick and got him over the head while he was down. I swear on the blessed grave of my mother."

The woman burst out laughing, throwing her hands onto the bar.

"Oh Murray, you could sell a snail his shell."

"Don't listen to her." The other woman was slurring a little too, but her voice was much softer. "I believe you."

"It's true, I'm telling you it's true." With that declaration the whisky seemed to have finally got the better of the man, and his head began drooping to his chest. His voice became almost indecipherable. With great effort he brought his head back upright and sank the whisky that the freckle-faced bartender had placed in front of him. He fumbled in his pocket for payment, heaping a few coins on the wooden counter, before slipping down to the ground.

The women took an arm each, supporting each other as they swayed to the door in their mismatched party. The saloon door swung open, letting out again the light and smells and sounds of the place onto the darkening street. The man, flanked by his companions, began his stumbling march. It was unclear where the party's next destination was, but it seemed likely to be another of the street's drinking establishments.

The drunkard looked Clellan straight in the face as he passed, but appeared not to see him. His eyes were focused on a point beyond him, somewhere perhaps at the back of his head. It made Clellan feel as if he were a mere ghost, or as if the man were somewhere else, in some other fragmented, faraway world.

Clellan watched their figures disappearing into the night and followed, drawn by the spectacle.

A person in such a state, he thought, would look through you, rather than at you. A person like that was not one you could ever reach. He hated the glassy eyes of those in their cups, the distracted way they seemed to slide in and out of focus and never quite connect. He hated the sadness and the pain that liquor so often seemed to hide; lifetimes, sometimes, of pain.

As he stepped out, he glanced up into the great basin of the starry sky and began to walk in the opposite direction from the man and his group, his hand in his pocket as he went.

WHITE STREET
28TH JANUARY 1901, 3 P.M.

THE DAYS SLID BY AS a series of headlines.

POLICE NOT ALL ASLEEP. THEY CAN FIND AN "UNPRO-TECTED" BILLIARD ROOM WITHOUT ANY DIFFICULTY.

CHIEF DEVERY LEADS A RAID. GATHERING IN A "CRAPS AND KLONDIKE" LAYOUT AND FOUR PRISONERS.

SEEKING "THE PROTECTOR", PHILBIN'S RAID ONLY FIRST STEP IN CRUSADE.

We're winning, I thought, as I wrote each of these pieces. Finally, the City Vigilance is ahead in the game.

I thought of how far we had come; how much closer the possibility of reform seemed now than it was when I had first started out in the city, a green League officer, carrying a fear beaten into me by my father's words, scared of almost everything I was trying to fight – terrified of even walking into a saloon bar.

These days, at least I could manage that – and look like I belonged. I had become increasingly good at melting into the background of the world of vice. That was the trick in my job. I had lost that fear and learned a certain boldness. This was why, on a clear Thursday afternoon, I was back following Philbin's men, with the plan, this time, to wait outside, rather than entering the betting rooms ahead of the raid. The committee were nervous that gambling bosses would now be on the lookout for reporters like me.

I stood in a narrow alleyway diagonally across from the entrance to the building and awaited the appearance of the committee's carriages on the street. In that time, I saw several men enter and leave the building. A police officer swung by at a gallop, pelting through the door and hastening down into the basement.

I checked my pocket watch. It was still five minutes off the appointed time of the raid, and I perceived that this policeman was not one associated with the committee.

Seconds later, a figure I instantly recognised – a fellow from the Iroquois, dressed in a bottle-green suit and mustard cravat – emerged, accompanied by another man in a top hat, with silvered cane, and took a glance both ways, then sauntered casually out into the street.

I sunk further into the shadows, hoping he would not see me.

Less than a minute more and there was the heavy rumble of hooves, as two carriages pulled up. Men, in mournful vigilance black, emptied out into the street and poured across the sidewalk and down into the basement. I followed this cloud of bats down the steps, but immediately slammed into those just ahead in the corridor.

A voice called out from further down the line, "The door is locked!" Then the sound of knuckles hammering. "Open up! Open up! Or we will take the door down!"

My nose was up against the back of the man in front, and I breathed in the smell of his wet coat. I turned away and took in the yellowed wall alongside me, where a paper sign hung.

Church prayer group and Sunday School rooms.
We kindly request no unnecessary noise.

Then I felt a frantic jostling and pushing back against me. Some of the men were squeezing back along the line.

I turned round and backed hurriedly up the steps as two officers squeezed by. "Sledgehammer!" barked one.

At the top, I watched the street. From a tiny alleyway, at a break in the block, a little group of men appeared, straightened themselves and took a sharp left down the street.

I was about to shout after them, when the two officers returned, accompanied by the athletic, bowtied figure of Judge Jerome, who was himself wielding the giant hammer.

"They're getting out that way," I said, feeling a little like a child trying, pointlessly, to be helpful in the affairs of adults.

But Jerome barely seemed to notice me. "Coming through!" he declared.

As he reached the top of the stairs, he pushed the tool high in the air, then simply dropped forwards. The officers in front started to flow onwards, almost toppling into each other as they propelled themselves down the steps. Jerome tripped, then righted himself, recovering just in time to avoid an accident.

The hammerhead went crashing into the wall.

"Damn!" Jerome cried. "Son of a bitch!" He stood for a moment staring at the implement, shaking his head in bewilderment. "They must have opened the door."

"Saves you a job!" I said.

The judge looked at me, askance. "I fear that's not a good sign at all, Mr Clellan." Then he descended into the corridor in front of me.

I followed his rapid march along the hallway and into the depths of the building, illuminated only by the daylight through the door behind us and the faint glow of a gas lamp.

Inside the room there was the smell of smoke.

"Check the back rooms!" someone shouted.

"Search the cupboards."

Justice Jerome, standing behind a counter at the back of the room, held up a sliver of singed paper. "I fear this may be all the evidence we have," he announced. "They have burned the betting cards."

I looked around. Tables were empty. Two elderly men were drinking from gilt-rimmed china cups, like ladies meeting for afternoon tea. One of them looked my way and grinned. "What is it you are looking for, officers?" he said politely.

The next day, standing perusing a folded copy of the *World* outside Ma's Oyster bar, I smiled at the artist's sketch of these two old men, and the peaceful scene, as if from a suffragist tea salon, on the front page of the paper.

I had arrived a little early at MacDougal Street for my lunchtime appointment and paused there for a few minutes, taking in the headlines and watching patrons examine the frosted roots in the baskets of the grocer above the oyster dive, before I descended beneath the sign, hung from ropes, declaring: "Oysters in every style!"

The dining room was heaving, a fog of cigar smoke and sea vapours, and Ma's son, out front rather than in the kitchen today, directed me to a standing barrel table in the corner. Buckets full of unshucked oysters were stacked in the nearby passageway. "An ale while you wait, sir?" he asked.

"No, thank you," I said. "Tea water would be fine."

For a brief moment, I observed the rocky and barnacled shells gleaming inside the bucket; they were smaller than usual, I thought, at little more than a couple of inches. The door banged and my gaze was caught by a broad, red-haired man entering the room, with his unkempt beard and flapping waxed coat. What was once a high bowler hat, crushed out of shape, in his hands.

As I watched him settling at the next table down, O'Connor arrived, grunting as he came in out of the cold, and in plain clothes, a peacoat and a flat cap. He still looked an impressive giant of a man.

Ma was already standing over me, a patient, expectant look on her face. "Ready to order, sir?"

I nodded. "You got any clams yet?" I asked.

"No, sir," she said, "the season's not until March."

"Those oysters don't look too big."

She tutted. "That's how they are these days. I'm using the same oysterman an' I've tried a few others. But this is how they are ... All the sweeter and saltier for being small."

"Fine, I'll have them."

"Ten raw, no ketchup?"

"That would be delightful."

"I'll have a platter too," said O'Connor, flashing her a smile. "Raw, like my friend here. But plenty of ketchup."

I noticed now, over O'Connor's shoulder, the scruffy, bearded man watching us as he drank his soup directly from the bowl. His presence, though he seemed innocent enough – a sailor fresh off some boat, or so I imagined – made me nervous.

I lowered my voice and craned in towards O'Connor. "More white folks in here these days."

"Uh-huh," he concurred with a nod. "Good to see your stories on Mr Philbin's raids. Finally, it seems somethin' may be happenin'."

"It's grand theatre anyway," I said, "and the readers love it."

"The raids are good news but they ain't what will make a difference. Ah'm more interested in Captain Herlihy's trial myself. You reportin' on that?"

"I've been a few times – but not much happened. They are dragging it out. Hoping to bore us into not noticing it, I reckon."

"Ah've heard Chief Bill is in a sweat," O'Connor confided, wiping the sweat from his own brow as if in sympathy. "He believes Herlihy is outta control. He may be so unstable that he could let things slip. The man is dangerous. He plays by his own rules, doesn't stick to the codes. What if he's asked about protection? We all know the Chief is on the take – some of that money ends up in his pocket."

I looked across at him, listening hard to his interpretations – and his fears.

"Extra couple for you there, sir!" said Ma as she slammed the oysters down on the tabletop of the barrel before she turned away, scooping up dirty dishes off a neighbouring table as she went.

"Remember, it's a police court," I said. "There's surely no chance of them asking about protection."

"No?" O'Connor gave me a quizzical glance as he took a short draught of ale. "You've got Boyngage in prosecution, York as the judge. Those two have got not a pinch of love for the combine."

"True." I swallowed an oyster; it was a sweet gulp of the sea, just as Ma had promised. "But even if they did, Herlihy would have to be one loose cannon to squeal on the whole racket. He wouldn't do that."

"All I'm saying is there's a chance," O'Connor insisted. "I'm just telling what ah'm hearing. Bill Devery is scared. They're all scared. I hear Tim Sullivan's Tammany faction are scared too. The Big Feller thinks someone may go rogue and snitch, and with Jerome running around all over town, wooing the crowds with his sledgehammers and improvised courts, there's an appetite for big heads to fall."

He swivelled his plate, as if to demonstrate his awareness of the diminutive size of the shells. "They sure are gettin' smaller." Then he picked up the pot of ketchup and began carefully spooning a liberal dollop onto each shell. "Still can't persuade you to try the ketchup . . . You and your spartan ways, Clellan. Live a little, why don't you, sir?"

C. S. PRATT, BOOKSELLER, 161 SIXTH AVENUE

30TH JANUARY 1901, 10 A.M.

A DANCING WIND WHIPPED FRAGMENTS OF twigs and shreds of paper through the air, clanking the signs along the fronts of buildings as I walked along Sixth Avenue, swept downtown by a river of shoppers that was in full spate. The sound of a baby crying caught my attention. Outside O'Neill's department store, a gaunt young woman was selling Wrigley's gum from a tray, her child strapped to her chest and writhing. I looked away, not wanting to catch her pleading eyes.

The wind seemed to swirl around her, then it picked me up to carry me onwards.

I was passing a block of shopfronts when my eye was caught by the display in the gold-lettered window of C. S. Pratt's store.

A memory of seeing Hall through that very window flitted through my mind as I entered. Pratt was organising books on shelves in the back of his shop. The man played against stereotype, being not a small, pale type, but a rather large and vigorous fellow. Nevertheless, he sported the bookish spectacles of his profession. "Ah, Mr Clellan. Good to see you.

And still on the hunt for the mysterious Mr Hall, are you?" He continued stacking shelves as we spoke, too full of energy to stand still, and he waved a book in my direction. Something about him set me on edge, but I couldn't put my finger on it. "By the way, have you read this yet? It's written for children but it's really quite something. Still as popular now as the day it came out – I'm recommending it to the grown folk too."

I stared at the cover and recognised immediately the idiotic-looking lion with a swirling red mane – adorned with a bow, of all things – ponderously bestriding a green background, and the title.

"*The Wonderful Wizard of Oz*," I said.

"Destined to be a classic. Anyway, a children's book is not what you are here for. It's the Murray Hall collection that you are seeking out, yes?"

I stared at the shelves, dense with dark fabric-bound books and their glistening titles. "I heard you still have quite a collection of Hall's books," I said.

"I do," he confirmed, "but I'm so sorry, I let a few of them go. They were of some value. But, as I said, there are a few I have held onto, most notably *The Science and Art of Surgery*, and a couple of other medical tomes. He bought them for his wife, but I feel he too must have studied them, especially given what we know now of his condition. Come along . . ."

His hand pointed to a stack of volumes on a central table. "Medical literature," Pratt said, "was Mr Hall's preferred genre for quite some time – so I imagine he must have been aware that what he was suffering from was cancer, and the invasive

nature of it. Indeed, that may be whence his interest stemmed."
On top of the pile was a large burgundy edition, embossed
with gold, and with various slips of paper inserted to mark
pages.

Pratt opened it at the first of these markers. "This one is
titled *The Science and Art of Surgery: Being a Treatise on Surgical
Injuries, Diseases, and Operations*," he said. The page offered the
title, *Cancer of the Breast*, and carried an intricate diagram of
shapes, which I soon realised were cells. "It's quite an expensive
book," he added, "on account of the illustrations."

I couldn't make sense of all these diagrams. My eyes scanned
a paragraph, glossing over the words, many of which were new
to me.

The mass, it said, *contained several cysts as large as cherries,
filled with dark or greenish fluid, and projecting from its surface;
and in a lady who is at present under my care for scirrhous of
the breast a tumour as large as a pigeon's egg, containing sanguinolent fluid, formed on the surface of the tumour.*

I had an ominous feeling, a kind of déjà vu, as if I were
looking through Murray's eyes onto the page. What would it
be like to read these words, as they confirmed what you knew
what was growing inside of you? Maybe, you prayed, they
wouldn't, that they'd offer instead some benign, impossible
rationale.

I thought again of that body on the slab, its chest caved in
and weeping.

"*Sanguinolent fluid*," I read aloud.

"Curious, isn't it?" Pratt said in his animated voice. "I'm sure he must have looked at a great many of these pages, these chapters on malignant growths."

"One has to wonder what he thought," I said.

"You mean about what caused it?" Pratt said, although that wasn't quite my meaning. "Who knows? So many theories abound. Some of these doctors tell us it is a microorganism, perhaps bacterial or protozoan, some tiny infecting forms. Others say it is hereditary, handed down through generations, the result of an undetected predisposition."

"Or a living fungus growth," I said, thinking of the advertorial by Dr Kilmer, "of which surgery takes out only the visible part, leaving many unseen rootlets and branches ready and waiting to start up again. It is the body turned against itself."

As I spoke, my eyes wandered over the next paragraph.

Sir A. Cooper states that the disease, on an average, is from two to three years in growing, and from six months to two years in destroying life, after being fully formed.

"*Six months to two years,*" I read aloud.

I felt, as I held the books that had once belonged to Hall, closer to him than I had thus far. Cancer, I thought as I stared at the pages, was something he knew. By the time it came for him, he had already seen its slow, steady, hateful progress in his wife. He knew the blow of a doctor's diagnosis: "Cancer." He must, when the unfamiliar flesh started to grow over his

chest, have wondered. He must have feared. There is a reson-
ance in books. They have been my companions all my life,
and one can't help but feel they take on some of the quality
of their owner. I recalled for a moment my father's Bible,
immaculate despite its constant handling. It was gilt-edged,
and always felt to me a thing to be feared, an extension of
the man – and his tempers – himself. I turned to another
page and noticed it had been marked by a scrap of paper, the
sloped script of its writing smudged beyond legibility. As I
held it up to the light, Pratt turned through a few pages and
began to read out loud.

"There's also this," he said. "You'll see it has been underlined."

*"In many cases, however, cancer can be distinctly traced to some
exciting cause, being immediately occasioned by a blow, injury, or
other violence, or by a long-continued irritation of the part that
eventually becomes affected; thus, in women a blow on the breast
often gives rise to cancer, and the irritation of a broken tooth may
occasion it to the tongue."*

"A blow to the breast?"

"Indeed," he said with a downturn of his mouth. "And you
will have heard of the bicycle accident."

"Yes, though I also heard there was another incident, a
sandbagging."

"And look at this," Pratt said, placing the book on the table
and reopening it at its frontispiece page. Written across its
faintly yellowed page, in a feminine hand, were the words,
"Celia Lin Hall, 128 Second Avenue, N.Y."

"Celia?" I said, with a jolt.

191

Pratt nodded. "Almost all the medical library has her inscription … It shouldn't be surprising. Celia not only herself died of cancer, but, as I recently learned – from one of your articles no less – she was a former medical student, who must surely have carried that interest in the workings of human physiology and pathology throughout her life. I imagine it was in reality she, not he, who was reading the books."

I stared at the inscription, florid and elegant.

"Interesting woman, Mrs Hall," I said. "I almost find myself wishing I could talk to her, and hear her stories, as much as I do Murray's."

"An interesting couple, for sure." Pratt nodded. "I will be curious to learn what you turn up about them," he said as, with a flourish, he closed the book.

CLELLAN'S APARTMENT, 22ND STREET
30TH JANUARY 1901, 11.30 A.M.

T HAT MORNING, I RUSHED HOME with my package
tucked beneath my arm, keen to leaf through the pages
and absorb words that I could be almost certain Hall's
own eyes had sought to absorb. But my interest was not in the
science of surgery, rather the knowledge of Hall's own mind.

Entering my block, I stopped at my mail box and slipped
the small key into the lock of its wooden door. Inside was just
one letter, waiting, my name inscribed in elegant calligraphy,
padded and bulging with some soft contents. When I opened
it, I found it contained an intricately embroidered handkerchief
made with lace, crafted in the same ivory thread I had bought
at Mendel Goldberg's. It was, quite simply, beautiful, and I
turned it over and over in my hands before taking a seat in my
worn wooden chair by the fire to read.

Dear Mr Clellan,

*My enormous gratitude for your gift. You cannot imagine how
such materials change my days in this thankless hell. Each day
I have thread is one in which I have hope.*

You will see by my writing of this letter that I am an educated man, if you had not already surmised it on our meeting. I am not like many of the unschooled who fill these Tombs, my name in fact being William Riley, and my family being well known in politics and business, though none of them now will have anything to do with me. None, I believe, ever mention my name. I have seen none of my people for the last fifteen years.

I like, as I told you, to keep my hands occupied. Even writing, as I am now, with this pen, provides some calming of the demons inside. There is something in the fine concentration required of calligraphy similar to lace.

I must confess I was greatly moved by your visit, there not having been any visitors to this dank cell in all my time here. I might better have addressed your questions if I had not been so moved; to weep, as you may remember, so overcome by feeling was I. You asked about Murray Hall, and I am sorry that I did not answer you more fully, even when you said your interest was not for any legal pursuit and would remain confidential.

I was struck by your sensitivity to the qualities of my lace, and when McAveety brought me these papers, I began to write down all that I recall of my encounter with Hall.

As you may know from the reports, the last time I came out of prison, they threw me right back in – and I had to beg for my freedom. I wrote to Judge Newburger. I told him I was a reformed man. I said, I have served many years of imprison-ment and I have been punished and suffered much for my crimes. Lord, have I suffered. I cannot complain, because

I know I deserve it. But here I am now, and I have made good of my time in prison. I have worked and studied night and day to learn a trade so as to earn a good, honest living. Let me make use of it.

I sent the judge an exceedingly fine piece of lace and when I was called before him, I wept. I wept bitterly. For all the years wasted. For the years I hadn't seen my people and what they must think of me now, for none of them ever speak to me. I wonder if it was those tears that made him show me leniency. Or if it was the lace. I wonder if he looked at my lace and thought, any man who could make something like this should be given a chance.

He gave me that chance and I feel great shame that I failed to live an honest life from it.

You are, no doubt, already aware that it was in the period of freedom that followed my release that I encountered Murray Hall. If I am to explain why I did what I did to him, I should probably start by telling you a little of where I had come to, not so much as to excuse my behaviour, but merely to help your understanding.

To my bitter disappointment, after being discharged by Judge Newburger, I failed to find employment as a needle worker. I knew nothing of machine work, and all the hand workers were women. My years of labour were of no avail. I sought employment finally as a cook, and eventually worked my way up to a $9 a week position. I always tried to better myself and from all my employers had good recommendations. I saved in that time $68.

If I had wanted to steal, I had many opportunities. But I did not. I remained committed to the honest way, and all was good until, one day, I went to Eleventh Avenue and 23rd Street to apply for a position that offered a larger salary than I was getting. I had that $68 with me. The position, I was disappointed to discover, had been filled – I was just too late. It was then about six o'clock in the morning, and very foggy as I began my walk home. Striding up Eleventh Avenue in my disappointment, I met a former convict I had known in prison. He told me a hard-luck story and I gave him $2 from my savings, advising him to lead an honest life.

Unbeknownst to me, another man was with him, and shortly after I found myself struck from behind and knocked senseless. When I came to, my money was gone.

This may seem a very long preamble, but it's important that you understand where I was in my life when I came across Hall that night in Geoghegan's.

You may well be acquainted with Geoghegan's – a saloon bar of reputation some blocks up from the edge of Five Points. It's a place you can go to find all types, where worlds meet and rub up against each other, where mawks dance on tables and Tammany businessmen drop in to make their deals.

I had gone to the saloon that night with a purpose. It happened I'd been recently sacked from a job as a cook berthed down at the docks and had less than a dollar left in my wallet. I wasn't sure where the next would be coming from.

I recall how the place hummed with sporting chat that night, the cheers from the rear room where someone had likely

196

won a good hand at pinochle. I could have bet my money on a hand, but that wasn't what I was there for. Instead, I'll confess, and I have no pride in this, to having tucked into my pocket a small brown bottle of the drug people call chloral. It was a substance I had used for such a purpose on only two previous occasions, and in the company of an ex-convict friend, Moe.

A couple of drops, my friend had told me, was all it took. More, if you wanted to be sure of putting a man out so he would feel nothing and remember even less. No act of violence was necessary, only these few easy drops, and then you could slip your hands into his pockets and take whatever treasure he carried. It was no big event. All over Manhattan and in Chicago, too, thieves were doing it. Why not us?

When Moe first suggested this, I was set against it, having known what it was to be drugged myself. But over time I was seduced by its ease. The idea of these few drops. I also saw some justice in the notion of taking my money back, even if it was from another person. It seemed to me that this was how the universe worked, and there was no point in striving towards honesty. It was a fool's goal.

I was watching the room, which was crowded that night, and spotted a man scanning the wall of bottles behind the bar. This figure, I recognised, was none other than Murray Hall. He was the bail bondsman I recalled having been a regular at Jefferson Market Courthouse, and of the whisky sellers around there. There was no doubting it was him: the oversized coat and eccentric hat. It could be nobody else.

197

Eight years had passed since I had approached him outside that courthouse, and in that time the bondsman appeared not to have changed. In those intervening years I had also not quite rid myself at the sense of injustice I felt around him, the grievance. I still remembered, clear as a bell, the words he'd said: "I'm afraid you don't look like much of a good bet when it comes to bail."

But that night, he looked as good a target as any – he would be my good bet, after all – and I pushed through the crowd to slip in next to him by the bar. "Mr Hamilton Hall," I said. "I thought it was you when you came in. Unmistakable in that baggy coat of yours."

The man turned and peered back, unsure if he was being mocked. "Have we met before?" he asked.

"William Reno," I introduced myself. "You might not remember me. But I remember you. One doesn't forget a distinctive-looking man like you. We met once. You gave bail for a friend of mine. I made a note of you as someone to contact if ever I should need bail myself."

There was a short silence, and I knew this man had no memory of me at all. All that time I had carried the slight with me, and he remembered nothing of it.

"I take it you haven't needed it, then?" he said.

"I have," I confessed. "Once or twice. But I never came to you. I might have needed it more if I hadn't spent much of the last twenty years in prison."

"And yet here you are!" he declared with a wry smile, clapping me on the back. "Can I buy you a drink?"

"Let me buy you one. The punch here is good. Will you have it?"

Hall nodded. It was clear this was a man who never said no to a drink when offered.

"Two of your Mickey's punch," I called to the barman.

"Twenty years, eh?" Hall asked as we waited.

"Only did eighteen of those years, though," I told him, "on account of my good behaviour. But it was the same again and again. I'd come out of the Tombs then I'd be straight back in again. Those prisons became my home. Problem is the world . . . it changes so fast when you're inside. You come out and you find there's these lights that come alive by some magic they call electricity. Or there's trains going along Sixth Avenue. But this time I'm not going back. I've learned a skill, you see."

The barman pushed over our glasses and I glanced around the room. "I see there's a table just come free. I'd say it's got our name on it." In my pocket I could feel the weight of that glass bottle knocking against my thigh, reminding me it was there, a beat that seemed to suggest that yes, this was the man.

It was only as I followed him over to the table, as I watched the back of his head in that old-fashioned hat, that I realised I really meant to do it. If I could find a way to spike his drink, I would, and not just for the money, but for what he said back then, and because of his forgetting.

I felt the slight of it.

"You're probably wondering what my skill was?" I asked as we slipped behind the table in that darkened corner.

"I'm thinking you're going to tell me anyway," Hall said.

199

I pulled a strip of lace out from my pocket and laid it on the table. "This."

Unfurled on the dark wood, it looked like a painting in thread. I watched as Murray removed his hat and bent in towards it. The hair of this man was thick and glossy and spoke of something I did not have. Was it wealth?

As I watched, I rolled the bottle around in my hand. I was telling myself how to do it, speaking to myself in my head, saying how I should follow what Moe had taught me, how I had done it before. As crimes went, it's the easiest thing in the world to do. It was putting things right in a world where the wrong people had the money. The people out there, as Moe said, were just asking for it.

"What is it?" Hall asked. "Some kind of lace?"

I nodded. "Bobbin design. Oriental influenced. Hold it closer to the light so's to see it better."

Murray lifted it, and as his eyes focused on the fine lines of slender thread I slipped my hand across the table and tipped a scattering of drops in his glass.

Hall smirked as his gaze returned to me. Had he noticed the swift movement of my hand returning to my own glass?

"Are you laughing at me, Mr Hall?" I asked.

"I'm just a little surprised. This is not something I was expecting to find coming from a man in Geoghegan's. Lacemaking is women's work. Why would a man like you learn such a craft?"

The comment with all its arrogance annoyed me, but I did not let that show. "In order to earn an honest wage. Why else?"

I said. "And for the love of it. You see, it gives me great pleasure, Mr Hall, to create a dainty little thing like this." I took a quick slug from my glass and leaned in close to him, as if to divulge some secret. "But I need to find the work. You would not believe the bad luck I've had. These past few months . . ."

Murray picked up his glass of punch and took a long drink. I remember thinking as I watched his throat expand and contract that there was my potion, there it was going down. The act had already begun. "It's a very fine lace," he said as he placed the glass back down on the table. "But I would be surprised if you found work with it."

"Surprised? Why?"

"I know for myself, as an employment expert so to speak, that young ladies are no longer making lace by hand – that's gone over to the machines. Time has moved on, Mr Reno."

Hall leaned back in his chair and reached again for his glass. I was pleased to see that this was a man who drank hard and fast. It meant he would soon be feeling the chloral's effects.

"You don't like my lace?" I asked.

"That's not what I said, is it?" His voice was now edged with irritation. "I'm just saying you will struggle to get a job with such a craft. Everything is being done by machine now. The world is ruled by machines."

There was something about the way the bondsman was leaning in towards me, know-it-all and haughty, that made me uncomfortable. He appeared as if he was about to say something, then stopped and sank back into his seat. I wondered if the chloral was already causing him to lose track *of his own words. Had something in him become untethered, unpredictable?*

"Perhaps so, Mr Hall. I have found myself a job as a cook, but it's not the work I want and pays badly. There are still women doing this work by hand, and I don't see why I shouldn't do the same. You run an employment agency, don't you?"

Someone had picked up a fiddle and started playing in the alcove at the other side of the room. The voice of a West Indian rose over it, deep and sonorous. Murray leaned towards me, and it was not clear whether he was trying to make himself heard or collapsing forward. "An intelligence agency for women, domestic help," he said. "That's it. That is what we do."

I waited a few seconds, thinking he might have more to say but was struggling to find it. Eventually he mumbled. "Not male cooks."

"Ah, now that's a pity," I replied. "I was hoping you might be able to help me out. I wonder, shall we have ourselves another punch? I'm happy to get you a second."

So yes, I gave him that second drink, laced with still more chloral. I probably gave him more than I should have, given he was such a small man. I was new to that game, unsure of the measurements. No doubt it was too much, and for sure it worked quick. I almost thought he might pass out there at the table.

That was when I decided we had to move and, by fortune, he seemed happy with my proposal to go on for another drink elsewhere. As I said, he seemed like a man, perhaps a skinflint, who couldn't refuse a free drink. He was leaning on me as we left the bar, swaying and going on about his shoulder-hitting days, and how loyalty was all that mattered in a man. At some point he stopped mid-sentence and I saw his eyes roll upwards, and I knew he was nearly out.

By the time we reached the narrow alley leading down the back of the block he was a dead weight. I had to carry him out of sight. But folk are used to seeing such things in that part of town – drunkards in every alley. No one blinked an eye. Perhaps they didn't even care if the man was drugged and robbed, nor if any man was.

I let him slide to the ground in the shadow of a doorway, then slipped my hand into his pocket to see what I could find. I took his money. I took everything I could find on him. It was a decent haul. Almost $30, plus a watch of some worth.

But the sandbagging – that wasn't me. I had nothing to do with that.

I know that is what he claimed in a letter to the district attorney, and all I can say is that the sandbagging was not me. Sandbagging suggests a beating of such weight and strength that it floors a man and leaves him black and blue. The most I did was let him slip too roughly to the ground.

I have since learned of his belief that it was this so-called sandbagging that caused the cancer. In other words, I caused it. I have no expert knowledge of this dreadful disease, but I will not accept I am to blame.

I will tell you, however, that I felt sorry about the drugging the following day and have felt guilt about it since – even more so when I learned of the letter and that this man was *in fact a woman, though I still find that hard to believe. I had wondered what happened to him after I left; how long it took him to rouse. I imagined him shifting in his slumber. I imagined God watching us both.*

Sometimes I have thought about what it must have been like for him that night, lying there on the sidewalk, just as I had done following the attack I suffered. I have thought of how he must have come round slowly and painfully. I remember the damp of the ground against my cheek, the faint tang of urine and vomit, the thudding inside my own head. And for that I have felt sorry.

What happened after I left him there, I have no idea. Some other rogue perhaps came along and attempted to raid his pockets, to rouse him, or attempted some other invasion of his privacy. If he was truly sandbagged, that must have been then, because it was not, I promise, at my hand.

A woman, they say, and dead of cancer of the breast. I find it hard to believe. When I think of how I slipped my hands inside his pockets and noticed nothing remarkable, only the boniness of his limbs inside that loose coat.

On finishing reading, I folded the sheets of paper, neatly and tucked them back into the envelope. The mustard-orange handkerchief lay in a vivid swirl on my desk. I smoothed it out, imagining my hands to be Reno's own careful fingers. I saw him again, sitting in that shaft of light, his desperate face, like a phantom, squinting at the tangle of dancing lace. The fine work on the edge of the kerchief appeared more intricate the closer in I looked. I felt like I was falling into some deep and impenetrable labyrinth.

The lace was the thread this tragic creature was holding onto. Its minuscule swirls and turns were his link to survival. A thread of life.

CORONER'S OFFICE, CHAMBERS STREET
31ST JANUARY 1901, 9 A.M.

I WOKE TO THE RUMBLE OF street life, and the realisation that I had stayed up too late burning down my oil lamp reading, and had thus slept in. The letter from Reno lay crumpled on my bedside table; the copy of Ellis's book was toppled onto the floor and *The Science and Art of Surgery* and other of Murray Hall's tomes were piled in a column on my desk. There was only an hour until I was due at the inquest. I found it hard to believe that it was now only the last day of January, little more than a week since I had first read of Murray Hall's death. I felt my impression of him and how he fit into this city had changed day by day.

The coroner's chambers were packed with journalists like myself, along with a crowd of layman onlookers itching for more gossip about the curious man-woman who had voted the Tammany ticket for a third of a century. I scanned those called up for the trial until I saw a familiar face.

Alone, staring straight ahead and dressed stiffly in high-necked mourning, was the elusive Imelda 'Minnie' Hall. A small hat was perched at the back of her head; the veil attached boldly drawn back. I studied her expression for any trace of emotion, but her father must have taught her the art of the poker face. She was relinquishing nothing. Alongside her on the witness bench was Dr Gallagher, the instigator of this whole affair, a pale man with wire-framed glasses. The physician had turned and was chatting with a gentleman in the row behind, leading him to lean into Minnie Hall, and she twisted away from him. I wondered briefly if the two had spoken since Murray's death, and if they were on civil terms. I couldn't imagine young Minnie would be too friendly with the man who had brought her family's greatest secret to light, and the press throng to her doorstep.

All of a sudden, the room erupted into a fierce hum of chatter, and I turned to see Antonio Zucca, Coroner of the Borough of Manhattan, emerging to take his place at the head of proceedings. A sweeping look across the room from this imposing man – tall, with salt-and-pepper beard and twisted moustache – was enough to still its chatter.

"There will be silence in these chambers," he said, raising a hand and shaking his head. "Now, I know we have a number of members of the public and the press here today, and I remind you all that this remains a legal proceeding, and as such any disruption will be dealt with in the strictest fashion." His hands spoke, in the Italian theatrical manner, cutting through the air to emphasise his point. "This should not properly be a coroner's case, but a supposed man was found to be a woman."

The faintest smile curled his lips, as if perhaps he was in some way entertained by the matter.

All in the room understood what that expression meant. Hall's case must have come as light relief in the relentless stream of barbarity that Zucca, a mere Parmesan importer who had climbed his way to the top, had to process as coroner. For when death came to Manhattan, suspicious and unattended – poisonings, drownings, boat sinkings, the plummet through nineteen floors of an Otis elevator, savage knife attacks, beatings – the coroner would preside over its investigation. But the death itself of Murray Hall was not in any way suspicious. It was a very ordinary example of how the plague of cancer can slowly and insidiously steal a life. The only thing remarkable about it was what it revealed about his sex.

"I must admit," Zucca said, leafing through a pile of typed papers on his lectern, "this is not the kind of case which would ordinarily fall under my jurisdiction; however, as there is an estate of some five thousand dollars involved, it seems pertinent that I should be called upon to settle it." His voice, deep and musical, was still marked by the faint lisp of his Milan childhood. "The legal disposition of such a significant sum necessitates an authoritative establishment of the circumstance of death."

After this brief introduction, the first witness was called: Dr William Gallagher, the man who had discovered Hall's sex. The usual establishing questions began the coroner's inquiry, and then Mr Zucca asked, "You say you attended Murray Hall throughout his illness? How long was that for?"

"Yes, I attended Hall during her last illness, at intervals of a year previous to her death."

"And when you examined him – her – did you discover her to have cancer of the breast?" There was a light ripple of laughter through the room, but the coroner allowed it.

"Yes, sir."

It was evident he had practised his answers well.

"Did you not find out then, some time before her death, that she was a woman?"

This was clearly not part of the doctor's rehearsal; Gallagher's careful replies took on a more guarded tone.

"That's a question I don't care to answer. A man can have cancer of the breast. It is not an assumption one can make." He paused, swallowed. "I have even seen some male bodies with what appear to be breasts."

Sensing he had touched a nerve, Zucca pivoted to a less accusatory line of inquiry. Rumour had it that the coroner, a Tammany man, had his own views. He believed that Hall must have taken this disguise in order to further himself in the world of business, and thus he, Zucca, wanted the whole matter sorted with the minimum of fuss.

"Do you believe the sandbagging alleged to have occurred at the hands of one William Reno may have hastened the death?"

"I could not say definitively either way – but it may have been an exciting cause that accelerated the end."

Coroner Zucca leaned back in his seat and studied the man closely.

"Dr Gallagher, will you tell the jury whether, in your opinion, the deceased was a female or a male person?"

"She was a female," came the reply. "A woman."

"Thank you, Dr Gallagher. Now, it appears we have only one family member as witness. Miss Imelda Hall, commonly called Minnie. Please come to the stand."

I held my breath as she took the witness stand, and I wasn't the only one. This was the first time I, or any member of the public, would hear her speak about her father. She was asked to confirm her identity with a few preliminary questions, and then:

"How long have you lived with the deceased, one Mr Murray Hamilton Hall?"

"I have lived with my foster father at 145 Sixth Avenue since 1885." Minnie's voice was surprisingly deep for a young woman, and her manner was polite but matter of fact, as if she was braced for further probing.

"And you call yourself his daughter. Were you ever legally adopted?"

"I have never been legally adopted, no. But my father called me his daughter. He always said that he and my mother were my family."

Her face was composed, almost fixed, though it bore the marks of recent stress: dark bags under the eyes, the blemish of a spot on the chin.

I wondered, as I watched, what it was like for her. Since the death of her father, so it was said, she had locked herself away in that house with its army of domestic servants, answering no calls and granting no interviews. Now she was here, under the gaze of the public's unblinking eye.

211

"And during all those years you lived with him, you never thought he was a woman?" inquired Coroner Zucca.

"No, sir," she replied.

Hers was a beautiful, if closed-off face, with dark hair and features. For an adopted daughter she did look remarkably like Hall, I thought, if only in the face and not the body. I recalled the story of the girl who had turned up weeping on the Halls' doorstep to be taken in; now that girl was a woman alone in the world, and yet she looked composed and self-assured.

"You knew he was ill, didn't you – you knew that he suffered from cancer?"

"Yes, sir," she said, her gaze shifting from the floor to the coroner.

"All this time you were living in the same house?"

"Yes, sir."

She sat bolt upright, her black dress, with its buttoned front and tailored shoulders, emphasising her rigidity. But it was her hand that distracted me. It constantly picked and pushed at the edge of the wooden witness stand, as if all her distress were directed at that one spot.

"And did any doctor visit or examine him?"

"Yes, we had a doctor for a year. A Dr William Gallagher."

"Could you tell whether the doctor was aware of Murray Hall's sex – whether he was a man or a woman?"

"No, I could not."

"How long had she – I mean he, no ... she – suffered from the disease?"

At this unexpected confusion over the he/she pronoun, the room burst into pockets of laughter, and a boisterous wave of snickering passed down the row on which I was sitting. Even the coroner allowed himself a small smile, choosing again not to reprimand the crowd. I noticed the only one who remained stony-faced was Minnie herself.

"For six years." She spoke as if she had not heard the laughter at her late father's expense.

"Did you ever hear her say that she had been drugged and sandbagged by a man by the name of William Reno, and is it your belief that the sandbagging made the disease worse?"

"Yes, I knew that he had been sandbagged," she replied, her voice now weary. "But I never heard him say that the sandbagging made him worse."

"Wouldn't it be better for you to say 'she'?" The coroner made the suggestion politely, but there was a hint of annoyance in his voice.

At this, her features darkened further and she sat up even straighter in her chair. Her demeanour and voice became that of a woman far more mature than her young years.

"No," she said firmly. "I would rather say 'he'. He was always a man to me, and I shall never think of him as a woman."

There was a further murmuring around the room in response, this time more subdued than humorous. The coroner seemed embarrassed and barked out an order of silence to those assembled.

"Thank you, Miss Hall."

For a moment, Minnie Hall looked perplexed, surprised perhaps, that this was all the coroner wanted from her. She looked across towards the public gallery, to the right of me, as if trying to search for reassurance, then nodded and quickly left the stand.

And at that, it was all over. The jury, who I observed comprised a number of middle-class officials and shop owners, took all of seven minutes to debate their verdict.

Coroner Zucca read it out in staccato bursts. "He was a lady," he concluded.

I heard the scribble of other pens in the press gallery, other reporters writing those words, ready to be sent out into print, for New York and the world.

He Was a Lady.

The decision had been made. In the eyes of the law, and of the people of this country, Murray Hamilton Hall was a woman. The greater debate, then, was whether this fact impacted the dissemination of his estate. Five thousand dollars was an impressive sum, and there were those at Tammany and else-where who I was certain would have tried to make a claim for it. However, after a hushed conversation between Zucca and his officials, Imelda was named as the sole descendant, and therefore heir to Murray's business and estate – regardless of his sex.

It was all over far more quickly than I would have liked. Not only was Minnie's testimony shorter than I would have wished, no information was sought or provided as to Hall's true original identity, nor the legal implications of a woman as a voter. It was as if the trial was simply for the papers, to provide a neat conclusion to this odd phenomenon and lay it to rest. For Coroner Zucca, Dr Gallagher and the rest of them, it felt as if the Hall case was an inconvenient anomaly, something to be brushed quickly under the carpet before it could garner any more attention. I felt cheated, bereft of the answers I so desperately needed.

As I stepped out into the chill January air, streams of people were making their way past me out of the courthouse. I overheard snippets of conversations as they passed.

"...Reckon she must have known. Her own father, for Christ sake! The whole family is a weird lot."

"... Knew him from the jail. You see all sorts 'round there, not that I ever thought ..."

"... Proud of her, keeping calm in that circus. She needs us now more than ever, despite the brave face she puts on."

At this last remark I looked up sharply, trying to identify from where it came. I thought I recognised an elderly woman, steel-haired and dressed in black servant's clothes, but the crowd was too densely packed and moved at too rapid a pace for me to keep track of her movements. I was sure it was the servant who seemed to constantly be at Minnie's side. It was a stupid mistake, to lose track of her like that, and I forced myself to keep a mental image of the woman in case I spotted her again.

As the crowd flowed out of the courthouse, I noticed two tall women with raked-back hair and green, purple and white rosettes pinned to their breasts. They were speaking loudly, and each held a handful of handwritten leaflets.

"Murray Hall was a woman, the court says!" The shorter of the women cried out. "She was a woman. And yet her life as a woman was such that she had to take on the role of a man in order to make her way in the world. To work, to vote!"

The second woman joined her.

"The Hall case is a symptom of an unjust system! Women, join the NAWSA for your voice to be heard. Men, speak out for your wives, your daughters! Let us join our cousins on the west coast; votes for women now!"

At this final impassioned cry, as the crowd had begun to part and form a ring around the two women, a police officer elbowed his way towards them, his brow furrowed.

"Ladies, you'll have to move on. You're causin' a blockage."

The two suffragists acted as if they had not seen him, and simply handed their leaflets to any that would take them. I stayed back against the wall, not wanting to be in the middle if a real confrontation broke out.

Sighing, the officer spoke again.

"I'm afraid I'll have to escort you ladies away. Where are your husbands?"

I was interested to see this play out. The last time a suffragist rally had taken place in my neighbourhood there had been several arrests, but the police were always reluctant to lay their hands on any woman who was too well dressed; indeed, who knows whose wife you could be throwing into a cell? These two ladies were most definitely of the middle class, and that awareness was making the officer nervous.

Thankfully, before the man got close enough for the situation to escalate, the shorter woman threw a handful of her remaining leaflets into the air, and in the distraction, they slipped away into the crowd, surprisingly nimble and quick-footed.

There was a buzz in the throng after that, with all the excitement of the trial and these two protestors. I stayed in my position, scanning the crowd as thoroughly as I could in the chaos.

I was at my post until the last few stragglers and then the court officials filed out. I was losing hope that Minnie would appear, thinking that she had either slipped out of another entrance or was hiding out in the building for fear of being accosted by journalists. If that was the case, her fears were well founded.

As I was kicking a stone to the side, cursing my luck, the great wooden door at the front of the building swung around. I looked up, and my gaze met that of Miss Minnie Hall, a flash of annoyance passing across her face as she realised that her exit was not quite delayed enough to avoid the press. At this closer distance I could see the paleness of her skin and a slight puffiness to her face that hadn't been visible from my seat in the courtroom. I guessed there hadn't been much sleep in the Hall household these past weeks, nor much laughter.

"What do you want?" She sighed. She seemed to have expended her energy fielding Zucca's questions, and had none left to fight me off. I felt a wave of guilt pass over me. It's far easier to justify probing questions when one is suspicious of the subject, or believes the information they hold will lead to

217

some kind of exposé. This now felt like self-indulgence, and a little cruel at that. I remembered the funeral and told myself there was no way this young woman could have recognised me from such a distance. I reminded myself of my principles, and the reason behind my investigation.

"Miss Hall." I took a breath and began, knowing this might be my only opportunity. "My name is Clellan, I'm with the *World*. I was interested to hear you speak in there; you deport yourself very well for someone so young. How could you be so sure of your answers? Is there not some part of you that is uncertain now if your father is truly the person he made himself out to be, when he kept this secret from you all your life?" I was careful to call Hall "he", remembering the young woman's reaction to Zucca's fumbling.

Minnie kept my gaze as she heard my questioning, her face unreadable.

"Murray Hall was my father. I said so to the court, and I'll say so to you. Anything else that he was or did was his own private business. I'll not pretend that he was perfect, but it's not just anyone who would take in someone else's child as their own. He kept me warm, fed and housed, and now he leaves me with the funds to begin my own life. I couldn't ask for anything more, from a father."

Her voice was calm and measured, and she didn't take her eyes from me once as she spoke. Her black mourning clothes struck a stark contrast against the pallor of her cheek, her dark brown hair and eyes completing the picture. I could swear I saw something I recognised in the curve of her brow and nose, and my mind was cast back to the small figure on the marble slab of the morgue. It was uncanny. Surely there was no blood relation between the two. And yet . . .

The girl seemed convinced that Hall was her adopted parent, but why would she tell someone like me if the truth was any different? That's if she even knew herself. It's entirely possible that Hall's sex wasn't the only secret he kept from his family.

Each question seemed only to unlock another.

Minnie finally broke my gaze and made to move past me.

"Miss Hall," I implored her. "One thing before you leave. You said in the court room you never knew your father was a woman. Was there never a moment of doubt? Not even in his illness, or in his relationship with your mother?"

I thought for a moment that she was going to walk past me without answering. I wouldn't have tried to stop her. But instead, she paused just long enough to give me her reply.

"My father was a man, in all the honourable and dishonourable ways one can be. Ask Dr Gallagher the question of sex. But I know who he was to me. He was my father, and I shall never call him anything else."

I had used my last chance and, as I watched, the dark-clothed figure disappeared into the swell of the crowds on Chambers Street. Her black dress blended in with the suits and hats of administrators and office clerks who hurried along, their heads bent to the ground with scarves around their noses.

I wondered if I had used that chance wisely, what else I might have learned had I asked a different question. I had the feeling she may have given me the same answer, no matter what I asked.

Minnie Hall was the closest living relative to Murray Hall. I should have been elated at the chance to speak to her, even briefly. No other newspaper had yet managed to obtain a quote. And yet I felt unsatisfied. Though I did not doubt the truthfulness of the young woman's feelings in her response, I still believed there was more she was not telling me, there was more she may never tell anyone. And then there was the question of how much Hall kept from her, too. His life was one so bound up in secrecy that I could believe that he kept his greatest secret even from his own daughter.

A chill whipped around me as I made my way from the chambers to the World's offices, my collar turned up against its knife edge. I wondered what this composed, self-reliant young woman would do now. I couldn't imagine that she would want to stay in New York, at least not without a change in identity. She had been marked out as the daughter of an oddity, not yet old enough to form her own stamp on the world. I imagined she would travel west, perhaps in search of a husband, perhaps not. She had enough money now to keep herself going for a few years. She had been right about one thing; Hall had left her a freedom of sorts. I sensed he had understood the value of that more than most.

WORLD BUILDING, PARK ROW
31ST JANUARY 1901, 3 P.M.

THE WORLD EDITORIAL FLOOR RUSTLED about me, a brisk breeze rattling at the windows. A wind blowing through the city, a hurricane shaking the very workings of things, rattling the woodwork, whipping at all we have built up about us, these flimsy ways we convince ourselves of our security.

At my desk, I paused to run through the words I had written. I was aware as I did so that someone was standing over me, and looked up to see a tall woman around my age, dressed in a tightly fitted double-breasted coat. She flashed a nervous, gap-toothed smile. "Are you the journalist chasing the Murray Hall story? Mr Clellan?"

The mention of his name gave me pause.

"Chasing," I said, placing the paper back down on the desk and standing to greet her, "and watching it constantly disappear out of sight."

"I feel your pain," the woman said. "The receptionist directed me your way. I've got my own story about Murray Hall I've been trying to pitch, but it's not been easy getting in the door."

"A story?" I asked.

"Yes. But I want to write it myself. I want to tell my own experience with ..." she said, pausing for a moment in search of a word, "that creature."

"You knew him?"

"Let's say I had some experience. I did a report on its employment agency some years ago."

The word "its", spat out between the teeth, made me wince. I felt it like a small dart to the chest.

"Mrs Hall's intelligence agency," I said.

"That's the one. I've written a column, should your editor want to publish it. Some reflections on my experience, which have stuck in my mind since."

"I imagine he would," I replied. "Are you a regular reporter or columnist?"

"Used to be. I wrote under the name Miss Wideawake."

"Miss Wideawake," I said with a smile. "Perhaps I have read some of your work ... in the *Times*?"

"No, the *Sun*. I didn't expect you to have." She placed her bag down on the floor then looked around, her glance landing on a nearby chair. "Do you mind if I sit down?"

"Go ahead."

She lowered herself into the swivel seat at the desk next to mine. "I once tried for a job at this paper. No luck. When a woman comes to a great city and seeks journalistic work, she must take what she can get – meaning she does not always get it. But I did secure some work over at the *Sun*, and as it happens, one of my first assignments in New York was a commission to investigate the city's employment agencies, and to discover whether or not they were engaged in unlawful and immoral business, as some of them were."

"A sort of Nellie Bly exposé?"

She smiled ruefully. "I thought so. It turned out I didn't make such a splash – nor a whistlestop tour round the world. As you no doubt know, for many years the so-called Murray Hamilton Hall kept an employment agency on Sixth Avenue. You will have visited the site. I visited it myself several times. It was run squarely enough, so far as the object of my investigations was concerned. I said so in my newspaper report."

"Yes, I looked into it myself," I said. "A well-oiled business, mostly due to Celia Hall, and later Minnie."

"Indeed," she said. "I also, however, made a comment which offended the woman-man – I called it 'a tiny man with a squeaky voice,' or words to that effect."

There was an acid tang to the woman's tone, something poisonous beneath her unassuming appearance. She frowned and went on. "This hurt the creature's vanity. It was only four foot seven inches tall, which makes the deception it practised still more extraordinary. The little deceiver was vindictive. It had me followed, and so found out where I lived."

I found myself flinching again at the word "it". She reminded me of the kind of woman who you might meet at a dinner party, who, with a gracious smile, would advocate for the segregation of the unfortunate into poorhouses and institutions for the mentally unbalanced, to keep them "off the streets" and out of sight, regardless of the conditions of their lives or the seasons.

More chillingly, she also reminded me of myself only a week or so ago. I might not have uttered the word "it", but I had insisted on calling Murray a "she", and was convinced that all I knew about him suggested egregious fraud and a person wedded to sin and corruption. In the presence of this woman, that fact made me feel the hot burn of shame. Had she seen me as an accomplice to her callous views?

"You are shocked that I say 'it'?" she said. "I shall continue to say 'it' for convenience, because the he/she pronoun is confusing, inaccurate and tends to give one a headache."

"He had you followed?" I tried not to dwell on this woman's language. After all, she might still yield useful information.

"One evening," she went on, "after dinner there was a caller for me at my hotel. It was Hall, the woman-man. The small chap carried a heavy Irish blackthorn stick, which it flourished vigorously. Hall was loaded for me, so to speak. It had swallowed a quantity of its favourite firewater and so possessed plenty of Dutch courage with which to carry out its attack."

The woman was now trembling as she spoke. I wasn't sure if it was with fear at the memory, or anger.

"It berated me in a curious contralto-falsetto voice, if there be such, which rose to a scream as the speaker became wrought up. It poured into my ears a tale of highborn descent from a fine old Scots family, but if it wasn't an Irishman, then it belied its looks. Then, in a stress of rage, Hall raised the blackthorn club over my head. I don't know what would have happened, but at that moment my guardian angel or some other power caused the cane to hit the chandelier, which splintered into glassy fragments. The clerk and hotel people came running in, and little old Hall cooled off. To this day I don't know whether it really meant to whack me upon the skull with that blackthorn club or only to scare me. But to the end of my days, I shall remember precisely how that stick looked, every grim black knot of it, as it struck the globes above my head."

She curled a hand as if clasping an invisible stick and then swiped it upwards through the air, shaking her head. "'I'm able to pay for it,' squeaked Hall grandiloquently. 'Send me the bill tomorrow. Here is my card.' Then it arose with a dramatic flourish of the club and went out at once."

The woman now paused with a nod and a quick, complicit smile. Her dark brown eyes searched my face for agreement or some kind of affirmation. For a second, I considered telling her my own story, but it felt in that moment as if I no longer knew how to tell it. "Well. That's certainly a story many would bite off your hand to publish," I said with a nervous laugh. "Did you investigate further? Or find out more?"

"No. The incident gave me such a scare. It made me realise I was not quite the Nellie Bly type, and I retreated more into the writing of columns – not that this was entirely successful. But it remained in my mind vividly, and with it there remained an indelible impression that somehow the little creature was masquerading. I seemed to know that intuitively, but how or why I could not make out. I was certain the name of Murray Hamilton Hall was an assumed one, but the real one neither I nor another ever found out." She smoothed her hands across the checks of her jacket. "You can assist me in getting it published, Mr Clellan?"

"I will recommend you to Mr Irving," I said, rising from my seat, as an encouragement to her that our meeting was over, and it was time to move on. I was struck by how visceral my response to her tale was, it being so close to my own.

"You are still following the story yourself?" she persisted.

"I have been attempting to leave it alone." I sighed. "But I struggle. Wherever you look, it becomes more complex. Every tale about Hall seems to present a different person, and I feel I am further than ever from learning any truth."

My glance fell on the page in front of me, its neat rows of carefully typed words.

"Hmmph," she snorted, as she bent to pick up her bag. "It's one I wish I had left well alone. You have some decent leads?"

"Decent. I'm not sure. I'm shortly to meet a woman who claims Hall confessed, in her company, to being a woman."

"Remarkable how few seem to have realised," she said. "I confess I was not sure about the nature of the masquerade. It now all makes sense. How funny that in hindsight it is so obvious. Could you direct me to where I may wait for your Mr Irving? I have the column already written, and I am keen to be sure to place it into his hands."

"I don't think he will be in for the rest of the day. Perhaps you would like to leave it with me. I can ask him to call you."

She handed over the sheet of paper, as neatly typed as my own, and I placed it on the desk.

"The telephone number for my current lodgings is written on the back," she said. "I appreciate this, Mr Clellan. I have found the *World*'s coverage of Mr Hall's story quite fascinating."

226

"I will make sure Mr Irving gets back to you," I replied. Her presence was unsettling me and I wanted more than anything for this woman to leave.

She smiled and turned awkwardly away, and it struck me that I did not know how to close our meeting. The shake of the hand, the nod of the head, which was so often exchanged between men, seemed inappropriate here. I watched as she walked towards the door and felt a sudden sadness, not for her, but for something about myself, or Murray.

For her it was simple. Murray Hall was a vindictive deceiver, a diminutive but violent creature who had menaced and terrorised her. For me . . . well, it was increasingly nuanced. I longed for a moment to be back where she was, in a world that was black and white.

Once she had left, I picked up the piece of paper and looked at the first line. I thought for a moment about crunching it up and throwing it into the bin, but instead I placed it back on my desk, a decision for another time.

I then slipped on my overcoat and walked out onto the viewing platform to look out over the city. The wind was so strong, I had to force the door open against its strength, and I found myself alone in its gusts. I walked towards the railing and looked over, eyes scanning the park below, where a yellow kite danced above the grass.

The lights were blinking on across the park as if in salutation. It was nearly dusk, and I recalled my appointment across town.

BRENNAN'S, 12TH STREET
31ST JANUARY 1901, 4.30 P.M.

THERE ARE WAYS OF SHRUGGING off the dirt and grime of a New York day, the toil, the mental effort, the faint smell of yellow that clings to you as a reporter, like cigar smoke on painted walls. Discomforts, like the one that was itching me.

One of them is a hot lather, smoothed across the face by the firm and knowing hands of a barber. Of all the men a fellow grows to love and trust, to surrender to, the most important is his chinscraper. The slip of the razor across skin, the supple massage of the face, the smell of witch hazel ... all of these, I have found, can transport me. The one man who can do it best is Gio at Galante's.

I hadn't had a cut and shave for quite some days, and I had the feeling that some of the residue of the world and my profession was clinging to me. Irving's comment from last week rang in my head, and I knew I only looked worse now. I needed to slough it off. I never did like looking in mirrors – I had some kind of aversion to the image of my own face – but I did enjoy the feel of being clean-shaven. Whiskers never felt right on my skin, and I only wore a moustache to blend in with the current fashion. It doesn't do to stand out in my line of work.

Half an hour with Gio is about more than a hair trim. The shaping of the moustache, the singeing of ends, the powdering, a dab of gossip. They use decent witch hazel there too, not the diluted half bay rum. Gio is not the most talkative of barbers, but he has a good ear and listens attentively to his customers, and from time to time he leans in close as he shaves to tell me he has "news". His gentle voice floats over my face. I make my mental notes, to be scribbled down straight after, and there are an extra few coins on the shelf come the completion of the cut.

"For the lilac water," I would say, though I never took any of that perfumed tonic.

I was about to head up to Broadway in the hope of finding Gio on shift when it occurred to me there was another barbershop that could be worth a visit. There was the establishment mentioned to me by the boys at Tammany, somewhere Hall would go for his trim; some even said a shave.

I would, I decided, go there and ask a few discreet questions.

Trying a different barber always felt like a risk. You get used to a man who knows what you like, and you grow to trust that he won't butcher your face, or any other part of you. The man who runs a razor over your neck has to be the one whom you pay well and who pays you the right pitch of attention. It always astonishes me the chinscrapers who can't manage this without leaving me feeling uncomfortable and unlike myself.

230

Brennan's on 12th Street. As I entered through the doorway a familiar, aromatic cocktail of singed hair, carboline and lilac washed over me like a calming draught.

The shop had a curious arrangement. Rather than mirrors round the outside perimeter, it had at its centre a wide hexagonal column, on each face of which was a mirror and a narrow shelf arranged with brush, razor, shears, witch hazel and various other tonics. Three customers were already situated around the room, cloaked like ghosts in white sheets, in chairs that seemed to tilt their heads further to the horizontal than most.

"What would you like, sir?" asked a slender young black man.

"Moustache trim and a shave behind and around the edge," I said.

"Certainly, sir," he said, turning a chair towards me.

I caught a glimpse of myself in the mirror.

"Hot towel?" he asked.

The heated fabric he placed around my neck, while instantly soothing, felt coarser and rougher than those they used at Galante's.

"What's your name, barber?" I asked.

"Daniel," he said. "Moustache trim, long at the ends?"

"Actually," I said. "Damn it. Why not? Let's have the whole moustache off."

"It's a fine moustache you have there, sir, are you sure?"

Daniel was by now lathering up my face – and with a decent layer of the stuff.

"You sure you want to take it off?" said the fellow sitting in the chair next to me. "Dangerous move, these days. I heard whiskers are becoming more than fashion – you need to prove you're a man, and nothing does that more than a big thick heroic beard that says I'm no Murray Hall."

"Not unless you're Tammany. They let them all in," said another fellow, whose eyes had previously been closed. "Did you hear Abraham Gruber? There should be a law requiring Tammany captains to wear whiskers!"

"And what would that prove? There are women in the world, so I hear, with beards."

"I heard," I said, astounded at my luck at encountering such garrulous types, "that Murray Hall was known to come in here for a trim. Gossip is he did have whiskers."

"Well, sir," said Daniel, interjecting, "Ah'm not the fellow to ask that question, sir. You want to ask Bob over there. Murray Hall was one of his steadies."

"So, he did come here," I murmured.

"Bob!" Daniel called. "Another gentleman here asking about Murray Hall. Want to speak to him?"

I twisted my head so that I could see the figure now, broad and short with a large, professionally twizzled moustache. "What do you wanna know for?"

"I'm a journalist. *New York World*."

"Ohh," exclaimed the nearby customer, with a scandalised note of delight in his voice. "Better keep our tongues still."

"There'll be a few dimes in it, then?"

"Sure."

Bob came over and stood leaning against the mirror column, utterly at home in his domain. "I can only tell you so much.

Murray was a quiet type, didn't talk a lot, but you could tell he enjoyed coming here. He liked the feel of the place, he said. 'Some place, this,' he would say. I've been trying to remember if I ever shaved her, or if it was just the cut. She ... I guess, she ... She had this thick, dark hair, good strong hair, though greying by the end. But I never thought. I guess I reckoned he was getting his shave at home."

"Know anyone else who knew him?" I pressed with a nod of encouragement.

"Well," he said, tilting his head playfully. "You could try going down to the Excise Exchange. Ask if they ever saw sight of Hall, though I doubt they will have done. There's all kind of stuff going on down there, but it's mostly men in corsets and lipstick, high heels and wigs, fairies."

I'd heard of this place, of course. Since the notorious Slide on Bleecker Street had closed down, partly thanks to my own newspaper's campaign, it was said they had moved down to a bar at the Bowery. The Excise was its name.

"There's a fairy called Jennie there – she might help."

"Jennie?"

"One of the old fairies, a bleached blonde. Seen it all. Knows everyone. I imagine if you pay her enough, she'll tell you some stories. Tell her you know me. Tell her Bob the bleacher sent you."

"Bob the bleacher," I repeated.

"My friend does a very fine bleach," said Daniel as he poised the razor over my upper lip. "Are you sure, sir?" he asked. "All of it?"

"Every whisker."

I felt the slow, smooth sweeps drawing over my skin. The blade pulling something away, then the hand running over to check for stubble. It felt like letting go. My eyes closed. I drifted.

Abruptly I was awakened. Daniel clicked the chair back upwards and turned me towards the mirror. A face stared back, naked. A little more recognisable, perhaps.

"Suits you, sir," said Daniel, as his brown eyes caught mine in the mirror. "It's like you've come out of hiding."

HERALD SQUARE THEATRE, BROADWAY
6TH FEBRUARY 1901, 8 P.M.

G RACE LOOKED AT ME WITH a puzzled frown as I arrived, a little late, in the theatre foyer. She was staring intensely. "You are naked!" she said, wafting a hand towards my face. "When did you do that?"

"A few days ago." I ran a finger along the smooth, hairless skin above my mouth. "I wanted a new look."

"Younger," she said. "You look younger. And ... a little more like me. I like it." She tugged at my arm. "I thought you were leaving me in the lurch. A lady on her own at the theatre."

"Never." I smiled, uncertain. "But why do I get the feeling I'm only here because Henry didn't want to see this?"

I looked around the room, assessing the faces. I felt some apprehension just being there. It wasn't that I had never been in a place like this – but it was different when one was reporting on something. Being here for my own pleasure felt distinctly uncomfortable. What, I wondered, if someone from the City Vigilance spotted me? But then that would mean that they too were here, watching a theatre show. Not even a serious play at that, rather a Broadway musical comedy.

"Don't be silly," Grace went on. "Anyway, I wanted to see you. And I thought you might enjoy this."

She hooked her arm into mine and started to guide me through the reception hall, past the dolled-up ladies and suited gentlemen milling about. "Even so, I can't believe I've persuaded you to come along to the theatre. First cards, now this. I do think you are going to enjoy yourself. Trust me, musical theatre is quite benign. I'm sure you'll leave with your moral fibre intact."

"I have been to the theatre before," I said, bristling slightly at her tone.

"To what?"

"*King Lear. The Barber of Seville.*"

She sighed. "Exactly my point."

As we reached the central stairs, I clocked the socialite Mamie Anthon Fish, sparkling in all her finery, but looking rather weathered. The audience here felt decidedly mixed. A few society figures, but also plenty of small businessmen, shopkeepers, financiers and the like.

"I hear it's a flop," I said. "Incoherent, one of the reviews said. Babbling frippery, according to another."

"It has Edna May in it. It's worth it to see her, to hear her, alone. Anything with Edna May can't possibly be all bad."

"But the premise sounds ridiculous. What was it? 'Olga has been trapped in the ice for five hundred years,' or something to that effect. It's pure fairy tale, as far as I can see."

We continued our light-hearted debate all the way to our seats, and I realised how long it really had been since I'd been in a theatre. Since I had done anything at all simply for pleasure, in fact. In spite of my complaining, I couldn't deny the spark of excitement I felt. We were seated right by the front of the centre tier of the theatre, and I could see the hats and feathers of society folk spread out below me. The stage itself was fairly small, but above it sat an impressive painted scene of rolling clouds and a figure at its middle, stretched out with cherubs dancing at its fingertips. It was an unusual figure, a bard in stockings and flowing dark hair, rather than the customary gods. As I stared at it, the lights dimmed, and the double layers of heavy burgundy curtains began to part.

The theatre felt remarkably warm, particularly whilst still wrapped up in my Kersey. The tinkle of the piano, and Edna's lulling voice as she sang out some number about being demure, made me stifle a yawn. I had been right; it was no *King Lear*. I was, I realised, exhausted, and it seemed to me there was nothing wrong in giving in to a few moments of sleep.

Suddenly I felt a sharp jab in the arm. Grace's elbow nudged me back to life, and the scene in front of me was entirely different. No longer were we in a world of ice, but a stage crowded with pirates.

"That's not Edna, is it?" I whispered, leaning in towards my sister's ear. "Dressed now as a buccaneer?"

"Yes, it's her character, Olga, in disguise," she replied without taking her eyes from the scene.

Edna was dressed in boots all the way up to the thigh, tight-fitting pants and sported a slender, sashed waist. With hands on her hips, she spread her legs in a swagger as she approached a hollering band of pirates. Her previously loose waves were tucked under a giant tricorn hat, topped with a pluming feather.

"How did we get here?" I asked, still puzzled as to how we had jumped from the North Pole to some pirate island, and a scene in which the star was masquerading as a man. I felt for a moment as though I were still asleep, and dreaming.

"She looks fabulous, doesn't she? I like her better like this than in her ice queen dress from earlier. She looks so powerful, and quite wicked! So much better than when she was doing that demure Susie number."

Someone from behind us shushed.

"So, she's in disguise?" I repeated, ignoring the *shush!* that came again from a fellow in front this time.

"Oh, Sam. You really haven't seen enough theatre, have you? Every show has some kind of masquerade, a character passing as a woman or man. It's one of their favourite tropes."

A hand landed on my shoulder and a face scrunched in annoyance appeared beside me, whistling another "*shush*". I raised a hand and mouthed the word "Sorry!" before returning my attention to the stage, where Edna was now pointing a musket and demanding that the captain pirate, "Hand over the cup!" Incapable of following the plot, I found myself transfixed by the performers, their bodies, and the sounds and actions that they could produce with them – their ability to be one thing in one moment, and another entirely in the next.

I watched Edna intently. It was theatre, true. But, I wondered, if this woman were to walk down the street with such a bold swagger, with her hair cut short and in a capacious sack coat . . . what would the reaction then be? Far from sleepy now, I became pertly aware of all the bodies around me, seated to the side, below, even above me. I was surrounded by hushed bodies, their faces all trained towards the stage. Of all of them, might there be one like Murray Hall?

I took a glance to the left, where a gentleman in a black suit, white waistcoat and jet-black whiskers was sat next to a woman whom I presumed was his wife; for this evening's entertainment, she was donned in a pink and cream striped dress, cinched at the waist and with a ruffle of bows at the chest. They were a perfectly ordinary couple, certainly not one you would look twice at whilst walking through Broadway. I looked closer. Perhaps, I thought, the gentleman's whiskers were too thick to be real. Perhaps some carefully styled horse-hair and glue could achieve the same effect . . . As for his wife, I noticed now how she sat almost a head higher than him, her elegant neck craning over the railing. Such height, I mused, is uncommon in a woman . . .

I sighed, sinking back into my seat. It was a useless game I was playing. If those closest to Murray Hall never knew the truth, I was certainly not about to become an expert in spotting sexual inverts. For so long I had believed them to be confined to the walls of such establishments as the Slide, but

239

Murray Hall had lived an apparently ordinary life, by all accounts. I remembered, too, the voice of the preacher, Joseph Lobdell, crying out his sermons from the street corner. As my eyes became heavy once more, the voice morphed into that of my father.

There is nothing in this world worth saving but the souls of men. Guard yours jealously; let none deceive it.

I awoke again to the applause of the crowd, despite its lacklustre nature. People were beginning to filter out, and I could tell that the general reception was an ambivalent one. Grace, on the other hand, seemed to have had an excellent evening.

"I can't believe you slept through it all! Oh, she was wonderful, Sam. I'll accept that it's a bit of an odd narrative, but she's a magnet on stage. I don't know where she gets all that energy from, I'm tired out from just watching her."

She carried on in this enthusiastic, almost childlike way as we shuffled towards the foyer, joining the crowds headed out into the night air. As we stepped into the refreshing breeze, I felt like I had been asleep for a week.

"Perhaps I should come to the theatre more often. I haven't slept that well in an age," I said with a smile.

"Oh, you're a brute! You've no heart for the arts." Despite her chiding, Grace matched my grin. "It's nice to see you smile, brother of mine. You ought to do it more often."

Given how many patrons were spilling out onto the sidewalk, we were in the cold for a few minutes before I managed to hail a hansom cab. As my sister stepped inside, I closed the door behind her.

"Won't you come by? I'm sure Henry would love to see you." Her face had fallen a little as she realised I was not going to join her.

"It's such a beautiful evening. I'd like to take a walk, think things through on this story I'm stuck on. I'll call around next week."

"All right, but don't catch a chill! There's supposed to be a frost tonight."

As the horses were pulling away, their breath coming out in short steamy snorts, I spotted the couple I had been watching from my seat. They were walking along the street, the moonlight picking out the highlights of the woman's dress and the gentleman's moustache, and they were leaning into each other in that intimate, comfortable way only lovers do.

The theatre that I had so long shunned as sinful and debauched, I now realised, was another invitation into the possible, a reminder that things need not be quite as they are.

THE EXCISE EXCHANGE, 336 BOWERY
6TH FEBRUARY 1901, 11 P.M.

I MUST HAVE BEEN IN A risk-taking mood that evening because there is no other way I would have made my way down to the Bowery, and the famous Excise Exchange. I hardly realised I was heading there, but the evening had me in an adventurous spirit. I remembered Bob the bleacher's advice and thought it was time I followed up on that particular lead. I'll admit to having been scared, but as I turned down the street, I found it milling with humanity, burly working men, bowler-hatted gents, black and white, mixing as you'll find nowhere else in this world. I was buoyed by my trip to the theatre, the simple act of stepping out of my usual comforts, and I had lost a few of my habitual inhibitions that ordinarily kept such a tight hold on me.

The lights were already on and glowed through the windows, which were frosted to above head-level, presumably for privacy. Still, fear rippled through me as I entered the bar. I felt like the outsider, the one who did not belong.

The room was thrumming, and there was barely space to squeeze between the bodies.

"I'm looking for Jennie," I said as I moved in against the bar.

"Oh, you're looking for Jennie, are you?" The boy behind the bar sighed, as if to express some pert disappointment that I was not looking for him. He seemed barely old enough to be working in a place like this, or maybe he just had a young face. "She's up back, in the purple dress."

"I don't suppose you've heard of Murray Hall?" I asked, chancing my luck and wanting to keep this youth talking. "The Tammany heeler?"

"We've all heard the story. But no, if you're asking if she came here, I don't think so. There aren't many of Murray Hall's type come here."

The boy led me through the crowd. The rattle of a piano and a high-pitched croon filled the air, and I felt I was swimming now through a sea of faces, smiling, laughter like a dose of sweet dope. One of those faces over the other side of the room caught my attention. Black hair slicked back with grease, skin almost pure white, with a strong handlebar moustache. It was a look distinctive enough to make me take a second glance.

Joe Young, I realised.

I wondered, for a moment, if he saw me too. But I kept on moving, following the boy.

"This feller is looking for you, Jennie. And asking questions about Murray Hall. I said we don't know anything about Murray Hall."

"No, we don't," said Jennie, looking me up and down, as if inspecting some faulty goods. "And I'm not sure I'd tell you if we did."

"I'm a friend of Bob's," I said quickly. "Name's Samuel Clellan. Bob said you might be able to help."

Jennie was petite, five foot five or so, and piled up on her head was the brightest bleached-blonde hair I'd ever seen. Her skinny arms jangled with costume jewellery, and though her dress was as vivid as her hair I noticed how it was fraying a little at the neckline.

"Bob?" she said. "Ha! Good old Bob. He sure does send the funny sort my way. It's Murray Hall you're askin' about? The bail bondsman? You could try the Walhalla. Though I doubt even he went there. The female androgynes keep themselves quiet and secret, not like us ladies! They mostly pass unnoticed. Every now and again we get a few of them here, for a drink and a carouse. But not your fellow Hall. He wasn't one for our kinda party."

There was something worn in her face, but the smile was animated and inviting, the lipstick adding life to the exaggerated, expressive shapes it formed.

"Come to the bar, sweetheart," Jennie said. "You can buy me a drink."

We shifted through the crowd.

"Are you sure you don't want something more? You look like you could be here for something other than a story." She grinned at me mischievously, flirtatiously. "Now, what might that be?"

"More?" I said. "I don't think so." I felt a manicured hand glide over my trousers as the flash of Jennie's eyes met mine. My whole body tightened. I should never have come here, I thought. I turned away to look at the bar, and in the mirror lining the wall I saw myself as if I were a stranger across some crowded room. I saw my own grey face and greyer clothes in the midst of this sparkling sea of colour and theatricality. Then I saw Jennie wink back at me, stick the tip of her tongue out and swipe it along her upper lip, then turn away. I heard the solemn whisper of a sermon in my ear, but I batted it away. "Maybe next time," she said, and her breath warmed my ear. "You can let me know how you get on at the Walhalla, if you're lucky enough to be let in. Someone like you!"

"You think I wouldn't get in?" I said, turning to her.

I felt flickerings, an insistent pulse as I looked into her painted eyes. Was it fear? It felt like something else, some feeling too dangerous to touch.

"Look at you, Monsieur Gris Ennuyeux!" She laughed. "You don't stand a chance."

"But you could help me get in?"

"Treat me to one of those Bijou cocktails, cross my palm with a few greenbacks, and I just might."

She was teasing me, but I could feel a chill creeping down my spine like ice water. I looked away, back to the mirror and the wild, beautiful throng beyond. My eye caught sight of an older, familiar man in the mirror behind me, staring straight at me. I whipped around to see him, but the space where he had stood was empty.

"Sam, Sam," Jennie whispered in my ear. "I see you there in that mirror. I see that look. I want to help you. Chasing after Murray Hall! You'll see it yourself soon enough."

She smiled, a genuine smile, and I felt a sudden shyness.

She kissed me on the cheek as if I was a child being dismissed. "If you'll excuse me. I'm due up at the piano. It's my song next! Wait around and we can chat some more later."

Laughing, she made her way up to the instrument. It seemed she was the one the room had been waiting for, as the riotous chatter died down a little when Jennie began to sing.

Strike up the band. Here comes a sailor,
Cash in his hand, just off a whaler.
Stand in a row. Don't let him go.
Jack's a cinch, but every inch a sailor!

Though it hadn't been Shakespeare, Edna May's performance now seemed sober in comparison to Jennie's easy glee as she strutted about the stage, her and the audience not caring for a moment when she hit a bum note. As she sang on, I looked around the bar, searching for the face of Joe Young, sure I had seen him earlier. A part of me was searching for that other face too, though I knew it couldn't be true. But the room now seemed a blur of faces, shifting and swaying around me, smiles and flickering eyes looming towards me and then away. Faces, smiles. Teeth. Lips. None of them Joe Young. I felt myself lurch, my heart beating a quivering rhythm in my chest. I slipped out the door and into the cool, frosted night.

There he was, standing in the dim light. An imposing figure in his giant frock coat.

A small crowd flanked him, and I could see some kind of exchange of goods was taking place. One of the crowd leaned in close and craned up to whisper.

I watched for a moment, until his gaze caught mine.

There was a slight smile, then he nodded. His hand raised in the kind of wave that said, "Not now."

But still, I walked in closer, watching him for a little longer. I don't know why I wasn't afraid of him this time. Perhaps it was where we were; I felt that whatever Jennie's world represented was far more complex and unnerving than the blood lust and fists of Tammany. His eyes caught mine again, he shook hands with one of the party and then left the group.

"Mr Clellan," he said.

"Mr Young," I replied. "You come here to collect?"

"Now would ah tell that to a reporter who is a known investigator of vice?" he said. An amused smile cracked over his face, crinkling his scar. I was glad he was entertained by my presence, rather than threatened by it. "Ah come here because ah like the company. That might surprise you, Mr Clellan, but ah do. Ah wonder why you are here. Would you care to tell me?"

22ND STREET, MANHATTAN
7TH FEBRUARY 1901, 9 A.M.

I WOKE THE NEXT MORNING, WOODEN-MOUTHED and in a cold sweat. Memories from the night before flashed through my head, which throbbed with shame and lingering drunkenness. My father's voice regaled me angrily, barking out from some fracas that appeared to be emanating from the street below.

Fool, a motorcar honked.

"Asshead!" someone shouted. "What in God's name were you doing?"

Fool. Fool, the horn repeated.

I rolled over and shifted into my daily prayer position at the edge of the bed, feeling my stomach lurch. The noise continued and now there were more voices, haranguing me:

"Get out the damned way!"

"What in heaven were you doing?"

I attempted to begin my prayer. Though my tongue is so practised it can recite without thinking, all that emerged was a vomited stutter. The words of the morning prayer when I finally forced them out, stung at my tongue. "I am no longer my own ... But ... thine."

Then I was struck by a flood of memory. A vision of the night before, of bodies swirling, and my own moving between them, and the smiles that greeted me. Broad, generous, welcoming smiles that knew little of the many reasons I shouldn't be there, smiles that wanted to have me belong.

But how could I?

I walked to the window and looked down onto the street. Below was a scene of chaos, a motorcar and cart at right angles to each other, potatoes rolled out over the street like heavy pebbles on a beach. The car driver, in a Raglan coat, rolling his shoulder as if in pain, then pitching forward to pick some of them up.

The mess cheered me, as did the noise, the bustle of the street, and the snapshot of two men standing shouting at each other, whilst a carriage strove to push past. After clumsily dressing, I went downstairs, fully intending to immerse myself in the commotion and see what aid I could give. But when I reached the hallway on the first floor, I paused, as is my habit, to check my mailbox. Inside, its dark cave was almost entirely filled with a single, fat letter. Its high-quality, slightly perfumed paper intrigued me.

Finger-thick, stamped with a British postmark and shipping frank. Forgetting the intrigue of the street, I wandered back up the stairs, carefully unsealing the envelope as I climbed.

Dear Mr Clellan,

I must say, it is a delight to receive messages from those interested in the peculiarities of gender inverts and their motivation, and under the recommendation of the esteemed Dr Wise. Peter and I may not agree on everything, but we at least share common ground and an open mind.

I was hesitant to respond to you at first; you can understand that the press are often at my door looking for a piece of gossip for the columns, when in actuality my practice is concerned with the scientific study of individuals such as Murray Hall. But as I came to understand that your interest is in constructing a larger picture of the woman's life, and by extension understanding from where such deviance emerged, I am more than happy to provide you with what I know of this particular individual.

Then, when in your second telegram you mentioned the connection with John Campbell, my interest was piqued. Whether Campbell and Hall are one and the same I will leave to your investigations, but I believe so. I can tell you only what I have learned of Campbell's life after her departure from Govan, some of which you will have already read in The Scotsman. There is some debate around whether she left Glasgow with or without her brother, but in any case, he was soon dead, and she was living in Kirknewton in her brother's assumed identity. It is from here that I can provide you with fresh knowledge, and another piece of your puzzle.

Campbell arrived at the fairly anonymous borough of Kirknewton in the early months of 1869, distinctive for her small frame, rough habits and West Coast accent. The town falls to the South-West of the capital and has lain rather dormant until recent years, when it has burst into activity since the discovery of shale oil within its borders. It is unclear *what brought our subject to that particular corner of the map; perhaps as she was still in the early days of her masquerade, she hoped to test out the limits of her deception on a smaller and less daunting scale than in a city. In any case, she had no difficulty in finding employment in the newly founded mine, and even less so in finding a wife. It is of ceaseless interest to me that sexual deviants such as herself should find themselves so popular with the objects of their desire. It is my belief that the danger and taboo of such relationships draws otherwise respectable women into aberration. They are tempted in much the same way as those women who fall into infatuation with murderers and rogues.*

Of course, the wife in question denied knowledge of Campbell's true sex; but we shall come to that. Her name is Mary Ann McKenna, and she was already burdened with two young children when she met "Johnnie" – as our lady was now calling herself – and, I am told, was pregnant with a third. It is not beyond the realm of imagination that this Mary Ann, regardless of genuine attraction to Campbell, would have seen an opportunity for stability in her proposal. Indeed, she may have been quite averse to the idea in principle, but in finding herself in a state of heightened vulnerability may have seen no other option but to accept. But, as I say, these inverse women never seem to find themselves short of suitors.

The two were married by a Reverend Henry Smith in the December of that year – Hall is fond of Christmas marriages, it seems – and began a life of apparent domesticity. It certainly calls into question McKenna's claim that she was none the wiser to Campbell's true identity that the two remained in a state of nuptial harmony for a number of months. Even then, reports appear to confirm that the reason for the pair's eventual separation was due more to Campbell's inability to remain faithful than to anything more unusual. Here is another reason I believe your Mr Hall and my Mr Campbell are one and the same; both seem to have an incompressible desire for the company of the fairer sex that leads them into disrepute with their respective wives.

Please indulge me a moment to pause from the narrative to give my thoughts on Campbell's motivations, which I know are as of much interest to you as the particulars of her story. I have, in recent years, been collecting any number of accounts of men and women like her. It is true, however, that Campbell's remains an unusual case. I find that sexual deviance, rather than inversion, is the more common – though both seem to be at play here. It is a condition usually more apparent in men than women, though this may be a misconception brought on by the natural familiarity of females that makes this kind of unusual behaviour more difficult to identify.

You know my work, of course, on the psychology of sex. Well, I am now working on a second title to that effect, and this time I hope to dive deeper into what I believe is a much misunderstood and misrepresented subject. Polite society tends to disregard these people as diseased, or else they are made a laughingstock, an oddity for the gossip pages; but my investigations tell me that their occurrence is far more widespread and consistent for them to be disregarded as such. In fact, I may use the case of

Campbell/Hall in my newest work. I believe she is a prime example of the emancipation of women causing not an insignificant increase in female homosexual activity and sexual inversion.

You have only to look at Murray Hall, whose status within American political life could not have been possible without her masculine guise; and yet, that is the world the suffragists should have us attain. I am not against women's emancipation in general, seeing it as a fairly inevitable progression of society, but one must acknowledge the effect that is caused by the independence of women. "Independence" is the crucial word; independence from what? It is independence from the function of men, and therefore the natural order of all civil things. If we are to deny our biological and Godsent reality, we cast aside that which makes us human, and who is to say what barbarity may follow.

You must understand that I am not advocating for the removal of homosexuals from society. My own wife is openly bisexual, and I find it invaluable to discuss my theories with her.

Hall is an intriguing case in this regard, representing that also ever-increasing population of the lower social classes who travel to America and find their fortune in its seedling states. She is a self-made man (if you'll forgive me the pun), and was remarkably successful in her endeavours, particularly when you consider the ramifications she might have faced had she been found out during her political career.

It is my belief that this aptitude to success within the world of men comes from overexposure to masculine activities and *personalities from a young age. She appears to have had an extremely close relationship with her brother, and is described as headstrong and ill-tempered in much the same way as her father was. It may well be the case that in growing up with such a docile and characterless mother, Hall instead chose to replicate what she perceived as the strength and health of her father's vigorous manner. Furthermore, I find it intriguing that she appears to have become more serious about her masculine charade around the time of paternal abandonment, signalling to me an attempt to fill the void of the father through personal theatrics.*

In some ways it is admirable. I do not begrudge her successes, just as I do not begrudge those thousands of young men who have made that long journey across the Atlantic to seek their fortune. America is the land of the bold frontiersman, after all. There are such aspects to Hall's personage as mark her case as different from some others that I have encountered. She was a Christian, despite the many sins she may have committed through her long life. And she was a European, born of ancient stock, and therefore rational and of good calibre in that regard. One cannot deny her canniness, nor her intelligence – she may have rubbed elbows with any number of down-and-outs in Manhattan's various drinking establishments, but she also outwitted some of the city's most notable and powerful men of politics with her act.

Indeed, despite her womanising (and how many men would have that charge laid at their door?), Hall seems in her later life to have led a reasonably honest existence. The second marriage appears to have been happy, for it lasted some twenty years, until the "wife" died. And by all accounts her secret was a complete revelation to all who knew her, even to her adopted daughter. If there are to be sexual inverts in the world, and my research tells me that it shall for ever be thus – Hall is not the worst example of them.

It may surprise you to hear that in the time I have been researching this subject, I have very seldom come across a sexual invert from the lower races. That is not to say, however, that I do not believe they exist. This is not something you will see written in my published work, as it is merely speculation, but I theorise that those inverts who come from those classes are the most conscious of hiding their condition, knowing that they face more than social exclusion should they reveal themselves.

In fact, the only such case I can recall is of not a female invert, but a young male. He is known by the name Lucy Lawson. You are likely not to have heard of him, despite your profession and evident interest in this subject, as the family have worked hard to keep this secret – but I have my ways. Lawson was born in Kentucky in 1886, and I believe is currently working as a domestic.

The fabulous aspect of this story comes from the intervention of a doctor, a fellow of my own profession. When the boy's mother was naturally disturbed by her son's abnormal behaviour and insistence on girl's attire, she brought him to the family physician. I don't know whether this doctor provided such extraordinary advice because he saw an uneducated child on whom he could encourage experimentation, or whether he genuinely believed his own advice, but he suggested to the mother that she raise her child as a girl. That is exactly what she did, and there are very few people, save myself and a few other interested parties, who know the truth.

What unsettles me most about this case is that this child – who is now almost a man – will enter the world believing with encouragement that he can carry on this façade without consequence. It is one thing for a character such as Murray Hall to insist upon such a lifestyle for whatever reason, despite the knowledge of what is right and proper. But it is entirely another for a child's delusions to be entertained, even supported by a medical professional. Regardless of the child's race, it sets a dangerous precedent, and can only encourage deviance among more of the population.

I do not wish to get ahead of myself. After all, the seed of suggestion can only develop when it falls on a suitable soil, and is watered and nurtured with diligence. But surely you can see the issue with such encouragement too. If a person like Murray Hall is to exist despite the taboo of correct society, who is to say what might happen should we throw caution to the wind and allow any child's fancy to develop into mature self-deception?

So then, what do I propose to be done? In the first instance, as you will have read in my book, I do not believe in one simple cure for sexual inversion. It is far too complex a social issue for that, and besides, many such cures have been touted in the past to no avail. There is to some extent the solution of hygiene, both physical and social, which goes some way towards *prevention. I believe, however, that – ultimately – some level of sexual inversion within the general population is to be expected.*

My position is that if we as a society are really serious about tackling the epidemic of sexual inversion, we must learn to speak about it openly, without judgement and in plain terms. The invert is not only the victim of his own abnormal obsession, he is the victim of social hostility. Once this condition can be recognised as a common issue, separated from shame and self-hatred, the patient becomes much more open to suggestion and treatment. Combine this with the fact that if inversion is treated in this way, far fewer cases – such as that of Murray Hall – will exist in secret, and we will know the true extent of his or her kind.

I hope you will forgive the divergence that this account has taken, as I have strayed a little from the facts of John Campbell's life, but I hope you can understand the reasons for my interest in delving deeper into the subject.

What pains me most about this case is not Hall's condition – that I have seen a hundred times over – but that we as a people have not created the conditions in which she might have shared her secret and received help in her lifetime. For her to have died of what may have been a preventable disease due to her fear of discovery tells me it is our social attitude that is the greatest threat to these people, not their inversion itself.

I have included, from my research, some correspondence I received from several people who knew John Campbell, including a woman by the name of Rebecca, who claims to be the only living person to have known Campbell as a child, and a Mrs Early with whom he lodged around the time of the revelation of his sex. I cannot confirm their veracity, but I'm sure they will be of interest, nonetheless.

I realised I was still standing outside my apartment door, quite captivated by this strange letter. Its tone filled my mouth with a bitter taste, and I found myself viscerally discomfited by how he spoke of Hall's inversion. I took a few moments to settle myself into the comfort of my rooms before reading on.

Dear Mr Ellis,

I was surprised by your letter – I can't think how you found me – and I was inclined to reject your request. I do not like to think of my old friend as the subject of some cold scientific study. I'm not long for this world now, however. Cancer of the liver. I suppose I'm thinking about how I want to be remembered, and Tam's story is part of mine.

I was just a child when I knew him. I called him Tam back then, a nickname of my own making for his love of his father's horses and, even at his young age, a nip of whisky. He had another name, given to him by his parents. He made me swear the day we met never to say it, and I've not broken that promise in fifty years. I don't know if my Tam is the man you're looking for, but even if he isn't, I always thought his life was worth

259

telling. I lost him the day he left Glasgow and never came back, and I'd be glad if he's this American you're looking into. I never told anyone, but I always regretted not travelling with him across that vast ocean all those years ago.

I was so young, and afraid of all the things in the world I didn't know. Well, I'm old now and don't know much more than I did then, except that I loved him and might've seen more of life had I gone too. I've not had a bad life, but I can tell you some old wife's advice – you'll never regret the things you do, only those you don't. You're most afeared for the day you never saw.

The story of the lad I'm to tell you may seem stranger than most – I suppose that's why you're asking me about him – but in his soul he was a lad like any other, with his share of love and heartbreak. There are those who say that if things were to be done twice, each one would be wise. I'm not so sure. I think my foolish heart hasn't learned a thing, and I'd be as sweet on him the second time around. I remember that bonnie wee face, hard-set and ready to take on the world. I loved it for its openness. You could always tell what he was thinking, what worries or pain was on his mind. It was written right there, on his face. That's why I know he was really a lad. If it'd been a fraud, I would have seen it right there, plain for all the world to see. Who's to know what brought us together. I'm glad life did.

Unlike me, Tam was born to the gloom of a Glasgow single-end tenement, the younger of two weans to James and Agnes Campbell. The elder was known as John. The two were never rivals like some born to the same house. They were sweet boys but as different as day and night, Tam always standing out above the crowd, charming and headstrong afore his meek wee brother. You wouldn't have thought he was the young one. They looked after each other in their own way, in a house that was cold in its heart and its hearth.

We had very different starts in life, the three of us, though we all knew the smoke and smirr of our shared city, that dear green place I still call home. It was quieter and slower, a different world back then, though the rumblings of industry were beginning to make their noises in an echo of what was to come. The elder brother John, so I learned, liked to wake up early, before Tam and the sun rose, to watch the smoking chimneys in the half-light and wonder aloud how anyone could ever leave it. He knew that plenty of skilled and well-read men vacated the city to travel south, or even further abroad across the sea, but there was enough movement and stink and expansion among his city's gaslit closes to last him more than one lifetime.

The same couldn't be said of Tam. Though he was the younger of the two, he always seemed to need less guidance to make his way in the world; as if he understood by instinct the mechanics of the social order, and their family's place in it. While one wain had often been too frightened to bide near the groomed and towering horses hitched to the coach their father commanded, the other observed with calculated silence how the man preened and smoothed himself just as he did the animals, making himself as respectable as he could for the silent judgement of his

261

superiors. Tam loved the horses. I think when he couldn't make sense of the world – or didn't understand why the world couldn't make sense of him – he'd tend to their care and it would soothe him. My Tam watched, too, how the man of the house treated their mother with a particular dismissiveness when the smart of subjugation became too raw, when he had been reprimanded, or wrong-footed, or had earned less than he believed he was owed.

I believe John wondered if this keen knowledge of the pecking order of men was what inspired his brother, at that time known to all as his sister, to start wearing his clothes. From as early as we all could remember, he had refused with shouts and fists to dress in any way that could be described as appropriately feminine, but it was only as he grew older and away from their parents' influence that he began to cut off his hair with their mother's dressmaking scissors, and to strut about in his brother's breeks, already on him a size too large.

The strange thing about it all wasn't the behaviour itself, but the way the confidence with which he carried out his deeds seemed to cast a spell on those around him, to the extent that folk in the gate-end who had known him for years failed to recognise him at first glance and took him for a visiting boy cousin. It brought him no end of joy to fool whomever he could with his act, perfecting the cock of his walk and mannerism of his speech to perfectly match his brother's, to be a small echo of his father's swagger. The strangeness of this behaviour was not discouraged as much as might have been imagined, perhaps in part due to the meekness of the parents'

262

dispositions, coupled with the fiery conviction of the child's. It may also have been a result of the young age at which his deviation began, so that by the time it could no longer be written off as childish daffery it had become accepted as an odd sort of normal by those who knew him.

I loved my Tam for his strength, the fierdy way he seemed to always be so sure of himself, always knew what he wanted, even if I didn't agree. His brother wasn't the same, though I was fond of him too. It would be a mistake to name him shy. It was just that he was so often away with the faeries, dreaming of other worlds rather than living in this one. He liked to talk of himself fully grown, the head of a family in his own right. Oh, he had all sorts of dreams. He'd be a scholar, set to come out with the next great medical or scientific discovery – and the next day an engineer, drawing out plans for a bridge that would cross to Ireland, or a railway line to travel the length of the country. Whatever the profession, in these daydreams he'd talk of himself as a great bulk of a man, with a family of his own to look to him for wisdom and guidance, his brother by his side to marvel at his worldly achievements.

I dare say he was jealous of his brother, the odd wee boy who wasn't feart of no man. They looked the same, even with my Tam a fair few years younger. Neither ever got enough meat on their plates to fill out their clothes. They were just wee lads who grew up to be wee men. I'm sure it riled John up no end when his own good pair of breeks would go missing for the third time in as many days, and he'd find his wee brother out getting them dusty in a game of hide and seek with the neighbours' wains. It wasn't uncommon that they would be mistaken for one another – they both had those hard-set faces, dark eyes and thick, waved hair. That they looked the same was always a point of pride for the younger, and of mild annoyance to the elder lad.

I mention John, the brother, so much as I think it'll help you see Tam better for how he was. As much as I like to think of myself as the one he trusted the most, it was really John who knew him best. I never had a sibling, but I could see they had something worth holding on to. I only knew them for a few years, but I got to know them both like they were my own family. They would tell me things – fears and hopes and vexes – about the other they were too afeart to say to their face.

John always knew his wee brother was different from the lasses their age, and from anyone else he had ever met. When they were both wee, Tam's selcouth choice of clothing had seemed a natural extension of his character, and John never paid it much attention. It was just who he was. There are things, though, that even he couldn't ignore as the years rolled on. Around the age of twelve, when the first blooms of womanhood were beginning to leave their mark on Tam's childish body, he started to treat the act of manhood much more seriously than he ever had before. What was only the will of a child grew into an obsession, an obdurate beast that shadowed his every hour.

John and I both watched him bind down his swelling chest with a ferociousness that left him cut, raw and bruised, and the dogged urgency of his actions exposed the brothers' differences

264

and pulled open a rift between them. Regardless, and even though John could not understand what drove his brother to wage such unrelenting war against his sex, I believe he remained loving till the end, his heart only feeling worry for the lad, compassion, and never sickness, never hate.

If you don't believe me, there's something'll prove it to you. See, John wasn't a fool. He knew Tam was his sister, but the mere idea of that as a truth caught in his throat whenever he went to say it. It was as if the dedication with which Tam lived the act of manhood bled into John's perception of him, and when he looked around at the other women in his life, the wives, sisters and lasses of his friends, workmates and superiors, he could not place Tam among them.

It wasn't only this. Sometimes we would see him treating Tam like a brother, stealing a draught of their father's whisky or roughhousing in the dusty street afore the house. I think he had a suspicion, one that he would not voice even to himself, but one that concerned him even more than the way Tam dressed or spoke or acted. It was something he would not have been able to prove even if he had been able to voice it, but it troubled him nonetheless, and he saw it in the way his brother turned his attention to the women in the room, always having a kind word or a willing hand to help them.

This is where I suppose I ought to tell you my place in this story. I've been avoiding it I think, in part to lose myself in the memories, and in part out of the pain of remembering. Once I've told you my piece, I'll be the one left with the end *of the tale. I wish I had a different story to tell you, but this is the only one I've got.*

From what I knew of John, this next part of the story was the time that troubled him most, was the time he understood his wee brother least in all their years together. He had just turned sixteen, and his brother was thirteen. Their father had become engaged for a time as a coachman for a factory owner for his affairs around Glasgow, well-paying and welcome employment. The gentleman had a daughter the same age as the elder child, and although their father discouraged them from ever appearing in front of, or speaking with his customers, the three children had found a way to strike up a friendship.

Lost in his daydreams, John had failed to notice just how much time his younger brother and the lass had begun to steal away together, and just how close they had become. I think much of the appeal for his brother came from gleaning information about the more refined circles in which this family moved – though that wasn't saying much. None of this interested John, and he chose to spend his time walking alone down the cobbled streets and closes, imagining the lives playing out beyond each closed door.

On one such trip around the neighbourhood, he was making his way back to the house in the fresh lilac twilight of a spring evening, one of the most beautiful skies I've ever seen. He had picked up a stick and was hitting it along bricks and railings as he passed. As he turned a corner only a few minutes from home, he was brought round to the sight of his brother, holding up the long hair of the gentleman's lass, whispering into her ear as she stood against the wall.

As soon as they saw him, the two sprang apart, but the damage had been done. He knew he was intruding on an intimacy that was never intended to be observed. Though none of them had been doing anything indecent, he felt the need to look away and hurry past. To my knowledge, the siblings never spoke about this furtive moment, but I would catch John staring at me sometimes afore he would look away, red in the face, and I knew exactly what he was thinking. I didn't appreciate back then how kind he was to think of me as a friend, to welcome me into their small family.

Of course, the lass was me. We were young, but isn't the love of your youth the strongest fire, the inmost mark? That was the beginning of a love that settled deep roots into my heart, and it's kept its hold on me even to this day. I'm sure if we had met even a year or two older then the rules of the world would have kept us apart, but we were young enough to be led still by the strength of our emotions.

I remember the day we met, when my father brought me with him on business — I think to impress me with his authority — and Tam was helping his father with the horses. He was so self-assured, so strong and gentle at the same time. I remember the moment I realised he was a girl like me, only with short hair and his brother's clothes. It sent a shiver up my spine and I wanted to know how he got the fierceness to do a thing like that. It made me wonder what was possible in this world; it set me to thinking of all the *things I hadn't yet even dared to dream of. Tam saw something in me too. That was when he made me promise not to use his true name – he knew I understood. We fell into an easy friendship that was as passionate as it was simple.*

I always expected John to say something that day in the alley, to come thundering in with some protective – or outraged – advice as older siblings are wont to do. But he never raised it, and the only reason I can think for this is what happened in the following weeks within his own home.

Their father had always been a proud man, a trait he had passed on to his younger wain more than the elder, and though he was glad of the employment, it pained him to work in such close proximity to the city's wealthy, ferrying them in their finery to their business meetings and extravagant dinners. The anger he felt at the hand he had been dealt expressed itself more often than not in disdain towards their mother. His anger boiled beneath, and although he never became violent, his sneering arrogance towards her wore her down through the years until she became a shadow of the woman she might have been, speaking only when spoken to and responding in the softest of voices, as if second guessing her own opinions and needs. His pride could also not allow him to accept the unconventionality of his child's appearance and behaviour, but thankfully for Tam, his father chose to reckon with this through a feigned ignorance rather than a violent and bullying aggression.

The whole family seemed to operate on the premise that if an issue was never acknowledged, it might go away on its own, or at the least they would have to think about it as little as possible. So, when the day arrived that the children and their mother awoke to their father missing from the creaking bed, his clothes absent from their drawer and his always-gleaming coach missing from its post, they simply laid one less place for supper and never mentioned his name again.

I don't think Tam ever thought of their family as poor. He knew they weren't rich, at least not like the men and women with fine clothes and stately houses his father talked about, but there were plenty of people they passed in the street whom he knew to struggle far more than their family ever had. After their father left, the wains noticed this gap closing. Their mother tried her best, increasing the cleaning and sewing work she usually did to try and make up for the lost income, but the suddenness of her husband's absence shook her so that her health weakened dramatically and never fully recovered, and it was left up to John as the new head of the household to provide. He wasn't a stranger to work, and had been running messages for local grocers and merchants for years, but now he needed desperately to find solid, dependable employment.

While Tam helped their mother where he could with her meagre load of laundry and tailoring, John began his search. I think he still believed in the fantasies of his youth, and as serious as their situation had become, he was blithe on the chance to be the man of the family, to take care of his brother and earn his admiration. Their home down in Govan neigh-boured plenty of new factories, shipyards and ironworks. You may think of New York as the centre of the world, being a newspaper man, but those of us who know industry know Glasgow to be the world's front door. It was to the ironworks that John found himself drawn, fascinated by the heat and smell and clanking weight of the metal, and the strength of the men who tamed it. The only thing I could ever really do for that family was to get him that job, and I'm glad to have been able to do it, no matter what happened next.

I know when he started work that first day, he was both exhilarated and shaken by the sheer stink and din that hit him as he passed through the foundry doors. It was the only time I think Tam was really in awe of his older brother. The rhythmic pounding of machinery, gruff shouts of men making themselves heard above it, and blisteringly bright liquid iron hissing and sparking through the air took the boy's breath away. My father took me inside one of these places once, and I'll never forget it. It was a far cry from what John knew of work through his father's coach driving – he said this was a real profession, domesticating fire, forcing the earth's elements to bend to man's will.

The ironworks had five blast furnaces, and his role was to be one of the men supervising the steam hammer's pounding of ore dragged straight from the furnace, spilling molten metal onto the factory floor. At first, he could hardly stand the heat, the pouring sweat making his clothes stick to his back and his hair to his forehead in an instant. Soon, though, his full attention was drawn into the work of the hammer. It had to bring down its deafening pounding at just the right moment, flattening the ore, held in place by giant tongs, into one smooth

270

bar. It was the scale of the whole operation that impressed him most. He felt he was part of a modern world, one of international commerce and industry that left the pace of his grandparents' rural lives far behind. I remember the excitement of that time. The industrial world was coming into its mechanised maturity, while we all passed into adulthood alongside it, and one another.

John grew with the work, his soft nature hardening like the ore he came to see more than his own family, until soon he could imagine no other life than the ironworks, molten sparks flashing behind his closed eyes at night. He was never mean, not like his father, but his quietness changed from timidity to resignation. It wasn't that he was especially passionate about this job more than any other profession he might have stumbled into, but now he was the breadwinner for his household I believe he was driven by a keen responsibility for his mother and brother that before had been only a daydream.

The importance of his wee bit of earning was brought into focus by the decline of his mother's health. She had always been a frail woman, almost transparent beside his father's simmering, niggling temper, and since his disappearance had slowly been fading ever further into herself. Soon Tam – and even sometimes I – had to take on all their mother's work, not that this had ever amounted to much. Every day we'd plead with John not to work every night as well as day at the foundry. He couldn't be persuaded. The fantasy of responsibility from his youth had become a strong-held belief that only he was standing

271

between them and absolute poverty, and he may well have been right.

For all the hours he spent at the works, his skin blackening, lugs ringing, and eyes blurring from tiredness, his peedie income was barely enough to cover doctors' bills on top of their daily bread. For all our work and care, their mother had no strength left to resist the inevitable, and one night with a weeping Tam at her side she faded from this world with less than a whisper.

It was then that Tam and I became truly close. With his brother away at the factory day and night, we would spend as much time as we could together, me sneaking away from my lessons to bring what I could from the kitchen to their house. Tam confessed to me all his hopes of leaving the city, sailing away on one of the trading ships to another corner of the Earth.

I was as fascinated as I was frightened by the things he said, comfortable as I was in the city that had been my home my whole life. We lived in a fantasy that we could get married, even have wains of our own one day. We talked about it as a time far away, not the real life we were living, but I believe we hoped for those fantastical mirages so much that we thought we could will them into being. We were so young, and it was easier, more thrilling to live in our dreams than in the world around us.

But, for John, there was no time for dreaming. There was now one less mouth to feed, but he felt the weight of responsibility even more. Those parents were the only family the lads had known, and he was now presented with the sober duty of being all his brother had to rely on in the world. He'd confide in me when I came around in the early morn, Tam still asleep from his late-night sewing, John unable to sleep despite his exhaustion. I don't think he had anyone else to talk to, and though Tam saw how the work was changing him, he didn't recognise the depth of his brother's grief. As much as I wanted to help, I knew my father would never accept a friendship with this poor family, these two young fellows adrift and parentless, and I had to hide my relationship with Tam, for fear that my father should stop me from leaving the house entirely.

The brothers hardly saw each other in the home, only glimpsing traces that it was occupied by another person; some bread left out on the table or soot-streaked boots by the door. When Tam did catch his brother, he did his best to persuade him to take a day of rest, but it was to no avail. John was living in a world of hazy, noise-filled exhaustion, barely keeping track of the days and falling asleep where he stood regardless of the brutal din of the factory around him.

Then came that day, one like any other but one I remember after all these years as if it had just occurred. Our young minds could never have imagined what was to happen; how our three worlds could spin on a moment. We were so full of belief back then that we could control the great world around us, make it bend to our will in our youthful arrogance.

You never see these things coming. You only see them afterwards. That's another thing I've learned in this life.

I was with Tam at his place when there was this thundering at his door, knuckles chapping and Tam's name, his real name, *being called again and again. Whoever it was sounded desperate. "You in there?" the anxious voice shouted.*

Tam opened the door to one of the workers from the ironworks, and I recall the very words he said for they are burned into my mind like everything about that day. His chest was heaving as he tried to speak.

"Your brother. I've been sent to get you, to tell you, he was . . . There's been an accident. He wis in an accident, an' it's bad. I have to warn you it's bad. I was sent to get you. He's no' in good shape but he wants to see you. He keeps saying stuff, keeps saying yer name."

I saw Tam's face turn pale, like he'd been struck suddenly ill.

"Come down to the foundry, now," the man insisted, "ye have to come now!"

Tam looked at me, and I could see the terrible fear in his eyes. I saw what he was asking of me; that he needed me and wanted me to go with him.

I was thinking of my father, and began to tell him that as much as I'd like to, there was no way I could join him. But I stopped when I saw his face.

"I'm coming," I said. "We're leaving now."

So I went with Tam, though I knew it would only mean trouble for me later. All the way there, that poor man from the ironworks kept saying he was sorry. In the rush I never even learned his name. He just kept saying that word, not like it was his fault, but like it was the only word he could hold onto.

We were at the corner coming down to the foundry when he stopped for a moment and stared at the ground. "He wasn't even doing his ain work at the engine," he said, the words spilling out, like he was talking to no one, talking to God. "He was helping the planer. The damned planer. Ye know how helpful John is. Will, the planer, was getting him to hold the strap while he fixed it. And he was bent down lacing this thing and it came loose from his hand."

We knew from how he was saying it, the shake in his voice. Tam and I both knew it was going to be bad, more than bad. I felt this lump growing in my chest like it might explode out. My heart hammered as we walked and ran, then walked again, our breath ragged and hopeless.

From then the man couldn't stop talking, his words flooding out even as we ran. "I saw it happen. I looked over from the other side of the workshop and the way John was moving caught my eye. That thing where you see something and you know it's wrong. Ye see, his arm was all tangled up in the strap. I ran tae stop the engine because I could see he was getting pulled in, but I was too late . . . He went right in, got pulled right round by the shaft.

"I reversed the engine. And that released him. But I could see the blood. I'm sorry. There was only a wee space between the shaft and the joints of the floor above and he got dashed on them, again and again. Twenty times, I reckon. I can't stop seeing the look on his face. I came straight tae get you. They called for an ambulance but I'm no' sure he'll make it. Ahm so sorry. We didnae want to move him for fear of making it worse."

When we got to the foundry, John was lying on the floor right where the man said they left him, and you could see the *blood smeared across like a paint stroke leading from the machine to where he lay. The place was hot, still one man in the corner stoking the engine, a great towering metal cavern that glowed and shed an orange light around the hall.*

The others were crowded round John. Someone had bandaged him, but even under the layers of white, blotched with blood, you could see his arm had been half pulled off and how his chest twisted under him.

"They're here!" someone shouted.

From that distance, I could see how John turned his head a tiny fraction and tried to push up, but then sank back down. Tam was there in an instant, kneeling by his side, looking like he didn't know where to put any part of himself, his hands hovering as if they wanted to touch his brother but were too scared to.

He glanced round at me and I could see in his face a fear I'd never witnessed in him, or any other creature, before. It frightened me far more than the horror of John's injuries.

We heard a murmur. John was trying to say something, but I couldn't make it out. "Here," he said. Tam leaned in. I was standing right over him and I could just about hear what he said.

John spoke to Tam in a voice that was as firm as it was spent. You could see he had the fear of death in his dark eyes. "Listen, wee brother. You . . . The thing we feared . . . I'm done. I'm done. Look at me. I know it." His chest rose in a shuddering sob.

His jaw clenched and he growled. "And I've . . . I've been lying here thinking what will happen tae you. You know what we said. We said this before about what if something was tae happen to me. You already wear ma claithes. You ken what I'm saying."

Tam nodded. I could see he was biting back the rush of tears.

"Keep wearing them," his brother whispered. "Take it all. You'll be mair a man than I ever was."

"No!" Tam's voice broke as he threw himself down close, so his face was a mere inch from his brother's. "Yer no' going. Yer no'."

John shook his head, a minuscule movement. His brow creased and he let out a long sigh. His breath caught in his throat. "Call yourself John. Call yoursel' John Campbell. Take that money; make a life for yourself somewhere." He coughed and in the noise of it was something wet and wrong. But still he spoke. "Ye know it's right. Do it for me. Do it for yourself. It's what you want."

His voice was becoming tangled, the insistent presence of death blocking his throat, but I could just make out the words.

"I know you better than anyone, wee man. Even her. I know who you are. Tell me now. What is your name?"

"John. John Campbell." Tam was crying now and repeating the name, and I wasn't sure if he was calling his brother, or naming himself. "John. John . . . John . . ."

"Good," John said. "Good." His mouth moved as if he was about to say something else, but the words got overtaken by some shuddering force taking over his body, which turned all sound into an unearthly moan, and he twisted like a hellish puppet then sank back down on the cold stone floor, into silence.

I begged Tam to stay, of course. Cried and did just about all I could, but it wasn't any use. I'm ashamed to say I threatened to tell my father, to scare him into doing what I wanted – which was to attach himself to me and allow me to attach myself to him. But my Tam had too much spirit to listen to the wailings of a lassie too feart to join him. And so, I knew he would go, would leave me, this person my heart yearned for, this hard-set boy from the closes with the name of his dead brother.

I never forgot about him, the first lad I ever loved. I went on to have a life after him, had my own family and finally stood up to my father. We had a happy life, me and my husband, but you always wonder what might've been.

Two weeks after his brother's passing, John Campbell stepped out of the building he had known all his life for the last time. I can still see it now – I play it over in my head like a zoetrope. He plunges his hands deep into the pockets of a coat two sizes too big, making his way down the cobbled street and turning the corner, only once glancing back at a lass too frightened, too fixed in her allotted place in the world, to follow him beyond the end of the road.

A motorcar horn blared in the street, and light rain began to tap against my window. Unsure what to make of what I had just read, I decided to continue through the pages.

Dear Mr Ellis,

I received your letter asking what I can tell you about the person known as John Campbell and whether I have any information as to his whereabouts. Of that I can tell you nothing. He disappeared from our lives twenty years ago, some said on a boat to America, and I have heard nothing of him since.

I will tell you now, I have nothing bad to say about him. Johnnie was always good to us and ours, and whatever secrets he had never harmed no one, as far as I could ever tell.

I met him in the summer of '71, and he came to us from Tranent, where he had been working as a farm hand. My husband and I were not long married, and had just started taking in lodgers. I never did quite work out what brought him there, or to Renfrew for that matter. I suppose young lads at that age can tend to drift, and it seemed to me he was never much settled with us, though he treated us as family while he was under our roof.

Aye, he'd been working on that farm in Tranent and didn't make too much of it. He told me later that was one of the reasons he left Kirknewton too, that a town is all well and good for a few months but it doesn't keep you the way a city does. I've never felt that way myself – before we had to leave I'd never travelled much further than Glasgow, but you could see it was true for him. He had grown up in Glasgow with all those ships coming in from all over, and the possibility of them had left an impression on him.

279

He came to us about the same time as he started work as a labourer in the forge, and it was work that troubled him. He was paid enough for it – that's what brings most of the lads to those parts – but I think he'd had a brother who'd had an accident in the same kind of work. He'd not have admitted it, but he wasn't cut out for that kind of manual labour neither. He was strong enough, which is surprising given what's now come out, but his skills were in talking to folk and bringing them round to his point of view more than working with his hands.

It's true what folk say about him having a way with the lassies. I never knew him not to have one or two sweethearts calling round asking on him, and as he didn't talk much about what he'd done and where he'd been before he came to us, I wouldn't have been surprised if he hadn't left a few broken hearts along the way. All being said, he was a young lad, like any other, and I was happy to have him boarding with me. He paid his rent on time and was always polite and helpful enough, not like some of these fresh-faced lads who don't know how to boil an egg or darn a sock.

It was only a couple of months in when he started being seen around with young Kate Martin, and you could tell he was sweeter on her than he had been on any of the others. To begin with, he could be a bit of a skinflint with his wages, but he'd take Kate out to Edinburgh for the day, to see the castle and the botanical gardens. She was a pretty young thing – in fact, she reminded me of myself in my younger days – and she'd have married him if he'd asked, I know that much.

It was around the time that he started seeing Kate that he started drinking more, and coming home less and less. To begin with, it was to impress her, but soon enough he was down the Black Bull all hours with the rest of the lads from the forge, coming home with the sun and never minding the neighbours' tittle-tattle or the boss's anger the next day.

I missed him then, when he started acting just like the others. I had a soft spot for young Johnnie – I still do – and I think he was fond of me too. He wasn't so much younger than the other lads, but he felt it. He was such a skinny thing, wet around the ears, and gentler than the others. He'd help me round the house, chopping the vegetables and clearing up after tea. My favourite was of an evening when he'd sit with me by the fire and we'd have a good gossip while we fixed up my husband's and the other lads' work clothes.

He said he'd learned it from his mother, and that he was only doing it for the extra penny in his pocket, but I'm sure he loved those evenings as much as I did. He'd tell me news from the forge, and which lassie he was sweet on that week. He knew how to make me laugh, to tell a story, and he was sharp too – never missed a trick of who was going to get promoted or who was soon for the sack. That's how I'll remember him, whatever comes out. I'm an old woman now, older than most people thought I'd last, and with my husband long gone – but that lad left an impression, and I'll never forget him.

Even with what I know now, I don't think back on those times and see him as a woman. Sure enough, he was different from the other lads, softer and better versed in women's work, with a sweeter nature about him, but that doesn't make him a woman in my eyes. If it wasn't for doctors and the like telling me so, I still wouldn't believe it. It makes me think of all the other lads I've had come and go over the years, if any of them were the same. And it makes me think there's more on God's green earth than I'll ever understand.

All that's memory now. It was only a few months he was with us, really – but you can see how fond I was of him just from that. He came in the spring, met young Kate, and maybe things would have been different if the smallpox hadn't found us by winter. I'm sure I wouldn't have lived to this ripe old age if that young lad hadn't helped me as he did when I fell ill.

It started as it always does, with a fever. I was the first to catch it, God only knows who from, and I caught it the worst, too. As soon as the doctor saw me, he knew what it was. I wouldn't admit it at first, claiming it was influenza or just the winter cold – I suppose I was still young enough then to be vain about my face and not want to lose my looks. I had always felt pity for the older folk who walked around with the mark of the pox on them, skin puckered and wrinkling like a plucked hen. I don't mind it so much now – it's good to know sometimes that people take a liking to you for what you have to say, and not just what you look like with your mouth closed. Still, I'm more than old enough now to know that nobody looks at me like that anymore.

I got ill, and once there was no doubt about the cause, most of the lads cleared out. Nobody wants to risk sharing a house with a diseased woman, especially if she's the one cooking your tea and darning your socks. But whether it was pity, or friendship, or simply because he had nowhere else to go, our Johnnie stayed. He was like a real son to me then, nursing me as I got worse, even putting his work and his sweetheart to the side for me. If he hadn't been with me to call the doctor when things got worse, as I said before, I wouldn't be here telling you this now.

Not that my husband, nor young Kate, were best pleased. My old man couldn't understand why a lad with no relation to us should dote on me in my sickbed, nor put his own health at risk for a woman he'd met only a few months prior. He couldn't ask while I was ill, but I knew after that he suspected there had been something between us. He got mighty jealous, that man did. I thought at one point he would kick the lad out, but even he could see how much good it was doing me to have him around.

Kate understood it even less than him. She didn't see at all why he should put himself – and her – in danger of catching the pox for the sake of me, nor why he devoted himself so entirely to my recovery. I was grateful, and flattered of course, but I knew the truth. He'd had so much loss already, that lad, and he couldn't bear to lose someone else. While he was young it made him soft, but from what I've heard of your Murray Hall in America, I wonder if over the years that pain made him hard, indifferent to suffering. Maybe it's good I only knew him that short while.

It wasn't a long illness, but it was an intense one – within a couple of weeks I had lost all my strength and had the marks of the pox unmistakably upon me. But whether it was our Johnnie's care, or that the illness had burned too brightly and run its course, it left me as soon as it came. Then, like a seesaw, just as I was gaining back my strength, poor Johnnie started to show the signs.

It was inevitable. Most folk were amazed he hadn't caught it already. A few other folk in town had got ill, but it wasn't too bad, all in all. You hear stories of the red plague sweeping over big cities, killing a third of all the folk it touches. We were lucky that year that me and Johnnie were the worst cases.

We thought when he got ill that he'd be the same as me, that it would be hard but short. Well, it hit him hard all right – he could barely move for fever within a day of it starting – but he didn't get better. We did our best, even I tried to help him when I could while I was still recovering, but the doctor said he'd have to go to hospital. Even with his fever and being in and out of sleep, Johnnie knew enough of what we were saying to make it known that we were not to take him to hospital, not ever. Not even if he were dying.

But we weren't going to listen. Men can be funny that way, refusing to be treated even when they're on their last legs, and I assumed his fear of the hospital came from the time when his family had got sick and passed. Anyway, the doctor would never have allowed it. He'd sworn an oath and couldn't let a young lad die just because he was too stubborn to accept medical help.

Still, for kindness, Dr Allison waited as long as he could, then told the lad that hospital was no longer a request but a *demand. Despite his illness Johnnie had fought him with fire until then, but even he recognised that he was in no position anymore to argue. In a couple of weeks, he'd become a scarred shadow of the popular young lad from the forge, and even Miss Kate had stopped calling round for fear of the sight of him, claiming she didn't want to catch his awful sickness.*

When the doctor made his demand, Johnnie seemed to give up all the fight in him, hanging his head like a whipped dog and speaking in barely a whisper. He asked to talk to the doctor alone. I was worried, and a wee bit upset, for our illnesses and Johnnie's care had brought us even closer together, and I didn't think there was anything he could say to the doctor that he couldn't say to me.

The worst part of it all was that was the last I ever saw of him. I never even got to say my goodbyes. The doctor came out of the room after several minutes, closing the door behind him, and said that Johnnie was to be moved to Paisley hospital that afternoon, but that he wouldn't take any visitors. I have to admit I forgot myself, crying and shouting at the doctor. I thought the lad was dying, and I couldn't understand why he wouldn't see me.

Of course, once he'd been moved, the doctor told me the truth. Johnnie had admitted his true name and sex, but he'd wanted him to wait until he'd been moved to the infirmary to tell me. I suppose he was ashamed, and maybe scared of what I'd say to him. I wish now I could go back and tell him I didn't care, and I really didn't. Truly. A person has the right to secrets, and all I wanted was for my dear friend to be well. To live.

All that's in the past now. There was a wee bit of scandal about it in town afterwards, and it didn't help my husband's jealous attitude. I think the attention we got in the weeks after made it worse. But Johnnie had been well liked, and Kirknewton's not a big place — everyone knows everyone, so it was clear that no one had known the lad's secret save himself. Even Miss Kate was as shocked as any. At least she pretended to be . . .

When it all came back around later, and the police came knocking, folk were still all too happy to say what a good lad and worker he had been, no funny business at all. It's strange reading about all this Murray Hall gossip in the papers now, as if this is the first time something like this has happened. Sure, it's not usually these folk with money and status you hear about, but the papers are acting like it's the first time anyone's heard of such a thing. It takes all folk to make a world, that's what I will say.

I tried to go and visit Johnnie in the hospital a wee while later, once I was restored to health and that police business was over. I wanted to see if what the doctor had told me was true, and if he'd tell me to my face why he'd left without a goodbye. But I suppose, more than that, I just wanted to see him. He was such a lonely lad in some ways, making sure he got on with the lasses and joked with the lads so that everybody liked him. I think he was scared to be by himself. He'd seen that in me too, how even with my husband and all my boarders at home I was still alone so much of the time, cooking and cleaning and following everyone around with a broom and a threaded needle and a pan full of broth.

He'd been a good friend and a good nurse to me, and I wanted to thank him. But by the time I made it over to Paisley he had disappeared; I believe he'd set off on a ship to New York. I couldn't tell you if young Kate went with him. She'd left Kirknewton a few weeks before, at the height of all the gossip. No one blamed her, and things would've settled down again eventually, but I think just knowing when she walked down the street that folk were whispering how she'd been courting a woman was too much for her and she vanished, no one knew where.

I often think about Johnnie and hope he made a good life. He was a smart lad, and kind in his bones, and he deserved happiness in the end.

Sincerely,
Mrs Early

Dear Mr Ellis,

You're not the first to ask me about wee Johnnie Campbell, and every time somebody does it takes me right back to my youth. In all honesty, I never thought I'd outlive him. In those days it was me who could drink Johnnie under the table, though I hear he embraced his Celtic roots in his years across the water, and I know it wasn't the drink that got him in the end. We were both lads then, even if we did think ourselves worldly men. I would've liked to see him again, but such is life – and I'm not sure either of us would have lived up to an old man's rose-hued memories.

I first met John in my hometown of Kirknewton, and I suppose I could sense he was a bit of a lost soul. I had a younger brother around his age who was off at school in Edinburgh, and, while he wasn't far, I missed having a man around who looked to me for guidance. I had a wife and two young lassies at home, and I was feeling in need of a little male company.

I was one of the first people John met in Kirknewton, and I reckon if he hadn't met me he might well have drifted on to the next town. He had no direction back then; he was floating from place to place looking for work without much of anything to tie him to one or the other. Kirknewton was as good as anyplace. He had come east from Glasgow, and it was a sad story, what I could get out of him. He'd lost his whole family one by one to illness, though I pieced together that there might've been a shabby, feckless father still around somewhere. He was a smart and capable young lad, but in those early days I got the impression he was waiting for life to reveal itself to him, often with apprehension.

I helped him find a job, and a modest place to live, and before long we were spending every Friday night together down at the pub, and many weeknights too when I could get away. My wife was fond of him, and it felt at times as though he were another child at the table, waiting for his supper to be served him.

He'd dote on my wife, though I never felt there was any threat – he seemed to want her to mother him as much as she did. I think it helped both she and me in a way, as we were both new to parenthood and struggling a little to find our feet. When you have a new wain, people tell you natural instincts take over, at least for the women, and you just know how to be. Well, we were happy to be parents and loved our wee lassies to pieces, but I can't say we were naturals. It took pains for us to settle in to a life that felt it no longer belonged to us, where our lives with other adults for company, doing as we pleased, gave way to early bedtimes and warm milk.

My wife found it especially hard, though she was the last of many of her cousins and friends to have a child. I think she felt guilty to be missing aspects of her old life, and felt she couldn't complain to the women around her who saw child-rearing as God's greatest gift – and the lack of children as a curse. Anyway, Johnnie's appearance helped us both feel a little more confident in our maternal and paternal roles respectively, and it didn't hurt a bit that he was great with the wee ones himself.

Having another adult in the house, albeit a bit of a rough-housing lad who was scarcely out of shorts himself, made us feel less alone on our domestic island. He was a welcome addition to our lives, and soon became part of the furniture.

I wondered if it was seeing myself and my charming wife finally settle into marital bliss that set the boy's sights on Miss Mary Ann. It's funny to me now to think that his coming into our home was the very thing that finally gave us the sense of *being a proper family, as I'm sure to him it seemed it had always been thus. Spending time with us and our young wains soon had him making noises of marriage, much to the mirth of many of the lads down the pub, who were more likely to run across the fields in the opposite direction should their sweethearts start suggesting matrimony.*

As much as I wanted to support these instincts in the lad, and believed that marriage could help counter the stray-dog quality that hung about him, I was wary of Mary Ann. She was known about the town as a wayward girl, having had two bastard wains already, with another on the way. I didn't want the boy to be burdened with some other man's mistake, nor to be taken advantage of by a girl with few prospects ahead of her, but he took no heed of my warnings.

Indeed, it seemed to me that the points which repelled me from considering the lass as a suitable choice for Johnnie only seemed to draw him closer to her. I suppose knowing the truth now it all makes more sense. Claiming the children for his own could only strengthen his own disguise, and he needed a woman who was in need of him too, and would not expose him once she learned the truth. This, it turned out, was a chronic miscalculation on his part.

I believe the two met at a local dance, but there wasn't much else that was usual about the courtship. Many Ann herself was without parents, or else they had disowned her – either way, she had only an uncle to oversee her affairs, and he didn't take much interest, I believe out of embarrassment at her position. So, the two were pretty much left to their own devices from the beginning, save for myself and my wife doing our best to give our advice.

I do believe he loved her – however opportunistic the pairing may have been. I think the two came together out of necessity, but found something within the other that each could understand. Both were outcasts in their own way – Johnnie more than I could know at the time – and both were young and without family in an oftentimes hostile world that was changing so fast.

John was full of big ideas at that time, and that's how I'll always remember him. From the sounds of it, he never lost that sense of wonder at the world, that desire to travel and become someone of influence. He filled that young lassie's head with promises of making a fresh go of it in the Americas, of raising their children to be pioneers of the New World. She must have known it was all hot air from the beginning, but I'm sure she wanted to believe it as much as he did. I'm glad he did make it in the end. If anyone were going to, I would've put my money on our John.

As things go, the two were married in a small ceremony by the Reverend Henry Smith, with just myself, the children and the reluctant uncle present to see the couple off. Still, it was a jovial affair, and even I had come round to the idea of the marriage, seeing as I could the unstoppable infatuation of youth.

Johnnie moved into Mary Ann's tiny rooms on the outskirts of town, promising that they would be off and away within a few months. For those first weeks we saw little of him, lost as he was to his new life, flung into husbandry and fatherhood.

It didn't take long, however, for the intensity of their relationship to turn sour, and soon he was turning up on our doorstep, cursing the girl's name when just a few days before he had been singing her praises.

I tried my best to dissuade him, being as I am a God-fearing man and a believer in the sanctity of marriage. Whatever he thought of her now, I told him, he had made that promise not just to her and her wains but to God – and to make light of that promise was to turn your back on God's will. It has always been to my dismay that Jonnie had never been the religious type, and my guidance did little to calm his mind or his temper.

My wife took a different tack, appealing to his love of the children and asking him to make it right with the woman, if only for their sake. This made more of an impression on him, and to his credit, I do believe he did his best to support her and act as head of their hectic household. I couldn't tell you what really went on between the two, but I can say with fair certainty that by the end it was little surprise to anyone in the town to hear that Johnnie had packed a bag and left in the night, with no sign of returning.

For Mary-Ann's sake, I made some half-hearted efforts to track him down, but I had always known that drifting was more natural to him than staying put, and that if he didn't wish to be found then there was no hope of my finding him. We all thought, I suspect, that would be the end of it – another unfortunate chapter in Mary Ann's chaotic life so far. We were a small community, and though most of us disapproved of the choices she was making for her life, we supported her as best we could with the occasional cut of meat, or half-loaf of bread, perhaps a worn blanket or a cast-off dress for a child.

That, as it turns out, was not the end of the tale. Mary Ann, far from accepting her lot and getting on with the business of childbearing and rearing, became increasingly hysterical at Johnnie's absence. I don't know if it was the last in a long line of let-downs that finally brought the madness out of her, or the fact that he had promised her so much and then snatched it away, or just that she really did love him, and she was inconsolable from his mysterious, some might say cruel, departure.

We took it as only natural in response to the situation, but as the days went on she started to make those of us who had been trying to comfort her all the more uneasy. She began talking about his "secret", saying that if we knew the truth about him we wouldn't judge her so. I must admit, at the time I thought it was the malice of a slighted, discarded woman that made her say such things. I wish I had taken more stock of her ramblings, and treated her with more kindness.

Sensing that she would get nothing more than sympathetic pity from us, she took her case to the local policeman, to whom she was already well known. She told him of her abandonment, of which he was aware, and then made her claim. She said that her absent husband, Mr John Campbell, was actually no such thing – that he was a woman, and that he had lied to her in order to get her to marry him.

Perhaps if she hadn't been such a character in the town, perhaps if she hadn't been so hysterical, and so heavy with *child – perhaps then her words may have been taken more seriously. Perhaps not. As it was, the policeman asked her a few teasing questions about how she could have possibly not known that her husband was a woman, and why she would not have brought such news forward sooner. When she sensed that the man did not believe her, she began to push her case more firmly, and he saw that he would have to bring her to the station.*

He tried to dissuade her, but she was adamant. Of course, anyone who knew Johnnie couldn't believe a word of it, and as soon as the official statement was made, it was ruled that she was a wayward woman who was lying to save her own reputation. This was the last lick of indignity that Mary Ann could take, and she gathered her unruly little family about her and left to stay with cousins in Arbroath.

I thought that would be the last time my path would cross with wee Johnnie's, and I went back to my ordinary, homely life. I thought of him sometimes and wondered where he could be – if he had made it to America, if he was still drifting from town to town. As the months went on, I thought of him less and less, and so it was a shock when all of a sudden I was summoned to Paisley under shrouded circumstances, being told only that I was to be reunited with my old friend. Strangest of all, Mary Ann – who had since returned to our small town, her new babe cradled against her chest – was to accompany me.

Ordinarily I might not have gone, sensing trouble or trickery, but I had grown so fond of the lad and was keen to see what had become of him. Mary Ann's claims did not even enter my mind, save perhaps as a humorous anecdote to tell John. The policeman who had come to fetch me was a stoic type, married to his work and would not give me even a hint of what we were to be summoned for.

As the journey passed, I began to grow uneasy at the thought that the boy had got into some kind of trouble with the law, and had thrown me in to save his own skin. I did not like to think of my friends in this way, but there was a wildness that sometimes came out of John. It was a Godless edge to his character that made him popular with the lads and lassies alike, but it was also the thing that left me unsurprised at his sudden departure, and that felt not wholly surprising about my summoning now. Mary Ann's presence puzzled me most of all, and I could not come up with any reason why he should want to see her again, except perhaps a dramatic change of heart.

Still, I did my best to cast these thoughts from my mind and looked forward to being reunited with my old pal. My daughters had grown up much since he had last been through my door, and I anticipated his questions about whether they were now walking and talking, and felt proud to tell him. I wondered if he had settled down again, found a nice sensible girl this time with whom he could raise his own children, not some other man's. Mary Ann said very little on the journey, and wore a curious expression on her face – one almost of smugness, though at the time I couldn't understand why. These myriad thoughts occupied my mind enough that the journey to Paisley flew by, and presently we arrived.

We drew up to a hospital, and my heart sank. What if Johnnie was gravely ill, with no one in the world save us – his abandoned wife and old drinking partner? What if he had summoned me to share his final words? I cursed myself for not taking greater pains to look for the lad after his departure, for assuming that he could fend for himself when he was just a child still, and one without friend nor family save myself. I composed myself, and followed the silent policeman inside.

Upon entry, I was asked by a nurse whether I had been inoculated against smallpox. My heart sank further as I told her that I had. So, this was to be his end, I thought. A zesty young thing, the last survivor of his family's ill fate, struck down by this most common of diseases. Perhaps he was blind, I wondered, or suffering from that most horrendous strain that causes the carrier to bleed to death before pustules even form. I wondered how long he had left.

I was led down several winding hallways, past doors that opened in on sorry-looking folk, to a private room at the end of a corridor. The door was opened for me by a nurse in starched uniform, and sitting up in bed, bright-eyed but pock-faced, was Johnnie. He nearly jumped out of bed when he saw me, exclaiming, "Is that you Will Waddell; how's the wife and bairns?"

After my initial shock at seeing my friend not on death's door, but in full recovery from a mild case of smallpox, my relief turned to confusion. What in the devil had I been brought all this way for? I did not have to wait long for an answer. As Mary Ann entered the room behind me, John's face turned pale in an instant. She stood there for a moment triumphant, before unleashing a barrel of curses upon him that I do not wish to repeat, and fairly lunging for the lad. It was good the policeman was there to stop her, or I believe she would have sent him to the grave I had earlier anticipated for him.

I shall spare you the details, as this account has gone on long enough, and I'm sure you can guess what occurred. Johnnie had contracted smallpox, but his unwillingness to admit himself to hospital had aroused suspicion. One thing led to another, and his true sex was exposed. The authorities somehow got wind of Mary Ann's previous account, and we were summoned, as wife and marriage witness, to confirm the identity of the man–woman.

Mary Ann returned to Kirknewton victorious, and I'm sure it was her doing that half the town knew of this sensational story before I had even made my way home. I stayed on a few days, to answer the policeman's questions, but mainly to make sure that Johnnie would be all right. There had never been such a case in the parish before, and I suspect no one knew what to do with him.

I believe it was his young age, his sickness and lack of family, along with a few of my persuasive words and equally persuasive coins, that saved him from jail. Instead, he was served the unusual sentence of working in the hospital to which he had been admitted, which seemed to suit him well enough.

I must admit, though I did my best for the lad I could not look at him the same once the truth was out. He tried to ask again about my wife and wains, to retrieve some of our old familiarity, but in truth my heart was chilled towards him and I could not look at him without thinking of deception; deception of me, my family and home; of the world, and of God. I wished the lad well, and meant it, but I could not stay there any longer, and that was the last time I saw young John Campbell.

I heard after a few weeks that he had fled his post at the hospital, and it left me entirely unsurprised. If there was ever a soul meant to wander, it was Johnnie – and I hope he found some joy, wherever his wanderings took him.

Though I'm glad to have known him, I could never shake the feeling that he stirred up in me of uncertainty. I felt, ever since saying my farewells to him, that there are unknowable things in this world, things of which I am glad to be ignorant.

By the time I finished reading and re-reading the letters, the sky had darkened, and the streetlamp had cast a pool of white on the snow-covered road outside. The scene below was motionless, save for one man shovelling gleaming slabs off his steps. Though I could feel the biting chill stealing through my window, I felt the urge to go outside and clear my head.

I buttoned the fur collar onto my coat, pulled on my beaver hat, and slipped my feet into my Balmorals. It felt, as I walked out, like emerging into another world, so very different from the one inside my head of a foundry an ocean away in another city, red hot and clanking, but connected by a vastness of water.

Impossible, I thought, that the two might match up, be brought together by the trajectory of a single person's life.

And yet, in that moment, I felt how New York was just the scene for such a rebirth, where the poor young Scotsman could reinvent himself once again, could pursue childish dreams into reality.

There were few people out on the streets, it being such a cold night. One desolate family trudged along the sidewalk, a mother and two children, unshod, feet wrapped in bandages of rag. The smallest trailed behind, whimpering. The woman turned and spoke softly to her child, her accent guttural and Slavic.

I imagined, as I traipsed the sidewalk in my own warm boots, arriving in this city for the first time from another country, an experience I had never fully known, but one familiar to so many.

Before long, I found myself once again on Sixth Avenue. The street itself was dark and deadened, little noise or light emerging from the buildings which lined it. A solitary glow emerged from the store only a couple of doors down from the employment agency; Meyer's Tobacconists. I wandered over and watched for a moment through the window, the figure of a young man, his leather-gloved hands boxing cigars. He wore a thick woollen hat, pulled down low over his brow.

The bell rang as I entered.

"Good evening, sir," he said without looking up.

"Chilly night."

"Yes, reckon I'll be closing up soon," he replied, glancing from under the fold of his hat, face alabaster white, but for the pinked tip of his nose. Behind him, shelves of coloured box labels glowed in the electric light. "I was going to stay open for the saloon crowd, but it's just too cold."

"I've a friend who used to come in here," I said. "Murray Hall. You knew him?"

"Of course," he said with a wry smile. "I knew Murray. We all of us did. Back in his days at the court, a morning didn't pass when he didn't pass here on his way home, gossiping. Muti knew him very well."

My gaze drifted over the rows of single cigars in a rack between us, like giant brown moth pupae.

"Do you remember what cigar Murray smoked?" I asked.

"Sure. He had a few he liked. Murray was a cheapskate. Didn't like to spend too much, and back in the day he was fond o' the cheapest tenement-scrolled cigars. Said, 'How else are those weans going to get fed?' More recently he would get Lichtensteins rolled down in the Bowery." He gestured to a row of boxes to his right, printed with the profile of a man with a gun and red whiskers, and topped by a card marked $1. "And he liked the five-cent Henry George. He said they were good for liver regulation. But when he had a few extra cents, he'd treat himself."

He pulled a box down from the shelf. "Rose O'Cuba. I recall him buying these a couple of times. You ever tried one?"

"No."

"To my mind they're almost as good as a Partagas. Woody and a touch peppery."

"Rose O'Cuba," I repeated. "How much for a box of those?"

"Depends how many you're after?" he said, turning round to check again the shelves behind. His gloved fingers walked up the boxes.

"What's your smallest?"

"Ten," he said, and then he smiled as if he understood my hesitation. His breath hung like a nimbus in the air. It looked like smoke, but I could tell it was just the chill. "Or, if you want, I can do a single. Twelve cents. But they're cheaper by the box. Works out more like ten cents each."

"I think I'll take a single Rose O'Cuba, and maybe a Henry George?"

"Of course. The Rose is strong and a trifle woody. If you're not a regular smoker, you might find it a bit heady. Take it easy. Small puffs. It's not a cigar for a novice."

I took the Rose O'Cuba from his gloved hand. It felt in that moment as if I was handling something illicit, of which my father would have disapproved. Finger thick and tapered at the end, I could smell its leafiness through its wrapper. "Thank you, sir," I said. "I will be careful."

PART III

MEYER'S TOBACCONISTS, SIXTH AVENUE
12TH SEPTEMBER 1898, 4.30 P.M.

THE CIGAR SHOP BELL RANG softly as its door was pushed open, the stale, familiar air of the shop reaching the man's nose in an instant. The man, usually a head or two shorter than those around him, appeared even smaller than usual. He was bent almost double on his blackthorn stick and seemed to be moving with great effort, though no words left his lips. There were no other customers within, and the only sound was the slow thump and drag of the cane as he drew himself towards the counter.

"Good afternoon, Mr Hall." The cigar man smiled. He knew better than to offer his help. "Lovely weather these past few days."

"Hmmph." It was unclear whether this came as an unwillingness to converse or as a result of the man's efforts to stay upright.

"I'll have a box of Flor de Leon, Frank, and a two-cent stamp." The old man leaned heavily on his stick but his eyes were as sharp as tacks, staring out from under his black derby hat. The cigar man wondered, as he often did, if he didn't get hot in those heavy clothes, which seemed to be his uniform all year.

"Helping out Uncle Sam again this week, Mr Hall?"

"Aye, that's it. It's for my sweetheart." His eyes were shining now and he let out a chuckle, slipping a white envelope onto the table. It bore a San Francisco address, the same as every week.

The cigar man was turning to reach for the box when the bell that hung above the shop door rang out once more, and the fiery sun shone briefly into the dim building. A young woman entered, looking around with a worried look on her splotchy, fretful face as though she expected to be shouted out at any moment. Her lank hair and stained clothes made Hall's worn overcoat look pristine.

"Please, sir." She had spotted Hall at the counter. "Please spare a few cents, sir, just a few cents so I can get some food and a bed for the night. Anything you can spare, sir." The words rushed out of her before she could be interrupted, and their flat delivery gave a sense that this was a script that had been performed many times before. Her eyes were searching as she begged, but it felt more like she was speaking to herself than to either of the men in front of her.

As soon as he heard her voice, the cigar man whipped around.

"You must leave, miss." His tone was low and firm. "You can't do that here. I don't want any trouble, but you've got to leave."

"It's all right, Frank." Shining eyes looked up at the hapless creature in front of them. "What's your name, lass?"

"Evie." The voice was dulled. It seemed she would have accepted any response from the men in the same way, with a passive acceptance.

"I'll tell ye what, Evie. I don't like to see pretty young ladies like yourself wasting away on the streets. But I don't do charity

306

either. What I can offer you is a chance at some real employment, a decent way to earn a living. It'll be nothing unsavoury, simply respectable waitressing or domestic help of some sort. I run an employment agency two doors down from here. Call in tomorrow morning and ask for me – Murray Hall – and I'll make sure we sort you something out. How does that sound?"

The woman blinked, coming fully into the room for the first time. She seemed uncertain of how to respond, and of whether she could trust this strange old man.

The cigar man sensed her unease. "Mr Hall is offering you a very fine thing here, young woman. You'd do best to accept his offer."

'Thank you, Mr Hall." Her voice was smaller this time, less rehearsed. "I'll be there." She paused for a moment, still uncertain at this turn of events, but catching the cigar man's expression soon turned to leave before she outstayed her welcome further.

"Good lass. I'll see you first thing." Hall smiled broadly, genuinely at her, then winced at something unseen.

"That was a kindness, Mr Hall. There are so many young women like that these days they seem to merge into the very scenery of the city, unfortunate as that may be."

"Och, it's only business."

Hall winked as he placed the money on the counter and drew down his cigars. The cigar man didn't need to count it – it was always exact.

"Until next week, Mr Hall," he called as the cramped figure began its slow return to the door.

THE CLAIRVOYANT'S, 146 SIXTH AVENUE
8TH FEBRUARY 1901, 5 P.M.

PPROACHING THE CORNER OF SIXTH and Tenth,
I pulled from my pocket the leathery log of the Rose
O'Cuba and took a long sniff, taking in its scent of
oak and must, the sharp whiff of woodpile that threw me back
to my childhood in Wayne County. My morning job of refilling
the firewood basket from the splintery log stack; beetles scut-
tling through the shadows of my mind.

I felt in my pocket for the small box of matches I had been
carrying, nicked off the cigar end and lit it in the damp
afternoon air; only the fifth or sixth cigar I had ever smoked
in my life.

The drag filled my mouth with a cloud of bitter spice, as if
my tongue were being seared by cracked pepper. For a moment
it made me gag. But, as I spat the smoke and spittle out onto
the damp sidewalk, I tasted something else – a hint of sweet-
ness. I detected caramelised nuts. The flavour, like a cloud of
scorched sugar from a street vendor, made me want to press
the cigar head once more to my mouth and draw again. I closed
my eyes and pressed my lips around it. *Black walnut*, I thought.
The smoke rolled around inside my cheeks, raking at my tongue.

It felt, for a moment, as if I was drawing in Murray's air; his breath. I tasted the flavour of his life. On this street, on this corner, leaning into the brownstone wall, it seemed to me I could be him; his tongue, his mouth and his welcome relief at the smoke filling his lungs, filtering into his blood.

I was still reeling from this extraordinary moment, my mouth still harbouring the faint taste of woodpile, as I approached the door to the clairvoyant's apartments at 146 Sixth Avenue. "Mr Clellan," the old dame said as she arrived at the door. "It is a surprise to see you here. And a delight . . . But . . . I'm sorry to say I already have a guest."

"I was passing along the street, and I felt compelled . . . you see, I have something I've been wanting to ask you. I can come back another time."

Mrs Porter smoothed her hair, aware perhaps only now that she was somewhat unkempt. "No, no . . . I'm sure my guest would not mind. It's only an old friend. Not a client. Please, do come in. You will have to forgive me. I am in some slight disarray. Please come in."

A frizz of fiery tresses led me through the hallway to her half-lit rooms, which seemed, although now seen in daylight, all the more like a darkened cave, to the reading rooms, where the table was now scattered with scraps of paper and crumpled bills. A tiny, wiry woman was sat in the armchair by the window.

"I believe you have met before," Mrs Porter said, gesturing to her.

"We have?" I asked doubtfully.

A smile of mischief wrinkled across her face, and I thought for a second I saw an expression I recognised. The woman was familiar, with deep lines criss-crossing her face and eyes like wet pebbles. She nodded, her sharp gaze assessing me.

"Down in the street," she said. "You were there one o' those days after Murray passed. Ah remember you. You were standing beneath the tracks for some time before you came over, listening in to our stories ... Did you get what you wanted?"

"Oh!" My face flushed, realising that I had not been as inconspicuous in my lurking as I had thought. As I studied her face, I saw it was the very same as had rolled its eyes and shrieked on that first night out in the street. She had been so wrapped in shawls that all I had seen were those eyes and her smirk.

"Mary. Mary McBride," she said. "Ah could have told you some story. Ah could've told you that, if you'd asked. Ah knew what Murray was. But ah knew more than that. There was more ah could've told."

"Yes, Mary McBride."

"But you did not come here to see me. 'Tis my friend, Agatha, you came for. Ah'll leave. You'll want your privacy."

"No, no. Stay. I am interested to hear what you have to say. I don't want to miss your story again."

"As you should be. But first, go about yo' business."

"Mrs Porter. There is something I would like to ask you. I am willing to pay, of course," I said, pulling my wallet from

311

the inside pocket of my jacket. "Did Murray ever use the name of John Campbell? So far as you remember?"

The old clairvoyant pulled out a chair and gestured for me to take a seat. Her friend, in the corner, made a faint mumbling sound, but Mrs Porter seemed not to register it.

"No," she said. "I never heard mention of that name. Did you, Mary?"

"Never," Mary replied firmly.

"Or," I went on, placing a dollar note on the table, "of his life in somewhere called Govan or Glasgow?"

"I hear what you are saying, Mr Clellan. I do get the news-papers and I have read your stories. But what this Mrs Canning said was all new to me. I don't credit it much."

"Nor me," the voice from the corner interjected.

Mrs Porter began gathering the sheets of paper, letters and bills together into a pile, in order to clear some space on the table in front of me. "Dear, oh dear. Look at this mess."

"I wonder if I might avail of one of your services."

"One of my services? Well, of course, of course. I would be very glad to oblige. What is it you would like?" With a sweeping, arching movement, she gestured towards the tools of her arts, arranged like decorative trinkets in the cabinet nearby. "Tarot, crystal ball, tea leaves, a communication with someone passed . . . I sense you have matters unfinished with your father."

I shook my head. "Communication with the dead, yes. But not my father." I paused for a moment and looked directly into her pale, squinting eyes. "I wonder if you could attempt, as it

312

were, to speak with John Campbell. It is just a little idea. I thought it might settle a niggling question in my mind."

I found myself ridiculous even as I said it. I could almost see my father's face, his neat grey beard and furrowed brow, twisting and contorting in consternation at the choices I was continuing to make, moving further and further from his dogmas.

"Mr Clellan!" Mrs Porter exclaimed with glee, pressing her jewelled fingers together. "And I thought you were not a believer. Well, of course, yes, yes, yes, and you will understand that such communications are only possible for a professional like myself, one of the highest capabilities, but even then, should the spirit wish to remain silent, there is nothing we can do. The dead don't always speak. It is quite up to them." She looked at me, her expression businesslike. "I charge a fee of two dollars for the call out to the dead, and a further dollar if the attempt is successful. Are you happy with the fee?"

She spoke quickly now, pulling up a chair and leaning in towards me as if keen to settle a deal.

"I am," I said.

Another of those disconcerting noises from the corner. I was uncertain if it was a wheeze or a chuckle.

"Very well," said Mrs Porter. "And it is John Campbell you wish me to ask for, not Murray Hall?"

"That is precisely right."

"As you wish. We are fortunate that the person you believe to be John Campbell was a resident of this block, so we can attempt to call him without any need for a personal object."

"Her," said Mary McBride. "She was a her."

"Please, Mary. As I have always said, we are all of us part of the universal, all of us embodiments of the divine, which is entirely complete in its duality. Freed from the body, the dead, as monads, can be more purely themselves. Neither male, nor female."

Mary snorted.

"Mr Clellan, perhaps you would like us to proceed in private?"

"I do not mind," I said, staring at the old woman, whose face was fixed in a broad, unambiguous smirk, "if Mary stays. It makes little difference to me. Would you like to stay?"

"I can always be convinced by diverting entertainment!"

Though the light was already low in the room, Mrs Porter reached up to turn the gas lamp down still further. Mary McBride, her face shadowed, gestured a brief sign of the cross, her pale fingers dotting across her chest.

The clairvoyant paused for a moment and lit a match. A dancing orange glow flickered across her cheeks. I saw now that there was a candle placed towards her end of the table. She bent forward to light it, speaking as she did so: "The dead still live in these buildings. I hear them. I listen to them. Not all of them stay, but some of them choose to. John Campbell, we would like to hear from you. If you are there, John Campbell, give us a sign. John Campbell, are you there? Are you there? Speak to us now. What is it you want to say?"

The silence in the room was such that I could hear the breath of the woman next to the window, and outside, the rumble of the distant El train.

"John Campbell, are you there?" Mrs Porter repeated.

I looked around at Mary's silhouetted hair, and then back to Mrs Porter, whose eyes were closed, the fingers of her two hands linked as they rested on the table. She breathed in, deeply and loudly, then let out a sharp breath. "Are you there?" she murmured.

Her head was now swaying from side to side, and she was humming gently. This hum, an expressive, high-pitched vibration seemed to go on for almost a minute, before she stopped, and shook her head. "Would you like, Mr Clellan, to ask for the spirit under a different name, the name he was known as here? I believe it would be more likely you would receive a response."

"No. It is John Campbell I wish to speak with."

"Very well," she said, her voice an irascible snap. But, at that moment, she was distracted, her gaze caught by something beyond me, at the end of the table.

"John ... Johnnie, are you here?"

She gazed at me for a moment, as if looking for direction or advice.

"Murray, are you here? Mary, are you here?"

There was a sudden snort from my right and I turned towards Mary McBride, whose eyes rolled upwards into her brows. At first, I thought perhaps she had gone into some trance-like fit, but then I realised, as her eyes levelled on Mrs Porter, that the expression was in fact one of boredom or ridicule. "Goddamn it, Agatha, do we have to go on like this? Murray is long gone and not coming back to speak to any of us!"

"Mary!" Mrs Porter retorted, her eyes swimming fiercely towards the woman.

"And why should she?"

The woman stood up, her chair squeaking on the floor, and she moved as if to leave. "Ah'm not saying that spirits don't talk, but ah just think this one never will and all of you that are wanting her to might as well give up."

"Please, Mary, sit down."

There was a tap on my arm and Mary was at my side, dark haired with bright streaks of white; how oddly like a bad-tempered, cynical badger, I thought. She spoke urgently, her hand clutching at my wrist. "You won't convince me Murray was this John Campbell. No chance, given all the stories she told."

"What makes you think so?" I asked, shaking my wrist free of her grasp.

"I was one o' the few who knew he was a woman. I've known Murray Hall as long as anyone has in this city, first having met her a quarter-century back when I was arrested. I was drunk and making a racket, so they said. Disorderly was what it was called. Though that's not how I remember it. Me, disorderly?" She snorted again, indignant even now.

"Sit down, Mary," said Mrs Porter. "Will you please sit down?"

But the badger kept standing there, her arms folded. "Mr Hall gave me bail and not long after I ended up livin' and workin' in the family home and that's when I worked it out. I said to her one day, 'I know what you are!' Gave her quite a fright. An' I'll tell you what's more, she confessed to it.

"And I understand why she did it. See, what you don't know, sir, being a man, is the brutal ways women get treated by some men, the ways they get used and treated, like little more than glass ornaments to be broken and then stuck back together and then broken again. I'm not sayin' you, sir. But you can see why a girl might think the best way to duck that whole sorry catastrophe might be to set up in life as a man! I believe Murray must have been one o' those girls who in childhood was badly – wrongly – served by men."

"As," I interjected, astonished by this outpouring, "was John Campbell."

Mrs Porter, who was stunned into a momentary silence, piped up in her loud, declarative voice. "Also, very sensible in terms of security and property ownership – and, as we well know, such things are not yet accessible for many women."

"Sure," said Mary in a dismissive tone. "An' Murray was good in business . . . I'm a watcher, see. I learn things an' I watch an' I talk, an' other folk talk to me. We got onto all kinds of things – and what he said made me think that she'd had a baby. Her own, probably now a woman, and that she lives out west." She smiled, as if pleased with some sort of triumph.

"A baby that Murray Hall herself gave birth to?" I asked.

Her fixed smile became unreadable. "Now tell me," she went on, "if Murray was this John Campbell, how he also managed to have a wife and a baby, most likely out west, before she came to be married to Celia? I don't believe it. And neither should you, sir. I thought you reporters were interested in the truth, not made-up stories as you get in establishments like this, places that thrive on fabrication an' bamboozlement."

"Mary!" Mrs Porter cried again, though I couldn't discern how much sincerity there was in her shock.

"Oh, Mrs P, my dear," Mary McBride countered. "I'm just saying the truth as I see it."

Mrs Porter rose from her chair in sudden affront. "You come here, you sit and have tea with me twice a week, and this is what you think of my profession?"

Mary shrugged. "I like your company, Mrs P, but that doesn't mean I like your business."

I started to back away, aware that there was a yawning chasm of difference to be settled between these two women and that such a settling was not going to happen fast.

"You listen to my stories. You drink my rum!"

"An' ah tell some good ones myself," countered Mary, "which are no doubt of use to you in your *profession*."

The women were now standing nose to chin, squaring up at each other like two silverback gorillas, the smaller one standing on her tiptoes to give her extra height.

"The two dollars is there, on the table," I said, pointing to the crumpled bills lying on the glinting mahogany. "I apologise for any trouble caused! My sincere respects to you both." Then I crossed the room, almost tripping over an upholstered foot-stool in the half-light and slipped out of the door, glad to escape the rising snarl of those two women.

MANHATTAN POLICE HEADQUARTERS, MULBERRY STREET

14TH FEBRUARY 1901, 11 A.M.

*I*THOUGHT YOU REPORTERS WERE INTERESTED *in the truth.* The words of Mary McBride turned over again and again in my mind as I attempted to focus on my work that week. Truth? It seemed truth was rarely easy to grasp, always slipping out of reach, like a yellow perch gliding down the Hudson.

That Thursday I found myself back at the police headquarters for the third time in a month, on another stint covering the interminable Herlihy case. More hours sitting patiently in those chill, grandiose buildings, vast spaces in which every shuffle or creak amplified, and breath floated through the air like clouds, where the law shifted in its seat and time slowed. Seconds dragged their scuffed heels across the chequered marble floor.

The truth was always hiding. Nowhere was it better at concealing itself than in a police court designed to investigate its own: in this case, a scornfully corrupt police captain who operated as if it were the remit of his badge to nurture debauchery like a flourishing, sticky weed across his precinct. This court, this procedure, many of us well knew, was no more than a theatre for those stories the police and its accomplices in the combine of protection wanted to tell. But still we came with our serious notebooks and pencils; still we reported on it. Still the cylinders of Park Row presses turned, inking those stories into print, the newspaper boys on streetcorners called out their fallacious headlines and the public pored over its newspaper columns in kitchens, drawing rooms and saloons.

That morning, the Reverend Paddock took to the stand; lofty, slender, jacket buttoned up to his starched dog-collar, indignant when he was asked what had made him visit Captain Herlihy in the precinct office.

"Do you think I could go on any longer, ignoring what I could see from my door, my very windows?" he retorted with all the rhetorical instinct of the pulpit. "Did you think I could ignore it when these young people, lighthouses, came with their cards, advertising outrageous vice, to the very steps of the church?" he said, his face colouring. Hair cropped puritanically short and parted in a straight line down the middle, he had the air of an over-earnest head boy.

I took notes, though this was not what I had come for. I already knew most of the Reverend Paddock story – and I believed it to be true. That the precinct had allowed prostitution to flourish in every corner, for women of ill repute to tip out onto the streets, and their runners to approach whoever passed, as if they were innocent grocers selling carrots at market. What I was more interested in was Herlihy himself, soon up on the stand, and the possibility that a man could be so cavalier, so self-aggrandising that he might let something slip about the machinations of the power he wielded, and the bigger question of into whose pockets that protection money ultimately flowed.

"A local girl, just fifteen, lured into intimacies and then imprisoned in one of these disorderly houses? A woman raped, and then forced into marriage, then incarcerated in a brothel under her attacker's control?"

"Objection," interrupted the defence lawyer.

The judge, President York, ever-calm except occasionally when his rosaceous cheeks would further pinken, tipped his head thoughtfully. "Sustained. Reverend, can you please stick to answering the question. Did you or did you not accost Captain Herlihy on June fourteenth, at his precinct?"

"I did," the minister replied. "And I did indeed call him a liar. I am not proud of it, but I do not think my words were the only reason the captain came from behind his desk and thrust a fist in my face."

* * *

The accused did not take the stand until later that afternoon, at which point I returned to find a much fuller room. I took my seat on the end of a row, next to Ernest Crosby, the child saver and anti-vice crusader, dressed in a worn, but perfectly tailored rust-brown suit. He looked up and smiled with what seemed like relief.

My eyes scanned the horseshoe rows of seated figures; to my right, a bank of Tammany rogues, including one well-known bondsman, a ward captain, and along the very end, a familiar,

dapper figure, dressed in dark blue check, whiskers shining –
Joe Young.

The portly ward captain was shaking his head. "These raids
are takin' it too far. Before many months I'll be lookin' under
the table when I set down to a peaceful game of solitaire."

"It's Wall Street trying to purify the Bowery," said the man
nearest, with a gentle chuckle.

So few, in this room, it seemed to me, were senior figures
from the police, politics or commerce. These were the middlemen,
the heelers and local leaders, mere representatives of power,
and they would be reporting back to their chiefs, the higher-ups,
the men in whose fists power lived.

Murray Hall, I thought, could easily, had he still been around,
have been amongst that hustling bank of sporting types and
misfits. He had been one of those middlemen. It would not
have been an easy or a secure life; it would have held few
guarantees. But Murray got away with it, as most had done in
this city for decades.

Herlihy walked up to the stand, dressed in a wide coat, boots
squeaking across the floor, and was sworn in. A square block
of a man, his low brow already shone with sweat.

"According to one of the witnesses, you visited the disorderly
house at one-four-two Allen Street on numerous occasions.
Did you collect?" asked Mr Boyngage, the prosecutor, his final
word tripping out lightly, as if almost accidentally, a small
innocent spillage on the floor of the trial room.

The captain's eyes widened, then creased into a pained frown.
"Collect?" he repeated.

A murmur rippled across the row in front. It flowed, across the bank of men seated forward of me and to the right, all the way to the end of the row, where it broke gently over Joe Young, who took his own moment to look around, a moment in which his eyes caught mine.

"Did you ever, Captain Herlihy, collect from any of the vice establishments on Allen Street? Or ask any of your ward officers to collect?"

There was a long silence. The prosecutor, who looked as if he had been paralysed by surprise, barked, "Objection."

"I see no reason why the question should not be answered," said President York, peering at the prosecutor through his pince-nez.

"Perhaps I should be clearer? Did you extract payments? Bribes? Any form of blackmail from anyone involved in these establishments, in return for turning a blind eye to their illicit activities?"

"No, sir, I did not."

It was a blatant lie and everyone in the room knew it – but that the question had been asked at all felt like the unprecedented acknowledgement of some truth. It hinted, it seemed to me, towards that bigger question which would not let me go. Sure, Herlihy collected. It was understood that almost every captain, wardsman and Tammany officer in the city did so – the matter was properly proving it. But who of us really cared about the wardsmen or the district deputies? What we really wanted to know was to whom that collection was passed as it rose, rung by rung, along the city's ladders of influence. Who was at the top of the chain of dollar-dirtied hands, ever passing such envelopes upwards?

I longed for the prosecutor to ask this question, to ignore the lie that had slipped out into the room, so easily, just as many such lies had before in flat denial of a system we all knew to be real. I longed for him to say those words:

Mr Herlihy, to whom did you pass the graft that we very well know you collected?

Come on. Ask the question. Ask it. Whose were the high heads that should be rolling? Big Bill Devery? Tim Sullivan? A well-known Tammany senator?

At the far end of the row, a cough was emitted loudly and forcefully. The sound was so false, I wondered if it meant something. The prosecutor glanced towards it, then back at the accused. The cough emitted, theatrically, again – from the red-haired gentleman sat in front of Joe Young.

"Very well," Mr Boyngage said. "But you say that Chief William Devery gave you a warrant. Can you tell us the precise nature of that warrant?"

"It was, as I have said, a warrant authorising members of the force to enter the premises and to arrest all patrons there found offending."

Crosby leaned into me, his faint eau de cologne mingling with the fustiness of the room, its smell of sweat and nerves. And untruth. "Someone will have to fall for this," he murmured, "and it won't be the chief."

I dipped further towards him and replied, sotto voce. "Devery always backs his men. That's the code of the chief."

"Not this time. I'd be surprised," he countered, his voice rising a little so that I wondered if we might be overheard. "See how people are distancing themselves from Herlihy. He took it too far. He was too public. Too brazen. Too openly contemptuous of our Reverend Paddock and his sensibilities."

"Perhaps," I said quietly, shifting bodily away, in the hope of ending a conversation that might be silenced by the judge.

But Crosby's voice was at my ear again. "Devery will want to keep his distance from that stain, even if all the while he's been collecting from it. Write that, Mr Clellan. Write that story. If not now, then one day. Will you? I'm counting on you."

He straightened in his seat, as if to signal the end of the conversation, and fixed his gaze back on the witness in front.

"It seems," said the judge, "we may need to hear from Chief Devery on this matter." He removed his pince-nez with a flourish, and scanned the room, finally landing his gaze on the prosecutor. "Chief William Devery has been called to the stand, has he not? I don't suppose we yet know when he will be gracing us with his presence?"

The room erupted like a spooked barnyard.

The judge waited for the ruckus to settle. "Mr Herlihy," he said. "You are permitted to leave the stand."

It felt as if we were watching a train slowly, inevitably, gathering motion. Some engine was departing the station. Some truth, however slight, had been permitted to emerge, even in the act of asking of a question. Herlihy was a link in a chain, and one that led upwards, to figures in power, who were at the very heart of the web, the drivers of corruption in the city. To have that question answered? Now that would be something. That could be the start of a revolution.

The World offices were bustling when I dashed through the door that afternoon, crossed the floor and, swinging open the gate, arrived at Irving's desk area. His head was bent over a sheet of paper, a cigar in his mouth and a pen behind his ear.

On hearing his gate creak, Irving looked up and plucked the cigar with his fingers damping it down, in a circular motion, onto his ashtray.

"How did it go? Did Herlihy spill all?"

"Not quite."

"Enough for a page-two column?"

"Certainly. And there is news. President York is calling Chief Devery to the stand."

"Big Bill? Well now, that could even be a front page," he said, nodding.

Irving bent his head towards the bronze, pipe-smoking mannequin on his desk, which served as a novelty cigar lighter, and clicked it into flame. As he relit his cigar, he studied me curiously. I watched as his mouth spooled out smoke, instinctively and absentmindedly as if it were no more than breathing. He watched me, as if trying to figure out some difficult puzzle. I was reminded of the Rose O'Cuba, and flooded with a momentary desire to return to its woodpile of memory.

"By the way," he said, "that other story of yours ... Murray Hall. Is there anything else in it? The will? The daughter? Anything at all? Would be good to get something out while there is still interest."

"Murray Hall?" I said, pausing at the other side of the fence. "No ..."

"Nothing new?" he said. His keen gaze drifted across my face. "Nothing at all? I thought you were still working on it."

"No," I said. I felt a lightness in my chest as I spoke, and I breathed in deeply, smelling the cigar smoke. "Nothing ... nothing at all."

He nodded at me with a bemused frown, then swept his hand through the air as if to usher me on my way.

That night I arrived home to find a letter had been delivered that day. Even a glance at the script of the address and watermark made me pause. Another from Ellen Elba Hobbs, without a doubt; that very same heavy cream paper. I hesitated to open it, on account of the bitterness I anticipated inside, on account, too, of my doubts. There would, I told myself, likely be no truth here.

Besides, I was hungry. My stomach growled and needled. I knew there was little in my cupboards, but nevertheless I raked through my cabin-sized kitchen. A rotten, dried-out piece of cheese, hidden under the lid of a butter dish. Mouse droppings like seeds sown along the shelf. A packet of old crackers, which

I tipped out onto a rose-patterned plate. The gracious design didn't make them look any more appealing, but I carried them through to my room.

The stale rounds held little appeal. I wondered what did. If I could distract myself, perhaps that nag of hunger would leave. I picked up yesterday's *Wall Street Journal* and put it back down. The envelope winked at me from my desk.

I took my paper knife, sliced it open, and began to read.

Dear Mr Clellan,

Enclosed is the letter Celia wrote to me around a month after this episode, as well as one – from the earlier years of her marriage – in which she spoke in strange terms on the subject of pleasure.

After receiving this letter, with such an open invitation to discuss, I made a point of always avoiding the subject entirely. I feared what she might say, and what she seemed to imply, though I had no idea what it meant. Besides, I was far too caught up in the business of running the farm at Shawmut and looking after my daughter Ethel, who was still young then.

I must admit, of all the things she sent to me, this baffled me the most. Intimate relations for a woman, I thought, are surely not about desire or pleasure. At times, I must confess now, perhaps I have felt something close – but it is not our purpose. Perhaps this is what Hall's hold over her was, the reason she felt so bound to him. I always knew there was something unnatural about it — the relationship between them — and now I have the proof. There are feelings that we women cannot describe, that are, as it were, unnameable. We do not even share them among ourselves.

And so, by sharing these matters with me so openly, I might almost say explicitly, it felt as if Celia was breaking some rule, and I am glad to say that I wanted nothing of it.

I have also taken the liberty of sharing a page, found amongst her possessions. I considered keeping the following document from you, not only in light of its deviant contents, but because I have so few keepsakes to remember my dear sister by. But I believe the world should know some of her true identity, some of the passion with which she lived her early years. I believe, too, that it shows the truths of Hall's influence on her, the way his disreputable craftiness deceived her and dragged her down with him, away from the beautiful girl of integrity and worth she once was. This is part of a diary she kept in her early courting days with Hall. I found it only recently, hidden under a mattress, when I was clearing out her old room. It brought me to tears and to my knees in prayer. I ask that if you do choose to share it, you do so with care.

I looked at the pages she had enclosed. The letters were dated November 1875 and June 1873 respectively. So extraordinary that there were these letters, now in my hands, not by Hall, but by the very closest person, his wife, Celia. My chest pounded with anticipation, and I remembered with a smile my earlier conversation with Irving. I was glad; in a way I wanted these letters to myself, not to share them with the rubbernecking public.

Dearest Ellen,

My apologies for not having written sooner. It is only the horror of what happened when you last visited that has prevented me. What you saw must have appalled you, and indeed it mortified me.

I was so close to coming back to beloved Shawmut with you and with only that small bag in my hand. I would certainly have done so were it not for my own cowardice, and the tight hold that I am ashamed to say Murray has over me. There are things inside my marriage that I will never tell anyone, not even you, my dear sister. That is the promise, for better or worse, that I made on my wedding day, and I am nothing if not my word. They will go with me to my grave.

As I told you on that day, I suffer so, though perhaps in part that is my character – this melancholy that comes and goes in me. Sometimes I can't tell what is in my mind, and passes solely inside my head, and what in my marriage is truly unbearable.

I should be clear. All is not always terrible with my husband. There are times when I still feel, even now, that he is the great love of my life; that we were bound for each other. Of course, he can behave monstrously – but don't all men have their less than edifying moments? You are lucky to have found a gentle man in Richard. Perhaps there is something wrong with me, a defect, that means gentleness could never fully engage me, would repel rather than attract me. As much as I hate Murray's outbursts, I can't resist the idea that they show the depth of his feeling for me. I'm not asking you to understand this peculiarity of mine, dear Ellen, only to hear me in my solitude.

Murray is worse, always, when family is around. You will remember that time, in Waterville, when he threw the glass against the wall? I think perhaps that is because he has no family himself. Orphaned young, and in such a scarring way that he only some few times has spoken of it.

The women of the agency, our boarders and so on, and myself, we are all the family he knows, and this is why he is so fiercely protective. Minnie is his daughter. But, as to the family in Scotland from which he came? His orphaning in adolescence, and calamitous loss of his brother, I believe left him very much on his own at a tender age.

This explains why he is such a fighter. He has had a tough life, a brutal life, at least in respect of his emotions, and it is my belief he can be forgiven some of the behaviours he displays, the things he does on that account.

As much as Murray has brought me to my lowest moments, he has also brought the sweetest.

Let me explain, for my own dignity as much as your understanding, that it is not always as you saw. There are times of great love and harmony, and we understand each other better and with more clarity than I believe many couples do. I know his mind, his very thoughts. I know what he fears most, and I know he fears that I know it too.

He fears that if I leave, I will share his deepest secrets with the world. And that fear drives him to bind me to him with the tightest of knots, just as he recoils from such intense bondage for himself. But I would not betray him. I never would. My heart could never speak it, not even to you.

Such is the privacy of marriage.

That privacy can be a lonely place.

The dreadful mood you saw was gone by the next day and he wept and went down on his knees, begging forgiveness, beseeching me never to go. I told him I would not. And, as for my forgiveness, he knows he can count on it.

That rage you saw is not who Murray is. It is only that Murray feels easily threatened, and when he does, this dark fog of rage and vulnerability descends. It is as if he is quite nearly another person, and, of course, the liquor does not help. This is what you saw. Fear blended with whisky. I can vouch that the following day he was sheepish and contrite and went overboard with his apologies, though I told him quite clearly that what he had done was inexcusable.

I must confess, it is not easy. My marriage, right from the day we made our vows in Grace Church, has not been easy. For me, Murray's fluctuating moods are not the worst of it. In some ways I can plan for that, I have learned the rhythms and tides of his tempers, the things that pull the trigger on his fury. The real horror is the way he goes on with other women, his flirtations, his nights out with ladies of all reputations in the city's saloons and bars, many of them friends of mine from the agency. I don't know if he does it to hurt me, to humiliate me,

or if he simply doesn't care. Sometimes I think his rages are
expressions not so much of his past losses, but of his present
guilt and shame. You once asked if he was a womaniser. Well,
yes, perhaps he is.

But almost always his betrayals stop at flirtatious laughter
and conversation over an evening of raised whisky tumblers.
I believe he fears going any further than the promise of intimacy
with any other woman.

My darling Ellen, now and again I truly wish I had come
with you. I wish I had got in that cab and returned to
Shawmut, that happy place of childhood, free from the anguish
of married life. But then I return my thoughts to the life I
have built here, and in spite of my difficulties with Murray,
there is too much in New York which I would not want to
relinquish. The agency, and the strange family of boarders and
friends who come and go here. And Minnie, of course. I worry
that if I were to leave, Murray would transfer his anger onto
her. This is the life I have chosen, and I must bear it, for her
sake as much as my own.

A breeze rattled at my window. I sat back in my chair, still
holding the final sheet of that letter, thin and with a hint of the
yellowings of age. The writing, I observed, was careful and regular.

I could imagine the sister, Ellen, riffling around in an old
box for the correspondence, reading over and over the words
she must have rejected so strongly on first receipt. Some

phrases stood out. *The privacy of marriage can be a lonely place. I know what he fears most.* And hints here and there about aspects of Murray's life. His orphaning in adolescence; his difficult early years.

There was much to pick over, but I was keen to read on, and so I folded open the next letter in the package.

Dearest Ellen,

It was a delight to visit you, Richard and the girls last month, and I am sorry we left under such a heavy cloud. I simply wish you wouldn't always ask so many questions on the matter of childlessness, or dismiss so entirely my working life. I know I am not the doctor I once yearned to be, but here in Manhattan, I am, you would find, quite admired as a formidable – and successful – business lady. That is not nothing.

You asked me, while we were sitting out in the garden, whether the problem was to do with intimate relations between my husband and I; if we were mismatched. It is not that, I tell you. I have no desire for children, and, as you may remember, never have. My mind has never shifted on that, and I have no concerns over the waning of my fertile years, so please don't imagine that I will have some sudden volte face followed by a storm cloud of regrets. No.

Remember how, when we were young, we used to imagine together how it might be to be with a man – and I would say that I had no yearning for it? None at all. Even the strongest, most handsome and capable men left me cold; even that strapping

334

Mr Albee with his horsemanship skills and redoubtable moustaches. Then Murray came along, and at last there was a man who could ignite that womanly part of me, could make me feel the imperative of my sex. He could walk into a room and I would become in thrall to his attention, as if to one of those touring preachers at the village hall. I think you could see that when he first came to visit us at Shawmut. His presence brought me to life in a way no other man ever could, brought me out of my apathy and alive into the world again.

I only tell you this because of your repeated questions about our lack of children, and the way you suggest that we are some kind of odd couple. The fact that we have not been blessed – or perhaps cursed – with children is not because we are, as you call it, incompatible. Far from it. We are very much in tune. There is an astonishing bond between us. We are flames feeding off one another, burning ever brighter in our passion. I can only say that what I feel with him is a force of inexplicable, powerful reckoning. It always has been.

I recall how in those early days at Shawmut you warned me not to go on my daily walks with him. I think you could see what was happening between us and were concerned for me, on account of my modesty – which, by the way, was already lost. I am sure I was quite a sight when I returned from our wanderings, dishevelled and flushed, my eyes flashing with energy, and you must have read the signs.

Yes, that was lust. It was desire, and of the sort I often think is only allowed to men, and yet I have experienced it – and I have acted upon it and felt its satiation.

You were right to think that there was danger, though not of the type you might have imagined. It was a kind of mental danger, a risk of falling outside of acceptable society, and of allowing myself to become enraptured by it, and that lure changed my life.

My sister, I trust you will be sure to keep this letter private.

There were things that happened between me and Murray on those walks that shook me, sent some quake moving through me, as if through a long-solidified landscape. I felt myself crack open. The things Murray did to me – that I did to him – were not as you might envisage.

They were both less and so much more.

Who would imagine that a kiss could do such things? Who would imagine that the lightest of touches could produce such trembling, compulsive force?

I was moved solely by kissing – and such kissing as you can never imagine. In those early days a kiss from Murray, with him, was a quickening, a summoning of pure spirit in me. I had felt so dead when I returned from Boston and he brought me alive, through him I emerged into the world and saw its wonders. I was a landscape wet with rain, lush with foliage, awash with streams in spate.

You may laugh – you have always seemed to laugh at my desire for Murray. He may not have the powerful form of a strongman, an Adonis or a Hercules, but my body aches for his. It aches for his secrets. It craves his smallness and tight muscularity. I tell you these things so that you might understand. The love that Murray gave me from the beginning, and that

I gave to him, has heightened the presence of love in the rest of my life, so that I might care for you and our parents more deeply. I am a being more full with love for knowing him.

When I came back from those walks, all I could think about was when and how I might return to that pleasure. I know you once said that your own congress with Richard could cause you pain. That has never been the case for me with Murray.

And so, your advice on marital intimacies was misplaced. I doubt that much of what you said would improve the experience for myself and my husband, and you now know I am not the innocent you might have imagined. I am not naïve, nor am I repressed. In truth, is any woman, who has been married for such an extent of years?

I have mentioned that I might have good reason to be unhappy, to be troubled within my marriage, but do not assume that it is due to our childlessness, nor to our marital bed. On this count, I have only ever been happy. There is only pleasure, and such a visceral intensity of pleasure as I could never have dreamed of.

If you should wish to know more about how to gain such pleasure in your own marriage, I am happy to share what I have learned over these years. I have become aware of how limited most experience of congress is, and I honestly believe this knowledge I now possess of how it might be expanded should be shared. I trust you as my sister to be discreet with this information. I know how dangerous it would be not to do so. The woman who revels in the pleasure of sex is always denounced; she is treated as a liability in her own life and that of her family. Though my experience reveals the opposite – that a woman's frustrations all too often stem from the denial of those unmentionable carnal longings – she who allows pleasure to flourish is perceived as a wanton madwoman.

With all my love,
Cee

The pages that came next were more confusing. A few yellow sheets, seemingly ripped from a notebook, with words decorated with doodles, spiralling with hearts, flourishes, flowers. I wondered where they might have come from and then recalled Ellen's note in the letter.

They had been thoughts squirrelled away, hidden under a mattress, pages of a journal written not for the world, but for Celia herself.

Murray called again today. Murray, Murray, Murray, Murray.

When he's here, he's the only thing in the room, his compact body taking up all the space, all the air around me. I see myself in him, even when we look so different. I think he sees it too – when he looks at me there's a recognition that sends lightning down my spine into my belly and beyond.

We went for a walk, further than I've been in months. I'm getting stronger again, in my body, if not my mind. He makes my mind weak so that it's full only of him. I feel like those village girls I used to despise so in my youth, their thoughts only of men and marriage and nothing of themselves. But

338

Murray is different – he understands the ambitions of a woman. He says he would support me in anything I wanted to do; he would not keep me cooped up at home like my mother. I yearn to believe him.

A new page.

We left early today, early for Murray. I left a note for Ellie. We walked for hours, further than I thought I could walk, and we talked and talked. I think he wanted to tell me something, but he didn't have the words. He doesn't need to. I understand him in the way he walks, the way his eyes meet mine with a hunger. Our bodies speak to each other when our mouths fall short.

We went to the lake I haven't been to since I was a child. I could see my breath, but when my skin brushed close to his, it gave off a heat I could barely stand. And in the midst of all that electricity, he gave himself up to me.

He never told me directly. The truth crept up on us like the tide, as if it were a revelation to us both. I think in my bones, in my flesh, I always knew. It's what drew me to him, an inverse reflection of myself, a self-made man.

The day by the lake. Cold wind and empty skies.

I told him I was starting my bleed.

He told me he knew how to make me feel better.

He did.

A hand on my belly and another slid under my skirt.

The hand that pressed as if it had always known where to find me. Had always known the way there.

No one had told me touch could feel this.

No one had told me my body could break like a cloud bursting.

We lay on the ground together in the winter earth and felt like the only people alive. He told me there were things I should know.

I told him I knew.

I know. I know.

And then I pressed my hands on him too.

Not like other men.

Not like anyone I've ever known.

Only like himself.

Now I know him, and he knows me; we're tied to each other. There's a darkness and a light all bound up at once in this secret. It scares me a little, this intensity. But there's no way I can turn back now. He says he's going to ask Father for my hand tomorrow. I want him to – I want to give myself to this man, keep giving myself to him over and over again. I want him to consume me completely.

"Not like other men," I murmured to myself as I read that line again. The words were extraordinary, but I felt ashamed for reading them, as if I were prying, glancing through the window and into a bed chamber, watching some remarkable, unfathomable intimacy, disturbed yet unable to look away. My heart raced. For a moment I felt isolated and estranged.

I repeated those words: "Only like himself."

All this time I had been thinking that Hall was a fabricator, a dissembler, a fraud who had created only masquerade. But what if she ... *he* had been truthful all along?

WASHINGTON SQUARE SOUTH
15TH FEBRUARY 1901, 5 P.M.

GRACE WAS FLUSH WITH A subtle radiance when I arrived at her house; I too felt the heat of some urgency, some wanting – yearning as I did to share with her what I had read.

But her simple practicality gave me pause.

"Maggie, can you bring us some tea?" she said.

Every time I came to visit her, I was struck by how much more relaxed she was becoming in her wealthy home looking out over Washington Square. There was often a new item of furniture, like the sumptuously upholstered chair she gestured for me to sit in. "You like it?" she asked.

That secret that Celia had written of, I wondered, did Grace know it too?

"And Maggie," she called out. "Some of those little French cakes!"

Gone was the frazzled Grace of a few years ago, who had always seemed nervous and vigilant, yet also somehow elated by the work she was doing with the fallen women of the lower East Side, the prayer sessions in brothels, the audiences in soup kitchens.

"The news looks exhausting," she said. "I can hardly follow it. The Committee of Five. The Committee of Fifteen. Big Chief Bill going down. Queen Victoria finally dead and all of London thronged in the streets for her funeral. I don't know how you cope."

"I have had another letter," I said to her with a shrug as I dropped into the velvet cushioned chair and marvelled at its comfort. "From the sister-in-law – enclosing passages from the wife's diaries."

She ignored my words, staring at me suspiciously for a moment. "You seem strangely excited, Sam. What's going on? You've not been playing cards again?"

"No." I frowned, wanting to steer the conversation. "The correspondence was all about pleasure. The pleasure she experienced with Murray."

"The pleasure," she said, her voice lowering to a growl I'd never heard from her before.

"The description was extraordinary," I persisted. Then, emboldened, "Does your body ache for Henry's?"

"Sam!" she warned as if I were about to take a step too far.

I took that step, determined to know. "Does he give you pleasure of such intensity that—"

"I've been thinking a lot about your Murray Hall," she interrupted, dismissing my prurience. "Or, more specifically, I've been thinking about Joe Lobdell. I found that paper I told you about. It was so interesting to look at it again."

"You're changing the subject. You're deflecting away from the subject of pleasure – your pleasure."

"I'm not. This is relevant." She waved a hand to me, bidding me to stay. "Just one moment. I'll get it. And will you join us for dinner? We're having broiled mutton chops and scalloped potatoes, and I'm sure it would stretch."

"Mutton chops." I repeated, almost as a murmur. "Broiled."

It had been a familiar meal throughout childhood; the meat grey, its fat limpid and squeaking.

"Not like that! Not like Mama's mutton chops. Maggie does an excellent job with them."

Now, my sister turned and offered a flickering smile. "I'll let Maggie know. You look like you could do with a plate of proper food, not just these French fancies."

CASE.

Lucy Ann Slater, alias, Rev. Joseph Lobdell, was admitted to the Willard Asylum, October 12th, 1880; aged 56, widow, without occupation and a declared vagrant. Her voice was coarse and her features were masculine. She was dressed in male attire throughout and declared herself to be a man, giving her name as Joseph Lobdell, a Methodist minister; said she was married and had a wife living. She appeared in good physical health; when admitted, she was in a state of turbulent excitement, but was not confused and gave responsive answers to questions. Her excitement was of an erotic nature and her sexual inclination was perverted. In passing to the ward, she embraced the female attendant in a lewd manner and came near overpowering her before the attendant received assistance.

Her conduct on the ward was characterised by the same lascivious behaviours, and she made efforts at various times to have sexual intercourse with her associates. Several weeks after her admission she became quiet and depressed, but would talk freely about herself and her condition. She gave her correct name at this time and her own history, which was sufficiently corroborated by other evidence to prove that her recollection of early life was not distorted by her later psychosis.

It appeared she was the daughter of a lumberman living in the mountainous region of Delaware Co., N.Y., that she inherited an insane history from her mother's antecedents. She was peculiar in girlhood – in that she preferred masculine sports and labour; had an aversion to attentions from young men and sought the society of her own sex. It was after the earnest solicitation of her parents and friends that she consented to marry, in her twentieth year, a man for whom, she has repeatedly stated, she had no affection and from whom she never derived a moment's pleasure, although she endeavoured to be a dutiful wife. Within two years she was deserted by her husband and shortly after gave birth to a female child, now living.

Thenceforward, she followed her inclination to indulge in masculine vocations most freely; donned male attire, spending much time in the woods with the rifle, and became so expert in its use that she was renowned throughout the county as the "Female Hunter of Long Eddy". She continued to follow the life of trapper and hunter and spent several years in Northern Minnesota among the Indians.

Upon her return to her native country, she published a book giving an account of her life and a narrative of her woods experience that is said to have been well written, although in quaint style. Unfortunately, the reporter has been unable to procure a copy of this book as it is now very scarce. She states, however, that she did not refer to sexual causes to explain her conduct and mode of life at that time, although she considered herself a man in all that the name implies.

During the few years following her return from the West, she met with many reverses, and in ill health she received shelter and care in the alms-house. There she became attached to a young woman of good education, who had been left by her husband in a destitute condition and was receiving charitable aid.

The attachment appeared to be mutual and, untoward as it may seem, led to their leaving their temporary home to commence life in the woods in the relation of husband and wife. The unsexed woman assumed the name of Joseph Lobdell and the pair lived in this relation for the subsequent decade; "Joe", as she was familiarly known, followed her masculine vocation of hunting and trapping and thus supplying themselves with the necessaries of life.

An incident occurred in 1876 to interrupt the quiet monotony of this Lesbian love. "Joe" and her assumed wife made a visit to a neighbouring village, ten miles distant, where "he" was recognised, was arrested as a vagrant and lodged in jail.

On the authority of a local correspondent, I learn that there is now among the records of the Wayne Co. (Pa.) Court, a *document that was drawn up by the "wife" after she found "Joe" in jail. It is a petition for the release of her "husband, Joseph Israel Lobdell" from prison, because of "his" failing health. The pen used by the writer was a stick whittled to a point and split; the ink was pokeberry juice. The chirography is faultless and the language used is a model of clear, correct English. The petition had the desired effect and "Joe" was released from jail. For the following three years they lived together peaceably once more and without noticeable incident, until the time when "Joe" had a maniacal attack that resulted in her committal to the asylum before-mentioned.*

The statement of the patient in the interval of quiet that followed soon after her admission to the asylum, was quite clear and coherent and she evidently had a vivid recollection of her late "married life". From this statement it appears that she made frequent attempts at sexual intercourse with her companion and believed them successful; that she believed herself to possess the virility and the coaptation of a male; that she had not experienced connubial content with her husband, but with her late companion nuptial satisfaction was complete. In nearly her own words: "I may be a woman in one sense, but I have peculiar organs that make me more a man than a woman." I have been unable to discover any abnormality of the genitals, except an enlarged clitoris covered by a large relaxed praeputium. She says she has the power to erect this organ in the same way a turtle protrudes its head – this analogy is her own comparison. She disclaims onanistic practices. Cessation of menstrual function occurred early in womanhood;

the date having passed from her recollection. During the two years she has been under observation in the Willard Asylum she has had repeated paroxysmal attacks of erotomania and exhilaration, without periodicity, followed by corresponding periods of mental and physical depression. Dementia has been progressive and she is fast losing her memory and capacity for coherent discourse.

On finishing reading, I closed the journal and paused for a moment, looking out over the desk onto the bare bones of a tree stretching up from the square below. I sensed my sister, sitting behind me by the fire, waiting for my response. I heard her swallow.

Other than that, no sound, but for the occasional crackle of the log burning in the hearth. I was waiting for her to speak. I sensed her expectation bearing down on the back of my neck, and it triggered familiar anger, one I knew from past moments when I had felt ambushed by her.

I felt stuck, my eyes pinned on a small line of winter sparrows on a branch, as if stranded out there on that wooden limb myself. I neither wanted to turn round, nor stay at this desk with these words. The text, and some of its most intimate details, were stirring in the depths of my mind.

The sparrows' brown-tipped heads switched, this way and that, above their pale plump breasts, as if gossiping on the trivial matters of the day. It felt as if Grace and I were both party to some shameful secret, though I was not entirely clear what it was. Where exactly did the shame lie, save that we had both read details of a life that would be in most company almost unmentionable?

"It is unthinkable," I said, turning towards her, but not lifting my eyes from the intricate geometry of the Persian rug between us.

Grace nodded. "Two women married ... And intimate ..."

I glanced at her and studied her dark eyes, which were turned towards the fire, gleaming in its orange light. I was perplexed. I wondered if she meant that she too felt it; I wondered what exactly it was that she had wanted to share by showing me this paper.

"I think I need to ... absorb this," I said, choosing my words carefully, but feeling some rushing surge of other words boil inside my mind.

Why? This surely is insanity itself? To read such things? This is the kind of thinking that only leads to dissolution, to the asylum.

She turned her gaze towards me shyly. "Of course."

A vague dread churned inside me. I felt a horror growing, not at what I had read, but at her for presenting me with the guilt of this new knowledge.

"I thought you would be interested," she said. "Given Murray Hall."

My eyes landed on the cake stand, with its crumbs and half-eaten patisserie, and it seemed so decadent, so gross, so jarring.

"I thought," she went on, "at first, that maybe she did it because she wanted to get on in the world, for the sake of business and security, for the impulse of making money. But then, when I read this, I thought maybe there is something more."

I knew some of Grace's strangeness from childhood, but now I saw that she still held onto it, while increasingly living a life that was respectable. Here she was steering her way through society, creating a semblance of genteel, polished ease, and yet still she read such things?

"But ..." I said. "It's too much. I'm sorry. And this doctor ... he talks as if Lobdell were some animal. It's too much ..."

"Sam," she said. She stood up, and swiftly she was standing over me, placing a hand on my knee. "This is not about me ... You don't need to worry about me. That's not why I showed it to you. Your interest in Murray Hall. Some other things, too ... I thought you might want to read it. Perhaps I shouldn't have shown you."

I turned away, staring again at the fire and its swirling flames. It seemed to spit across the hearth at us. "Yes, perhaps you should not have."

Her hand was still pressed softly, pleadingly, on my knee. "I see you, Sam," she said. "I've always seen you. I see who you are. Your interest in this story is more than journalistic. I see who you are, how curious you are, and how father never liked that. You don't have to hide all that from me. Father is gone."

I stood up abruptly. That hand, that voice – the tender pressure they exerted on me – seemed almost unbearable.

"I have to go," I said, snatching my gaze away from hers.

"Oh, Sam. Won't you stay for dinner at least?" Her voice was resigned but pleading, knowing she had already lost me. I couldn't look at her.

"Not now," I almost snarled, desperate to pull away from a conversation I did not fully understand, one which bruised me somewhere deep and tender. "Not here."

I bounded out into the mist of the street, still buttoning my coat against the drizzle. I needed some air. I needed to escape the Persian rugs, the flaky, overwrought cakes, the learned, leering psychiatric papers, the godawful clag of mutton chops ... and, most of all, the secret world of my sister's mind. The damp on my skin barely cooled my fury. I took breath after breath but still my mind raced, accelerating as the cold hit my face, a tumble of words and voices, all speaking of Murray Hall, him, her, it ... Of Scotland, New York, Shawmut, Govan, Paisley, Kirknewton, the hardscrabble lives of the goldrush West, the towering, glittering monuments to politics and commerce of Manhattan.

I see you, Sam, my sister had said. But what could she see? She didn't even have the courage to tell me, to explain what she saw, other than to hint that it had been buried in some way. This glimpse of a half-truth was so typical of Grace.

At Bond Street, I continued walking east, through the East Side and onto the bustling Bowery, already jostling with voices raised by liquor and a vital, evening energy. Falling into step with the rhythm of the neighbourhood, I kept walking, speeding past canopies of umbrellas, popping up in a synchronised bloom against the light shower.

Under the pall of the Third Avenue elevated railway, I watched the long, impoverished queue of ragged men outside the Bowery mission.

A dime museum, advertising "Gargantua" and "Bawdy Entertainments" rattled mechanical music out into the street. At its entrance, under flagpoles floating with stars and stripes, a woman called out, "Behold here, a lady twice the weight of Queen Victoria, three times the weight of Boadicea! Behold our tattooed Mars and Venus! Behold the dog-faced man!"

I wondered, as I watched the bedraggled punters pass through its turnstile, if that was what I had been doing in telling Hall's story: if my own fascination had at least a passing relation to the common man's love for oddity, the magnetism that draws people through into the seamy labyrinth of the dime museum. Had I not both been attracted and repulsed by Murray Hall?

As I moved, horrified at myself, to walk away, I caught a glimpse of my own form in a mirror propped at the entrance of the museum. The green buttons of my jacket so distinctive, stretched across an elongated torso that segued into a face that was no more than a narrow, featureless bar. For a moment I was confused – *What was this creature?* – but I soon realised that this was a curved mirror of the sort found frequently in fairgrounds.

Was this what my sister had seen? This strange, warped being?

And what exactly did she think it was?

I hurried onwards, fleeing that sight, merging myself into the flow and clamour of the Bowery. Now I knew where I was heading, and before long I found myself outside the door of the Excise Exchange, hesitating at the two swing doors, through which I could see the glow of the hanging lights of the saloon. A fight was brewing outside, with a man and a woman haranguing each other with ever more vicious insults and postures of aggression.

The mood felt different from my last visit, balanced on the edge of something, and the bar was rowdier and more densely crowded than before. Shock mingled with delight caught in my throat as I realised that the perfumed, dancing and catcalling women who made up the majority of clientele were not women, but painted and costumed men.

My head swirled, and this time it had nothing to do with alcohol. I didn't know where to look. These tall, swaying figures both repulsed and magnetised me. They brushed by me on all sides, apparently oblivious to my presence, calling out to each other across the room with expletives and raucous, uninhibited bursts of laughter at witticisms I was unable to catch. I looked around for a free table. Almost all were taken; the closest to me was occupied by two bowler-hatted men, one of whom leaned forward and sensually stroked the hand of the other.

As I stood there, frozen, a familiar face appeared by my side.

"I knew you'd be back," Jennie announced with a smile. "They never can stay away!"

I felt myself drawn to her again, that unstoppable mix of arousal and something else, something deep and raw that I wasn't sure I wanted to touch. I looked at her soft brown skin, her hazel eyes. I searched her body, the angle of her hips, the curve of her neck. Was she? How could I know?

She seemed impatient, disappointed by my brooding, stilted silence. Where were my sharp-tongued ripostes and delicious innuendoes? My exquisite promises of physical pleasure? It was the end of the week, payday, and she was in demand, the fat woman at the piano summoning her.

"Mine's a rum punch!" she called behind her as she left my side. "Come bring it to me when you've finished gawping like an overgrown schoolboy!"

I found myself a stool by the bar, gripping the sticky wood and attempting to slow my breath, soothe my beating heart.

I pulled my handkerchief out of a pocket and swiped it across my dampening brow. I stared at the glowing orange square, darkened in patches by my sweat, and its dancing edge of lace. My mind swirled with its swoops and turns. Was this, I wondered, how Murray Hall felt, as he was felled by those drops of chloral? I had drunk nothing and already I felt drugged, woolly-headed and lost in a fantasy.

After a few moments, I couldn't say how long, I was able to look about me again without feeling as if my vision were closing to a pinhole. I scanned the room, deliberately skipping my eyes over those hypnotic figures who had so shocked me on my entrance. My gaze was drawn to the flight of stairs that dominated the centre of the room, on which a small procession of men, of all different colours, garbs and outlines, had formed, seemingly desperate to reach its top. I had heard tales of the room there, of the wild orgies that it hosted.

I felt excruciatingly out of place. Cold sweat was collecting on the back of my neck. I searched for some neutral spot on which to focus, but wherever I cast my gaze it fell upon extraordinary scenes, lewd images. Men dressed in satiny bodices and lace stockings; masculine bodies entwined with one another. I snapped my gaze away.

But, irresistibly, my eyes wandered again across the tables and, in the corner, alone in a booth, I saw a figure I recognised. My body flooded with relief at the familiar sight, and for a moment I couldn't believe he was real, but I also felt myself beset by a hammer of nerves, by the fear of being spotted and exposed.

He was apparently unfazed by the chaos around him. He had on the table a number of small piles of coins, and was absentmindedly moving coins from one pile to another.

He smiled as I lowered myself into the chair opposite, as if this were an appointment to which I was just slightly, forgivably late.

"Mr Clellan," he said, in a low voice that swept me right back to that moment at Fatone's when I had found myself opposite him and Murray Hall.

"Mr Young," I replied.

"Twice in as many weeks. I'd say you're almost a regular."

"I wouldn't say a regular ..." I said, cringing at my own defensiveness.

He smiled, a half-laughing smile. "And yet you are here again."

"Yes." I allowed myself a nervous smile, wondering why it felt so different to see Young in a place like this. It disarmed some of his threatening bulk, and yet in other ways brought it into sharp focus.

"Or perhaps you're here to report on one o' your raids? Are we going to see Mr Philbin and his cronies streaming through the door?"

"No. Certainly not so far as I know."

He pulled the coins together, sweeping them into a pile, as if to demonstrate that he didn't care. "Ah would be surprised maself. Those reformers are too scared. They are scared of the Bowery."

"If you want an honest answer, I don't know why I'm here," I told him. "I don't know why I came here. To find something, perhaps."

"Ah see," he said. "Have you worked out what it is, yet? Ah've been wondering maself, ever since you turned up at the Iroquois. What is it that boy's looking for? Because it's not Murray, nor is it a vice scandal, it's something else. See, ah did know exactly who you were, Mr Clellan. Ah imagine you have been wondering that ever since you beat me at the Widow – whether ah remember the time we met at the Italian bar on Mulberry Street."

"Yes, I have."

"Well, ah do. Ah do remember."

I felt the fume of indignation flood my nostrils. "I lost my job because of whatever you and that damned Murray Hall did." I heard my own words and flinched at a sting of guilt.

"Yuh think so?" His lips contorted. "Maybe you were just not the best at your job? Bosses rarely fire a man who is good at his job. Could be you were a little too biased to see a story straight."

"That's not true," I said slowly, yet I sensed my own doubt, that thing that had been there in my mind all those years back, the itch of self-recrimination, the sickening fear that I had even now misrepresented Murray Hall by linking him to Johnnie Campbell. "I am no imposter," I insisted, my voice a little too loud. "I was good at doing what journalists should do."

Joe Young shrugged. "Well, ah didn't have anything to do with you losing your job. Ah came that day out o' loyalty to a friend. Just as ah was at the police court the other day out of loyalty. Do you know anything o' that yourself, Mr Clellan? Loyalty to a friend?"

"Loyalty to Tammany is what's wrong with this city," I said, my tone too strident, looking away and watching the languid movement down below by the piano, where . . .

"It's not about being loy'l to Tammany. It's about being loy'l, as ah said, to a friend, and Murray was a friend. Ah'm sorry you lost your job. It had nothin' to do with me. And if it had somethin' to do with Murray, ah couldn't tell you. Perhaps it did. Perhaps it didn't. Perhaps, as ah said, you were just bad at your job."

He went on, his finger raised accusingly at me. "You say you don't like how Tammany does things. How do you think most people arrivin' in this city survive and get by? By doin' the kind of things Murray did. That's smart. Even smarter, perhaps, if like Murray Hall you was a woman. Respect to him . . . or her . . . Ah know how hard the hustle is out there. We are all jus' making our way. Perhaps you never had to struggle much yourself."

I smiled; I hadn't come here to do battle with vice, but still I felt roused. "You know Philbin and Jerome are going to be the end of Tammany – certainly the Tammany that exists as it does now," I countered.

He curled his lip, a mix of indifference and contempt. "They are chasin' the wrong beast . . . And anyway, this . . ." He spread his arms to indicate the room. "This kind of thing – this kind of people – is never going to go away. And nor should it. You can't stop a human urge. It's who we are. And none of your soapbox Methodist moralising's gonna put an end to it."

"This isn't moralising—"

"You think you're above us, Mr Clellan. You think you're above the dirt of lustful humanity."

"I don't," I replied, and I meant it. "I really don't . . . Perhaps I did once."

Joe looked at me then, and I was struck again by the intensity of his eyes. I noticed now the thick lashes, thicker than I'd ever seen on a man. "Ah miss Murray," he said, as if my honesty had unleashed his own emotions. "It's unexpect'd how much ah miss him. Ah keep thinking back to times we had together, say, for instance, that trip to Boston. Ah went to a fight recently and ah felt him with me. Ah could feel him right there, moving in echo of the boxer."

I nodded, noting his insistent use of the male pronoun. There was something especially moving about seeing a man like this touched by grief. "I've started calling Murray him too," I offered, relaxing a little into his company. "The more I've unearthed about him, the more it's felt right."

He smiled, with a warmth of recognition, and nodded. "There's many memories keep coming back to me. After the Boston fight, we stayed in the city for two full days, drinking ourselves to altitudes, enjoying the hell out of the day, one saloon bar after another. Hackett, Hall, myself and a couple of the other boys. Sloshing our way from the Green Dragon Tavern to the Old Oak to the Union House Oyster bar. I can't remember where we slept, or whether any of us sobered up at any point, but we must have got rooms in some inn or other.

"Ah do remember, though, that on the second night there was some fight between Hackett and Murray over a billiards game. Murray stormed off. Ah thought he was going to cool off outside. We didn't see him till the end of the following night, when he stumbled back into the Green Dragon. Ah asked him where he had been, and he simply slurred and smiled. He was prone to disappearing like that. He would be with you one moment and then gone the next. The vanishing man, we'd sometimes call him. Ah always assumed it was into the arms of some woman. He spent so much time in their company. Now, ah wonder . . . if there were other reasons."

He tipped back the last inch of his beer, then, staring at the empty glass down on the table in front of him, sighed. "Those were the days. Ah don't have days quite like that anymore."

"I don't think I've ever had days like that," I said, a little ruefully, I must admit.

"No?" he said. "That doesn't surprise me. You oughta. You really oughta give it a try some time. Ah've never felt so close with some of my fellow men as on those nights."

"Yes. Perhaps I ought to."

"We all have our secrets, Mr Clellan. Ah've never met a person in this world who doesn't. So, Murray's was a little bigger than most ... Doesn't bother me."

There was the roll of notes from the piano and Joe looked up and over my shoulder. "It sounds like Jennie's up to give us a song."

I glanced round and saw a cloud of blonde hair stepping onto the small stage, where the piano sat.

As Jennie began to play, I saw Joe relax back into his seat, his muscular arm draped over the chair behind him. He smiled a genuine smile, head bobbing gently to the music. As one song ended and another began he caught my eye, noticing that I had been watching him rather than the performance.

His smile widened as I felt a warmth rise up the back of my neck.

"Ah seem to have finished my drink, Mr Clellan. Why don't you get me another?"

MOUNT OLIVET
16TH FEBRUARY 1901, 5.30 A.M.

THAT NIGHT, WHEN I FINALLY returned to my bed, I struggled to find my way to sleep. It felt as if the movement of the dance was still in me, prompting me to toss and turn, to flick my galloping heels across the cold mattress. I was fully conscious but my body was dreaming of the Excise.

Too many glasses of Vin Mariani had rendered me sharply awake. After some time, lying rigid, eyes closed, forcing myself to still my limbs, I got up and polka-ed over to my reading desk. The step is not one I know, in truth, but it felt like I was guided by the music inside me, like I was flying across the room.

Perched on my chair and humming, I picked up one of the books I had piled precariously at the desk edge, but my hand seemed to lunge involuntarily forwards, knocking over the stack and sending them tumbling, thudding to the floor. I paused to stare at them, scattered, one of them thrown open with its spine up, then I swung an arm to the ceiling, as if to launch into a wild, grunting Mazurka spin.

From there I lunged down to sweep up the book at the top of the heap, and was drawn, tumbling, towards the floor, in some state of collapse. Crouched there, I stared at the titles of the tomes and felt an acute sensation of what I can only describe as shame. It felt like Murray Hall were staring back at me, accusing and knowing.

The books were those once belonging to him, the small collection I had bought from C. S. Pratt. I turned in my hand *The Science and Art of Surgery*, observing how its pages had creased, creating a line that now divided across a diagram of small creatures that were labelled "cells".

As if borne by a devilish merry-go-round, my head spun with a memory of that day, so many years ago, within the dark wood and hush of C. S. Pratt, Bookseller. Clearer now, or perhaps more defined by the many attempts I had made to summon it, and all the other occasions I had met Hall.

The pile of five books on the wooden counter. The bark of his shrill voice. The striking small figure, making his way across the shop floor, a package of books hanging curiously from his outstretched arms like a labourer might carry a heavy stone. The faint wheeze of his cancer-constricted breath.

It felt, as I held the surgical guide, turning its broad, heavy pages, that this, and the other books, were stolen objects. They were not mine to look at; just as the letters from Celia were not, nor even the letters from all those many witnesses to John Campbell's life.

They did not belong to me.

Rising from the floor, I waddled clumsily across the room and began pulling things out of my cramped wardrobe. I knew I was looking for something, but had already forgotten what, till I found the bag I had used when visiting the bookshop.

I unclipped the catch, placed the books inside one by one – *The Science and Art of Surgery, The Lamplighter, Gunn's Domestic Medicine, My Lady Nobody* – and secured it shut. I collapsed back into my chair and stared for a moment at the bag, feeling that even now, the covers of those books were glaring back, as accusingly as Murray himself would, through its worn, tan leather.

I put the bag on the desk, but decided there was something insufficient in its placing, as if this were a task not yet complete. This receptacle and its contents needed to move more definitively out of my home. I lit a candle, then picked the bag up by its handles and staggered, swaying down my hallway to place the offending item down by my apartment door, undeniably on its way out.

On returning to my room, I looked out the window and saw a hint across the sky of first light in the indigo blue above the tops of the tenements. Despite the fact that I was very likely still drunk, I felt the urge to take myself off. As I let the door shut behind me, it seemed that no one was yet up in the building, and I allowed myself to wander through the streets aimlessly, my only companions at that hour the bakers, stray cats and other staggering drunkards. We did not acknowledge one another.

I turned corner after corner and ended up near Park Row, where I scuttled guiltily past the early morning lights of the newspaper buildings, before turning down towards the river. At Willets Wharf the waterfront already frothed with activity, seamen bellowing orders as they stacked barrels onto a carriage. I kept walking to the water's edge, where I looked down and across to the dense cluster of Brooklyn at the other side and the murky water of the East River, which swirled and churned.

Murray, I thought, is over there. In spite of my desire that morning to eject his possessions from my rooms, it felt that he was drawing me. His grave, over the other side of the water, was beckoning.

Whipped by the breeze, the river's surface formed small white flecks. I looked at these peaks of surf and thought of Murray, at the water's edge, alone, whilst others jumped and dived and frolicked.

I determined to take the transit car across to Brooklyn.

At the station, commuters poured like roaches out of an arriving train. The carriage heading the other way was near empty, but for a small cluster of grime-smeared cable layers, weary night workers slumped in its seats. As I sat in the juddering carriage, I supposed my wandering was not so aimless after all.

From outside the station, I leapt into the crush of a trolley car, heading north towards Maspeth. For a few blocks, I clung to the ceiling strap as it swung this way and that, but soon, on stopping, an Italian woman in a headscarf got off and I slid gratefully into her seat. The car lurched forwards again along its Grand Street track, running beneath sagging lines of criss-crossing cables.

The journey was long, and I nodded off for a time to the swaying of the carriage, only to be jolted awake when the car slammed to a stop. Outside, a couple of boys, no more than seven or eight years old, skipped past, just missing the front of another streetcar, their squeals an indiscernible blend of fright and delight. "Watch ya-selves!" yelled the driver. "Damned dodgers."

The car rattled forward again, its bell ringing angrily. Soon clustered neighbourhoods had given way to scattered buildings and more greenery than I had seen in days. Up ahead, I saw it now; the grassy rise, bordered by the spears of a wrought-iron fence. Beyond it was the bell tower and steep roofs of the gingerbread-house cemetery office. I tugged at the cord above my head, and as the car juddered to a halt, I slipped out into the cold morning air.

I knew now where I was heading. Walking ever faster, with ever more determination I made my way towards the great headstone-bouldered expanse of Mount Olivet.

I began the gentle climb on thawing ground, wending through the headstones of defenders of the Union, towards the grave I knew awaited me. There was some unexpected delight there, to find the worst of the winter was over, with early snowdrops emerging from the raw earth.

I stopped to catch my breath, and found I was not alone. Standing next to the bare earth which stood in for a grave in quiet contemplation was a woman I recognised. Esther O'Donoghue; the servant who had turned me away from Hall's door; the housekeeper who I had seen at this very spot some weeks before.

She didn't seem startled by my presence, which almost amused me in my intoxicated state. I can't imagine I looked my best, and I must have reeked of the saloon. I ran my tongue over my fuzzy teeth and realised I even had a split lip. Somehow her ease in my company embarrassed me, and I moved to smooth down my hair. She smiled.

"Looks like you've had a night," she said.

"Mrs O'Donoghue?" I replied.

"Smells like it too," she said. "I know you. You're the journalist who spoke to Minnie. Strange the people you meet up here. I've been coming here every so often and I've been surprised to find often there is someone here, or someone has left something. It comforts me to know there are those who still care." She paused and glanced my way. "You too? You upset Minnie, you know. She's an indomitable young woman, but she keeps a lot of that strength of hers inside. Reminds me of myself when I was younger. It's a way to fend off the world, I suppose, but it can't do for ever. She'll find it keeps out all sorts of other things too."

She had directed her statement towards me, but I sensed I was not really a part of this conversation. Rather it appeared she was now talking half to the grave, half to herself.

"I was with him twenty years. More time than I gave my husband. I was the one who convinced him to take Minnie in, you know. Him and Celia doted on her, but they weren't ready to admit she was their daughter. I helped them see that. She's mine to look after now, though I'm not long for this world myself. No, sir. I'll be picking out my own plot in which to spend eternity soon enough."

I did not know what to say, if anything. I did not want to interrupt the woman's thoughts.

"I knew everything from the start, and so did he. Took Celia a bit to catch on, though. Oh, me and Murray would laugh about that."

Her smile split into an uninhibited grin, more gum than tooth.

"When he'd had a few drinks, he'd joke with me that we got mixed up in the factory. They fitted us with each other's parts."

I realised I was holding my breath. Why was this woman telling me this? She knew I was a journalist, no matter how dishevelled and reeking my appearance that morning. Perhaps she did not care. I risked breaking the spell with a question of my own.

"Are you saying you ... are you the same as Murray? But the other way?" My voice came out cracked and I longed for a glass of water.

"There are more of us than you think in this world. Me and Murray were the same in some ways, but mostly we weren't. We both had the devil's humour, I'll tell you that, and I was one of the only ones who could keep up with him on the whisky. But I never liked the way he treated Celia. He was so afraid of losing her, of revealing his true self, he'd forgotten how to love her, how to care for her and keep her feeling safe."

The smile was gone, and for the first time she looked as old as she must be. I searched her profile for a hint of what I believed she was telling me.

Abruptly she turned to face me, and I felt myself burn red under her gaze. Her eyes were bright and alert and I felt as if under a streetlamp, illuminated by her fierce attention.

"You know, there's plenty of journalists knocked on our door. Plenty looking for a story. A story! We've all got stories to tell. But you've been hanging around. It doesn't seem enough for you, what you have been able to gather. What is it you're looking for?"

I couldn't maintain her gaze, the resolute directness of it, and I stared back to the bare mound of earth where all that was Murray lay: a dress, a small arrangement of bones, that dark, cancerous wound which I could not banish from my mind.

"I don't know," I answered truthfully. "I thought maybe . . . Maybe this story. Maybe if I could figure it out, I could know something else. Something bigger . . ." I paused and glanced back down at the strip of brown earth. "But it's been a dead end."

"Oh, I wouldn't say that!" The odd smile was back. "I think if you keep on with your digging, you'll find something. The dead don't talk, though, my dear. If you're seeking an answer, you might have to find it among the living."

Why, I wondered, is this old woman speaking to me in this way? Why has she changed her attitude so from our first meeting?

I almost felt like pinching myself, as if this encounter were a dream. But the familiar whisky headache was returning and I knew that throb at least, was real.

"You journalists. Always looking for someone else to create all the meaning. What about you, eh? Who's going to dig into your story?"

She turned away from me again and bent down with some difficulty to touch the cold earth.

I watched that hand as it settled there, the fingers long and broad, not so very much smaller than my own.

I thought of my father's hand, too, as he lay in his coffin, wrinkled, curled into a claw, no longer quite human, and the black fly that had landed on his waxy skin.

"My Murray. A good friend despite it all. And a good father to young Minnie. You should have seen what a father he was. And he lived truthfully, no matter what some of your lot might think." I watched as that strong worker's hand of hers pressed against the earth. "That's all you can do. Live honest and hope those you love will understand."

I think perhaps there was still more alcohol in my system than I realised, for I was crying. Soft, silent tears this time, which turned into gulping, hiccupping sobs.

"Yes. I think you're closer than you appreciate to the heart of it all," she said as she turned back towards me. She put that wrinkled hand on my arm to straighten herself. "I knew there was more to you when you kept turning up. It's not just about Murray, I can see that now."

That touch, felt there. I felt instinctively it was the touch of a woman. I looked down briefly. The fingers, gloveless on my dark sleeve, looked so vulnerable in the morning light.

Perhaps she saw my reaction because she pulled her hand away. She waved it through the air with a dramatic flourish. "Good luck to you, dear. And don't go bothering my Minnie again."

With this final warning she teetered her way on creaking legs down the opposite side of the rise, leaving me and Murray to the daybreak.

The light greyed; the sun was obscured by clouds. I looked back down the slope and saw the figure now receding. From a distance, it seemed neither that of a man nor a woman, simply an ageing body moving slowly. Old, I thought, that is all one can tell, and I watched her becoming ever smaller. Becoming like Murray himself – more distant; less discernible; further out of grasp, however hard I might try.

So far out of grasp.

So far beyond the neat lines of meaning.

I wanted to reach out with my fingers and hold that moving speck in the landscape. That thing you can never hold onto. A person. A father. A husband. A life. A smile. The tap of a blackthorn stick. Warm flesh inside a coat. A fear. A desire. A body expressing a self. Regardless.

Murray Hall.

POSTSCRIPT

FROM MILO CLENSHAW

Legacy is a strange beast. We talk about wanting to be remembered, about leaving an impact on the world, but we have very little real control over what that legacy is. Scandal, violence and stupidity are as memorable in the collective consciousness as brilliance and acts of great empathy, and an individual's lifelong efforts can, in an instant, be overshadowed by a moment of chance.

Murray Hall's legacy was shaped by public opinion from the moment of his death, and I think he knew that would happen. The privacy and caution with which he carried out his affairs right until the end suggest a person acutely aware of the delicacy of their image. Hall was white, relatively successful, and he passed as male in a world where those things mattered most, and I believe he knew what he was set to lose if that image of masculinity slipped.

Murray Hall was a real person, and there are facts about his life that can be fairly convincingly confirmed, but the truth and motivation behind the way he lived is entirely lost to time. We cannot ask him why he lived as a man, and any significance ascribed to his life says more about us than it does about him.

Before going on, it is perhaps important to say a few words about the collaborative nature of this project, the authorship of this novel. Vicky and I, respectively one cis writer and one trans, worked together to bring the story of Murray Hall to life. We decided to work together not only because of Vicky's writing expertise and my lived experience, but because a project like this is by nature collaborative. We, in turn, are collaborating with the many journalists, historians and queer scholars who kept the memory of Murray Hall alive long enough for us to discover it, and it is through a joint perspective that we wanted to reactivate his story.

It's true that inevitably our individual voices have leaked onto these pages, but I hope we have kept each other right enough that this is a more nuanced account of Hall's life than would have been possible from one of us alone. We come from different backgrounds, but were united by a passion for the potential this story presented.

Personally, I am fascinated by queer and trans stories, from the past, present and future. When you are part of a community that has no direct personal ancestry, you begin to look for identification in a broader way, tracing community and inheritance across the borders of time and geography. There is danger in this, too – to ascribe too much definitive meaning to someone who cannot speak for themselves is to use and ventriloquise them for your own ends.

There are many reasons why Hall might have lived as he did, the two most obvious being that he was transgender, or that he saw and understood the privileges men enjoyed and wanted to access them himself. It is possible that both were true. For myself, I do believe that he was trans, or at least genderqueer, because I can't imagine someone committing so fully to a life that didn't truly reflect who they were. But that's just more conjecture – if there is an objective truth to the story of Murray Hall, we haven't found it.

More significantly, the reasons why the question of Hall's life and gender have fascinated for the last hundred years bear examining. There is a morbid curiosity around trans people that is still very much alive today – just browse the endless articles sensationalising the pregnant man, or witness the pearl clutching around trans people existing as teachers, doctors, or any other human occupation. The narrative thread between the emerging yellow press of the nineteenth century and the red tops of the twenty-first is unbroken, woven together by intrusive writing around trans lives.

We don't need to know why Murray Hall made the choices he did, but I do still believe his story is an important one to tell. When Vicky and I began to work on this book, the one thing that excited me most was the chance to bring another queer history to light. Queer and trans people, and our histories, have been erased, misrepresented and scandalised for centuries, and it is only now, and slowly, that other ways of telling our stories are beginning to emerge.

It is cliché that history is written by the victors, but that doesn't make it any less true. Gender has meant different things to different civilisations at different points in history, but predominantly in our Western tradition it has meant an enforcement of a gender binary, positioning men over women and trans and nonbinary people outside of the frame entirely, other than as cautionary and peculiar anomalies.

The truth is that gender variance – whether defined as transness or something else – has always existed. The problem is that trans people do not fit into a clean, binary understanding of gender, and so it has been easier to write us out of history entirely than to recognise the genuine complexity of human experience. This can mean that, for trans people like me, we do not see ourselves reflected in the wider tapestry of human history. We are unanchored, without a past, which can feel like you are the first person in the world to experience the challenges, joys and emotions of a trans life.

It also leads to the false belief for people more generally that transness is something new and frightening, rapidly corrupting our world and leading young people in particular to a degenerate view of gender that will eventually – somehow – lead to the breakdown of society. If only. Of course, this is not the case, but it is a genuine fear that leaks into the hearts of many who lack access to accurate information. When transphobia is the standard, why would you believe anything different?

Trans people have always existed, and more importantly, we will continue to exist. The real question is whether those future queer and trans people will have a better understanding of our shared history, or whether they will continue to emerge as loose threads, unable to connect to the wider picture of our culture. The hope, for me, is that this greater understanding is already happening, with a younger generation of queer and trans youth acutely aware not only of their interconnectedness but of the holes in history waiting to be explored.

Our aim with this novel wasn't to write in a complete history that isn't there, although I don't believe there is anything wrong with that approach. If transness has been written out of the history books, then it is our right to write it back in. After all, all histories are subjective narratives in some form – it just depends on whose authority you choose to believe.

What we hoped to do, at least in part, was provide an overview of the complexity of telling a story like this, where the voice of its central player is absent. Although there is a wealth of information available around Murray Hall hidden in snippets and contradictory stories in all sorts of places, none of them, as far as we have discovered, reflect the voice or the writing of Hall himself.

All we could ever do, then, was take these fragments of information and present them in as coherent a narrative as possible, highlighting some of the paradoxical, exaggerated and illogical stories that we uncovered along the way. All of this is to allow you to form your own opinions about Murray Hall – after being presented with everything we could gather about his life – and to make known what is lost when queer people's stories are told by others and not in their own words.

We wanted to show that Murray Hall was as human and as reflective of his world and society as anyone else, cis or trans. He may have had his own struggles with acceptance and survival, but he also enjoyed much of the privilege and power that any successful, married, well-connected and able-bodied white man enjoyed in nineteenth-century New York, and which survive in varied forms today.

Hall was able to not only survive, but thrive due to these privileges, and I have no doubt that if he had been poor, a different kind of immigrant, or a person of colour, the papers would have treated him very differently upon his death. Even his masculinity was an asset, as maleness is always understood to be the goal. People could, to a certain extent, understand why a woman would want to enjoy the advantages of a male life, but for a man to give those up in pursuit of womanhood was to turn their back on a birthright and to actively seek weakness. One could suggest that this is why trans women still endure some of the most acidic abuse today.

The complexity of Hall's humanity can perhaps be best understood through his relationship with his wife Celia, although whether she was his first, second or third wife is unclear. The relationship between the couple appears to have been a genuinely romantic one, and it is unknown whether Celia was aware of Hall's gender status before their marriage or not. Regardless, they stayed together, and it seems almost impossible that she wouldn't have known at some point. She was an educated woman, and it appears she was instrumental in running Hall's employment agency, potentially to a greater extent than Hall himself.

The couple's relationship also looks to be fraught with difficulty, with reports of abusive and controlling behaviour on Hall's part. Who knows if his treatment of Celia was due to

376

jealousy, fear, a general anxiety of disclosure, or something else entirely, but it certainly reflects a behaviour all too common in people who exist as men in society; Hall's gender variance did not render him exempt from this. It is telling that Hall's story has been reproduced and hypothesised upon in multiple tellings since his death, and yet Celia's life and their relationship has often been reduced to a footnote.

The same can be said of Imelda, or "Minnie", Hall's adopted daughter. I find her one of the most fascinating characters in this winding narrative, and yet just as little is known about her as her adoptive mother. Minnie's defiance and refusal to misgender her father after his death is a striking, pivotal moment, one of solidarity that can be read as illustrative of the existence of queer families in history.

It was important for us to highlight how the press of the day fixated on Hall's body. From his height to his hands to his walk, everything about his body is analysed and marvelled at – how could we not have known? How did he manage it?

This fascination with the trans body continues, though the press today is less polite, inevitably fixating on the genitals, surgery or hormones of the trans person in question. Such a perspective dehumanises trans people, reducing us to freak show objects rather than recognising us as evidence of the breadth of human diversity. There is something grotesque in mass consciousness that is repulsed and fascinated by "the surgery", as if trans people represent a new form of Frankenstein's monster.

The other kind of surgery present in this narrative is that of Hall himself, with his seeming obsession with medical literature concerned with surgery. As far as we know, he never actually performed a procedure to remove his cancerous breast tissue, but the gory details around this part of his life are vague.

While there are plenty of curious and entertaining snippets in the patchwork of Hall's life, this for me is the most difficult story to contend with. It can be easy to justify telling his story when relating spirited anecdotes, but with this – potentially the darkest episode of his life – you can begin to feel exploitative of someone's pain and suffering.

The justification is that it highlights the tangible, physical effects of marginalisation. Despite Hall's relative privilege and wealth, he knew he could still not access medical care for fear of discrimination, even at a point where it cost him his life. John Campbell faced the consequences of this when he acquiesced to treatment for his smallpox. For me, it feels important to include this episode as it speaks uncannily to the self-medicating many trans people are driven to by contemporary institutional medical neglect, this being felt not only in accessing trans-specific healthcare but healthcare in general.

This, inevitably, traces back to our society's intolerance of difference. When human diversity is accepted, it tends to only be within rigid binaries – a behaviour that is not only applicable to gender, but other forms of variance too. Simply put, capitalism insists that people are classifiable – in accordance with its own categories. As such, trans, non-binary and gender non-conforming people present an intolerable provocation.

The labels with which we describe ourselves and each other do serve to create moments of identification, but they also divide us. Murray Hall's story is illustrative of this. If we claim his story as categorically a trans one, we might lose its potential as a narrative of female resistance and empowerment. These reclamations do not have to sit in opposition to each other, but can instead represent two struggles united in the same cause.

This, then, is an invitation to absorb from the story of Murray Hall whatever speaks to you. We will never be able to hear Hall's life in his own words, and while that fact should always be acknowledged, his history should be available for those whose imagination it sparks. History is not an immovable object but a series of ever-changing interpretations, and the more we recognise our own subjectivity in its analysis, the more we will recognise the plural narratives that make up something resembling truth.

The reporting around Hall's death often refers to the incredulity of those who knew him, because he presented such a complete image of masculinity. Many people today will claim that they have never met a trans person – a statistically unlikely event – because transness is viewed in a particular way. Because Murray Hall really did look, sound and act like a man to those around him, they could not square their memory of him with the papers' description of him as a woman in disguise.

This is, of course, because trans people really are who they say they are, rather than a person setting out to deceive. To know a person can only ever be to know a part of them, as we shift, chameleon-like, through the time periods, stages and relationships of our lives.

It could be argued that who we really are is an amalgamation of the reflections of ourselves as seen by the people around us, rather than something essential within us. I tend to believe in a combination of these elements, a self-knowledge working in tandem with the impressions we leave as we move about the world to create a complete being.

Murray Hall's legacy is not complete with the publication of this book, and no doubt it will continue to morph and evolve with future understandings of gender, identity and history. I don't want Hall's legacy to be defined by our narrative telling of it, but rather for this book to offer a jumping-off point for future imaginings. What I hope above all is that the nuance and subjectivity of his history is remembered, so that all these interpretations can exist side by side, each presenting their own version of the truth about Murray Hall.

A NOTE ON THE SOURCES

FROM VICKY ALLAN

Though Samuel Clellan, the central narrator in this novel, is entirely fictional the vast majority of other characters are based on those who featured in the news stories that, in the wake of Murray Hall's death, flooded the newspapers in New York, the United States, and the world, some of them reprints, relayed by wire services, These were sensational articles like the *New York World*'s "Known As A Man For Sixty Years, She Died A Woman" (January 18, 1901), or the same paper's "'He Was A Lady', Says Jury Of Murray Hall" (January 29, 1901). There were also more practical reports following the legal aspects of the case, including the story in the newspaper clipping that follows this note.

We know that Murray was married to Celia Lowe, and her name even appears as his wife in his naturalisation certificate, as reproduced by Lydia Nelson ("Reanimating Archiving/ Archival Corporealities: Deploying 'Big Ears' in De Rigueur Mortis Intervention", *QED: A Journal in GLBTQ Worldmaking*, Vol. 1, No. 2).

We also learn from interviews with his wife's sister, Ellen Elba Hobbs ("Wife's Relatives Amazed", *Boston Sunday Globe*,

January 20, 1901), that, if her accounts are to be believed, he was abusive and controlling exerting some kind of "power" over her. Ellen also related the story of how, on Celia's death from cancer, Murray shipped her body back to Shawmut, and she described his defining characteristic as "supreme meanness".

However, others presented a very different picture of the bondsman and ward captain. Yes, many described Murray as a womaniser, gambler and "sport", but there were also those who would mention his generosity. A clairvoyant neighbour, Mrs Porter ("The Mystery Of New York's Man-Woman", *The Commercial Tribune*, January 27, 1901), told the tale of how Murray's adopted daughter, Minnie, came into Hall's unconventional household, and spoke of the kindness of the couple.

Our "Joe Young" is a fusion Joseph Young, an officer in the Iroquois Club, with a number of political and sporting friends who told tales of Murray's gambling and political life: his trips to see fights, games of poker, and a visit to Coney Island where he declined to strip off and take a splash in the waves with his companions.

Senator Barney Martin, meanwhile, was a real high-profile and colourful Tammany political mover, whose depiction we have based on a political sketch of the time. A fairly close associate of Murray Hall, he reportedly did say the words, "She's dead, the poor fellow. My old friend Murray Hall is dead." ("Mystery of Murray Hall", *New York Daily Tribune*, January 20, 1901).

Our Esther was based a member of the Hall household who answered the door to journalists following Murray's death, and who insisted Murray was a man, and was the executor of his will. She was one of several women listed, in articles, as having lived in the residence.

Our story told by Policeman O'Connor, of Hall's arrest, was reported in the *New York Times*, including a description of how Murray whipped O'Connor when he tried to arrest him, and left with a "storm cloud draping" beneath the eye. ("Murray Hall Fooled Many Shrewd Men", *New York Times*, January 19, 1901).

Murray reportedly wrote to the District Attorney complaining of a sandbagging by William Reno ("Murray H Hall: a 'lady'", *New York Times*, January 29, 1901). We based his character on a report about one William Reno, lacemaker and convict ("An Ex-Convict's Story", *New York Times*, October 20, 1900). We have no idea if this was the same William Reno. He merely served as inspiration.

Miss Wideawake really did write a column on Murray Hall, applying the pronoun "it" to the "creature" who had her followed, and threatened her with a blackthorn stick raised above her head (*Altoona Mirror*, March 4, 1901).

The chapter on the Inquest is based on numerous newspaper sources and it presents the only words, left to us today, from Minnie Hall, including her powerful declaration: "I shall never think of him as a woman." Little other testimony exists from Minne Hall about her father.

The "body in the basement" conversation overheard by Samuel Clellan in the street (which appears in the chapter taking place on 17th January 1901) is a fusion of stories from numerous testimonies of people who claimed to have known him well, or even suspected that he was not a man, as he presented. And, yes, one labourer, Arthur Hughes, did claim to have come across a body in a skeleton in Murray's basement. ("Voted Tammany For 30 Years, Died – A Woman", *New York World*, January 18, 1901). Was the story true? Who was it? Like many questions around Murray's life, the answer will never be known.

A key story that determined how Murray's life would be understood was broken by the *New York World* in an article titled "Sure Murray Hall Was Mary Anderson" (January 22, 1901).

The source, an elderly Scottish former nurse, Mrs Canning, related a story that linked Murray Hall with John Anderson, and an older story that had gripped Scotland. It's typical of the somewhat confusing nature of the historical and newspaper trail that, whether due to the inadequacies of memory or some shiftings of identity, this John Anderson turns out also to be called Johnnie Campbell.

There were other speculations about Murray's past, but this was the one that came to dominate, whether true or not. Scottish newspapers enthusiastically reported the story that Murray Hall was a Scot, and formerly Johnie Campbell or John Anderson, with the *Dundee Evening Post* describing how this Johnnie worked as a labourer but "no one suspected her sex".

It also said: "She could 'carry the hod' like any of the other workers," mentioning also that "her "stride" is said to have been as firm and steady as that of her fellow workers walking the "plank".

But was Johnnie Campbell/Anderson actually the same person as Murray Hall? The timing is tight. There is less than a year between Campbell's story being reported in various UK and US newspapers, including the *Birmingham Mail* ("A Woman Disguised As A Man", December 2, 1871) and *The Redruth Times* and *Camborne Advertiser* ("Unhappy Termination Of An Extraordinary Career", January 19, 1872), and Hall's marriage to Celia Lowe Hall in December of 1872.

Lydia Nelson, in her inquiring and forensic paper, "Reanimating Archiving/Archival Corporealities: Deploying 'Big Ears' in De Rigueur Mortis Intervention" (*QED: A Journal in GLBTQ Worldmaking*, Vol. 1, No. 2.) points out that in the census records for 1900, Hall gives his age as sixty and his date of emigration to the United States as 1846, listing both of his parents as from Scotland. But it's possible that Murray made some of this up, as he did many things.

Most importantly, in terms of our own narrative, the "parallel" life of John Anderson/Campbell was the explanation *The World* latched onto and was widely published, indeed confirmed by the medical officer of Edinburgh, Sir Henry Littlejohn, and seemed to be believed by many. It was even added to the 1915 edition of Havelock Ellis's *Sexual Inversion*.

Was this a fusion of two separate lives and stories? And if it was, was this because these lives were so threatening, in their day, that they had to be fused?

Or was it that there was enough in the detail of these lives to suggest a connection that may well have been real? The mystery remains, and the possibility that they were one and the same gripped us too. Though we speculated about other theories, such as the notion that he had come over much earlier and been a goldrush forty-niner, with a lover out West ("The Mystery Of New York's Man-Woman", *The Commercial Tribune*, January 27, 1901), none were quite as compelling as the trail that led us back to Scotland, to Johnnie Campbell, to a scandal triggered by a doctor's diagnosis and, ultimately, to an exhortation by a dying brother, to take and wear his clothes so as to "better make her way" in the world ("A Woman Married To A Woman", *Dundee Courier*, January 5, 1872, and "Unhappy Termination Of An Extraordinary Career", *North British Daily Mail*, January 4, 1872).

Where is the truth in this tale? You may make your own mind up. All we can say is that some of it, at least, must be true.

IN MURRAY HALL'S WILL "MY WIFE" IS MENTIONED

Even in This Document the Eccentric Woman Maintained her Life-long Fiction

Even in making her last will, Murray Hall, the eccentric woman who posed as a man, maintained her singular deception. The will executed on April 9, 1900, and offered for probate yesterday by Lawyer Thomas Moran, of No. 145 6th avenue, is as follows:

"I give, devine and bequeath all my property, both real and personal, and wherever-situated, to Imelda A. Hall, and especially request that at my death the said Imelda A. Hall shall cause to be erected a suitable headstone over the grave of my deceased wife, Celia F. L. Hall."

The execution of the will was witnessed by Louisa Perkins and Esther O'Donoghue, both of No. 145 6th Avenue, the house in which Murray Hall resided.

Imelda A. Hall is the young girl who was adopted by Murray Hall and "his" wife, Celia L. Hall, who until Murray Hall died was of the belief that he was her father.

No value of either the real or the personal estate was given.

ACKNOWLEDGEMENTS

A thanks from both of us to the researchers, bloggers, historians and *New York Times* journalists without whom we would know nothing about Murray Hall. Thank you too Glasgow Women's Library and the NYC LGBT Historic Sites Project.

To Emma Hargrave, who was more like a third collaborator than an editor, helping breathe rich life into our telling of Murray's story. To Lee Randall for her essential editorial eyes. To all the team at Black & White, especially Ali McBride and Campbell Brown, who believed in this book before it existed.

Milo here; I would like to thank my wonderful colleagues at Alchemy Film & Arts. Their support and critical insights have shaped the way I think and write. Caro Clarke for their support at a crucial early stage. My trans family: Nerida, Miles, Maxi, Sofia, Lyall, Naphon and Naomi. Vicky, I'm still not sure how you found me, but I'm glad you did. Thank you for your confidence and generosity right from the start. To my mum and dad. And Luna, for everything.

Vicky here; mostly I would like to thank Milo for being such a wonderful companion in this journey into the life of Murray Hall – and also for asking that I do play a role. It has been such a mind-expanding collaboration (and Google doc adventure!).